THE FRAGMENT OF
POWER

By Ben Hale

To my family and friends,

Who believed

And to my wife,

Who is perfect

The Chronicles of Lumineia

By Ben Hale

—The Shattered Soul—

—The Master Thief—

—The Second Draeken War—

—The Warsworn—

—The Age of Oracles—

—The White Mage Saga—

Table of Contents

Map of Lumineia

Prologue: The Fragment of Power

Draeken picked his way through the dead soldiers, lifting his cloak so it would not be stained in their blood. Shouts rang out in the city of Keese, mostly by those fleeing the destruction of the estate.

The walls of the structure had been reduced to spikes of stone piercing the ground like claws through flesh. Stone and wood, blackened by fire, sent curls of smoke into the afternoon sky. The dead lay where they had fallen, while the living sought to crawl away.

Draeken ignored their whimpering as he advanced into the interior of the estate. Serak, Zenif, and Zoric claimed places on his flanks. Bartoth strode through the grounds of the estate, hunting targets to kill. His enormous frame cast a shadow on the survivors, who cried out as his black armor filled their vision.

Gendor also sought targets, albeit against his will. He killed quickly, an act of mercy for those close to death. His will was bound to Draeken and Serak, and he continued to exploit Draeken's orders, manipulating them to his own purpose.

Draeken ignored them all as he advanced to the front doors of the estate. Whispers and hissed fears came from behind the ornate wood paneling, the voices of those who'd fled to the perceived safety of the estate.

Draeken chuckled and leaned back, gathering flame and light into his hand, golden beams merging with the fire, so bright the others were forced to shield their gaze. Then he leaned into the blow, striking the ornate doors.

The wood shattered, bursting inward, the splinters shredding the guards braced in the hall beyond. The handle struck a man in the side, breaking his ribs and flipping him onto the stairs. Another length of wood pierced a man's stomach like a spear, pinning him to the wall.

10

The shards of wood embedded into walls and shattered glass. As the dust settled, fires licked at the broken remains. Draeken advanced to the threshold and called into the interior, his tone amused.

"Will you come out and speak to your guests?" His voice echoed down the hallways. "Or must I further destroy your home?"

He waited, half hoping they would continue hiding, and half hoping they would come out. One meant he could destroy more, the other meant he would get what he sought. A thudding of boots sounded in the distance and Draeken glanced to the streets with a frown. He did not wish to be interrupted by the city guard, so he motioned to Serak.

"Don't let the city guard interfere."

"As you will," Serak said, his tone worshipful.

Draeken glanced to Zenif and Zoric, the two mind mages, father and son. "Is she still inside?"

"They have not escaped," Zenif said, and Zoric nodded.

Draeken gathered the fire in his hand. The flames spilled onto the floor, turning into paws and legs, a large, muscular body, and powerful jaws. Draeken cast the reaver entity as easily as he would pour a mug of ale, and the beast pawed the entranceway, its claws digging burning grooves into the finely tiled floor.

"Last chance," he called.

A door slammed open and a woman appeared. The Lady Dentis. Her husband sought to drag her back into the room but she shook him free. The nobleman hesitated, the terror on his face evident before he leapt after his wife.

"Let the guard deal with them," he growled.

Draeken grinned. "Your hope is misplaced, Lord Dentis, for we are no common thugs."

"Then who are you?" Lady Dentis snarled, all the haughtiness of her birthright twisting her features. "Do you have any idea who I am . . .?"

11

She slowed to a stop in the corridor, her eyes going wide in recognition. Zoric smirked, while Draeken merely offered a short bow. From the memories of the fragments, he knew the Lady Dentis recognized him, but she also saw that he was no longer a fragment. He was Draeken, the fragment of Power.

"Indeed I do know of your identity," he said. "You are the Raven, powerful head of the bandits known by your name. It is a pleasure to meet you."

"You think my wife is the Raven?" Lord Dentis scoffed. "She is a noble of Talinor, and I am—"

Draeken pointed to the man, and a needle of light burst from his finger. Three inches wide and three feet long, the bolt of light pierced his chest and sent his body tumbling down the corridor. He crashed into a cabinet of fine ales and fell in a heap.

Lady Dentis stared at the body of her husband, her eyes wide and unblinking, her chest heaving. She swallowed and turned back to Draeken, her haughty pride leaking from her features and turning to fear.

"Walk with me?" Draeken turned and motioned out of the house.

Trembling, the Raven glanced to her dead husband, and then did as Draeken requested. She joined him on the threshold, and followed him into the ruined grounds of her once beautiful estate. She glanced back again, and Draeken chuckled.

"Do not pretend you loved him. He was not as vile as you, but neither was he a good man. You used him and his position to cover your bandits; a well-executed persona, I must say."

"What do you want?" she asked.

He mentally applauded her bravery. "You," he said simply.

"For what?" Her eyes narrowed.

Draeken motioned to Zoric and the mind mage pulled a dark cloak into view. Like liquid ink, it poured off his fingers, a sheen of material that made the woman shudder and retreat a step. Zoric advanced and handed the cloak to Draeken.

"I'm not going to wear that," the Raven said flatly.

"It is unkind to refuse a gift," Draeken chided.

"I know who you are," she said. "You are Draeken, the guardian that was once broken into five fragments."

"True," he said with a smile. "But I am so much more than you know. You see, the fragments are not part of me. They are separate and broken. I, on the other hand, am the fragment of Power, and my will is untarnished by their impossible quest to protect the people."

She swallowed and shook her head, her eyes on the cloak. "What is that thing?"

"Isn't it beautiful?" he asked, his smile turning soft. "I wish I could take credit, but my servant Serak prepared it."

Men shouted in the street, followed by orders as the city guard arrived. But the orders were cut off with a brutal *crunch* that echoed into the estate. Armor cracked and bones were broken beneath Serak's magic. The flicker of hope in the woman's eyes died and she shook her head again.

"What will the cloak do to me?"

"It will give you power," he said.

"What sort of power?"

Draeken smirked at the touch of desire in her voice. "I know you from the memories of the fragments. Your ambition is insatiable. You hunger for power, for gold and possessions. And that is why you are perfectly suited to be one of my four horsemen, the destroyer who will be known as Famine."

The Raven gazed at the cloak, the greed alight in her eyes. The cloak would indeed give her power, but it would also destroy her flesh. Half-truths were so much better than lies. The Raven glanced to him and back to the cloak, and then to Gendor as he glided close.

13

"It will rob you of your will," Gendor said. "Do not fall for Draeken's—"

"Gendor," Draeken said. "Must you continue to resist? Must I punish you?"

"You already did," Gendor said, and swept his skeletal hand across his body.

"Does he speak the truth?" the Raven asked.

"He does," Draeken admitted. "But look at Bartoth." He pointed to the towering rock troll. "I have no need of enforcing my will because he has *chosen* to become my general."

"You will forever be his," Gendor warned.

"Death," Draeken ordered, addressing Gendor by his proper name, "go kill a child."

Gendor's red eyes glowed in his cowl, and then he swung his scythe into the ground. Lifting the weapon, he showed the young mouse. Draeken chuckled at his clever loophole, unable to refute his logic.

"And if I refuse?" the Raven asked.

"Then I go to Princess Melora," Draeken said. "She too, is ambitious . . ."

The words struck the woman like a dagger to her heart, as Draeken knew they would. The Raven hated Melora, for she was a rival. The prospect that Melora might win the prize was sufficient motivation for her to straighten and reach forward.

"I'll be your general."

Draeken handed the woman the cloak, and then retreated. She eyed the cloak, and Draeken ordered Gendor to silence. His continued belligerence was amusing, but Draeken's patience was not eternal.

The Raven lifted her chin and then swung the cloak about her shoulders, shoving her hands into the sleeves. Then she yanked the cowl over her head, as if the motions could hide the tremble in her fingers. The cloak rippled—and then sank into her flesh.

The Raven screamed, the sound echoing into the city, stilling even the cries of the wounded outside the estate. She sank to her knees and clawed at the cloak, desperate to remove it, but it was part of her body now, the flesh sinking inward, her bones showing against her skin, her body sunken and hollow.

Cries of fear came from the nearby homes, where men and women peeked through windows. The food in their homes crumbled on their tables, spoiling before their eyes, mold appearing and consuming bread and meat, root and leaf.

The Raven screamed again, and then sucked in her breath. Draeken had ensured the magic would not touch him and his companions, but his stomach rumbled. He smiled and stepped forward, pulling the woman to her feet.

"Rise," he said, "and claim your place at my side."

She stood and looked at her arms, at the flesh worn away, but her eyes bore a haunting victory. She felt the power, knew it in her bones. She could kill with a touch and rob men of flesh by standing in their midst. At a distance she could destroy food and resources, ravaging an attacking army with desperation and hunger.

"I live to serve, my master."

Draeken smiled, the sense of victory like sweet nectar on his tongue. Three of his generals stood before him, and only the fourth remained. When the horseman of Plague had been collected, he could finally open the Dark Gate.

Serak crossed the courtyard and joined him, nodding his approval. "Our plan advances."

Draeken met his gaze. "It does indeed."

Serak examined Famine with pride, but Draeken's smile was not of gratitude. Serak had prepared armies and hidden fortresses, even created the chance for Draeken to become whole, but Draeken was the master, and his plan was his own.

"Come," Draeken said. "Our work is done for the day."

He reached upward, and a red dragon dropped from the sky, landing in the courtyard. Bendelinish, Serak's mount, was one of the strongest reds the dragons had produced in ages. Draeken stepped into the air, and flew.

Those still watching fell silent, their shock robbing their voices as Draeken lifted himself off the earth by force of will. Draeken alighted on the dragon's neck, while Serak used a foreleg to join him. As the dragon flapped its wings, Draeken pointed to the estate.

"Burn it."

The dragon lowered its maw and fire burst forth, engulfing the building. Serak's mount rose into the air as it poured fire onto the roof of the estate, filling the halls and corridors with dragon's breath. Draeken watched the inferno before calling down to his generals.

"You know what to do."

They nodded and then departed, disappearing into the rising smoke. Draeken directed the dragon into the sky, rising above the wall and the soldiers huddled against the battlements. He paid them no mind as he soared over a country illuminated by the setting sun. His land. His kingdom.

"Witness the dawn of my kingdom," he said. "And my reign will be endless."

Chapter 1: Aftermath

Elenyr advanced into the remains of the estate, her footfalls sending ash rising in small puffs. The city guard had managed to contain the fires before they spread, but the estate itself was nothing but ruin. The supports of the home resembled a burned carcass, its bones reaching skyward. Another corner had caved in, the beams and stones a pile of debris.

"There were a handful of survivors," the captain of the guard said from her side. "Would you like to speak with them?"

Elenyr shook her head. "No. Leave them to their healing."

The man bowed and then departed. The fragment of Mind took his place. "Why did you want to come here?"

Elenyr frowned at the sense of fear rising in her throat. Draeken had separated from the fragments, but she had no idea what to expect from him. As the fragment of Power, he was more dangerous than he'd ever been.

"It's been two weeks since you separated from Draeken," Elenyr said. "I expected more from him, but he didn't appear anywhere on Lumineia. Then he suddenly showed up here? I want to know why."

"Witnesses say Lady Dentis put on a cloak," Senia said, joining them. "I'm guessing it's the same type he forced Gendor to wear. With the way the food rotted, I'd say he turned her into Famine."

"That means he has three generals," Elenyr said. "Only one remains."

She turned to the rest of their group, all sifting through the wreckage, looking for reasons why Draeken and Serak had come here. Despite their foes and the dire situation, a small smile appeared on her face. The fragments and their friends were powerful, and Draeken was a fool to ignore them.

All five fragments were alive and whole. They were not really fragments anymore, but after viewing them as such for so long, she had a hard time shaking that concept. They were her sons, her family she'd nearly lost, but thanks to Mind, they were alive and well.

In addition to the fragments, others had gradually joined the conflict. Willow, the dark elf called the Inked One, with weapons tattooed on her flesh, a walking armory. Lira, the Eternal, as well as Ero, head of the Eternals, who lived under the persona of Jeric.

Senia, the oracle, had brought Rake, a man bonded to a white dragon. And then there was Tardoq, the bone-armored dakorian. Once a servant to an invading krey, the mighty Bloodwall towered over the rest of the group. Elenyr was still uncertain of his role, even if Rynda spoke in support of the soldier.

Queen Rynda, head of the rock troll people, and revered by her entire clan, stood talking to Tardoq. By all accounts the two were friends, though both had scars to prove they were once adversaries.

Lorica talked to Shadow, her special cloak fluttering in the breeze. Now head of the Assassin's Guild, the woman retained her persona, the Angel of Death. She was formidable and fearsome. More importantly, she hated Serak, and had become friends with Shadow.

The last two members of their group were the strangest. Sentara, once a woman named Marrow, and Rune, her young charge, who had bonded to the Unnamed, a woman of tremendous magical power.

"What are you thinking?" Mind asked.

Elenyr gave a wry smile. "That Draeken has chosen his generals, but I prefer mine."

"We can defeat him," Senia said.

Elenyr faced the elven woman. As the current oracle, Senia had the power of farsight, allowing her to see glimpses of the future. Against Serak and Draeken, she was their most powerful weapon.

Jeric approached and shook his head. "Our assumption seems accurate. Draeken gave her the cloak and it turned her into Famine."

"Then her will belongs to Draeken, now," Senia said.

"I don't understand how that's possible," Mind said. "No magic exists that can rob a man of his will. It's one of the immutable laws of magic."

"Perhaps he's not using magic," Elenyr said.

"You think it's krey technology?" Senia asked, looking to Jeric.

The krey masquerading as an elf shook his head. "The Krey Empire cannot control another's will."

Elenyr pondered the mystery power as the others argued its source. It did not come from Draeken, for Serak had turned Gendor and Bartoth into generals before Draeken had become whole. Regardless of it source, Elenyr recognized the need to fight Draeken and Serak on several fronts.

"We must part ways," Elenyr said.

"When we left Blackwell Keep you said we should stick together," Jeric said.

Elenyr glanced to Mind and he inclined his head. He knew why she'd spoken as she had. After the separation, the fragments had been weakened, and if Draeken or Serak had sought to kill them at that time, they would have been defenseless. Staying together in a single body, they'd kept themselves safe. But now her sons had returned to strength—not their former power, but sufficient to defend themselves if Draeken sought to assassinate them.

Mind frowned. "Our adversary is cunning. If we do part ways, each group must be strong enough to stand against him."

Elenyr noticed how Mind didn't mention Draeken by name, but his jaw clenched and he looked away. He still blamed himself for stripping the fragment of Power from the fragments. Elenyr agreed to his suggestion.

Are you certain we can trust everyone present? Mind spoke into her thoughts, his eyes flicking to Tardoq.

"I am," Elenyr spoke aloud.

"We cannot risk failure," Mind said.

Elenyr regarded him for a moment, and then said, "His actions reveal his character."

Jeric overheard the conversation and joined them. "Perhaps it's time I bring in more Eternals."

Anger pricked in Elenyr's heart and she leveled a finger at him. "You and your Eternals claim to protect Lumineia, yet you have failed to protect us from the Krey Empire."

"What are you talking about?" Senia asked.

Elenyr pointed upward. "Serak was not born on Lumineia, he came through a Gate. He came from the Empire."

Jeric's eyes widened. "Is that true?"

Mind scowled, and Elenyr gave an apologetic look. He'd shared what he'd learned from Serak in confidence, but Elenyr had grown tired of secrets. Perhaps they were the very reason they stood on the brink of war.

"It's true," Mind admitted. "Guildmaster Elsin of the Verinai tried to open a Gate and a handful came through, Serak among them."

Senia cursed under her breath, and Elenyr raised an eyebrow to the woman. As the sole oracle of Lumineia, Senia had been taught her entire life to hold a certain moral standard, one that did not include swearing. She grinned sheepishly.

"We need to part ways," Elenyr repeated. "We need to attack Draeken and Serak on multiple fronts."

"But how?" Senia asked. "And who?"

Jeric shuddered. "It's like getting picked last for Welfall."

"Welfall?" Elenyr asked.

"A game for young krey," Jeric said. "I won't bore you with the details, but I was not the most athletic of youths. It was decidedly unpleasant."

Elenyr frowned and considered the gathered group. She liked the idea of her and Shadow infiltrating Serak's ranks. Both of them were skilled at deception, and she appreciated the need for subtlety. But what about the others?

As she considered the options, she noticed Light playing with a small object he'd found in the ash. It flickered bright orange as it rotated. Her eyes widened and she hissed the others to silence. Without explanation, she bolted for Light and caught the spinning object.

Light protested, but she urgently motioned him to silence. Then she waved her hand, summoning the entire group while she continued to use hand signals to request them not to speak. When Mind stepped close, his eyes widened and he spoke into her thoughts.

Is that a listening mote?

It is, she replied. *Can you tell the others not to speak at all?*

You think it's from Draeken. Mind scowled but nodded, and the confusion on the other faces evaporated.

He lived inside you and the fragments for ages, Elenyr said. *He knows how you think. But perhaps we can use this to our advantage . . .*

"Hello Elenyr," the object spoke in her hand.

She grimaced at Draeken's voice. It was similar to the voice of her sons, yet darker, more sinister. The other fragments scowled, while Senia cursed again. Elenyr glanced her way but the oracle jerked her head, a touch of guilt on her features. She hadn't noticed the mote in her farsight.

"Draeken," Elenyr replied evenly.

"I like your plan," he said. "Divide and attack me on multiple fronts. It may be destined for failure, but it's rather clever."

21

Elenyr grimaced as she realized Draeken had overheard their plan. "I take it you have joined with Serak?"

"He's spent five thousand years building a plan for me," Draeken replied with a laugh. "It would be rather rude of me to deny him."

The orb in her hands flickered and she dropped it onto the ground. It landed in a puff of ash and smoke, and then light seeped from the interior, rising and shaping into the body of Draeken. The entire group reached for weapons but the mirage rotated in place, a smile on his lips.

"Your alliance is adorable." He swept a hand to Lorica and Tardoq. "Such a motley collection of individuals. You're like a pack of mongrel dogs."

"We'll see who's the dog by the end," Tardoq said evenly.

Draeken burst into a laugh. "I know I should just kill you all, but I admit a trace of the fragments remains in my flesh, and I'm fond of you." His eyes settled on Sentara and he smirked. "Some of you anyway."

"I live to be annoying," Sentara said.

"Are you going to open the Dark Gate?" Rynda asked.

"Your bluntness is legendary," Draeken said. "And I will be blunt in turn. The Dark Gate belongs to me now, and as you know, I require one more general before it can be opened. I do look forward to seeing you across the battlefield. I'll even keep Gendor from assassinating you."

"You just want to watch us die." Tardoq folded his arms.

Draeken shrugged, his expression guilty. "True. Enjoy the war, former friends. I promise I will visit your graves when it's over, if I'm not too busy being king of Lumineia."

He winked and the image faded. Rynda promptly stomped on the ball of magic, shattering it into dust. Elenyr's dread mounted until the fragment of Fire began to laugh, his eyes glowing with anticipation. The others stared at him as if he'd gone mad, but Fire pointed to the broken listening mote.

"Draeken may know us," he said, "but we know him. That arrogance? That used to be part of me."

"He has my sense of intrigue," Shadow said, nodding.

Mind looked to Elenyr, the determination on his features giving her hope. "Let's put the dog in his place."

Elenyr smiled at his words. "Draeken thinks his reign is about to begin. Let's make certain we see its end."

Chapter 2: Forewarned

Senia fell to her knees, gasping for breath. Elenyr caught her hand and helped her to her feet, shifting her so she sat on the old mine cart. She opened her water skin and gave it to the oracle, who thanked her with a nod.

"What did you see?" Mind asked.

"It is as you suspected," Senia said. "Ten days from today we will arrive in Keese, but we will be too late. We will only find ashes, and the Raven will have already been turned into Famine."

Elenyr passed a hand over her face, as if the motion could stave off the rising weariness. Senia had been exploring the future for days now, and had yet to find a possible way to stop Draeken.

It had been two days since the group had emerged from the mines of northeastern Griffin, two days since the fragment of Power had been pulled from the fragments in Blackwell Keep. Now Draeken had joined with Serak and become the greatest threat Lumineia had ever witnessed.

"Tell us everything," Elenyr said.

Senia detailed what she'd seen in her vision, of how they'd hastened west, arriving in Keese in an attempt to stop Draeken from taking the woman as his third general. She described the failure and the devastated estate in vivid detail, prompting Rynda to fold her arms.

"It's been two days since we exited these blasted mines, and all we've done is sit here while you examine our future failures."

"She's doing the best she can," Rake said, kneeling beside the oracle.

"It's not good enough," Rynda said, stabbing a finger at the oracle. "You've looked into a dozen futures and what have we learned? Nothing."

"That's not entirely accurate," Mind said.

"Oh?" Rynda swept her hand wide. "Then enlighten me."

Mind offered a faint smile. "Senia has looked at what we'd thought would be our best options." He ticked them off with his fingers. "A direct attack against Draeken and Serak at Xshaltheria. Joining the army at Keese and fighting Xshaltheria. And attempting to stop Draeken at Keese—with a few of us, and the entire group. Each time she has seen failure."

"She cannot foresee my effort to recruit the Bonebreaker," Tardoq said.

Elenyr looked to the large dakorian, her voice turning apologetic. "Her farsight is limited by indecision."

Tardoq held her gaze and then turned and exited the mine entrance. Elenyr winced, wishing she could have said it more softly. Tardoq had once served Wylyn, and if he returned to the Krey Empire, he might betray them all, leading to a worse fate than if Draeken succeeded. Rynda glared at Elenyr and then followed him out.

"I can try again," Senia said weakly.

"You've searched the future enough," Elenyr said. "And you are getting weaker. I believe the time of decision has come."

"What do you think we should do?" Rake asked.

"I'm not sure," Elenyr said. "But time advances without our actions, and our fate approaches. We must make a decision."

She retreated to the back of the cavern and sank onto a seat where the stone had been cut, making a rough bench. With a sigh, she leaned against the cold rock and surveyed those in the cavern, her allies, her friends, her family.

The mine entrance was small, about the size of a small tavern. Mine tracks extended into darkness, the metal cankered with rust, the wooden underlay long since rotted away. A pair of mine carts lay on their sides, a touch of frost on the wheels where snow had blown into the entrance.

In the clearing beyond, the snow had begun to melt, patches of grass showing through. It wouldn't be long until the branches began to blossom, and the snow in the canyons turned into raging streams and brooks. Then the army at Terros would march on Xshaltheria, and the new spring earth would see the spilling of blood.

Assassins and mages, soldiers of the Krey Empire, Eternals, and her five sons. Just sixteen allies against Serak, the Father of Guardians, and Draeken, the fragment of Power. If that wasn't enough, Serak had two mind mages in Zenif and Zoric, as well as a red dragon, two powerful generals in Bartoth and Gendor, and soon they would add Famine to their forces.

Mind claimed a seat at her side. "I don't need to read your mind to see your despair."

"I'm just worried," Elenyr admitted.

Her eyes settled on Fire. The fragment spoke with Water, the two speculating on the fourth and final general, the one they only knew as Plague. If they could discover their identity, perhaps they could stop Draeken from claiming the final general.

Mind followed her gaze. "You do not need to worry about us."

"You're more vulnerable than ever," Elenyr said. "You cannot stop me from worrying."

"Look at Light," he said. "Do you notice anything different?"

She spotted Light at the opposite side of the cavern. He'd conjured a pick axe out of light and begun striking the stone wall, getting excited when he found a glimmer of ore. Willow stood at his side, encouraging him, even though the ore was probably nothing. The dwarves would not have left anything behind.

Elenyr shrugged. "He's as impulsive as ever."

"Perhaps," Mind said. "But look at how he sees Willow."

"We both know he loves her," Elenyr said.

"But now they get to be together," Mind said.

Elenyr finally understood his meaning. "Now that he is mortal, he can live a life with Willow?"

"Exactly," Mind said. "I may have ensured our deaths, but at least they will get a chance to be happy."

She shifted in her seat. "Not you?"

"I'll be happy when I've destroyed Draeken for good."

Elenyr didn't comment on his dodging the question. Mind wanted to buoy her spirits, even when his own features were tight with doubt. Mind had given Draeken his freedom, but if he had not acted, the five fragments would have been killed. She hoped that in time he would recognize he had made the right choice.

"We cannot keep using Senia to find a future that works," Mind said, lowering his voice. "She cannot sustain that level of magic, and she is not gifted in farsight."

"That is true," Elenyr said. "But we've already looked at the various paths."

"And parting ways will make us too vulnerable," Mind said.

Senia's head snapped up. "What did you say?"

Mind frowned. "We discussed this. If we split up, Gendor and Bartoth will hunt and kill us one by one."

"No," Senia said. She put her hand on the cart and stood, Rake ducking under her arm to help. "In that last vision, Draeken left a monitoring mote so he could listen to our plans. He claimed that he would not send his generals to kill us because he wants to witness our demise."

"I know that arrogance," Fire said, drifting closer. "It used to be mine."

27

"Not all of it," Shadow said with a smirk. He detached himself from the darkness behind Elenyr and Mind, where he'd been listening to their conversation. He grinned at Mind's annoyance and plopped down between them.

"Why didn't you share this before?" Rynda asked, standing in the doorway. Tardoq joined her.

"Because I was trying to keep track of the entire vision," Senia said tersely. "You want to try?"

Elenyr rose to her feet, a touch of hope in her chest. "We can divide, at least for now, and seek all four paths."

"The path of war," Rynda said, a smile on her face. "I can handle the alliance at Terros."

"The path of the gate," Willow said quietly. "We have to close the Dark Gate, permanently."

"The path for aid," Tardoq rumbled. "I will seek the Bonebreaker's help."

"And the path of assassins," Shadow said. They all looked at him and he shrugged. "What else would you call it? We have to kill the four generals."

"Our foes will likely be focused on the war," Mind said. "We should place our strongest forces there."

"You should hunt the horsemen," Water said to Elenyr. "You and Shadow are best suited for infiltration, and that journey will likely require you to enter Serak's fortresses."

"I'll go with Tardoq to the Krey Empire," Mind said.

Elenyr spun to face him, surprised by his offer. "You want to go to the Empire?"

It was undeniably the most dangerous of the paths. In the Empire, humans were slaves, and Mind would be regarded as such. And if Tardoq betrayed them, he would be imprisoned and they would attempt to discern the source of his power.

28

Jeric's eyes hardened and settled on Tardoq. "I don't trust Tardoq enough to take him back to the Empire."

Tardoq did not retreat. He'd once been their foe, but now stood as an ally. Yet Elenyr knew the risk. Allowing Tardoq to return to the Krey Empire could very well ensure their destruction. If Tardoq told the Empire about Lumineia, an armada would arrive in their skies.

"It is the one option Draeken and Serak will not consider," Elenyr said.

Fire stabbed a finger at Senia. "The oracle said she cannot see beyond indecision. We cannot trust Tardoq."

Rynda growled at Fire's words. "You would speak of him as if he were not here?"

"Would you rather we lie behind his back?" Fire asked. "I thought that was the reason you hate men."

She snorted but did not refute his statement. Elenyr watched Tardoq. The dakorian had been a soldier for the Empire for ages, and his entire life had been an oppression to mankind. Could they trust him?

"This is foolish," Jeric said. "Tardoq is a Bloodwall. For us to trust him is like putting a snake in your coat and hoping he won't sink his fangs into your flesh."

"We cannot risk failure," Mind said.

"So you trust him?" Jeric asked.

Mind regarded him for a moment, and then pointed to Elenyr. "I know Elenyr does, and I trust her."

"I do trust him," Elenyr said, and Tardoq inclined his head to her, a mark of gratitude.

Jeric scowled and looked away. "You seek one who is unlikely to help. The Bonebreaker is an exiled Bloodwall, perhaps the mightiest dakorian to ever live. Even we, the Eternals, have feared asking her aid."

"Tardoq will succeed," Mind said.

"I cannot do as you request," Jeric jerked his head. "The Eternals protect Lumineia from people like him. We cannot trust him."

Tardoq reached up and slowly drew the greatsword on his back, the weapon of a young rock troll named Kentor. He held it in his hands, his expression reverent. Then he grasped the hilt and placed the sword on the floor.

"I give you my oath as a Bloodwall, sworn on the blade of my protector, I will not betray the people of Lumineia. As of this moment, I renounce my rank in the Krey Empire, and if you will have me, I will join your ranks in protecting this world."

His words were soft, but they seemed to reverberate in the cavern. Then Shadow shrugged. "Good enough for me. Ready to go?"

"Four paths," Elenyr said. "Each with the chance to cripple or destroy Draeken and Serak."

"A sound plan." Mind swept his hand to the others. "But who goes with whom?"

Senia abruptly laughed, and when all turned to face her, she shrugged apologetically. "Sorry, I saw you talk about that in one of the futures. Something about Welfall."

Jeric grimaced. "Not a subject I like."

Elenyr frowned and considered the gathered group, and then directed them into groups. "Water and Fire, you go with Lira and Rynda to Terros. There you can join the alliance and help fight the war."

They separated themselves and stepped to the side of the room, and Elenyr turned to the remainder. "Light and Willow can go with Senia and Rake to find Lachonus. We know he is integral to stopping Draeken, but not how or why. The oracle can guide you to him."

She looked to Jeric as she spoke the next group. "Tardoq and Jeric will go to the Empire, and Mind will accompany them."

Jeric scowled but did not argue as he took his place with Mind and Tardoq. Shadow grinned as he stepped to Elenyr's side, and Lorica joined him. Sentara and Rune walked to Elenyr's side and Sentara shrugged.

"Looks like we are going after the generals."

"We are," Elenyr said, and surveyed the four groups. "For now, this is our best course, but remember the foe we face. Draeken is smart as well as powerful, and if we are to succeed, we must be ready to adapt."

She swallowed at the sudden worry in her chest. Her sons were weaker, and now they were fighting an even greater foe. Yet she could not imagine a greater collection of family and friends. She smiled.

"We are a strange group of allies," she said. "But in this, we stand united. Let us make certain that the world we love remains intact."

Chapter 3: A Shift in Power

Water embraced Elenyr and bid farewell to the other fragments, unable to shake the strangeness to the parting. Their personalities had altered after the separation with Draeken. Since he was the only one to retain a fragment of Power, he was the only one unchanged by the separation.

Water watched the fragments and wondered where he fit. He was still a fragment, but without his brothers, was he still a part of someone greater? Or was he now whole? Shadow slid up to his flank.

"Don't die in the war," Shadow said with a wink.

"I don't plan to," Water said.

The feeling of the group had changed since Elenyr had devised their plan of four paths. Water appreciated the hopeful tinge to their words, while Shadow and Light were borderline jovial. Rynda was obviously impatient to depart for combat, while Tardoq alone seemed somber. Elenyr appeared worried, and to her Water smiled.

"They'll be fine," he said, stepping to her side and handing her the waterskin he'd filled.

"I hope so." She smiled as she accepted the skin. "Because I already lost a son. I don't want to lose one again."

"Me?" Fire turned, having overheard the comment. He smirked. "No war can stop us now."

Water chuckled, unable to deny his brother's amusement. Then he reached for the flow of water trickling down the slope from melting snow and swept it into a circle, the liquid wrapping up and around to form his traveling wheel. A seat rose from the base, and he added three more.

Rynda snorted and jerked her head. "I'm not traveling in that thing."

"You won't be able to keep up."

"*You* won't be able to keep up," she retorted.

"I think she'll be fine," Lira said, climbing into the water wheel and claiming the left seat. Fire nodded in agreement and claimed the seat in the back.

Water placed a hand on the center chair but turned back to the group. Senia stood with Light and Willow, the trio mounting Isray, the dragon bonded to Rake. The white dragon made the clearing feel small, and he snorted when Light kept trying to touch his wings. Smoke curled from the dragon's nostrils.

Mind stood with Tardoq and Jeric, the trio shouldering packs. Mind's expression was reserved, but there was a trace of excitement about his frame at the prospect of going to the Krey Empire. Their eyes met and Mind spoke into Water's thoughts.

Keep Fire safe.

Water nodded to the mental words. *If you promise to return.*

Mind inclined his head and flashed a rare smile. *I have to. I can't trust you fragments to survive without me.*

Water chuckled at that, and then noticed Elenyr. The Hauntress had joined her own group, and stood with Shadow, Lorica, Sentara, and Rune. Sentara still didn't like Elenyr, the animosity visible on her features, but Rune seemed excited at the prospect of their journey.

"Ready?" Lira asked, drawing Water's attention.

Water glanced to her, the woman he'd come to love. "Of course."

"Don't start kissing in front of me," Fire warned. "Not unless you want to see burning vomit."

Lira grinned. "No promises."

Elenyr called to everyone, and the four groups looked to her. A touch of emotion marked her eyes, and for a moment she did not speak. The pride was palpable and Water fought to keep his own emotions in check.

"My sons and friends," she said, "to look upon you fills me with pride. Draeken and Serak represent everything we abhor. They represent oppression and tyranny, and their plan threatens our lives and our freedom."

Light burst into a laugh. Everyone stared at him and he stifled his amusement. "Sorry."

Elenyr smiled at Light and swept a hand to them. "If there was ever a group with which I'd want to go to war, it is you. Be safe in your journeys."

Water nodded to Elenyr and then climbed into the wheel of swirling liquid. He cast the other groups a lingering look as each departed. The white dragon took to the sky, billowing cold air into the clearing. Tardoq, Jeric, and Mind threaded into the trees, the armored dakorian visible for several seconds until the branches took him from sight. Elenyr and her group re-entered the mine and disappeared into the darkened recess. Then Water sighed and accelerated his wheel, kicking mud into their wake as they sped into the trees. Rynda ran at their side, keeping pace with ease.

Fire leaned forward and spoke in Water's ear. "You should put her in our dust. Show her how fast you can really go."

Lira shook her head. "I don't think angering that woman is a good thing. She's rather intimidating."

Water agreed with Lira, and kept the wheel at a pace that would eat up the miles. Rynda did not seem perturbed, her long legs carrying her through the forest as if she'd been born to run. It made Water wonder just how the rock trolls trained to develop such endurance.

They dropped down the slopes of the mountains until they encountered the main highway. Connecting the middle cities back to Terros, the highway wound through valleys and mountain passes on its way west. Villages dotted the region, with a handful of smaller cities.

All lay between Xshaltheria and Terros, the path Draeken's army would take if they invaded.

Patches of snow melted in the gulleys and ravines, and buds blossomed on branches. Deer and foxes flitted about, hunting mice and voles, while badgers sought for new dens. Trappers were out in force, hunting for skin and meat, hoping to stock up for the alliance army that was rumored to be passing in the next few weeks.

"They should be fleeing the region," Lira said.

"Probably," Fire said. "But they don't think Draeken is a threat. To them, he's just kidnapped their king for a season. How much harm can he be?"

"What will Serak do now that Draeken is his master?" Lira asked.

"He thinks to serve Draeken." Fire dipped his hand into the spinning wheel of water, kicking mist around his arm. "I'm not sure he knows what he has unleashed."

"What's that supposed to mean?" Water asked, glancing his way.

Rynda drifted closer, her breathing labored but not fatigued. "Serak has spent lifetimes anticipating this moment, but there is no way for him to anticipate how Draeken will really react—especially without the influence of the five fragments."

"You don't think he'll do as Serak intends?" Lira eyebrows pulled down.

"We'll find out soon enough," Rynda said. "But Draeken is his own being now, and people rarely do as you expect."

Water frowned, disliking the idea that Draeken would be unpredictable. If he didn't follow Serak's plan, what would he do? Would he still open the Gate? Or would he turn against Serak and stand alone? Was there a chance he would rejoin the fragments and Elenyr?

The questions occupied them as they descended from the higher valleys into the lowlands of western Griffin. Camping only at night, they resumed their journey each day. The road became clogged with riders, many of which were soldiers. They shouted in alarm as Water and Rynda sped by, but their horses could not keep up with his magic and a rock troll queen.

They slowed as they approached Terros. It had been months since Water had seen the city, and when they stepped out of the trees his jaw dropped at the sight. The city and outlying farms had been swallowed by the war camps.

Tents and temporary forts dotted the farmland between the towers of Outer Terros. Hammers echoed from the dwarven camp where engineers built war machines, the metal and wood fashioned into ballistae and catapults. Others labored over large armored wagons, where dwarves could fire crossbows from within. Huge beasts conjured from fire were chained to the war machines, pawing the ground as dwarven fire mages completed the enchantments.

Adjacent to the dwarves, the elven war camp contained rank upon rank of water golems. Treewalkers took their places in a different formation, the large oak trees groaning as they obeyed the orders of the mages controlling them. Elven infantry and archers filled the camp, the twang of bows a soft backdrop to the morning.

Human camps from Erathan and Talinor filled the remainder of the farms. Cavalry from Talinor rode across the earth, the thundering horse hooves reverberating off the city walls. Children from the city lined the sides of training grounds, cheering the steel-armored soldiers. Erathan swordsmen trained on the south side, the clang of swords and shields adding to the din.

Rynda turned to her own camp of rock trolls. Although much smaller in size, the rock troll camp was the most organized. With forty-foot logs around the quickly erected fort, the camp contained a thousand rock trolls, the large warriors almost jovial as they prepared for the impending war.

"Food and water," Rynda commanded when they stepped through the gates. "And send a messenger to King Justin that we've arrived with news."

"Yes, my queen," a troll said.

He sheathed the giant sword on his back and sprinted from the camp. Rynda caught the skin of water tossed to her and drank freely, while another troll approached and set his giant maul on the earth.

"Please tell me we didn't come all this way for nothing."

"Warshard Dent," Queen Rynda said, pausing in gulping down water. "Our foes are almost gathered. When does the rest of our army arrive?"

"Tomorrow," he said. "I just received word."

"Will we be ready?" Rynda asked.

The troll general swept a hand to the trolls. "Always. When do we march?"

"As soon as King Justin confirms the order," she said.

Warshard Dent was smaller than Water expected, and stood at just eight feet tall. Despite his smaller stature, he boasted more tattoos on his body than nearly anyone else, the carpet of ink in his Sundering revealing his talent and skill. For a weapon, he carried a large maul bearing spikes on the back side of the head.

"Why do we not assault Xshaltheria on our own?" Warshard Dent said. "Surely we can exterminate the threat without the lesser fools."

"Not this time, Warshard," Rynda said. "I've seen what Serak is capable of, and now he has Draeken at his side."

Dent frowned and his eyes flicked to Water and Fire, the look revealing his knowledge that the fragments were part of Draeken. Water struggled with how to explain what had occurred, but Fire shrugged.

"Draeken is no longer part of us," Fire said.

"So you're fighting yourself?" Dent asked.

Water grinned. "It's even stranger than it sounds."

Dent grunted in agreement. "We have another problem. An assassin is stalking the camps."

"Gendor," Rynda said with a nod. "He serves Draeken now."

"He's killed over a hundred," Dent said. "No one has seen him."

"Any of our people?"

"Seven," he replied.

"That many?" Water asked, surprised and disturbed.

"The assassin is formidable," Dent said. "His scythe carries a lethal poison that kills quickly. We have yet to catch him."

"Who is he killing?"

"Leaders," Dent said. "He has yet to stalk my path, but I hope he does."

"We can only hope," Rynda said. "But watch your back."

Fire leaned over to Water. "I like the trolls."

Water stifled a chuckle. "Me too."

"Are they afraid of anything?" Lira whispered.

"A slow death," Rynda said, overhearing them.

The rock troll messenger returned through the gate with King Justin at his side. The king rode into the rock troll camp flanked by two young women, both in regal garb. Water recognized Princess Nelia, of Erathan, and Princess Annah, King Justin's daughter. King Justin dismounted his steed and advanced to Rynda, offering his hand in greeting. Rynda did not accept the gesture, and after a moment the king lowered his hand.

"I came as soon as I heard," Justin said. "You have word of our foes?"

Rynda motioned to Water, and he briefly relayed what had occurred in Blackwell Keep. He saw no reason to withhold the truth, so he shared the full details of Draeken and his power. When he was finished, the man nodded and swept a hand to the camps.

"We have two hundred thousand soldiers under my command," he said.

"Griffin doesn't have that many soldiers," Water said, disliking the man's tone.

"It does now," Justin said. "With King Porlin revealed as Zoric, Zenif's son, and King Numen dead, the nobles of the other kingdoms have given me temporary control over their armies." King Justin absently motioned to Princess Nelia, as if she were an afterthought. "All three human kingdoms are under my reign now."

"And you agreed to this?" Rynda asked Princess Nelia.

She opened her mouth to speak but King Justin spoke first. "Of course. There is no other feasible option. Erathan and Talinor require strong leadership to deal with this threat."

"I think the princess is strong enough to lead her own kingdom," Water said, folding his arms.

Water knew the young woman enough to recognize her strength. She had not followed in King Numen's footsteps, and upon discovering her father was Carn, she'd taken measures against him, and sought the support of the other nobles of Erathan.

"You have my gratitude," the princess said, inclining her head to Water. "But this alliance is for the good of Lumineia, and will end after the threat is resolved."

Princess Annah gave a sharp nod at her words, while King Justin's features darkened a shade. Water realized the man wanted to use the conflict to gain power, but it was obvious the two young women were well aware of his ambitions and were not deceived.

King Justin remounted his horse. "We march in two days. I'll let you know your orders."

He rode from the camp, and Dent leaned over to the scowling Queen Rynda. "Are you certain you do not wish to fight Xshaltheria on our own?"

"It's more tempting than I care to admit," Queen Rynda said, her metal hand flexing as if she wanted to crush King Justin's throat. "Begin final preparations. We march in two days."

Rynda departed with her Warshard, and Lira turned to Water. "It's disturbing how much King Justin reminds me of krey houses."

"Indeed," Water said.

Water watched the man ride away, wondering if a victory for the alliance would lead to a victory for King Justin. Would he seek to claim the other kingdoms? If he had enough support from the other nobles, it seemed plausible. Water grimaced, and recalled a time he'd fallen into the southern sea, and a group of sharks had begun to circle. He'd felt the same in that moment as he did now. He just hoped they could forestall a conflict before the alliance shattered from within.

Chapter 4: Weakened

In the two days following their arrival in Terros, Water tried to smooth tensions between King Justin and Queen Rynda. It didn't help that Fire thought the rising tensions an amusing display and even sought opportunities to stoke the tension.

"Let them fight it out," Fire said the night before the army was set to march. "Don't you want to see Rynda tumble Justin from his pedestal?"

"You want these armies to go to war?" Water asked.

"You have to admit it would be fun to watch," Fire said. "A thousand rock trolls against a hundred thousand men. I'd say the odds were about even."

"War is never amusing to watch," Lira said softly.

Fire grunted in irritation as his chair was jostled. The tavern was packed with soldiers enjoying a last night before the march. Men laughed and drank, boasting about crushing what had been described as a large group of bandits.

"They think their foe insignificant," Water said.

"Rynda said Serak has less than five thousand at Xshaltheria," Fire said. "The alliance would crush them, and there are enough mages to destroy even Serak and Draeken. If the Dark Gate isn't opened, the battle won't last the day."

"And if the Dark Gate *is* opened?" Lira asked.

"Then it will be the alliance that is crushed," Water said.

He looked at the men in the room, at their smiles and laughter. Most were in uniform, their mugs full, the heat from the fire on their faces.

They thought the alliance an overreaction, and their comments were dismissive, as if the battle was merely a formality to victory. How many would die if the Dark Gate were opened?

He imagined the men with blood on their armor, shock on their faces, their friends dead at their feet as they fled a horde of fiends. Draeken and Serak stood at the head of their foes, where none could touch them.

Fire's chair was jostled again. The soldier guffawed loudly, ignoring Fire's glare as he slammed a mug down on a table where other soldiers had been boasting. Wiping the ale from his beard, he pointed to the mug.

"Five copper says I can smuggle this mug from here into battle and not spill a drop."

Others laughed and cheered as he held it up. Water noticed Fire pointing to the floor, and fire appeared on his fingers, the flames shaping into a bee, one the size of a mouse. It buzzed through the crowded tavern and landed on the man's backside, the stinger hovering over his rump.

"Fire," Water warned. "Is that necessary?"

"Absolutely," Fire said.

The bee stung the man, who whelped and tossed the mug into the air. Ale spilled down his face, wetting his beard and tunic before the mug shattered on his shoulder. He ignored it as he furiously rubbed his posterior. The other soldiers laughed themselves to choking, while Fire dismissed the bee.

Lira hid a smile, while Water glared at his brother. Fire made no effort to hide his laughter as the man stumbled about, still rubbing the bee sting. It would probably leave a welt, and if he were a rider, would hurt for the entire march the following day. But Water could not deny the amusement, and a glance at Lira struggling to contain her laughter cracked his irritation. Fire noticed his expression and stabbed a finger at his smile.

"Ha!"

42

"What?" Water asked, clenching his lips to erase the smile.

"Too late," Fire said.

Water spared the man a glance and found him attempting to show his companions the bee sting. Laughter bubbled out of him at the sight of a grown man attempting to display his injury to a group of soldiers, all of whom protested loudly.

"See?" Fire said. "There's nothing to worry about."

The barmaid threaded by, dropping three bowls of stew on the table and was gone before they'd stopped rocking. Fire picked up his bowl of stew and frowned at the chill. He held it in his palm. Heat glowed on his flesh and the stew began to bubble. Lira slid her bowl to him and he did the same to her meal.

Water watched the exchange, and noted Fire's attitude. He was much like the soldiers in the room, without fear or care of the war with Draeken. The momentary levity faded and Water realized his brother did not share his concern for the battle. He smiled and laughed, his expression the same as it had been shortly before he'd died on the Stormdial.

Water shuddered and looked away, abruptly cold. Fire had been fortunate before, but Mind would not be able to bring him back a second time. If he died in the conflict with Draeken, he would not return.

"There's something we need to do," Water said suddenly.

"Now?" Fire eyed the server, trying to get the girl's attention, but she was busy talking to a knot of soldiers. "I haven't even gotten my bread."

"There's something we need to do," Water insisted.

He rose to his feet and Fire raised an eyebrow. "What's going on?"

"Trust me," Water said. "Please."

Fire held his gaze and then reluctantly nodded. Fire stood, and Water turned to Lira. "I'll need your help."

43

"But our food," Fire protested.

"We can get more," Water said.

Lira glanced between them and stood. Other soldiers were quick to claim their table as Water vacated the tavern and passed into the night. Fire asked Water what he intended but he didn't speak, the battlefield he'd imagined too fresh in his thoughts. There was one other thing he'd imagined, his brother among the dead.

Water guided them into the trees, threading his way out of the war camps and into the forest. The sounds of raucous taverns and soldiers grew dim, replaced by the faint whistle of the wind. They came to a clearing flanked by two towering oak trees, where Water turned and gathered magic into his hands.

"Lira," he said, "at my side."

"Water?" Fire drawled, his eyes on the staffblade forming in Water's palm. "What are you doing?"

Lira, her expression uncertain, joined Water, and he pointed to Fire. "You still talk like you have the power you once had, and I'm not losing my brother again. If we're going into battle, you need to know your new limits."

"I'm still the fragment of fire," Fire said, irritation on his features. "I've always been stronger than you."

"Prove it." Water raised his weapon.

Fire scowled. "Are you doubting my power? Or have you grown arrogant in yours?"

"Water is right," Lira said. "You're weaker than you were. You need to know—"

"Of course you'd side with him," Fire snapped. "We all know you love my brother. That doesn't mean you can talk to me like that."

Water took a step forward. "Hit me," he said. "Please."

"I'm not doing this," Fire growled. "I have nothing to prove, and you're just afraid."

"Of *course* I am," Water yelled. "I lost you before, and I'm not losing you again."

"I'm not playing your game," Fire said.

Water raised his staffblade and hurled it at Fire, who ducked, the weapon striking the tree behind him. As Fire rounded on him, Water cast another staffblade, the weapon bright in the moonlight.

Flames blossomed on Fire's fist as he glared, and Water braced himself for the fight. Fire would be angry and would try to punish Water for his impudence. It wouldn't be sparring. It would be a fight. Fire clenched his fist and the flames extinguished. As smoke curled up his arm, Fire growled his anger.

"I thought of anyone, my brother would trust me."

Fire spun and stomped away, leaving Water and Lira in the clearing. Water took a step to follow but Lira caught his arm, holding him in check. Water grimaced as the darkness swallowed his brother.

"Fire!" he called.

There was no response, and Water turned on Lira. "Why did you stop me?"

"He's afraid," Lira said.

"Afraid to fight me?"

"Afraid you are right," Lira murmured.

Water grimaced at the truth to her words, and he wished his brother were not so stubborn. They were headed into the greatest conflict of their lives, and all four of his brothers were vulnerable.

"I don't know how to protect him," Water said.

"You can't," she replied. "You need to trust him."

"Are you saying he was right?" Water rounded on her.

She gave a wry smile. "People don't like to be told they're weak."

"But this war could kill him."

"It could kill any of us," Lira said. "It's the risk we take every time we step into a fight, every time we draw a sword, every time we face a foe."

He shifted to face her. The moonlight cast her blonde hair into silvery light, softening her expression, and illuminating her slim form. He'd seen her fight with a strength charm active, decimating foes, but right now she looked small, even fragile.

"I've spent my whole life fighting beside my brothers," he said. "And I never really thought any of them could die."

"Until Wylyn killed Fire."

He released a sigh, his breath a swirl of white in the chill. "If what Elenyr said is true, my brothers have lost what made them ageless, and if we survive this war, I'm likely to witness all of them die."

"I've watched friends and family perish," she said, her tone distant.

He recalled the world of Morena, where she'd lived with a husband and family, ultimately losing them all when the krey had invaded. But the way she spoke implied a deeper loss, of others she'd seen perish, other friends, other family. She'd been born in the Dawn of Magic, making her thirty thousand years old, a fraction compared to Tardoq or Ero, yet several times Water's own life span. How many deaths had she witnessed?

"How do you press forward, when you know everyone around you could perish?"

"I am not defined by those I've lost," she replied. "I'm defined by the legacy they have left upon me."

He smiled and kissed her forehead, suddenly overwhelmed with gratitude. "I love you."

She smiled and wrapped her arms around his neck. "I know, and right now, that's what I'm fighting for."

"Oh?" he asked.

"You still have a piece of the fragment of Power," she said. "Don't tell me you haven't thought of what that means."

It meant he could still be an Eternal, and journey with Lira to other worlds, fighting to protect Lumineia from otherworldly threats. The prospect seemed more real than it had before, the bond between him and his brothers now absent.

"You think the Eternals would want me?" he asked. "As you said, I still have a fragment of Draeken."

"All of us have a fragment of darkness in our souls," she replied. "What matters is that you resist yours."

"What's your fragment of darkness?"

She shook her head and kissed him. "You expect me to just share it? You'll have to discover it for yourself."

He grinned and then caught her hand, leading her back into the trees. Although he hadn't been able to help Fire, the impending conflict did not carry the weight it had before. Because he had Lira at his side, and he had a future worth fighting for.

Chapter 5: Return to Blackwell Keep

Shadow advanced into the network of mineshafts, caves, and tunnels, relishing the sense of darkness and solitude. This was his domain, his home. He needed no light, no torch, no source of illumination. The darkness was his refuge.

The walls were as visible to him as if it were broad daylight. Every contour and crack, every knob and vein, all were visible in the Deep. At his side, Elenyr did not have the magic of shadow, but she too did not need the light, her ethereal eyes granting her the chance to see into the very walls.

"How's your vision without the fragment of Power?" Elenyr asked.

"Same as before." Shadow shrugged at the question.

Shadow turned ethereal, his body fading to the black smoke of shadows. He reached to the walls and glided along the length, the sensation different, requiring more effort. It lacked the effortless ease he'd previously savored. He frowned in irritation and returned to flesh, falling into step at Elenyr's side.

"You're weaker," Elenyr said.

"But still a guardian," he replied. "And I was always the weakest of the fragments. This is no different."

"Is that what you thought?" Elenyr asked. "That you were weaker than the others?"

"Shadow magic is the weakest of all the magics," Shadow said. "And I'm *made* of shadow."

"No you're not."

He released a bark of laughter and raised his hand, turning it to shadows, his fingers fading and swirling like smoke. The action would be invisible to anyone else except Elenyr, who could see the changing density of his fingers.

"You're a brother and a son," Elenyr said. "You protect and tease, inspire laughter and anger, even compassion. You have a friend that you would die for, and a family that loves you. A shadow can't do that."

"You're a mom," he said. "You're required to say that."

"I didn't sign a contract," she said.

He grinned. "Are you certain?"

"It was several pages long," she admitted. "And it required a blood stamp."

He laughed and pointed ahead. "We're almost there. What's your plan?"

"Get in and find out everything we can about Serak's generals," she said. "There are lightning wards, so I can't get through all the walls. But we both know lightning has no effect on you. Between the two of us, we should be able to explore the fortress."

They came to a halt at the end of the corridor, where it connected with a vast cavern. It had only been five days since they'd left the cavern behind, and he should have felt a chill, but instead it was anticipation in his chest. A slow smile spread on his face as he surveyed the citadel where the fragment of Power had been ripped from him and his brothers.

Blackwell Keep.

The fortress rested on a pedestal of stone that rose from an abyss, its walls and towers overlooking the well of darkness. Light orbs hung on the exterior, illuminating the bridges that connected to the citadel. Golems that had survived the previous conflict dotted the battlements, the statues scarred and chipped, but still lethal.

"Are you nervous?" she asked.

49

He snorted in amusement. "Last time I was dragged into this fortress unconscious. This time I get to sneak in and discover his secrets. It's like my birthday."

"Don't get arrogant," Elenyr said, and pointed across the cavern, where another entrance was visible as a dark spot on the wall. "Lorica, Sentara, and Rune are ready to attack if either of us gets discovered."

Shadow caught a glimpse of the three women at the opening across the cavern. The assassin was just visible, while Sentara seemed to be eating an apple as she leaned against the wall. Rune crouched in the opening, staring intently at the fortress.

Be careful, the voice of the Unnamed spoke into Shadow's mind. *I cannot determine if anyone is inside.*

"I won't get discovered," he said to both.

Elenyr held his gaze and he sensed her worry. But in this, he was not concerned. Blackwell Keep was a fortress hovering above a sea of shadows, a veritable mountain of his magic. He enjoyed the surface, but he loved the Deep.

"The doors have lightning embedded in the material," Shadow said. "Probably left by Numen before he was killed. How are you going to get inside?"

"We need to find an entrance that isn't protected," she said.

He squinted into the depths beneath the fortress, at the giant pillar holding the castle aloft. Far beneath, a length of stone extended from the exterior wall and connected to the pillar. Without light orb or other illumination, it was invisible in the darkness. A secret entrance.

"There's another way in," he said, pointing to the hidden bridge. "I wager it leads to an entrance you can use."

"I'll meet you there," she said.

Her ethereal form descended into the stone floor of the corridor, disappearing from sight. He stepped to the platform and dropped off the edge, turning to shadow form as he plummeted into the abyss. The wind passed through his body as the lights dimmed, and his smile widened.

He reached outward and cast wings, the shadows forming around his body and allowing him to bank out of the fall. He swerved up and curved around the giant pedestal of stone, relishing the cool air against his body.

The hidden bridge arched between the central pedestal and the outer wall of the cavern, a hundred-foot span that was hardly more than a few feet across. Underneath the fortress, an arched opening had been cut into a recess, invisible from any point above. He flew toward it and alighted on the stone, dismissing his wings and striding to the door. A faint clicking sounded and the door swung open, with Elenyr framed in the opening.

"Don't get arrogant," he admonished.

She grinned, the expression visible beneath her cowl, and led him up the curving stairs. "Embedded lightning charms are difficult to cast," she whispered. "I doubt he has more than the great hall and the main entrances warded."

"Any guards?" Shadow asked.

"Not yet," she replied.

Together, they advanced up the stone stairwell. With the scent of dust, it was obvious the secret entrance had not been used since its creation. As they ascended, a faint glow came from above, and Elenyr's hand shot out, catching him in the shoulder. Without a word, she pointed to the ceiling, and withdrew into the wall.

Shadow turned to darkness and leapt. Rebounding off a curve in the wall, he clung to the darkness on the ceiling. Just as he did, the wall began to shift, and a golem pressed into view. It stepped free of the wall as another appeared, and then another. The trio of guards lumbered down the steps. Hidden in the shadows of the ceiling, he waited for them to grow quiet, and then crawled up the curving ceiling.

He noticed faint indentations on the walls, a curve of a finger here, the protrusion of a nose there. The walls were filled with embedded golems, ready to strike any intruder attempting to gain access. Elenyr passed right through them, and Shadow did what he did best.

51

They advanced up the remainder of the staircase, which culminated in an ironbound door. The spark of energy in the portal suggested it had been warded, so Shadow dropped to his feet and morphed a finger into a shadow key. Pressing it into the lock, he filled the mechanism with shadows and then rotated.

With a dull clank the portal opened, and Shadow strode into the storage room. Elenyr rose from the floor and entered the room as well. Shadow shut the door but left it ajar in case they needed a quick escape.

Stacks of barrels and crates were piled to the ceiling of the small room, a plentiful reserve in case of assault, even though Serak had been the sole person who came to Blackwell Keep. Shadow passed them by, pausing at a barrel of dwarven magma ale.

"Do you have any idea how much that costs?" he whispered.

"We aren't here to drink," she said.

"Maybe on the way out?"

"Shadow," she warned.

He groaned and fell into step behind her. Elenyr crept up the stairs into the fortress, and Shadow listened for any sign of presence. Serak and Draeken, as well as two of their generals, had been present five days ago. Shadow doubted they were here now, but Elenyr's caution was prudent.

The chamber at the top of the stairs contained an assortment of weapons, swords, staffblades, and shields. The small armory sat adjacent to the main hall where the fragments had ejected Draeken. The armory had another door at the back which led to a wide, double staircase.

"I'll search above," Elenyr said. "You explore the rest of the basement."

Shadow agreed and retreated back the way they had come. Pausing at the cask of magma ale, he conjured a dagger from darkness and thrust it into the wood. Withdrawing it, he morphed the dagger into a mug. He filled the mug and then sealed the breach. No need to waste the ale.

Sipping the expensive ale, he savored the burning flavor as he began to search the series of rooms beneath the fortress, all connected to a central hallway. He casually strolled between them, peeking into the rarely used chambers.

He didn't expect to find anything, and was not disappointed. Serak was cautious, but only a zealot would protect his stores of food when they were already locked inside a secret fortress and protected by an army of golems.

He sipped his mug until he found a stash of tableware. Pouring the liquid into an actual mug, he continued to enjoy the exorbitantly expensive drink as he explored. When he found nothing, he made his way up the stairs.

Dim light glowed from a handful of orbs, and he was grateful he had swapped his shadow mug for a real one. The first floor above the great hall was empty, just a spacious receiving room and a collection of maps on a large table.

He ascended to the one above, and then into one of the towers. He guessed the place was empty. Serak had built the refuge in order to trap Draeken, so why would he remain once he had Draeken as his master?

He climbed the last tower, where he found Elenyr peering into the window of a small chamber. The crackle of energy indicated the room was bound by lightning. Elenyr whirled at his entrance, her sword coming free.

He retreated, avoiding losing his mug and protesting loudly. She glared at him and hissed for quiet, at which he advanced and joined her to peer into the small chamber. Elenyr pointed at the mug.

"Really?"

He took a sip. "Really."

She snorted and motioned to the room. "This chamber is the only room outside of the great hall that's protected by lightning. I suspect what we desire lies within. Think you can open the door?"

He morphed his finger into a key. "The challenge is doing it without spilling my ale."

One handed, he pushed shadows into the key hole while Elenyr covered the nearest orb on the wall. With the increased solidity of the magic, he managed to rotate the door and ease it open, without spilling his mug. He grinned in triumph.

"Will you please get focused?" Elenyr asked, exasperated.

Shadow smirked and slipped into the chamber, which proved to be rather small. Containing a cabinet on one side and a desk on the other, the room contained much of interest. Shadow stepped to the cabinet while Elenyr examined the table.

"There's a memory orb here," he said. "And four containers."

"For what?"

"If I knew, I would not have called them containers."

She opened the tome on the desk and scanned the contents. "This is a private office," she murmured. "Here he's writing about his plans for Draeken." She flipped to the end of the archive. "The final entry is after Draeken's separation. It says he's taking the final two vials."

She rotated and looked to Shadow, who pointed to the four strange reservoirs in the cabinet. Each resembled the claws of a beast. Carved out of obsidian, the claws were pointed upward, as if they were intended to hold an object.

"One for each general?" Shadow asked.

"But what was in them?" she asked.

She bent and examined the book, searching the text. Shadow joined her, almost spilling his ale when he bent to read the final words. Elenyr cursed when she read them, and Shadow took her place, reading aloud.

"The vials of the Dark must not be broken, for they are the only way each general's will can be leashed to my master . . ."

"That's how he's doing it," Elenyr whispered. "He's using the Dark to control the generals."

Shadow sipped his drink, delighted with the turn of events. "This is the best war we've ever had."

"I hope you're enjoying it," she said. "Because if we're not careful, it's going to be our last."

He raised his mug as if to toast the event. "Then here's to the final war."

Chapter 6: An Old Friend

Shadow settled into the seat and put his feet on the desk as he listened to Elenyr. She opened the cabinet and took one of the claw shaped holders, murmuring to herself, a habit she'd had since Shadow's youth.

"No magic can rob a man of his will," she said, "but the Dark is not magic, and it alters the flesh of those it touches, turning them into extensions of itself. Serak must have trapped some of the Dark from his first attempt to open the Dark Gate."

He drank his mug of magma ale, wondering if he had time to return to the basement for a refill. The mug was running low and it had been ages since he'd managed to get his hands on such expensive stock. The dwarves tended to keep such priceless liquid under heavy lock and key.

"But why is this here?" Elenyr asked aloud.

She collected the memory orb from inside the top of the cabinet. It too, sat on a matching clawed pedestal, and she examined it with a frown. Shadow began rifling through the drawers of the desk, wondering what else he might find from a man of such expensive tastes.

"The memory is locked," she said. "We'll need to find a mind mage to unlock it."

"Can I see it?"

She shrugged and handed him the orb, but he moved his hand at the last moment, causing it to fall. It shattered in a tinkling of glass, the memory floating up from inside. Elenyr threw him a scathing look.

"Why would you do that?"

"I thought you wanted to see the memory."

"I wanted to keep it as evidence."

"Too late," he replied.

The memory was of the sea, the water rising and falling in shallow swells. But the liquid seemed off, more reflective, solid even. The image of the waves filled the room, making them feel like they were on the seas, the walls and ceiling obscured by the memory.

"Where are we?" he asked.

The sea swelled up and morphed into the shape of a man. Gendor. At his side, the water rose up and turned into Bartoth. As the third took shape into the Raven, Elenyr sucked in her breath, her features wide in recognition.

"This is an *oracle's* memory."

"Senia?" Shadow asked.

"Or her grandmother," Elenyr said. "They are the only ones I know whose farsight was the sea."

"One of them foresaw the creation of the generals?" He was out of magma ale, and he rose from his seat and stepped to the door.

She caught his elbow and held him fast. "This is Senia's memory," Elenyr said as the final one took shape. "Serak must have manipulated her and then used his memory mages to strip the memory so she wouldn't know."

"But who is the last general?" Shadow asked.

The final figure took shape. The woman's slight frame was that of a dark elf. Her body was slim and appeared frail, her features mottled and diseased. Shadow blinked in surprise as he recognized the woman.

"Is that Mimic?"

"First of the Queen's Hand," Elenyr nodded in understanding. "Her magic would make her an ideal candidate for becoming Draeken's general."

"And she's really cruel," Shadow said.

"I didn't know you'd met."

She turned and noticed he stood with his hand on the door, his mug empty. She frowned at his posture and he shrugged sheepishly. Just as he took his hand off the door, the knob began to turn. On instinct he retreated into the shadows next to the cabinet. Elenyr followed his lead and turned ethereal before leaping into the cabinet, both disappearing from sight just as the door swung open.

The cloaked figure of Gendor stood framed in the opening, his scythe pulsing with power, his skeletal hands clenched on the wood. His eyes burned like coals as he surveyed the room and settled on the mug resting on the desk. The memory had faded, but the mug marked the presence of an intruder.

"My apologies," he said, and then slashed through the cabinet.

Elenyr cried out as the scythe cut through the wood, slicing across her side. Shadow leapt from his hide and picked up the mug, which he smashed on Gendor's head. The man whirled with inhuman speed, his scythe cutting high.

Shadow ducked, the scythe scraping his hair as it passed above his head. Shadow leapt into the stairwell and hurtled down the stairs to avoid the spinning weapon. The man gave pursuit, much faster, and far more deadly.

The scythe cut Shadow's cloak from his shoulders, the fabric settling on the steps as Shadow turned to dark form and leapt to the ceiling. Gendor kicked off one wall and then another, bringing himself to the top of the hall, his weapon reaching for Shadow. Giving up on escaping on the ceiling, Shadow dropped to the floor, narrowly avoiding losing his hand as he landed on the steps.

"I thought you were on our side," Shadow called over his shoulder.

"I didn't choose this," Gendor snapped. "He holds my will. I am to kill the intruder."

"What if I'm not an intruder?" he shot back.

"What else would I call you?" Gendor demanded.

Shadow reached the basement stairwell and ducked into the armory. He caught a sword from the wall and then picked up a shield. He sent it spinning into the hallway, clipping Gendor on the shoulder as he entered. Shadow raised his sword and parried the man's scythe but the weapon was too fast, and Gendor drove him back into a storeroom.

Shadow was used to being faster than anyone except Light, but Gendor's sheer speed took his breath away. Shadow ducked and twisted, avoiding the scythe by a hairsbreadth as he retreated to the next stairwell and into the final storeroom. Just as he passed the barrel containing the magma ale, he yanked the plug from the hole and spun, slashing the dagger and sword against each other.

The spark ignited the ale in a burst of fire that poured from the barrel. Shadow had hoped it would explode, but the flow of liquid created a current of flames that streaked across the room and splashed across the opposite wall.

Gendor slid to a halt on the other side of the firewall, and across the barrier the two combatants regarded each other. Shadow smirked at Gendor's reserve, and the assassin passed his scythe into the fire, the metal burning bright.

"Very clever," Gendor said. "I cannot disobey my orders, but neither can I die for them."

Elenyr dropped through the ceiling and groaned when she landed on her feet. She had her hand on her side, where a line cut through her tunic. She straightened and caught Shadow on the shoulder, dragging him towards the exit.

"Let's go."

"You cannot stop them," Gendor called.

"Then who will?" Elenyr snapped.

"My blade is poisoned with the Dark," Gendor said. "If you do not clean the wound in the next few minutes, it will take root and you will be dead soon."

"Why would you help us?" Elenyr asked.

"I didn't ask for this," Gendor snapped. "I didn't ask to become a butcher."

"Then be smarter," Shadow said.

"That's easy for you to say," Gendor growled. "I'm a specter of death, and my entire future has been taken. When this fire gives out I will pursue and kill you, and neither you nor I can stop that."

The current of fire began to diminish, the flames falling. Elenyr caught Shadow's arm and pulled him toward the exit, but Shadow shook himself free and returned to the flames. Gendor began to pace on the opposite side, as if fighting the urge to leap through the flames.

"You must kill intruders?"

"I am compelled," Gendor said. "The moment your presence was known, I found a Gate and returned."

"What if we're not intruders?"

Gendor slowed. "What are you suggesting?"

"That we are an assassin's old friends," Shadow said with a smile. "Here to reminisce over an expensive barrel of magma ale, which unfortunately ignited. A sad and expensive mistake, I must say."

His words brought Gendor to a halt. Elenyr had opened the door, but she spun to face Shadow, her features writ in surprise. Shadow gestured to the barrel of magma ale, which had begun to sputter.

"You think we're friends?" Gendor asked, his tone incredulous.

"Doesn't matter what *I* think," Shadow said. "Only matters what *you* think. Are we intruders? Or are we friends?"

The fire sputtered and the liquid died. Gendor did not advance. He stood in the doorway, his scythe low to the ground, the metal still red from being plunged into the fire. Shadow smirked at his reserve.

"I see no intruders here," Gendor said.

"Exactly," Shadow said.

Elenyr did not lower her sword. "What is Serak's weakness?"

"There is one that can defeat Draeken," he said.

"One of us?" Shadow asked.

"No," Gendor replied. "Serak manipulated a prophecy out of Senia, and then took her memory of the vision."

"We saw it," Elenyr said. "It's how Serak knew they would need four generals."

"The same." Gendor twitched as if he were struggling to keep himself in check. "But you did not see the rest of the vision. Senia foresaw one born of three bloodlines, human, elf, and dwarf. He's the only one capable of destroying Draeken, and Serak's greatest fear."

"Why not kill Senia?" Elenyr asked.

"Serak fears her power," Gendor said. "But he also needs her."

The scythe came up a few inches, and Shadow realized the gambit would not endure forever. Gendor hated them, for the fragments had almost destroyed his mind, taken his future before Serak had done the same.

"Do you know their name?" Shadow asked.

"No," he said. "But I know he's in Talinor. Now go, before I reconsider your presence."

"You can stop Serak and Draeken," Elenyr said. "You can be your own master, again."

"No," Gendor's red eyes flared. "My fate is sealed, but I will have revenge against those who call me servant. I swear on the edge of my blade, Draeken and Serak will fall."

"What are you going to do?" Shadow asked. "Your will is bound."

Gendor's voice hardened. "But my mind is free."

Elenyr pulled Shadow into the stairwell and this time Shadow did not resist. As they departed through the secret entrance, Shadow stifled a laugh, pleased with how the morning had turned out. Then Elenyr stumbled and he recalled her injury.

They exited through the base of the fortress and Shadow flew them up to where Lorica, Rune, and Sentara were hidden. As he deposited Elenyr in the mouth of the cave, Rune leapt forward and knelt at her side.

"You were in there a lot longer than we planned," the girl said. "What happened?"

"We found a friend," Shadow said.

"Did your friend slice Elenyr?" Sentara asked.

"It must be cleaned or it will kill me," Elenyr said.

"It stays with you even in ethereal form?" Rune asked.

Elenyr nodded, her features tight with pain. "Only weapon to ever do that unless it had lightning."

Rune stepped forward and knelt. "The Unnamed knows what to do."

She placed her hand on Elenyr's waist—and white fire burst from Elenyr's skin. Elenyr arched her back and screamed, the sound of agony echoing in the cavern of Blackwell Keep. Rune stumbled backward and the light died, revealing a searing callous over the wound, but no trace of the Dark.

"Sorry," Rune said. "I didn't know that was going to happen."

"I'm okay," Elenyr said, sucking in her breath. "I can feel it. The poison is gone."

"What happened in there?" Sentara asked.

"We enjoyed a lovely drink with an old friend," Shadow asked.

"Not the time to be you," Elenyr groaned and accepted Lorica's hand to rise. "We met Gendor, and he told us of a memory Serak stole from Senia. Apparently she discovered the greatest threat to Draeken, and then erased the memory."

Lorica shook her head. "Is that possible?"

"We saw part of the memory," Shadow said. "It's certainly possible."

"What happened in this memory?" Rune asked.

"Senia learned that one person can destroy Draeken. He is born of human, elf, and dwarven blood," Elenyr said.

Lorica regarded them with doubt in her expression, but Elenyr's scream had brought the golems out of the fortress, forcing them back up the tunnel. As Shadow took the lead, he chuckled to himself.

"It appears our path just shifted."

Chapter 7: A New Mount

Draeken surveyed the devastated home, a frown creasing his features. The once beautiful estate in Keese lay broken, beams poking skyward, flames leaping into the sky as if they wanted to devour the clouds. The handful of survivors moaned as Gendor and Bartoth dispatched them.

Draeken shook his head. "They should have been here."

"Who, my Lord?" the Lady Dentis asked at his side.

He spared her a look. She stood trembling, her beautiful green dress stained with blood and smoke, dirt covering her face. She'd been a powerful wife to a powerful lord, but only in public. In private, she'd been the ruthless Raven, head of a thieves guild expanding across the south. Few had known she'd also served Serak as an appendage to the Order of Ancients.

"The Hauntress," he said dismissively. "She should have come. I made my plans clear so they would come."

Serak approached and bowed his head. "Gendor is killing the last of the bandits. Bartoth is scattering the city guard."

Shouts and screams came from outside the estate walls, followed by a brutal crash and the splintering of wood, the sound of an armored body bashing his way through the base of a building. Unstable from the conflict in the street, the structure collapsed, billowing dust into the smoky twilight sky.

"Why did they not come?" Draeken growled.

"Perhaps because they saw your intent," Serak said. "Elenyr is crafty, and the oracle would have seen what you intended."

"I know her capacity," Draeken said, his lips twitching with irritation.

Elenyr would prove to be a problem. She'd survived three attempts on her life by a lightning mage, and her continuing guidance to the broken fragments kept them focused. In addition, Serak had seen the oracle and Tardoq headed east after they'd failed to stop Bartoth's conversion to Draeken's general. The two parties likely joined outside of Blackwell Keep. The oracle would have foreseen Draeken's turning the Raven into a third general, and Elenyr should have tried to stop him. A perfect opportunity to rectify Serak's biggest failure.

"Why did she not come?" he growled.

He'd hoped to end Elenyr for good. If she would have come to the Raven's estate to stop him turning the Raven into his general, he would have been able to kill the woman, before she could thwart his plans. But she had not come.

"It seems they chose a different path," Serak said.

"Obviously," Draeken said.

Serak's intelligence grated on Draeken's flesh. The man had spent five thousand years preparing for Draeken's arrival, preparing so Draeken could open the Dark Gate, yet he treated him like a fool.

But if Elenyr had not come to stop Lady Dentis becoming a third general, where would she have gone? What quest would she possibly deem more important? A thought crossed his mind and he smiled. If Senia had foreseen him coming to Keese—with Serak, Bartoth, and Gendor—it meant she had foreseen their absence in other locations.

"She seeks to stop the fourth general," he replied.

"That means they have discerned her identity," Serak said. "We must move quickly."

"And we must divide," he said.

"Master?" Serak asked. "I believe that is unwise. If we take separate ways, the oracle might learn that we are alone."

"That is my hope," he said. "Elenyr must die, and she will not attack unless she sees a chance of victory."

"But if we separate, she could kill you," Serak said.

"You think me vulnerable?" Draeken laughed, the sound causing the Raven to shudder and look to the exit. "She cannot harm me, not anymore."

His amusement faded into a scowl. Five thousand years, trapped inside the fragments, caged by Elenyr's teachings of protecting others. His might had been used to repair walls, grow plants, end conflicts, while his identity was known by only a few. He deserved better. The people of Lumineia should tremble at the mention of his name.

"Shall I get the cloak?" Serak asked, glancing at the Raven.

"No," he said.

Clearly surprised by the answer, Serak raised an eyebrow. "Master?"

"You said there were two candidates for the position," Draeken said. "Let us insert an element of indecision into the oracle's visions."

"A clever ploy," Serak said with a nod of approval.

"Take her to your mount," he said. "It's time we depart."

Serak bowed again and then lifted the Raven on a pedestal of stone. The woman bared her teeth but did not move, the stone shackles on her legs preventing escape. A red dragon dropped through the smoke and landed in the gardens, its claws tearing furrows in the earth. More shouts came from the streets and Draeken smiled. The music of fear.

Bendelinish, the red dragon, dipped its head and opened its jaws, eager to join the conflict. But the battle had ended quickly, and Draeken patted the red dragon on the flank. It was middle aged, large, but not giant, lean and powerful. A worthy mount for Serak, even if Draeken could hear the sullen tinge to the beast's thoughts.

Serak placed the Raven on the dragon's neck and mounted. Nodding to Draeken, he directed the dragon skyward. The red dragon

66

disappeared into the haze as Gendor exited the burning structure and advanced to Draeken, who noted the blood on his scythe. Bartoth too, returned, albeit through the outer wall.

He burst through the stone, his deep laughter scattering the few soldiers still in the street, and then advanced to join Gendor. Draeken smiled at his two generals, so powerful, at his command.

"Shall we return to Blackwell Keep through the Gate?" Gendor asked.

Although the assassin tried to keep his voice even, there was a trace of hope. He did not want to continue killing, not for Draeken. The man's reluctance and defiance brought a measure of pleasure to Draeken, for now. Draeken valued Bartoth for his brutality and power, but Gendor provided much more amusement.

"You said there was no intruder at Blackwell Keep," he said.

"There was not," Gendor said. "A golem's magic had failed and it had begun to wander about. I dealt with him and returned."

Draeken wondered if the man was lying. He was certainly crafty enough to evade giving the truth, even if Draeken pressed him on it. But this time, Draeken found he did not care. He had more pressing concerns.

"If Elenyr failed to come here, that means she might know of Lachonus. Find him. Kill him."

"Serak said he needed to remain alive," Bartoth said.

"He's not the master anymore," Draeken said. "Make sure he's dead."

"As you order," Gendor said, and turned away.

Bartoth sheathed his sword and motioned to Draeken. "What about you?"

"Serak has a mount. It's only fair I have my own."

"You want your own dragon?" he snorted in amusement.

"Doesn't everyone?" Draeken replied with a laugh.

"There are always outcast dragons on the outskirts of the Dragon's Teeth," he said. "I would enjoy the hunt."

"No," he said. "I want you to go with Gendor. Make sure Lachonus dies. The oracle's vision proves he is a threat."

Draeken wished Serak had killed Lachonus before. The man was obviously a threat, and Serak had possessed the power to end his life. But the vision Serak had taken from Senia had been clear, if Lachonus died early, another would rise in his stead. Still, Draeken decided to cast the vision aside. His future was his own, and it was time for Lachonus to die.

"You're going dragon hunting alone?" Bartoth asked.

"Not hunting," he said, and reached into his cloak for the small pocket Gate that had brought him to Keese. "I know the location of my prey."

Bartoth shrugged, clearly confused, and then turned and followed Gendor into the darkness. Draeken opened the pocket Gate and activated it by touching a small rune. Silver liquid poured from the small mirror and expanded, rising to become an oval touching the earth. Draeken swept the burning estate with a satisfied gaze and then stepped through, his body transporting into the depths of the towering mountain range south of Talinor, the Dragon's Teeth.

The terminus lay in a small room of stone, the air also tinged with smoke, albeit the smoke of dragon's flame. Draeken returned the pocket Gate to its pouch and ascended the steps through the underground outpost.

Once a krey structure, it had been abandoned when the treaty had been signed with the dragons, and the dragons had taken the outpost as their throne. He threaded his way upward and entered a vast chamber, the hollow interior between three giant peaks.

An enormous roof bridged the trio of summits, the floor stretching to the great doorways where the dragons entered the royal roost. Scored by thousands of dragon claws, the floor had blackened from dragon fire,

68

and reeked of soot and smoke. An enormous home for the greatest living creatures on Lumineia.

The King of Dragons.

Thistikor, the giant gold dragon, lounged on his royal perch, the stone melted and shaped by ages of past dragon kings. Two other dragons were also present, a red dragon that was even larger than Thistikor, and a blue dragon, a female, by the markings on her neck. She was smaller than either of the males, but lighting crackled in her throat as she opened her maw.

"Thistikor," Draeken said, coming to a halt.

Draeken, the great dragon dropped from its perch, sending a shudder into the mountain. *Your presence is unwelcome.*

Draeken eyed the trio of dragons, a slow smile spreading on his face. Their posture indicated they were second and third in command, likely generals, or possibly a prince and a princess. Which mount did he prefer? A giant gold dragon? An even larger red? Or the smaller blue?

"I'll just be a moment," he said.

The last time you were here, you killed several of my kindred, the red snarled, flames spilling from his jaws.

"You shall do nicely," he said to the red.

The gold dragon reared back and roared, the sound reverberating in the chamber like thunder. *ENOUGH*, the king bellowed. *Gorewrathian, I want his corpse hung on my wall.*

The red lunged forward, fire bursting from its throat. Draeken reached for his own magic and gathered the fire, shaping it to his will. Arms and a torso formed, followed by legs and enormous fists. The golem took shape and swelled to fifty feet, large enough to cause the red to cut off its breath and stumble back in shock. The golem leaned forward and punched the red dragon.

The enormous beast rocked to the side, several teeth coming loose and scattering across the ground. The blue dragon opened its jaws but

69

the towering golem reached out and wrapped a hand about her throat, lifting the dragon off the ground and slamming her against the wall.

"I will have what I came for," Draeken said from behind the dragon.

He gathered the light from the room and leapt forward. Thistikor dropped to the ground and snapped its jaws, its maw large enough to crush a house. But Draeken possessed the speed of the fragment of Light, and he leapt aside. The jaws snapped shut and Draeken conjured a six foot spear of pure light, a sliver of power that pulsed.

He plunged the spear into the dragon's throat. It pierced the nearly impenetrable scales and sank deep—and then began to grow. Thistikor stumbled back, flames pouring from its jaws as its fought for breath, but the spear continued to grow, stretching and extending, a shard that became twenty feet, and then thirty, until it pierced the dragon's skull.

Thistikor's strangled roar again reverberated in the confines of the throne room, the sound of a dying beast. Still the spear grew. Thistikor thrashed on the ground and dug its claws into its own neck, desperate to dislodge the weapon. Then it charged Draeken, a desperate attempt to crush his killer.

Draeken didn't move, but the giant fire golem raised a knee, bashing the king of dragons in the chin, a brutal blow that sent the beast into the wall. The spear stuck through both the jaw and the skull now, and it jammed into the ground, lifting the dragon upward. It clawed at the hundred-foot spear of light magic, but its claws cracked and broke against the rod, its body sliding up the wall. Its hind legs came off the floor, and then its tail, until the rod struck a protrusion and sank into the stone, pinning the dragon against the wall. Only the tip of its tail still touched the ground, where it flopped from side to side.

"You did want a corpse on your wall," Draeken said.

The red dragon and the blue hung back, their heads swinging between the dying king and the mage that had killed him so easily. As Thistikor twitched his last, Draeken turned to the red dragon.

"Gorewrathian was it?"

The red snarled, but made no move to attack. *Prince of the reds, second in command to the king.*

"You have my congratulations on ascending to the throne," Draeken said.

A red has not sat on the throne in ages, the dragon said, greed filling his voice.

"Sadly you will not be able to enjoy your new position," he said. "You may be king, but you are also my mount."

I am not a horse, the dragon growled.

"Would you prefer I find another?" Draeken asked. He cast a second spear of light.

Gorewrathian looked to the dead king Thistikor, and then bowed its head. *You have your mount.*

Draeken smiled and turned to the blue. The female had shifted towards one of the entrances, her posture one of escape. Draeken asked her name and she spoke in a surprisingly light voice, the tone indicating a female.

Lagailien, the blue dragon replied.

"I have a special task for you," Draeken said. "A Hauntress that needs killing."

She glanced to the dead king, still pinned to the wall. *If my companions die, and I succeed, I want the throne.*

Draeken laughed as Gorewrathian growled. He loved dragon greed. It was so predictable. "You shall have it."

Then consider her dead, the blue said.

Draeken strode to his new mount and rose into the air, flying himself up to straddle Gorewrathian's neck. The ability caused new shock in the dragons as he settled into his seat. Never before had a mage existed that could fly on his own, and the sight inspired a sense of fear in the dragons that Draeken savored. Serak possessed a red dragon. But Draeken rode on the back of a king.

"North," he directed the beast. "It's time the people remembered why they fear your kind."

Chapter 8: Dedliss

Mind walked with Tardoq and Jeric, the trio making their way north and west, deeper into the mountains. Spring had yet to arrive in the higher altitudes, and the snow was deep. Rather than dry and crisp, the warm air led to melting snow, and winter had lost its bite.

They ascended through a pass so narrow that Tardoq had to turn sideways in order to ease his way through the gap. Higher and higher they climbed, aiming for a towering peak. Allies of necessity, the three spoke little, and Mind mulled over the events at Blackwell Keep.

His thoughts frequently shifted to Tardoq, his oversized and armored companion. The last time Mind had seen him, Tardoq had been a foe, and wielded a powerful otherworldly hammer. Now he carried a rock troll greatsword, and not a common one either, but a warrior's soulblade. Rock trolls never relinquished their soulblades unless dead, and the family could gift the weapon to another. But who had given the blade to Tardoq? And why?

As they approached a towering peak, Jeric pulled his cloak tighter about his body to ward off the icy wind. "We're almost there."

"Where are we going in the Empire?" Mind asked.

"We should start at Dedliss," Jeric said.

"The Bone Crucible?" Tardoq asked.

"She's been spotted there a handful of times," Jeric said, "always under disguise, of course, but she enters when she is in need of resources. I suspect she has a contact there that we can utilize."

"Care to enlighten me?" Mind asked.

Jeric glanced in his direction. "Dedliss is a world known for a single element, brutality. It was once a world rich in forests and

73

beautiful lakes, but House Torn'Ent converted most of the surface into the Bone Crucible, an arena where thousands fight for survival. The contests are beamcast throughout the Empire, making House Torn-Ent one of the richest."

"Wealth gained from blood," Mind said, wrinkling his nose in distaste. "Who are the combatants?"

Tardoq motioned to himself. "Dakorians like myself are frequently entered, as are outcasts, criminal krey, and human slaves. Occasionally a house in need of glint will enter one of their higher ranked dakorians, or even a Bloodwall."

Mind understood the strange words from context. Glint was coin, beamcast meant some kind of viewing mechanism that allowed other worlds to witness events on Dedliss. In just a small conversation, Mind was forced to acknowledge the sheer vastness to the Krey Empire.

"How would you fare?" Mind asked Tardoq.

Tardoq met his gaze. "Few can stand against me, but in the Crucible, Bloodwalls have fallen to humble krey. The only sure bet is that humans always die."

"And how will we draw the Bonebreaker out?" Mind asked.

They ascended a rise and came to a natural cave. In the recessed space, an arch of stone curved over the opening, the shape distinct and obviously made by the hand of man. The cave was empty, just a shallow crack near the summit of a towering peak.

"I think you should enter a ranked contest," Jeric said, nodding to Mind as he pressed his palm against the side of the arch. "If you defeat a dakorian, your fame will be instant, and should draw the Bonebreaker out of hiding."

"Who would I face?" he asked.

"Probably a criminal dakorian," Tardoq said, but he had a frown on his face, as if he disliked the suggestion. "They never pit humans against krey. They don't want slaves seeing other humans killing krey. It happens in the war contests, but not in the ranked events."

Mind liked the suggestion. It was bold and would draw a quick response. With Draeken and Serak so close to opening the Dark Gate, time was against them, and a quick return with the Bonebreaker would add critical aid to their effort. It did beg one question.

"Do the krey have technology that would help us locate the Dark Gate and destroy it?" Mind asked. "Or perhaps destroy Serak from one of your skyships?"

"It is possible," Jeric said. "But the Eternals do not own any ships with such capabilities, and even if we did, any action of such magnitude would reveal the Empire to the people."

Behind the effort to keep Lumineia hidden was the real truth. The Eternals were not as strong as Mind had assumed. A skyship undoubtedly cost a great deal of coin, or glint, as Jeric had said. He wondered how many Eternals even served Ero. Ten? Fifty?

"And the other Eternals?" Tardoq asked.

"Occupied," Jeric said. "To bring them now would just open Lumineia to other threats."

The Gate glowed to life, the silver liquid shimmering into place to resemble a mirror. Jeric reached up and touched his pendent, his body changing, his arms slimming and skin darkening into his true form.

Ero.

"Keep your eyes open," Ero warned Mind. "And remember, in this place, you are viewed much like cattle."

"I'm not giving up my sword."

Tardoq chuckled. "This is the one world where humans are allowed to carry weapons. Of course, if you draw the blade, guards will crush you to pulp. But it's to be expected that human combatants be armed. It helps the oddsmakers to understand what value to place on your life."

"Ready?" Ero asked.

Mind stepped past them and into the Gate. As in his trip to Kelindor, he felt a tug, and then stepped onto a raised platform. He swept his surroundings with shock, a single thought reverberating in his mind.

He was no longer on Lumineia.

The room he'd entered was enormous, larger even than the entire city of Herosian. Platforms lined the cavernous space, stacked twenty high and hundreds long. Each contained a single world Gate.

The exterior of the room was all glass, unbroken sheets that extended for hundreds of feet, allowing a clear view of the churning currents of magma cascading down the mountain. The Gate chamber sat on the slope of the volcano. At the base of the volcano, a war waged, with blasts of fire, light, and other energies.

At the center of the Gate Chamber, an enormous sphere hovered in the air. Images of battle and combat washed across the surface, before being replaced with runic text, which Mind took to understand as a call to spend glint in order to watch more.

"We'll need to get you registered," Ero said. "This way."

Ero crossed the platform to a much smaller Gate, this one obviously connecting only to the locations on the world of Dedliss. He tapped the symbols on the side and the silver shimmered. Tardoq followed, and Mind passed through, entering a much smaller room.

Obviously underground, the room was spherical in shape. They stood on a platform at the center, which connected by walkways to the exterior. Combatants prowled the interior of cages that lined every inch of the sphere. Abruptly the sphere shifted, turning on an axis to bring a certain cage in line with one of the walkways, where a krey woman explained the value of a dakorian inside the cell to another krey. Although the cells on the ceiling were now horizontal, the captives stood on the sides as if the gravity had turned.

The center of the chamber contained a circular desk with a krey man and woman behind it. Both obviously bored, they spoke to a dakorian and a krey at his side, who argued that his soldier should receive a better ranked position in the upcoming duels.

"He's two hundred years old," the krey behind the counter scoffed. "He won't last long in a ranked contest."

"He was nearly a Bloodwall for house Thorn'Vall," the krey protested. "And he saw combat on the moons of Urgin."

The female krey shrugged. "Just let him die in the seventh tier."

The male frowned but tapped a floating sphere. The symbols changed, and he rattled off instructions to the seller, who nodded eagerly before making his way to one of the small Gates lining the platform.

"How can I understand them?" Mind murmured to Tardoq.

"Language is universal throughout the Empire," he replied. "Even slaves are encoded with the knowledge."

"But I wasn't born in the Empire," Mind said.

"Your ancestors were," Ero replied.

The accent was strange, but Mind had no difficulty understanding the conversation. He struggled to discard his sense of unease. He'd spent five thousand years on Lumineia thinking it was the entirety of existence. Stepping on Kelindor's moon had made him feel small. Now he felt like a gnat.

Ero stepped into the space vacated by the seller, and the two krey behind the counter perked up, their eyes on Tardoq. The krey released a sound of appreciation and reached for the hovering sphere.

"And who might this be?" he asked.

"A Bloodwall," his companion said, her eyes flicking to the prominent four scars on Tardoq's horns. "And what a specimen. What house?"

Tardoq jerked his head. "I'm not here to fight. He is."

He pointed to Mind, who folded his arms and tried not to look annoyed. Both krey were disappointed, and the male exited the desk and came around to examine him. It allowed Mind to get a good look at the oddsmaker.

The krey was about Mind's height, but his skin was a dark grey, several shades darker than Ero's own flesh. His eyes were a bright green. He was obviously not a soldier, because Mind was able to sift through his memories as he poked and prodded Mind's body.

His name was Ursun, and he came from the house of Eter'Quen. It explained his green eyes. Apparently every house in the Empire had different eyes. Wylyn and her son had color changing eyes, the colors shifting according to their mood. House Eter'Quen had green eyes. When children were born to parents of different houses, they belonged to the house matching their eyes.

Ursun was six thousand years old, young by krey standards, and just working on Dedliss at the crucible because his family owed gambling debts to House Torn'Ent. He hated the female he worked with, who was a higher rank daughter of House Thorn'Vall, a krey woman named Rasina.

Rasina fiddled with her clothing and kept glancing at Tardoq, attempting to draw his gaze. Mind couldn't pick her history as easily, but there was enough for him to realize she disliked her position at the Oddsmaker sphere, a position she'd been given after her own debts had come to light. Apparently gambling was rampant in House Thorn'Vall, and her mother disapproved of her foolish wagers.

"He'll have to fight a dakorian," Ursun said. "Rank fourteen, criminal they call Basher. I can't get you a lower ranked foe until next week. We've had a flood of slave fighters in the last few days, most from Wylyn's house."

Mind guessed that without Wylyn, the house had begun to sell off their slaves, looking to make glint before her return. They didn't know she was already dead and her house would eventually disintegrate.

"That is acceptable," Ero said.

"Your funeral," Rasina said with a snort.

Ursun shrugged. "If he lasts ten minutes, you'll win the standard thousand glints. If he dies, you get nothing."

"I'll place a wager that he wins," Ero said.

Ursun actually laughed. "How much do you want to lose?"

"A million glint."

That got their attention, and both stared at Ero, slack-jawed. Ursun recovered first and fumbled to update the information on the sphere, the lettering changing to reflect the wager. Mind picked their shock from their thoughts. Both thought Ero stupid. If victorious, Ero would win a hundred times that amount. Failure would probably result in Ero being tossed into his own duel.

"You understand the risks?" Ursun asked.

"I do," Ero said, "and I accept them."

"This ought to be good," Ursun said.

Ero reached up and touched the floating sphere. It flickered green and Ursun turned the sphere, rotating the entire chamber so an empty cell lined up with the walkway. He pointed to it as the grate lifted, and Ero guided Mind down the walkway.

"Is a million a lot?" Mind asked.

"It is everything the Eternals possess," he replied.

"You bet your entire organization that I would win?"

"I did," Ero said, and offered a faint smile as Mind entered the chamber. "We're both invested in this victory."

Tardoq stood at Ero's side as the grate lowered. "Don't forget, dakorians have two hearts." He pointed to a spot on his chest and then stomach. You'll have to puncture both of them. Or the throat."

"I know what to do," Mind replied. And hoped that he did.

Chapter 9: Duel

After the grate shut, the spherical chamber rotated up and around. Mind instinctively reached for the wall, but his feet remained on the floor. His stomach heaved as the world turned sideways, but gravity remained rooted in the same direction. He chuckled at his own nervousness and felt the threads of gravity emanating from a machine at the side of the cell.

The sphere locked into the place, and through the grate he spotted Ursun and Rasina watching another floating orb, this one located at the back of their desk. It depicted a small arena high above the earth. The interconnected walkways were narrow, with ramps and steps circling and winding back on itself. A place of dueling.

A large sphere rose to the platform and attached to the side, and a section of the wall opened. A dakorian stepped out and hefted a hammer. Modified to include spikes, the weapon was as ugly as the dakorian, which had numerous scars twisting his flesh.

Another sphere appeared, rising and attaching to the opposite side of the dueling arena. A section opened—and the back of Mind's cell lifted as well. Mind had thought the chamber underground, and now realized it floated in the air. He cautiously stepped into the open and surveyed the dueling area.

Several paths extended away from him, some switching up and over, others turning to steps and descending under. A handful of walls bordered the walkways, but most of them came to his knees. Mind stepped to an edge and leaned over, but the ground was thousands of feet below. Clouds drifted beneath them, and the sun was just beginning its descent.

He returned to the doorway of his cell and looked across the space, to the dakorian called Basher. The dakorian bared his broken teeth in a snarl and pointed his hammer at Mind, obviously anticipating a quick victory. Then a countdown appeared on the small tower at the center of the arena, the numbers depicting a countdown. Small hovering spheres floated around walkways. Mind assumed they would pick up the image and send it so others could see. Then Basher began to advance.

"A slave?" he sniffed in disgust. "I expected better."

Mind scanned the sky. Hundreds of giant spheres floated nearby, some connected to other dueling arenas. Silver and reflective on the exterior, they resembled giant bubbles floating through clouds. Mind spotted dakorians dueling krey and humans. A human man screamed as he fell off the ledge and plummeted to his death.

The sun hung low on the horizon, and in the distance lay the volcanic battleground. Sparks of light flared on the earth, the evidence of energy weapons. In the opposite direction lay an ocean, a series of islands forming the Sea Battleground. An entire world, dedicated to death and war. The sight filled Mind with revulsion.

"Basher, rank fourteen dakorian," a voice said, "and Fragment, rank fifty human."

Mind smiled faintly at the term. It was fitting, if now incorrect. The dakorian roared, a sound that would have been terrifying to any other human, but Mind saw into the criminal's consciousness. He'd once been a soldier, but he'd frequently succumbed to baser instincts, until he killed several of his own soldiers and been placed in the Crucible as punishment. He'd killed hundreds in a variety of contests, and gloried in the blood and killing.

The timer at the top of the tower clicked and began to change, and Mind drew his sword. Basher laughed as he leapt to a higher ramp and began to accelerate. He dragged his hammer behind him, the weapon bouncing about, empowering the runes on the shaft, the scraping meant to frighten Mind.

"I'm going to crush you to paste," he called.

Mind strode toward the dakorian, unhurried. He set his sword low and at his side. The dakorian hurtled down the ramp, his bone armored body causing vibrations to cascade through the floor of the arena. He'd picked one of the wider pathways, and Mind made no attempt to evade.

Thirty feet became twenty, and Basher raised his spiked hammer. Mind gathered his magic and shaped it around the tip of his sword. Basher roared and swung, his blow meant to crush Mind's ribs and heart. Mind sidestepped, allowing Basher's hammer to whistle over his head. Mind set his toes on the edge of the pathway, and leapt.

With a burst of gravity magic he jumped four feet and swung his sword. Backed by four times the natural gravity, the sword smashed into the dakorian's jaw, slicing through bone and throat.

The impact sent the dakorian tumbling over the side, his hammer falling from his grip. Basher stared in shock as Mind stepped to the edge. With dispassionate eyes Mind watched the dakorian plummet to the volcanic surface below.

He flicked his sword and sheathed it, and then noticed one of the observation spheres hovering around him. Another zipped to his position, and then a third. More and more came, until four became dozens, and then a hundred, all floating around the arena.

He was a spectacle, he'd realized. Humans in the Empire were not trained for combat, not prepared to fight, and against a dakorian they stood little chance of survival. What Mind had done would quickly gain a reputation, and Mind wondered if he should have taken his time.

". . . Fragment is the victor!" a voice proclaimed, rushed, as if the speaker had scrambled to speak after the sudden end of the duel. "Due to the speed of his victory, Fragment advances a full thirty-six ranks, and will now take Basher's place in the standings!"

Mind turned and strode back to his cell. As he stepped out of the wind, he faced the swarm of orbs floating around the arena, all pushing each other for a closer view. Some examined the blood on the arena floor, others circled the dakorian hammer where it lay. Still others zipped down to watch the still falling Basher.

The outside of the cell shut and the interior rotated again, bringing Mind back in line with the walkway to the oddsmaker desk. Both Ursun and Rasina were shouting at spheres, or rather, someone was shouting at them. Ursun was laughing, while Rasina looked stunned.

The grate lifted and Mind stepped free, joining Ero and Tardoq, who looked impressed. "Well done," the Bloodwall said. "From what I saw, his ability was impressive, yet you made him look like an untrained youth."

Mind shrugged. "It wasn't really fair. It's not like he knew about magic."

Tardoq began to laugh, the sound rueful, a reminder that when he'd arrived on Lumineia, he'd also thought little of the humans. Then Tardoq's dakorian soldiers had been killed, one by one falling to the fragments and others with magic.

"Thirteen seconds," Rasina breathed. "You killed a fourteenth rank in *thirteen seconds.*"

"We'll be staying at Warview," Ero said as they passed the desk. "You can send my winnings there."

"Of course," Ursun said. He shook his head and eyed Mind with what could only be described as greed. "Thirteen seconds," he breathed.

Rasina stepped in front of Ero, cutting him off. "You are in luck," she said. "After such a strong showing, the houses of Thorn'Vall and Torn'Ent would like to purchase your slave. As a member of house Thorn'Vall, I suggest my own house, and am required to say the offer is even higher than—"

"He's not for sale," Ero said.

"We'll add ten million to your winnings," she said.

"No," Ero said, stepping around her.

She rushed back to the front. "Twenty? Thirty million? Name your price."

"He's not one I can sell," Ero replied.

The sphere floating above Rasina's shoulder laughed. "Everyone is for sale," a greasy voice said. "We'll double your winnings."

83

"You'd pay two hundred million glint for me?" Mind shook his head in disbelief.

"Not for a billion would I sell," Ero said.

"Are you mad?" the sphere demanded. "No slave is worth that much."

"A life is without price," Ero said.

"Then what about your Bloodwall?" the sphere asked. "I'll take both for five hundred million—"

Tardoq drew his sword and slashed above Rasina's head, the weapon slicing the sphere in half. Sparks burst from the machinery, and liquid splattered Rasina's hair. She cried out in fear and anger as the broken sphere crashed to the walkway, half spinning over the edge. Those in the cages began to shout, bellowing in excitement.

"Try to buy me again," Tardoq said evenly, "And I'll show everyone how much *you* are worth."

Rasina sputtered and tried to wipe the liquid off her face and dress. "Do you have any idea how much this costs?" she demanded, sweeping a hand at her fabric.

Tardoq stepped around the shrieking krey woman as one of the other spheres began to shout, pulsing as the speaker demanded information. Mind couldn't resist a smile. They'd thought him a soon-to-be-corpse, and he'd devastated their odds. As they returned to the Gate at the edge of the oddsmaker sphere, he realized what he'd done would have ramifications throughout the Krey Empire.

"Did I kill him too quickly?" he asked, casting a glance back at the shouting sphere and the two krey.

Ero smiled and shook his head. "You did exactly as I hoped."

Mind heard the trace of triumph in his tone. It was the sound of one who'd planned for a certain moment, prepared for it, manipulated it into being. Ero had not just wanted to draw Bonebreaker out of hiding, he'd wanted Mind to win, and do so in a manner that would command attention. He stabbed a finger at the krey.

84

"You *wanted* me to draw that much attention."

Ero stepped closer and lowered his tone. "The Krey Empire views mankind as beasts. What you just did will be seen and replayed in every house, in every home. Humans here are not like on Lumineia. They have no hope, no spark of might. They labor and love, but without a semblance of joy. They are broken. In a few days we're going to disappear back to Lumineia, but your legacy will remain. A slave, who demonstrated the might of his race."

"You wanted to change how the Empire views slaves," Mind said.

"It will change how slaves view themselves," Tardoq corrected, his voice tinged with understanding. The dakorian looked to Ero with new eyes, and Mind wondered if that was part of Ero's plan. He'd wanted to show Tardoq the purpose of the Eternals.

"This is why you agreed to bring me here," Mind said. "So I could become a rallying cry."

"It won't galvanize change," Ero said. "The Empire is too big for a single act to alter, and the generations of broken spirit cannot change so quickly. But this moment will be remembered."

Mind spotted Ursun listening to the sphere at his side. The speaker was not shouting, and his voice was too low for Mind to hear. But the dark greed in his eyes were easy to understand as he looked to Mind.

"The Empire will try to kill me," Mind said.

"It's true," Tardoq said. "He's ordering Ursun to have us followed."

"I suspected as much," Ero said. "But we'll be gone soon, and Lumineia is the one place they cannot follow us."

Ero pressed his hand to the Gate and it glowed to life. He nodded reassuringly to Mind and then disappeared through the Gate. Tardoq stepped into the Gate but turned back, a faint smile on his features.

"Ero may have manipulated you, but he was right. The duel will be examined by many, but they will not see guile or intent. You defeated him merely because you could, not because you were under orders."

"I don't like being manipulated," he said.

"That's what the krey do," Tardoq said. "Even Ero. For what it's worth, I enjoyed seeing a human stand so tall."

He inclined his head in respect and then stepped through the Gate. Mind looked back, his eyes sweeping the interior of the sphere. Most of those in the cages were dakorians, but some were krey and humans. One human caught his eye, the man staring at him as others shouted. He did not speak, his expression filled with a single thought.

Wonder.

Chapter 10: A New Direction

Light trudged down the road, yawning and wishing the sun would just come up. It seemed like they'd been walking for days and the sun had set hours ago. Surely it was nearly dawn. He nudged Willow, who walked at his side.

"How long until the sun rises?"

"The sun set thirty minutes ago," she said. "Night has just begun."

Light groaned, long and loud. Willow grinned, as did Rake and Senia. The quartet had departed the gathering and headed south and east, intent on reaching Xshaltheria within the week. Initially they'd flown on the back of the white dragon, until Senia had foreseen Serak aboard his own dragon. No one wanted that encounter. But did they have to walk so late?

"Can't we fly again?"

Rake shot him a scathing look. "You almost fell last night because you decided the back of a dragon was a great place to take a nap."

"I was tired," Light mumbled.

"You can rest when we find a good place to camp," Senia patted him on the arm.

Resigning himself to wait, Light tried to keep up with the others. How did they not get tired? None of them were guardians, so where did they draw their strength? He shifted closer to Willow and lowered his voice.

"Why are you three so strong?"

"Determination," she said.

He chuckled at her answer. "That's what Mind would say."

"What's it like, without the fragment of Power?"

The question surprised him, and he shrugged. "Strange. At first I just felt weak. Now? I don't feel like myself."

"How so?"

"I'm not sure."

He didn't know how to answer. Everything felt subdued. His magic, his curiosity, even his love for Willow, all of it had been muffled like a handful of cotton had been pressed over a squeaky hinge.

He stole a look at Willow and flushed when he found her watching. When he'd seen her in the past, a fire had ignited in his chest. He still felt the stirring, but it lacked the same power it had carried before. Did he still love Willow?

"I watched Draeken separate from you," she murmured.

"You saw it?"

She looked away, into the dark trees. With her vision she would be able to see through the shadows, see the wind rustling the branches, and the deer attempting to escape around them to reach its herd. Light had seen it as well, but the usual impulsiveness that would have driven him to find the creature was noticeably absent.

"The door was broken open," Willow said, "and I watched the fragment of Power be ripped from the fragments. It looked painful."

"Like removing my own limb," he said ruefully.

"And since then you've been . . . different."

"I'm still me," he said. "I think."

"There's a clearing adjacent to the road ahead," Senia said. "We should be able to camp there for the night."

"How far are we from Xshaltheria?" Willow called up to Senia.

"Another two days, as the dragon flies."

Rake asked the oracle a question and Willow slowed her steps. Light did as well, giving more space between them and their companions. Curious, Light fell back to walk with Willow, and for the first time noticed the distance between them.

He'd loved Willow for years, and whenever they journeyed together, there had been a proximity. They'd walked side by side, fought together, laughed together. Now she walked a short distance away from him. He wanted to close the gap, but instead of acting on the impulse, hesitation bound his feet.

"Draeken was part of you," Willow said. "And now that he is gone, you feel the lack."

"I'm sorry."

"You don't need to apologize for who you are," Willow said. "But you do need to figure out your new identity. I suspect that nothing will feel the same, and it will take time to discern your new self."

"We're fighting a war," he said. "I'm not certain our foes will stop so I can meditate on my new future."

She smiled at his tone, the expression brightening his heart. Willow's dark form was hardly visible, yet her smile had the same power as a blazing torch. He tentatively reached out and touched her hand, and smiled when her fingers threaded into his.

"Conflicts have a way of forcing self-discovery," she said.

"Like a forge?" He raised an eyebrow. "Elenyr used to say that we are all metal in a forge. The heat and hammering shows what we're really made of. A mighty weapon? Or the scrap heap."

"The Hauntress is ever wise," Willow said.

His smiled faded and he looked into the dark forest. "I think she knows exactly how we have been changed."

Willow swept her hand to the forest. "A part of you is gone. Everything from the sky to your foes will look different."

"I can still see your beauty," he said, and then flushed.

89

She smiled, and then looked beyond him, to the center of the road. He felt a prickling on his neck and rotated, searching the darkness for an attacker. Senia and Rake turned as well, all four facing the floating spark of light.

"What is that?" Rake asked.

Senia frowned and took a step forward. "I'm not sure," she said. "But it could be—"

BOOM.

The sound burst across them like thunder cracking in their midst. Light flinched and raised his hand, squinting into the expanding light. It resembled an arch but the light was blinding and silver. His eyes widened with wonder.

"Hey, is that—"

Willow grabbed his elbow and yanked him to the ground. On the opposite side, Rake tried to do the same with Senia, but she brushed him off and he flopped in the dirt. Light burst into a laugh as Willow yanked her sword and dagger from her skin, the ink pooling and hardening into weapons.

A person appeared out of thin air and stumbled to her knees, where she promptly vomited. Light stood and brushed Willow aside. He leaned down and twisted, trying to identify the intruder. Then she turned her head and Light realized it was Rune.

"Are you well?"

"No I'm not well," she gasped. "It's like my guts have been ripped inside out."

"Rune?" Senia asked, advancing and helping her to her feet. "How did you get here?"

"*She* brought me," Rune said, and then shuddered. "We needed to get you a message and she said she knew the fastest route. I thought she meant a messenger, and then I was yanked into—"

She crouched and retched again, and Willow patted her on the back as Light craned his neck into the dark trees. "Shadow could have sent a messenger."

"Rune used a Gate," Senia said.

"I don't think I'm ever doing that again," Rune said, wiping her mouth.

"You said something about a message?" Light asked.

"It must have been urgent," Rake said.

The man was dusting himself off, his face burning red from embarrassment from his fall. Senia spared him an apologetic look. Rake withdrew his waterskin and handed it to Rune, who gratefully took a swig and offered it back.

"Keep it," Rake said.

"What's the message?" Senia asked.

"Shadow and Elenyr managed to get inside Blackwell Keep," she said. "They spoke to Gendor."

"The assassin?" Light yawned, the momentary excitement having failed to alleviate his fatigue.

"Elenyr and Shadow saw a memory," Rune said. "It was a memory of the four horsemen, and one that could close the Gate."

"Where did they get this memory?" Senia asked.

Rune's expression turned apologetic. "You."

Senia frowned in dismissal. "I don't recall such a vision."

"Serak visited you in disguise," Rune said. "You saw his future, and he removed the memory of the vision."

"Impossible," she said.

"They saw it," Rune said, taking another swig of water. "And there's more. Apparently you foresaw there was someone that could defeat Draeken, one born with the blood of dwarf, human, and elf."

"Lachonus?" Light blurted.

"Who?" They all turned to face him.

He hadn't really been listening. In fact, he'd begun to fall asleep, but the mention of the three races mingled could only be one person. Was it him? Light shook his head, now uncertain. Then he noticed the others were still waiting.

"Lachonus helped us destroy the Order of Ancients in Talinor," he said. "His father was a dwarf. Not sure if there was an elf in his line." He yawned.

"This is all based on a vision I cannot remember," Senia said.

"Can you not see it again?" Rake asked.

Senia shook her head. "I could only replicate the vision if I had Serak in front of me."

"Could it be a trap?" Willow asked.

"Elenyr thought of that," Rune said. "She didn't think so. The vision and its source did not strike her as deception."

Willow returned her weapons to her tattoos. "If it's true, it's our first real weapon against Draeken."

"Hey!" Light protested, and then recalled that Draeken was not part of him anymore. "Sorry."

Willow patted him on the shoulder. "So is it true?"

Rune shrugged. "I don't know. But Elenyr believes it."

"And I trust Elenyr," Senia said.

"Then my message is delivered," Rune said with a nod of satisfaction. "I guess I'll just . . ." her eyes widened in horror. "Not again."

BOOM

She disappeared in a burst of energy which crackled across the road. Light shielded his gaze and when the energy had diminished, Rune was gone. He advanced to the spot and found the ground to be burned, scorch marks going in multiple directions.

"Can I go next time?" he asked Willow.

She rolled her eyes. "You *would* enjoy such a thing."

Light grinned as Rake swept a hand to the departed Rune. "What does that mean for us?"

"It means we are going the wrong direction," Senia said. "Rake? You think you can fly us to Terros?"

"Is Light going to fall asleep?"

"That happened one time," he protested.

"Six times," Willow corrected. "But the bigger question is, will Serak be in our path?"

"I think not," Senia said.

Light sighed. "Do we have to travel at night? I thought we were going to camp for the night."

"We need to leave now," Senia said, and motioned for Rake to change form. "We got the information from Serak, so he will be searching for Lachonus as well. We must hasten."

Rake bowed his head and his body began to change shape, the large wings sprouting from his back, his forearms swelling and his hands morphing into claws. As Isray appeared, Willow stepped close to Light.

"You almost fell off last night. Are you sure you can stay awake?"

"It's not my fault a dragon's hide is so comfortable," Light muttered.

Willow smiled and the trio mounted the dragon's back. The white dragon launched them skyward and soared over the forest. In the still

93

night, Light relished the sensation of power granted only on the back of a powerful dragon. But several minutes later fatigue got to him, and his eyes began to droop.

"You're falling asleep," Willow whispered. "Do you really want to fall off?"

"I can't help it," he murmured. "I got tired in the dark *before* the separation, and now it's worse."

"Your body is more flesh than magic, now," she replied. "You need more rest, like everyone else."

"But you all sleep for a third of your days," Light said. "That must be such a waste of time."

Senia glanced back. "It kind of is. Doesn't mean we can avoid it."

"Am I going to have to sleep that much?" Light shuddered at the thought. "My head is beginning to hurt."

"People sometimes get headaches when they are tired," Willow said. "It's fairly common."

"Am I going to get sick too?" he asked.

You'll be fine, Isray rumbled, the thoughts coming into Light's mind. The dragon sounded annoyed.

Behind him, Willow pulled her whip from her flesh and wrapped it around Light's body, binding them together. Light shivered as her hands brushed across his waist. Willow smiled faintly, the expression dim in the darkness.

"I'll hold you," she said.

"Thank you my love," Light murmured, and closed his eyes. A dragon really was a great place to sleep . . .

Chapter 11: Targeted

"Light!" Willow hissed.

He snapped awake, and then groaned. He raised his hand to the bright sunlight streaming into his eyes. Why did the sun have to be so bright? He shoved Willow's hand away and tried to go back to sleep, before he realized what he was doing.

"What time is it?" he asked, appalled at the late hour.

"Almost noon," Senia called back. "Since you were sleeping so soundly, we just kept going."

"I slept *late?*"

He'd never slept late a day in his life, not unless it was overcast or exceptionally dark. He'd slept extra in the Deep, but they'd been underground and he hadn't been able to see the sun. Whenever the sun came up, he experienced a surge of energy that erased any fatigue.

"I love sleeping late," Willow said.

"Me too," Senia said over her shoulder, her tone wistful.

"But it's me," Light said, rubbing sleep from his eyes as if that would help. "And I slept until noon? *Noon?"*

"You did." Willow seemed to be suppressing a smile.

He wanted to protest further but his stomach rumbled. "And now I'm starving. What did you eat for breakfast—wait, was it determination? Did that taste good?"

"It's rather unsatisfying for a meal," Senia said. "If I'm totally honest."

I prefer a few juicy horses, Isray said. *Or a nice roast pig.*

"Stop," Light protested. "You're making it worse."

"Bacon and cheese on a nice slice of bread," Willow said with a smile.

"Or elven frybread with sugar and fresh berries?" Senia asked.

"Please," Light pushed a fist into the ache in his side. "Stop talking about food."

The two laughed and Senia directed them out of the sky. Isray dropped through the clouds and banked south. He spotted Terros to the north, it's spires and war camps arrayed in the midday light, but they were traveling away from the city.

"I thought we were going to Terros," he said.

"I looked ahead," Senia said. "Shortly after we would have landed, we would have been told that Lachonus is leading a cavalry unit through the elven forests. We're going to meet him in route."

Light looked down at his stomach. "And how soon can we get this monster fed?"

I haven't eaten in days, Isray said. *Stop complaining.*

"Your stomach is bigger than my whole body," he protested. "You can eat a few times a year if you want to."

"Here," Willow said. "I was saving this in case of an emergency, and this clearly qualifies."

She passed a small pouch of dried fruits. He wanted to savor them, but the first tasted like the dews of heaven, and the pouch was empty in seconds, except for the last one, which he offered back to Willow.

"You left one for me?" Willow sounded surprised.

"I'm hungry, not stupid."

"How many did he leave you?" Senia asked.

"More than I thought he would," Willow said, and popped it into her mouth.

96

Light's stomach still ached, but he did not think it prudent to speak any more. The dragon banked left and soared across the rocky terrain, keeping his body partly in the white clouds. Moisture speckled Light's face and he smiled. How much he loved to fly.

"There," Senia said.

Light followed her arm to see the dust rising from a group of mounted horsemen. The snow had melted this far south and the region had warmed considerably. Light squinted for a good look.

"Looks like five companies," he said.

"We should land out of sight and meet them on the road," Senia said. "No reason to startle several hundred armored cavalry."

"That does seem unwise," Light agreed.

Isray folded his wings and dropped from the sky. He curved between two hills and then backwinged to land in the space between, out of sight from the road. Light and the others jumped off and stumbled on the rocky ground. As the thundering of hooves came from the road, Senia pointed back to the sky.

"Perhaps it's better if you keep an eye out," she said. "We have no way of knowing when Draeken will strike."

I'll stay close enough to hear your thoughts.

The white dragon retreated back the way they had come and then leapt into the sky. Light waved and then picked his way down the short slope towards the road. The dust cloud was visible around the hills, rising into the sky in a hazy plume. Then the lead riders rounded the curve.

"They're in a hurry," Senia said. "They won't want to stop."

"You think they have food?" Willow asked.

Light looked to her and she shrugged. "You're not the only one that's hungry."

"Army rations," Senia said.

Light wrinkled his nose in disgust even as his mouth watered. Dried meat and nuts did not sound satisfying, but his stomach seemed to disagree. The lead rider caught sight of the three of them barring the road and reined his mount to a halt.

"Step aside," he commanded. "By order of the armies of the alliance."

"We need to speak to Lachonus," Senia said. "Is he with you?"

"Captain Lachonus!" another rider called back to the force appearing around the hill.

One of the group flicked the reins and the horse accelerated beyond the others. He caught up to the leading scouts and spotted the four of them. The scout scowled and began to speak but Lachonus cut him off.

"Light?" he asked, dismounting and striding to greet them. "What are you doing here?"

"Looking for you, actually," Light said.

Dressed in a captains uniform for the Talinorian cavalry, Lachonus wore silver plate armor with white accents. His helmet hung from a length of leather in the saddle, and his long spear was attached to the opposite side. A sword and scabbard hung on his back. Perhaps the most striking was his hair, which was bright, dwarven red.

Lachonus looked between them, his eyes settling on Senia. "Oracle Senia," he said. "Forgive me, I didn't recognize you."

"Armor is not usually customary clothing for an oracle," she said. "Can we speak in private?"

"Of course."

He motioned to the scouts and barked an order for them to continue. Then he led his horse off the road to a space between a group of boulders. The army continued, the horses passing them on their way north.

"What's going on?" he lowered his tone. "Last I knew, the fragments had been taken by Serak."

"Things have changed," Senia said. "We need you to come with us."

"Now?" Lachonus gestured to the army. "I've been ordered to join the army at Terros, where we march on Xshaltheria."

"It won't matter unless we can destroy Serak directly," Senia said.

As they talked, Light eyed the captain's pack, which looked heavy, he hoped with supplies. Lachonus glanced his way, noticing his attention on his pack. Eventually he frowned and motioned to the bag.

"Is something amiss?"

"Is there food in there?"

"Help yourself," Lachonus said.

Light grinned and opened the saddlebag, where he discovered pouches of dried nuts and fruit, as well as smoked meat. Officer rations. He dug in, and then noticed Willow's disapproving look. He gave a sheepish shrug and then closed the saddlebag.

"Sorry." His voice was muffled with the food in his mouth, and he resumed his former place next to Senia.

"We believe Serak will seek to assassinate you," Senia was saying.

"Does this have to do with the other killings?"

"Other killings?" Willow asked.

"Someone has been killing officers and warriors of renown," he said. "The killer has been described as the specter of death himself."

Senia grimaced. "That would be Gendor, Serak's assassin."

"Why would he come for me?" Lachonus asked. "I'm nobody."

"You have human and dwarven blood," she said. "Do you have elven blood as well?"

Lachonus looked confused at the turn in conversation. "What does that have to do with the assassin?"

"It's important," Senia said.

Lachonus regarded the three of them and then shrugged. "I don't know. My family is convoluted. My mother would know."

"Then we need you to take us to her," he said.

"She's right here," he replied, and pointed to the supply wagons. "She is leftenant over infantry."

"We must speak to her immediately," Senia said.

Lachonus regarded them for a moment and then called an order over his shoulder. "Corporal Wilten, summon Leftenant Rilia."

"As you order!" came the reply.

The speaker detached himself from the line of cavalry and then rode south to reach a set of wagons. He spoke with someone there, and a moment later a woman climbed onto a horse tied to the side of the wagon.

Dressed in the ornate armor of a leftenant, second only to a general, the woman conveyed an imposing air. Her blonde hair was tied back, her helm hanging from her saddle. Her features were haughty and rigid, a woman of strength and dominating will. Light took an immediate dislike.

She rode to Lachonus and dismounted, her eyes sweeping the group. She noted Willow with a touch of suspicion, her eyes passing over Senia, whom she recognized. Light thought he saw a trace of ambition in the woman's features before she looked at him.

"There is berry on your face."

Her disapproval made Light flush and wipe at his cheek. "Sorry."

"What's this about?" Rilia demanded.

"I'm here on an urgent request," Senia said. "I need to know if Lachonus is descended of the elves, humans, and dwarves."

"Why?"

100

"I cannot say."

"Then we cannot help you."

She folded her arms. Light leaned over to whisper to Willow, but she jerked her head, and he remained silent. He fidgeted, his eyes flicking between the standoff and Willow, annoyed by the woman's stance.

His eyes flicked to the saddlebags again, and then drifted upward, to the marching army. The hundreds of soldiers tried to pretend they were not watching, but many eyes glanced in their direction.

"I am the oracle," Senia said, her tone turning hard. "What I have foreseen is my duty."

"And my soldiers are my duty," she said. "As is my son. Why do you need him?"

"You wouldn't understand," Senia said.

"I'm second rank to a general," Rilia growled. "You may be the oracle, but that does not mean you are more intelligent than a soldier trained for war."

Is everything alright? Isray's voice was distant.

"We're fine!" Light called, and then flushed again when Rilia stared at him like he'd gone mad.

"He does that," Lachonus supplied.

"He lacks discipline," she said. "An attribute my son possesses, and will one day help him achieve the highest rank in Talinor."

"Leftenant Rilia," Senia said. "The war you are headed for will—"

"—Bring my family more glory than anything you can offer," she snapped. "Captain, back to your post."

"You can't be serious," Lachonus said. "I've fought beside Light, and the oracle has a rank that rivals the kings."

"Not my king," Rilia rounded on him. "I didn't train you for decades just so you can miss the most important battle of your career. This war with Serak and his Order of Ancients will reveal many distinguished soldiers, and I'm not allowing you to depart on a mysterious assignment with the oracle—one with deeds that will likely never be known."

"Even if he is the key to destroying Serak?" Willow asked.

"He will destroy Serak," Rilia barked. "But he will do it on the battlefield. He is stronger and faster than a normal man, with the cunning of his distinguished lineage. No *mage* is going to stop him."

Light didn't notice the rising tension. His eyes were drawn beyond the marching soldiers to the figure approaching the opposite side. He frowned and pointed in that direction, but as he began to speak, Lachonus grunted in irritation.

"If you want more food, go and eat."

"Do we need to worry about him?" Light asked.

"Who?" Rilia demanded.

The others rotated, and spotted the approaching figure. Wearing a cloak of midnight, the man seemed to glide down the hill, a wicked scythe in his hands. Beneath the cowl, only a pair of dark coals glowed for eyes, and his fingers had been stripped of flesh, leaving only bone.

"Who is that?" Lachonus asked, drawing his sword.

"That is the assassin come to kill you," Senia said.

The cavalry responded in unison, the riders yanking on their reins. The horses spun, spears were extended, the weapons pointing toward the solitary figure. Facing a half circle of the best cavalry on Lumineia, Gendor came to a halt. The stillness stretched for several seconds until Rilia growled.

"What's he waiting for—"

A roar shook the ground and caused horses to whinny in fear. It was not from a dragon or beast, but another warrior, one twelve feet tall and layered in black armor. The warrior advanced into view and spun his giant sword, which emitted a dull whine.

"Oh look!" Light called, pointing. "It looks like Gendor did not come alone . . ."

Chapter 12: Enmity

Light waved to Gendor, but the assassin did not wave back. After Light's conversation with Rune, he'd assumed the assassin was on his side, but perhaps that was overstating their friendship. Light waved again but Willow caught his hand and pulled it down, and then shook her head.

Senia whirled to Rilia. "You need to retreat, now."

"Retreat?" Rilia scoffed. "We are the Talinorian cavalry, and five companies are more than a match for these criminals."

"You don't understand," Senia said. "These are not normal soldiers. Serak has empowered them beyond normal means. Gendor and Bartoth are his generals, capable of—"

"All men can be killed," Rilia said. "Lachonus, order the right flank to advance. These criminals are wanted for execution. Kill them."

Lachonus scowled but nodded. "As you order, Leftenant."

He barked orders as he mounted his steed and snapped the reins. Senia released an explosive breath and turned to Willow and Light, who watched Gendor and Bartoth. As Rilia mounted and also departed, the oracle lowered her voice.

"We have to get Lachonus out of here, before this turns into a bloodbath."

"Too late." Light pointed to Bartoth.

Bartoth released another roar and began to advance, accelerating into a run. Lachonus shouted an order and a spear was thrown, the weapon bouncing off Bartoth's armor. Another order, and three more spears were thrown. All clattered off Bartoth's armor, and the rock troll began to laugh, the sound of anticipation.

"Cut him down!" Rilia shouted.

The cavalry surged into a charge, the spears pointed at the armored rock troll. Horse hooves thundered across the ground, and Light took a step forward, wanting to intervene. Senia caught his arm.

"Light," she said softly. "You cannot stop what is about to happen."

"They're going to die," he protested.

"I know," Senia said, her features a grimace. "There is nothing we can do for them. We need to find a way to get Lachonus out. It's the only way to stop this."

Bartoth and the cavalry closed the gap and Bartoth raised his sword. With a snarl he slammed into the leading ranks. Horses and men, spears and shields, all bounced off his body, cascading away as his charge carried him deep into their ranks. Men cried out as their bones cracked and horses whinnied as their bodies fell in broken heaps.

Men screamed and orders were shouted as five hundred armored cavalry sought to destroy Serak's general. But Bartoth was a rock troll with body magic, one empowered so *every* spell enhanced his flesh, granting him speed and strength far beyond even the mighty trolls. Horses and men died in seconds, their bodies rent and torn, their armor ripped apart like parchment.

Anger pooled in Light's chest like a fever, until he shrugged out of Senia's grip and sprinted into the conflict. Willow called his name but he ignored it, his gaze fixed on Bartoth. Then Willow reached him and yanked on his elbow, spinning him around.

"You cannot stop him," she said. "You are no longer a fragment, remember?"

"I'm still a guardian," he said. "I can't stand idle. Do you not hear the dying?"

"Of course I do," she said.

"I have to try." He stabbed a finger at the raging battle.

"Where is your rage?" she challenged.

105

He blinked in surprise, shocked to find that his rage was absent. Anger, yes, but no unbridled rage, the emotion that had granted him power against the strongest of foes. He'd defeated Bartoth before, his rage enhancing his magic. Now he was vulnerable.

He reached out and took Willow's hands in his. "I am not who I was, but if I do not fight, then what I am to be?"

"I cannot lose you!"

Her hands trembled in his, and he suddenly saw the moment from her perspective. She loved him, and feared his diminished strength, feared losing him to Bartoth. He was mortal, his flesh weak, his magic weaker.

"Will you love me if I do not fight?" he asked.

Tears came to her eyes but she nodded.

"I may be different," he said. "But I am still one who fights. Will you fight with me?"

She smiled through her tears and reached to her waist. Her tattoos pooled into ink that hardened into her sword. She leaned up and kissed him, and when they parted, she reached to her waist and drew her whip.

"Always."

He reached for his magic and cast a bow. He turned and aimed at Bartoth and drew an arrow back, the arrow shimmering with power. The arrow flew at the rock troll and exploded on his chest, knocking him backward. He skidded on the ground, smoke billowing around his helm. Lachonus wisely took the opportunity to retreat, and the cavalry rushed back to the road. Rilia skidded to a halt and jumped off her horse next to Senia. Blood was on her armor and cheek, her eyes ablaze with anger.

"Tell me why you need my son."

Senia regarded her with anger. "You would deny me after what you have seen?"

"He is my son," she snarled. "If you want him, tell me why."

"He is the only one that can defeat Serak."

All four whirled to find Gendor in their midst. The assassin held his scythe low and ready, but did not attack. Rilia leapt in and swung her sword, but the scythe moved with shocking speed, knocking her sword from her grip.

"Why do you not strike us?" Senia asked.

"Serak ordered me to kill Lachonus," he replied. "And I must obey. Sadly, he neglected to say when, or if I should kill those that stand in my way."

Rilia growled and jerked her head stubbornly. "Why him?"

"We need one born of man, elf, and dwarf," Senia snapped. "Is it him?"

Bartoth groaned and rose to his knees. He shook his head as if to clear it, and then picked up his fallen sword. Willow cursed when he rose to his feet and cast about, looking for who had fired such a dangerous arrow. When he spotted Light, he leveled his sword at him.

"*You*," he snarled.

"You remember me?" Light asked, pleased.

"I've looked forward to our next meeting since that day in the north."

"The day he made you apologize?" Willow asked.

Bartoth released a snarl and charged. Lachonus shouted an order and the cavalry parted, providing a path for the giant warrior. Light braced for the impending duel, his anger rising and bursting through his body.

"My son is who you seek," Rilia said, raising her chin. "He will destroy Serak for you."

"Get Lachonus and the cavalry out," Light said to Senia. "We'll keep Bartoth busy." He glanced at Willow and she nodded.

Lachonus was on the opposite side of the road. His horse was dead, and he was staunching the wounds of one of his men. Light aimed his bow again and fired at Bartoth, but the troll swung his sword, deflecting the arrow into the sky, where it detonated. Light altered his bow into a sword and leapt into the road, sprinting for the rock troll with Willow at his side.

The two parties converged and Light leapt over Bartoth's flashing sword, coming down behind him. The troll skidded to a halt and spun, driving a fist into Light's chest. The air burst from his lungs and he went tumbling onto his back.

"Not so fast as you were before," Bartoth said with a chuckle.

Light spit blood. "Fast enough."

Bartoth looked to his shoulder and found a small shard of magic blinking there. He reached for it, but it burst into a rope that embedded into the earth, yanking him to his knees. He snarled and reached for the cord, but Willow landed on his arm and stabbed her sword into the chink between his shoulder plate and his helmet. She leapt away, her sword bloody.

Light's anger flooded his body and his magic burst from his skin. He cast his large sword and swung, slashing across Bartoth's back. The rock troll whirled, his sword moving at breathtaking speed. Light deflected it upward and conjured a crossbow out of light, which fired a bolt into Bartoth's stomach, but it bounced off his armor.

Bartoth yanked the crossbow from Light's grip and used it like a club, smashing Willow away. Light's fury mounted as he watched Willow slump to the ground. He summoned the light around his body, the magic forming into flesh, making him swell to match Bartoth's size. His sword grew into a giant maul, a weapon to punish.

He charged and struck, the impact of his maul on Bartoth's helmet echoing across the bloody road. For several furious seconds the two traded blows, the whirlwind kicking up dust. But Light's anger lacked its former might, and gradually it melted away until Bartoth smashed his sword through Light's maul, the light shattered into splinters.

Light ducked Bartoth's next swing and struck the troll's back, his broken weapon sharp enough to pierce the armor and dig into troll flesh. Bartoth reached an armored glove to the wound and laughed. Then he caught the weapon and yanked it free.

"Is that what you have been reduced to?" Bartoth said. "It is truly a pity to see one so mighty fall to such depths."

"There is one benefit to losing my rage," Light said.

"And what is that?" Bartoth stalked forward.

"Clarity," he replied. "Unbridled rage is unbridled power, but it lacks wisdom and intelligence."

"And what's that going to do for you?" he raised his sword high.

Light pointed skyward, and Bartoth looked up—catching the full blast of a white dragon's breath. He bellowed in anger but the freezing current covered his body in ice, seeping into his armor and binding him to the ground. Isray shook the ground as he landed, his frost breath continuing to freeze the armored troll.

With ice forming around his legs and arms, Bartoth pushed for the dragon and raised his sword, his body slowing. He bellowed his fury and forced himself to advance through the dragon's breath, his blade coming at Isray's snout, where it came to a halt.

Encased in ice, Bartoth stood with his arms extended, his sword touching Isray's snout. His eyes glowed through the helmet, the fury evident as he trembled. Light rose to his feet and wiped blood from his chin.

"That won't hold him for long."

The ice cracked near his arms, and Willow joined Light. "We don't need long."

Senia approached with Lachonus and pointed to the dragon. "Let's go, soldier."

He looked to Rilia, who nodded. The woman's features were bright with haughty pride. "Your name will ring through the ages, my son."

The ice cracked again, and they climbed onto the dragon's back. More ice cracked, and Rilia shouted for the soldiers to retreat. Cavalry poured from the road, the wounded and dead loaded onto spare horses. More ice cracked, and Gendor retreated into the cloud of dust.

Light swung his leg over the dragon's neck just as a chunk of ice fell to the ground. Isray opened his jaws and roared. Then he spread his wings. The ice shattered, Bartoth stumbling from the shards.

He stood, gasping for breath, just feet from a dragon's maw. He began to laugh, the sound washing over the dead horses and dusty road. Light gathered his magic but Bartoth sheathed his sword and stood.

"Weaker but wiser," he said. "I enjoyed this fight, but rest assured, the next will be your last."

"We'll see about that," Light said.

Isray launched them skyward, and as they departed the battlefield, Light breathed a sigh of relief and reached for Willow's hand. She smiled and tightened her grip. He may have survived, but the battle was far from over.

Chapter 13: Battlefield

The allied army advanced out of the trees to enter the valley. Led by Griffin infantry, the soldiers spread out, gradually filling the breadth of the foothills below Xshaltheria. Under the twilight sky, the alliance arrived to destroy the criminal known as Serak.

Thirty thousand Talinorian cavalry, sixty thousand Griffin infantrymen, twenty thousand elven archers, another twenty thousand Erathan swordsmen, and still they appeared at the end of the road. Rock trolls from the north, sand trolls from the deserts, dwarves, gnomes, giants, they all took their place and set up camp at the base of the great volcano.

Fire and Water watched the advance from an escarpment on the northern side of the valley. The two had ridden ahead to survey the fortress, and to Water's relief, it appeared the Dark Gate had yet to open. For now, only a few thousand of the loyal Order members guarded the winding road leading up to the fortress above.

"The gates are well guarded," Fire said, pointing to the road.

The fortress and road were a testament to dwarven engineering, and paranoia. The road curved its way up the slope, passing through several smaller gates, the fortifications built so soldiers higher up the road could attack the lower approaches. The allied army would have to fight through the teeth of the defenses to reach the top of the mountain, where large openings led to the citadel. Suspended by giant chains, the entire fortress of Xshaltheria hung in the throat of the volcano.

"Serak's forces are small," Water said. "But it's going to be hard to fight our way up that road."

Lira appeared below them and hiked to their position. "As we assumed. Just a few thousand men. They look nervous."

"They should be." Fire swept his hand at the allied army below, already two hundred thousand strong with more entering the valley. "We're going to crush them."

"Not if the Dark Gate is opened," Lira said.

"We should attack quickly," Fire said.

"That's what Rynda wants," Lira said. "But King Justin opposes her. He and the orcs want caution."

Fire snorted in disgust. "They've gathered the mightiest army Lumineia has ever seen, and now he wants to wait?"

"It's a ploy," Water said. "King Justin now controls the armies of Talinor and Erathan. He wants to consolidate his power now, so after the battle his reign will be unchallenged."

"Perhaps Rynda is right about men," Lira said sourly. "King Justin has gained more power, but instead of using it to stop Serak, he wants to demonstrate his strength."

"I suspect he wants to acquire the other two kingdoms," Water said. "I overheard many Griffin soldiers boasting about the great kingdom of Griffin, which will own the entire southern lands."

"I still can't believe King Porlin never existed," Fire said.

After the fragment of Mind had unmasked Porlin for his real identity, the truth had spread like wildfire. King Porlin's predecessor had failed to have a son, and formed a secret arrangement with Serak. He gained an heir, while the heir would serve the Order of Ancients. None but Porlin, his supposed father, and Serak had known Porlin's identity. But over the years others had learned the truth, all from Porlin himself, who was actually Zoric, son of Zenif. In his pride, he'd enlisted the aid of soldiers and nobles of Talinor, all of which were quick to turn on the false king the moment his true identity was revealed. The Talinorian throne now sat empty, and several of the nobles vied for the vacancy. All four were present with the army, for they needed King Justin's support.

"Erathan is in worse shape," Fire said. "King Numen had finally managed to get his kingdom under control, but reports say the people are preparing a revolt. Princess Nelia has managed to keep the peace, but the people view her as weak."

"King Numen betrayed Erathan, served their enemy, and is now dead," Lira said.

"At least his daughter is there," Water said. "She is smart enough to lead in his absence."

"Not if Griffin decides to conquer Erathan," Fire said. "They wouldn't last a month."

Water sighed, disliking the truth to the conversation. The political tension on Lumineia was visible in the valley below. The Erathan soldiers had claimed the northern slopes, where the duke leading them insisted they make camp. Talinorian cavalry argued with them as to the choice in position, saying they should be at the center of the line, where all infantry were positioned. The cavalry could operate better from a flanking position.

Other sections of the valley were equally as tense, with various groups arguing, their heated conversations reaching Water's position. Higher officers struggled to maintain control, while the dwarves, elves, rock trolls, and dark elves tried to avoid the complications.

Water scowled at the tension of the allied army. Why did King Justin behave with such arrogance? Did he not see that it could destroy them all? Water then recalled a statement Elenyr had frequently quoted regarding nobles.

"They are raised to nobility, wealth, and privilege. It's not their fault they act with arrogance."

"It doesn't make it right," Water had argued.

Elenyr had shrugged. "I know. But who can teach them?"

Water lifted his gaze to the volcano, annoyed that Serak's plan made a sort of twisted sense. He could enforce the rule of law and justice, and the nobles would live in perpetual fear of the fiend army.

One of the dark elves spotted Water and separated herself from the rest of her soldiers. With a small personal guard, Queen Erisay climbed

113

the slope. She waved at her guards, who remained behind as she picked her way up the slope.

"Fire, Mind, Lira," she said, greeting them each in turn.

"Queen Erisay," Water offered a bow. "Your soldiers look ready."

"Don't patronize me," Erisay said with a smile. "We all know the alliance hangs by a thread."

Water sighed and pointed to the camps being erected. "Even against a foe like Serak, the nobles cannot set aside their ambition and greed."

"The surface races have always been on the brink of turmoil," she said. "A precipice they will tumble from without those that protect their unity."

Water met her gaze, and realized she was speaking of them. Elenyr, the fragments, the oracle, all had kept the nobles in check, their actions preventing those in power from falling to their darker impulses.

He frowned and looked to Xshaltheria, wondering what the fragments would do after the war with Serak. And Draeken. Few knew of Draeken's role yet, but it would not be long before the people understood that Serak was merely a servant.

If they survived, would the former fragments return to their former life? Water doubted that, not without the power that had kept them living such a long time. Water alone retained a piece of Draeken, a piece he was not certain he desired to keep, even if it kept him ageless.

"When will the assault begin?" Lira asked.

"Dawn," she replied.

Fire chuckled at the answer. "I wager Queen Rynda is the source of that decision."

"Indeed," Erisay said. "She insisted there was no reason to wait, and King Justin was forced to agree."

"Do the other human armies now obey his authority?" Water asked.

"They do," Erisay replied. "As you know, Princess Nelia ceded temporary command of her army to him."

Fire cursed and pointed to the bickering soldiers. "Justin isn't going to give up that authority after the war."

The dark elf smiled faintly. "Rynda, Dothlore, and I will not give him a choice."

Erisay's statement bordered on a proclamation for war, and Water chuckled. Justin desired the other two kingdoms, but could not conquer them if he had to defend against the dwarven, rock troll, and dark elf armies.

"You told him that?" Lira asked.

"That's why he agreed to attack at dawn," Erisay said. "He may command the largest army on Lumineia, but he is not immune to fear."

Fire laughed and pointed to the crafty dark elf. "You and Rynda are a dangerous combination."

"It is only prudent," Erisay said with a smile. "If the three human kingdoms become one, my people will be threatened. Talinor and Erathan must remain intact."

She turned and returned to her guards. Water recalled her ability with sound magic, so he kept his silence until she was far enough down the slope that she would not be able to hear his words. Still, he whispered.

"I'm fervently grateful that she is on our side."

"Aren't we all," Fire said.

"It's no small wonder that she and Rynda have become friends," Lira said. "Both are women who care nothing for ambition, and merely wish to serve their people."

"Dark elf and rock troll," Fire snorted in amusement. "Who would have thought they would be allies."

"Certainly not I," Water said.

115

He turned and watched the soldiers of Xshaltheria casually prepare for the coming onslaught. Most knew that Serak had manipulated the alliance into coming, but for what purpose? Was it just so the fiends from the Dark Gate could destroy the allied armies? Water shook his head. Serak was a brutal tactician, but he was not wasteful, and killing so many would not serve any purpose. So why bring the army to his door?

"We should return to our place," Fire said. "I don't want to miss Rynda's plan for tomorrow."

"You just want to charge the gates," Lira said.

"True," Fire said with a grin. "It's been ages since I was part of a good assault, and whatever happens, tomorrow will be a battle of legend."

"Don't get too comfortable," Water warned. "We have yet to understand all that is arrayed against us."

A distant roar echoed across the valley, stilling the army. Soldiers froze in the midst of erecting tents and sharpening weapons, their eyes turning skyward, searching the fading light for the source of the unmistakable sound.

"Serak must be coming back," Fire scowled. "This is going to frighten the men."

"How could it not?" Water asked, searching the skies. "Everyone fears a dragon."

"Everyone except us," Fire said.

Water frowned at his brother's willingness to fight. As a fragment of Draeken he'd been strong enough to stand against the great beasts, but now? Water stole a look at Fire, wishing his brother was not so quick to rush into battle. The thought of losing him again made him shudder.

Another roar echoed, and all eyes snapped to look south, where the rumble of a dragon's challenge faded into disturbing silence. Water and Fire exchanged a look, and for the first time Fire looked uncertain.

"That didn't come from the same beast," Water said.

From the east, a dragon burst into view, soaring above the mountains and banking around the valley. The rider on his neck was obviously Serak, his customary cloak billowing behind him. Water ducked back into the trees above the escarpment, out of sight as the red dragon passed above them. He caught Fire's arm when he noticed flames appearing on his fingers.

"Don't," he warned.

"It's Bendelinish," Fire said. "He's big, but the three of us could handle him."

"Not with Serak on his back," Water said.

"If that's Serak," Lira said. "Why is there a second dragon?"

Another beast appeared on the horizon, quickly growing larger as the great wings flapped. Water sucked in his breath as the gigantic beast approached. The soldiers shouted and scrambled for weapons, the tumult one of fear.

"You'd think they'd be braver," Fire sniffed.

"It's twice the size of Serak's mount," Lira breathed.

Water spotted the tiny figure on the neck of the great dragon and dread filled his chest. "It appears Draeken has his own mount," he said.

Chapter 14: A Daring Plan

"That's Gorewrathian," Fire said.

"Who?" Water asked.

Water didn't take his eyes off the enormous dragon. From snout to spiked tail, the beast was over a hundred feet long, it's scales thick enough to stop spear and arrow, blade and magic. Horns grew from its head, and spikes ran the length of its tail.

"See the scar across his eye and down the side of his skull?"

Water saw the jagged edges to the broken scales, the scar marking an ugly wound from a past conflict. Another dragon perhaps? Other scars marked its scales, the legacy of conflicts with other dragons.

"Gorewrathian is the strongest red dragon his kind has seen in ages," Fire said. "And a mortal enemy to the phoenixes."

"How do you know him?" Lira asked.

"I gave him that scar," Fire said.

"So I take it you're not friends?" Water asked.

"We're not the type to get together and share a pint of ale," Fire said.

The great dragon banked into a hover, each stroke of its wings gusting air onto the army below. Water's gaze remained fixed on the rider. Draeken, whole and unhindered by the fragments. A flicker of yearning kindled in Water's chest, and he sensed that his piece of Power wanted to join the whole.

"Armies of Lumineia," Draeken called. "You've come to destroy Serak and the Order of Ancients, but instead of Serak you find another. I am Draeken, the greatest of all, Master of Serak, the fragment of Power."

"We are not afraid of you!" Rynda's voice came from her army.

The enormous dragon dropped lower as Draeken chuckled. "Queen Rynda, bold to the end. Before blood stains this ground, I will give you one chance. Relinquish your thrones, your castles, your kingdoms, and kneel before me. Do that, and you may live to be my slaves."

"I'd rather rip your limbs from your body!" Rynda called.

Draeken laughed. "I did hope you'd say that."

Gorewrathian rose into the sky and turned to the volcano, Serak following as well. They alighted on the volcano's edge as the sun fell below the horizon, darkness settling on the valley. In the ensuing silence Fire muttered a curse.

"I'm going to enjoy destroying him."

Water continued to watch the great dragon as he wrestled with the sense of dread. The fragments had been unable to stop Serak when they'd possessed the fragment of Power. Now they had to face both the Father of Guardians *and* the fragment of Power.

"We'll find a way," Lira murmured.

She caught his hand and squeezed, and he smiled, grateful for Lira at his side. Muttering to himself, Fire turned and descended to the army below, leaving him alone with Lira. As the stars appeared in the dark night, he swept a hand to the lights of the valley.

"We have the greater force—even against Serak and Draeken—so why does it feel like we're caught in the jaws of a trap?"

"Maybe we shouldn't wait until dawn," she said.

He raised an eyebrow. "What are you suggesting?"

"Tonight," Lira said.

"There's no way we can get the kings to agree to such an assault."

119

"Not all of them," she said. "But a smaller group. Rynda, Dothlore, Erisay, the Bladed, they would all be willing."

Water liked the suggestion. It posed a risk, but the goal was simple. Destroy the Dark Gate. If they could breach the fortifications unseen, and infiltrate the fortress, they might be able to destroy, or at the very least, delay Serak's plans.

"Let's see what Rynda has to say."

They dropped from the escarpment and made their way down the slope. Outer sentries had been posted, and thousands were still erecting fortifications, tents, and war machines. A notable separation kept the various commands distinct, a fifty-foot gap where no tent or soldier lingered.

Water and Lira passed through a contingent of Talinorian cavalry and then crossed one such gap on their way to the Griffin infantry. The soldiers laughed and talked as they had the previous week, but the talk had gained a noticeable current of tension. Seeing Draeken and Serak astride twin red dragons, one of which was the largest they had ever seen, had left them shaken. They'd thought this would be a quick campaign, crush the Order of Ancients and be back in a week.

"The men sense a reason to fear," Lira murmured.

Water watched a pair of sentries speak in low tones, the subject that of how to kill a dragon, and how to hide if it landed in their midst. They hoped to be stationed near the river that coursed through the valley, where the water would give them a place to escape from dragon fire.

The river cut through the valley, descending from the northern foothills near the escarpment where Water and Lira had surveyed the advance, and continuing through the valley to a small lake. Creeks from the southern hills entered the lake, which emptied into the river winding west, where it culminated near Terros.

At thirty feet across, the river was not overly large or swift, its lazy current easy to cross with the various temporary bridges the men had placed. Half the human forces had placed their camp on the west side of the river, as had the elves.

Water strode to the surface and hardened the liquid, allowing them to cross to the opposite bank and avoid the heavily trafficked bridges. Talinorian cavalry, rock trolls, gnomes, orcs, and the rest of the human camps were sprawled across the remainder of the valley, flattening the indigenous brush.

On a small rise near the center, Queen Rynda leaned against the single tree. Water and Lira picked their way through the camps to reach her, arriving as Fire appeared as well. Fire grinned as they approached at the same time, and Fire's plate of food revealed where he'd gone.

"I'm not used to being so hungry," Fire said as they ascended the small rise.

"You get used to it," Rynda said, turning to greet them.

"Is your camp set?" Water asked.

Rynda nodded. "Twenty thousand rock trolls."

"Can you kill the dragons?"

"We've killed more dragons than the other races combined," Rynda said. "It's Draeken and Serak that give me pause."

The statement spoke volumes. As long as Water had known the formidable rock troll queen, she'd never expressed fear or doubt. After dismissing a battle against two of the mightiest creatures on Lumineia, it was their riders that made her question her strength.

"It doesn't help that our army is on the brink of infighting." Fire used a fork to point to the camp.

Rynda cursed under her breath. "This was a bad idea from the start. It's clear Serak wanted us here, and even though all outward signs point to a quick victory, we are not fighting a normal foe."

"Lira has an idea," Water motioned to her.

Lira pointed to Xshaltheria. "I think we should attack tonight."

"All of us?" Fire snorted in disagreement. "They've just set up camp and I cannot see King Justin putting on his armor to attack when its dark, and especially not when it looks like we have such an overwhelming advantage."

"No," Rynda said, nodding in thought. "Lira is right. A small force could breach the fortifications and reach the Dark Gate. Destroy it before he has a chance to open it."

Fire looked between them. "Are we seriously talking about planning a high risk attack against a weaker foe—when *we* have the superior force?"

"Yes," Water said firmly. "It's our best chance to stop Serak and Draeken. What fool would ignore their superior strength for such a dangerous gambit?"

"Smart tactics are never foolish," Rynda said, stepping away from the tree. "Erisay will want to be part of this, but Dothlore is meeting with King Justin. We'll have to do this without him."

"How many do you think we should take with us?" Lira asked.

"Two dozen," Rynda said. "No more."

"This is madness," Fire said. "Fortunately, I like this type of madness."

Rynda grinned and turned away before casting over her shoulder. "Meet me at the edge of my camp at midnight."

"She seems excited," Lira drawled.

"Of course she is." Fire took a bite of his bread and spoke through a full mouth. "She gets to abandon all the soldiers she thinks are useless, and strike at Serak in a way that could destroy him for good."

"You make it sound like it's easy," Water said.

"Not easy. Just exciting. I'll see you guys there."

"Where are you going?"

He looked at them like they were daft. "I'd rather be stabbed in the leg than watch the two of you sneak kisses."

Water flushed and Lira grinned. Fire had finished his plate and departed in search of more. When he was gone Lira took Rynda's place on the small rise and pointed to the fortress of Xshaltheria.

"You think we can do this?"

"Would Ero let me be an Eternal?"

She swiveled to face him, clearly surprised by the change in subject. "Why do you ask?"

"My whole life I've thought I was preparing to become Draeken. Now that future is obliterated. When I look forward there's . . .," he struggled for the right word and then shrugged helplessly, ". . . nothing."

"You want to be an Eternal because of me?"

Her lips twitched and he smiled in turn. "I want something to look forward to."

"Assuming we win this war."

He chuckled at that. "You know, I don't think I've ever really thought about not becoming Draeken."

"And now you worry that you still have a piece of him inside you."

Unable to meet her gaze, he looked to the campfires of the alliance. "I see what he is doing, what he intends to do now, and I cannot help but wonder. I'm the only fragment left with a piece of Draeken. What does that mean?"

"It means you can stop him," she said.

"Or it means I could turn on my brothers."

It was painful to voice the fear he'd felt since the moment he'd learned that Draeken was alive. Lira approached and reached up to his cheek, turning his head. From inches away her eyes reflected the fires in the valley.

"You would never turn on your brothers," she said.

123

"How can you be certain?" he asked. "Draeken was ready to kill the fragments to rise to power."

"You and your brothers rejected Draeken," Lira said. "You proved that you were stronger. He may be the fragment of Power, but you and your brothers are superior."

Unable to withstand her conviction, he smiled and wrapped his arms around her back. "What would I do without you?"

"Be sad and miserable," she said with an impish laugh.

"True," he replied.

"And yes," she said. "I believe Ero would permit you to join the Eternals."

"Assuming we survive," he replied.

"*When* we survive," she said, and leaned up to kiss him.

There was an audible groan and both looked up to find Fire turning away. He had a bag of supplies in one hand, a jug of ale in the other, and a look of disgust on his features. He dropped the food and retreated.

"This is what I get for thinking you might be hungry."

"Thanks, Fire!" Water called.

"I'll be back when you're done kissing," Fire growled.

"That's not going to happen anytime soon," Lira said.

Fire groaned loudly as he strode away, and Water chuckled. Despite what they faced, he believed Lira's words. They would survive, not because they had more power, but because they had something to live for. And now, Water had a future he desired. Draeken and Serak may have been powerful, but they lacked the very thing Elenyr had built. A family.

Chapter 15: The Melting

Shadow trudged through the dark tunnels, yearning for a bed. His feet hurt, his legs ached, and his stomach grumbled. Four days of walking through underground caverns and tunnels had left him annoyed and irritable.

Glowing vines covered the walls, illuminating the Deep caverns in iridescent blue, green, purple, and white. Mushrooms grew in neat stalks, and rivers flowed through channels cut by time. They passed small lakes, and narrow crevasses, the trail leading through a labyrinth of plunging ravines and rocky caves.

Shadow had always loved the Deep for the surge of magic, but after hiking for days, he wished for his bed at home. Of course, Serak had destroyed Cloudy Vale, so his bed was probably a pile of ash.

"Why can't Rune just teleport us there?" he asked.

Rune sighed in irritation. "The Unnamed cannot go where she has not been."

Shadow groaned at the response. "Are we there yet?"

"Ask that again and I might have to cut you," Lorica said.

"It's just around the corner," Elenyr said.

"That's what you said ten minutes ago," Shadow said.

"That was a lie," Elenyr replied.

"And this isn't?" Shadow asked.

"Not this time," Elenyr said as they turned a corner and the dark elf prison came into view.

Shadow forgot about his fatigue and irritation, his eyes rising to the large cavern. He'd expected a castle or fortress, for the rumors of the prison were too varied to believe. For the first time, the rumors did not do justice to the truth.

A thousand feet across, the cavern was large and open, with a curving road clinging to the left wall, where it connected to a small fort embedded in the side of the cavern. But the prisoners were not in the fort. Instead of locking their greatest criminals in walls of stone and steel, they had turned the entire cavern into a prison.

Hundreds of cages hung from the ceiling, each cage containing a single person. Channels of steel crisscrossed the ceiling, allowing the cages to be moved throughout the rail system. At the center of the prison, a platform extended upward like an island from what lay below the cells.

A lake of acid.

Heated from below, the green liquid spat and popped, casting the entire cavern in a green hue. Built by a dark elf named Werindel, the prison carried his name, but the criminals of the Deep called it by another name. The Melting.

"Don't touch the acid," Elenyr warned, leaning over the edge of the road. "It's strong enough to disintegrate steel, let alone flesh."

Men and women in the cages called out to them, clamoring for attention as the five advanced up the curving road that bordered the inside wall. The path was narrow, forcing them to walk single file, and Shadow noticed the holes at his side. Noticing his gaze, Sentara motioned to the holes.

"Acid traps," she said. "If the guards think we are a threat, they can open the pipes and we'll be washed into the lake of acid."

"Lovely," Shadow breathed, his smile widening.

Rune shuddered. "This is the worst prison on Lumineia."

"On that, we can agree," Elenyr said. "Werindel Prison contains the worst offenders of the dark elves, as well as a handful from the other races. The surface kingdoms pay a handsome sum for the dark elves to

126

house their more violent offenders. It is said Ero himself even put a criminal here."

"Jeric?" Shadow asked, surprised. "Who did he put here?"

"No idea," Elenyr said with a shrug. "But rumor says he's another krey, one using Lumineia to hide from the Empire."

"Really?" Shadow asked.

Elenyr smiled. "Like I said, it's just a rumor."

"Anyone ever escape?" Rune eyed the acid lake, her features tight with worry.

"Some got close," Elenyr said. "But none made it out alive." She pointed to the guard station they were approaching. "That controls the movement of the cages, and the acid traps. They can also seal the entrance we came in, preventing entry from without, or escape from within."

"Aren't you a pretty one," a criminal called to Lorica, whistling in her direction.

Shadow's eyes widened. "Do you have any idea who that is? That's the Thresher, a man known to kill his victims and rip them apart. And that's the Devil of Dorinvale, a dwarf said to have robbed every major vault in every kingdom. And that's the Red Elf, who spilled so much blood they say his hands will never be clean."

"Why do you sound so excited?" Lorica asked.

"I put them here," Shadow said, smiling at the memories. "I wonder if they remember me."

"The fragment of Shadow," the Red Elf called from his hanging cage. "Did you come for a visit?"

The elf wore a grimy uniform, grey with orange accents. He stood at the edge of his cage, leaning against the bars as he picked dirt from under his fingernails. The green glow of the acid made him seem more sinister.

"You *do* remember," Shadow said, pleased.

"How can I forget the one that put me in this hole," the Red Elf said.

"Is that the fragment of Shadow?" a gnome asked, rising and stepping to the edge of his cage. "Who would have thought he would come here."

"Siphon!" Shadow exclaimed. "I thought you were dead!"

"Who's Siphon?" Rune asked.

"The worst of the lot," Elenyr replied. "He used to create horrending daggers for the gnomes, and he is quite gifted with anti-magic. He decided to use the daggers he was making to steal the magic of other mages, claiming he could sell the magic and place it in someone else."

"Can you do that?" Lorica asked.

"Of course not," Sentara said. "But he managed to steal and kill his way through several kingdoms and several bounties."

"Until we caught up to him," Shadow said, waving at the gnome.

The gnome did not return the gesture. He merely regarded Shadow from beneath bushy eyebrows, his black eyes reflecting green from the acid. Shadow noticed he had an additional shackle about his ankle, the attachment preventing him from using his magic.

"You should visit more often," Siphon called.

"I've been busy," Shadow said. "Next time."

"Stop goading them, Shadow," Elenyr said. "You can't come spend time with them."

"Why not?" Shadow protested. "They could clearly use the distraction."

"For you it's a distraction," she replied. "For them it's a game of who can murder the fragment."

They approached the guard station, which was built into the wall of the cavern. Massive windows allowed for an unbroken view of the prison, and Shadow spotted a long desk of levers and controls, presumably to move the cells on their ceiling tracks.

The path led to a portcullis and guard house manned by two dark elves. The two stood behind the closed gate, playing dice on a small barrel set between them. The courtyard beyond connected to the viewing and control room, also blocked by a second portcullis. Against the cavern wall, a doorway led to a set of stairs headed into the wall, probably to the guard's quarters.

"We're an hour outside of Elsurund," Elenyr said. "The only people that come here are either prisoners or soldiers."

About the size of a small fort, the structure contained a tower at the road, a small courtyard, and the control room. Shadow peered into the courtyard and spotted a door set against the stone, presumably leading to the barracks. The elves obviously relied heavily on the defenses of the prison, and did not station very many guards at the Melting.

"Let me do the talking," Sentara said, advancing to the guard house.

Elenyr frowned, but made no move to intervene as the aged woman tapped the portcullis with her knuckles. The guards looked up and then went back to their dice, laughing as they rolled sixes.

"What do you want?" one asked.

"We need to speak to a prisoner," Sentara said.

"These prisoners don't often get visitors," the second said, a touch of suspicion lighting his eyes. "Least of all from an old woman." His eyes flicked to the others in the group, a man, two women, a young girl. No dark elves.

"We have word from Queen Erisay herself," Sentara said.

Elenyr extended a roll of parchment through the portcullis. A guard scowled in annoyance as he stepped away from the dice and accepted the parchment. He unrolled and read the missive, his frown deepening as he noted the mark on the bottom, the seal of Queen Erisay.

129

"Wait here," he said.

He turned and crossed the courtyard, calling to the guards in the control chamber. Someone inside pulled a lever and the second portcullis rose upward, permitting the guard inside. Shadow craned his neck and caught a glimpse of the controls. The seconds passed and his irritation returned, so he cast a thread of shadow through the portcullis, tipping the dice as the remaining soldiers sought to continue their game. The loser cursed.

"These dice are rigged," he growled. "There's no way they roll so low every time—and only on my turn."

"Just your luck," the second said with a laugh, and rolled a six and a five. He grinned as he dragged the small pile of coins into his hands.

The second guard cursed again and struck the dice, and Shadow tipped them upward, bouncing them off the top of the wall. The surprised guards stepped to the courtyard wall and watched as the dice fell into the lake of acid.

Shadow grinned as he watched the dice melt and disappear.

"Shadow," Elenyr murmured. "Do remember we need their help."

"I thought you said gambling was a filthy habit," Shadow said.

"It is," Elenyr said. "But that doesn't mean you can melt their dice."

"Gambling is fun," Sentara said. "But fun is not a virtue possessed by the Hauntress."

Elenyr glared at Sentara while Shadow laughed. Few dared to stand up to the formidable Hauntress, and he enjoyed the spectacle. Elenyr noticed his expression and her scowl deepened, but before she could speak the last guard returned and waved for the gate to be opened. The thick portcullis clanked upward, allowing them into the small courtyard.

"Captain Jefsor would like to speak to you."

Although he tried to hide it, his voice was hard. Elenyr glanced to Shadow, who shrugged like it didn't matter. Rune and Sentara were talking about the prisoners, and Sentara was pointing to one of the

130

prisoners, who had retreated to the back of his cell. He stared at Sentara with abject fear. Lorica frowned, making it clear she'd noticed the guard's tension.

"Thank you," Elenyr replied to the guard.

The five entered the courtyard and the guard swept a hand to the other two. They straightened and ambled to the portcullis, sealing it behind them. As Shadow crossed the courtyard, another trio of guards appeared from the barracks, and holes in the courtyard floor opened up.

"That doesn't bode well," Shadow said, pointing to the holes.

Captain Jefsor appeared at the gate to the control chamber, dressed in the customary green and grey of a dark elf captain. He was short for an elf, and oddly, had a beard. Shadow burst into a laugh.

"That's better than a dwarven beard," he said.

Captain Jefsor growled, his eyes on Elenyr. "An elf, two human women, a girl, and a vagabond."

"Hey!" Shadow protested, looking to his traveling clothes. "I'm not a vagabond."

"You expect me to believe the five of you are here on an order from the queen?"

"We are here to speak with Mimic," Elenyr said.

"Not until we find out who you are," Jefsor said.

He made a motion to someone out of sight, and there was a rush of sound. Shadow stepped away from one of the holes just before acid burst from the floor, spurting upward. A dozen other geysers rose, sealing them all inside.

"Captain, you're making a mistake," Elenyr said.

"No mistake," Jefsor said. "Tell us who you are, or we'll put you inside a cage and let you rot until you do speak."

"I'm sorry," Elenyr said. "But I really don't have time for this. Someone else will be coming for Mimic soon, and we cannot afford to let her be taken."

Elenyr turned ethereal and leapt through the acid. She drew her blade as she passed through the captain's body, who cried out in fear. Elenyr placed her sword on his throat as she turned back to flesh. The courtyard was visible by the prisoners, who began to shout and call, rattling their cages.

"Captain," Elenyr said, "please lower the acid. I'm only going to ask once."

"Do as she says," the captain said.

A guard obeyed the order and the acid dropped back into the courtyard floor. Just as it did, one of the guards at the gate called back to them, and all eyes turned to the three newcomers that had just entered the cavern.

"Two visitors in less than an hour?" Captain Jefsor asked.

Elenyr removed her sword and pointed to the new arrivals. "That, captain, would be the others come for Mimic."

"You know them?" the captain asked.

Shadow smiled as he recognized them. Now it was getting interesting. "That would be two mind mages and a former rock troll king."

Chapter 16: The Prisoner

Shadow watched Bartoth advance up the road to the prison entrance. It was the first time he'd seen the troll without his black armor, and he looked different. His brown skin was shadowed, tinged with grey, almost sickly. The helmet he'd worn had scarred his face and features, leaving lines across his nose and cheeks.

His two companions were obviously Zenif and Zoric, the two mind mages dressed as dark elf soldiers. As they approached, their features seemed to change, and he felt a faint tug on his consciousness, the whisper of mind magic.

"They're going to look like dark elves," Elenyr said.

"They *do* look like dark elves," Captain Jefsor said.

The captain led them up a set of stairs to a room above the entrance. Through a narrow window, they watched the trio approach, the two mind mages in the lead. Shadow noticed Zenif's uniform was that of a high captain, and Bartoth looked like a rock troll mercenary.

"They don't want a battle," Elenyr said.

"Too bad," Sentara said, her sword in her hand. "They're going to get one."

Elenyr pointed to the hanging cages. "The guards could drop Mimic's cage into the acid, and it looks like Zenif doesn't want to risk them killing her."

"They'll be here in two minutes," Lorica said. "We need a plan."

"What exactly is going on?" Captain Jefsor demanded. "I believe you are here on Erisay's order, but why so much effort to get one prisoner?"

"Mimic is no normal prisoner," Lorica said. "She was first of the Queen's Hand, the greatest assassin your people have had in ages. And Serak wants her."

"Where is she?" Rune asked.

The captain stepped to the window overlooking the acid lake and pointed into the hanging cages. "There are four quadrants of the prison, each with a type of prisoner, mage, murderer, thief, and surface dwellers. The central platform is the common area, and the prisoners are permitted limited time together. Mimic is in the furthest cell of the murderer quadrant. She has anti-magic shackles and bars."

"Is there a back exit to the prison?" Elenyr asked. "One where we can slip her out?"

"You want to take her?" Captain Jefsor asked. "She's the most dangerous person here. If she escapes, we won't catch her again, and there's no telling how many she will kill."

"If they get her," Elenyr said, "they will give her *more* power."

"I don't know what the problem is," Sentara said with a shrug. "There's only three of them. And we have Rune, an assassin, the Hauntress, and a former fragment. Let's just kill them."

"She's right," Shadow said. "Bartoth doesn't have his armor, and I don't think we're going to get a better chance."

Shadow didn't say that he cared little for Mimic. He just wanted to fight Bartoth when he didn't have his armor, and imagined telling his brothers he'd defeated the former rock troll king when his brothers had failed. A smile spread on his face as he foresaw that conversation.

"Mimic is the priority," Elenyr said. "We need to get her out."

"Elenyr?" Rune asked. "I think the choice is being made for us."

Shadow darted to the window. The three on the road had come to a halt, and Bartoth had drawn his sword. Shadow's smile widened as he realized the two mind mages had probably sensed their presence.

134

"Captain?" Elenyr said. "Whatever defenses you have, I suggest you get them ready."

"There's just three of them," Captain Jefsor said. "What can they do?"

Bartoth surged into a run, sprinting up the roadway with shocking speed. His feet pounded on the stone, and the prisoners of The Melting came to their feet, sensing the impending strike. Captain Jefsor barked an order and acid burst from above the road, pouring into Bartoth's path.

The rock troll leapt into a flip that carried him above one spout. He landed on the opposite side and flipped again, and then used his sword to deflect the next spout of acid. The liquid sprayed to the side, but the rock troll managed to evade, moving even faster than the flowing green liquid. His sword went unscathed.

"Lieutenant!" the captain shouted. "Full defenses! Now!"

Elenyr drew her sword. "Lorica, Shadow, get Mimic out. Do whatever you have to. Sentara and Rune are with me."

"It's about time," Sentara said.

She too, had her sword in hand and darted to the steps leading to the courtyard. Rune cast an uncertain look out the window and then followed. Elenyr stepped close to Shadow and lowered her voice.

"Whatever it takes," she said. "Don't let them have her."

"Done," Shadow said.

He sprinted over the steps and dropped into the courtyard, landing as Bartoth reached the outer portcullis. The rock troll leaned his shoulder into the blow and slammed into the steel bars. Flesh and bone met steel, and it was steel that gave way.

The bars bent inward, the stone moorings cracking from the impact. Seeing that Bartoth was momentarily on the opposite side of the gate, he reached to the shadows in the alcove and cast a sliver of darkness, which he stabbed into Bartoth's foot. The mighty rock troll began hopping like a child with a stubbed toe.

135

"I'll cut you to shreds," he growled.

"You should put some herbs on that," Shadow said. "Before it gets infected."

"Shadow," Lorica called, dropping to his side. "Will you stop messing around."

"Never," Shadow said, but followed her into the control chamber.

Guards rushed to the courtyard, gathering weapons tipped with acid. Shadow and Lorica passed through the soldiers to reach the interior, where a pair of operators franticly sought to work the levers.

The hanging cages began to shift and move, spinning around the inside tracks, moving further from the guard station. The dark elf in command, a woman with silver hair and a scar on her arm, looked up at their entrance.

"We're moving all the cells to the back wall, as far as we can from the conflict."

Clang.

Bartoth struck the portcullis again, the metal bending and screeching, the stone crumbling. Lorica leaned back and looked through the door. She grimaced at what she saw and stabbed a finger to the entrance.

"That's not going to last long."

"Any way to make the cages move faster?" Shadow asked.

"Only in emergencies," she said.

"I think this qualifies," Shadow said.

The woman reached for a lever, and hesitated. She blinked in confusion, her hands trembling before she reached for a second lever and pulled it. The hanging cages came to a halt, where they rocked on the chains before reversing direction.

"What are you doing?" Lorica demanded.

"I have new orders," she intoned.

"Zenif is manipulating her mind," Shadow said.

The woman shook her head and grimaced, and then her features smoothed out before she pressed a second rune. The cages accelerated, gliding toward the roadway, closer to Zenif and Zoric.

"Sorry," Shadow said, and struck her on the side of her head.

The woman collapsed to the floor and tried to rise, so Shadow struck her again. A shout came from outside and two of the guards sprinted toward the control chamber. Lorica blocked one swinging sword and deflected the other upward. The two weapons were both tipped with acid, and one tumbled from the dark elf's grip. It fell into the levers and runes, the acid causing it to sink into the controls.

A dull whine came from within, and suddenly the tracks in the ceiling shifted, turning into concentric circles. The chains began to accelerate, spinning around the circles and dragging the cells. The prisoners howled as their cages spun above the acid lake.

"What did you do?" Shadow demanded.

"It's not like I meant to," she said, pulling the lever that would shut the portcullis. "We need to get Mimic."

"There she goes," Shadow said.

He pointed to her cage as the dark elf sped by. The woman looked exactly as she had the last time they had met in Mistkeep, her skin sallow and mottled, diseased. Her eyes were cold and unblinking, even as her cell whirled above the acid lake. The shackles were on her ankles, binding her to the cage.

"We need to get to her before Bartoth does," Lorica said.

"You want to get *on* the spinning cages of deadly prisoners that hangs above a lake of acid?" Shadow asked.

"You don't?"

Shadow laughed. "Of course I do. I just wanted to make sure you did."

"At least my wings work down here," she said, and her cloak unrolled. "If you fall, you're going to land in acid, and I don't think even you can survive that."

"A lake of acid makes everything better," Shadow said.

"Nobody would think that except you."

He climbed up to the window's edge and looked out at the spinning cages. They were arcing twenty feet away, at least on the outer ring, and once he was on a cage, he would have to jump from cage to cage to reach Mimic's cell.

Lorica leapt out the window, her cloak unfurling into bright wings. She flapped once and Shadow jumped, catching her hand and swinging outward. A hundred feet above a sea of boiling acid, he soared, and then landed above a cage. He caught a chain and held on as they spun past the outer guard house.

Crunch.

The portcullis crashed inward, the stone mooring unable to withstand Bartoth's blows. He charged into the gathered solders in the courtyard, leading with his sword. At impossible speed, he spun into a whirlwind of blades, deflecting weapons and striking guards. Elenyr, Sentara, and Rune joined the battle, but Bartoth still had time to rip a spear from a soldier and hurl it at Lorica.

"Look out!" Shadow called.

She ducked, but the spear scored a line across her wing, the acid-tipped blade cutting into the fabric. It fluttered, and she dropped onto a cage several back from him. She examined the rent and grimaced, and Shadow realized that it would no longer be safe for her to fly, not while Bartoth was there.

Bartoth deflected Elenyr's sword and picked up a dark elf, tossing him into the acid lake. The elf screamed as he plunged into the liquid. His hand resurfaced, waving wildly as the gauntlet melted. Then he was gone.

138

The prisoners were in an uproar, shouting and screaming in the cavern. Spinning around the outside of the prison, Shadow searched for Mimic's cell, and spotted her seven cells ahead. He charged the edge of the cell roof and jumped to the next, just managing to land on the edge.

"Hey Shadow," the Red Elf growled.

The prisoner had climbed the bars and he reached up, attempting to grab his ankle. Shadow yanked his ankle free and kicked the elf in the face, knocking him back into his cell. The elf shouted and held his face.

"You broke my nose—again!"

"I wish I could play," Shadow lamented, "but I do have a task to complete."

Shadow sprinted to the next, leaping to the following cell. He looked back and spotted Lorica following his example. They'd rotated halfway around the cavern and starting to turn back, bringing the guard station back into view.

Half the soldiers were dead, and Bartoth had cut off the acid flow on the approach road, allowing Zoric and Zenif to leap forward. Then Bartoth landed a blow on Elenyr, knocking her into a wall. He spun and deflected a blast of fire from Rune. Driving past Sentara, he stepped on the edge of the courtyard and leapt high.

The prisoner in the cell cried out as Bartoth caught the bars of his cell, the rock troll's weight throwing it off balance. The cell careened into a neighboring cell and crashed together, the chains groaning from the weight. Bartoth dragged himself upward just as a chain broke. He leapt to the nearest cell, allowing the careening cell to break free. The dark elf inside screamed as his cell fell into the acid lake.

In the courtyard, the two mind mages engaged Elenyr, Sentara and Rune, the battle quickly turning bloody. Shadow turned away and leapt to the next cell, charging across and jumping to Mimic's cell. He landed hard, ducking as a piece of chain flipped about from a broken cell, nearly striking him in the head. He leaned over the roof and looked down at Mimic, who met his gaze with the same disturbing calm.

"Shadow," she said coldly.

"Mimic," he replied. "Would you rather end up with him? Or me?"

She regarded him for several moments, and her eyes flicked to Bartoth, who had destroyed three cells in his charge across the prison. Thresher screamed as he plummeted into the acid. Then Mimic reached down and withdrew a small sliver of metal from under her sleeve, which she jammed into Shadow's arm.

"I choose him," she said, and shoved him free of the cell.

Chapter 17: Vanquished

Dazed from the impact with the wall, Elenyr cursed Bartoth's speed. It had been some time since anyone had landed such a heavy blow and it had nearly crushed her chest. She rose to her feet and looked to the swinging cells—and saw Shadow be stabbed by Mimic.

He flinched from the sudden wound, and Mimic dislodged his fingers and shoved, sending him tumbling away from the spinning cell. In horror, Elenyr watched as her son fell towards the lake of acid.

Lorica dropped from the cell she was riding and her cloak spread into wings. She dove for Shadow, both hurtling towards the deadly surface. She reached her hand out and Shadow reached up. Their hands clasped and she swooped upward, but Shadow's feet grazed the acid, melting the heel of a his boot as she banked upward. Elenyr released her held breath, her head pounding with relief.

"He's not your son, you know."

Elenyr rotated to meet Zenif's gaze. The mind mage regarded her with contempt, his lips curled into a sneer. She flicked her sword, the anger sharp and sudden, empowered by her fear. She stalked across the bloody courtyard.

"My family is mine," she snarled.

She darted in, slashing low, her sword passing through his leg as if it was a mirage. She scowled and spun, finding another Zenif standing nearby. And then another. Zenif was not strong enough to pierce her thoughts, but he was strong enough to insert one of his own, and make her see duplicates of himself.

She winced as a blade cut across the back of her leg, drawing blood. She whirled and cut through Zenif, but again her blade passed through his body as if it was made of smoke. He laughed, the sound seeming to come from everywhere.

141

She spared the spinning prison a look. Bartoth had begun opening cages, ripping the hatchways off the top and ordered the prisoners to hunt Shadow and Lorica. One dwarf refused, and Bartoth slashed the chain, letting the cage fall into the acid. The others were quick to join Bartoth's cause.

Zoric had retreated into the barracks, and Sentara and Rune had followed, the three locked in battle, the sounds of ringing swords and blasts of magic echoing up through the door. The dark elf guards were on the floor of the courtyard, dead or wounded. Captain Jefsor leaned against a barrel, breathing hard as he held a gash in his side.

Elenyr turned ethereal, preventing the mage from striking in her direction, and then leapt through the portcullis into the control chamber. Zenif called from outside and tapped his sword on the steel.

"You cannot escape forever."

"I'm not here to escape," Elenyr replied, searching the panel of levers and runes for a way to help Shadow.

She began to work the controls, reading the symbols and pressing runes. The spinning cells began to slow, and the tracks shifted in the ceiling, sending cages going one way and then another. Then she spotted the symbol for acid placed on a symbol for the courtyard. She smiled and slammed her fist on the rune.

A shout came from the courtyard, and the mirages faded. Zenif appeared as if from thin air, only she knew his magic had shielded him from her eyes. He'd been standing too close to a column of acid, and the liquid had burned up his side, catching his hip and elbow. He removed his cloak and used the unspotted portion to wipe at the acid, furiously attempting to remove it before it ate into his flesh.

Elenyr took a step towards him, but then saw Shadow and Lorica battling the sudden army of prisoners. They jumped across the cells and attacked the pair, pushing them back by sheer ferocity. The Red Elf crept from the side and lunged, but Shadow slashed his dagger across the elf's shoulder. The next attacker was not so fortunate, and he fell into the acid, screaming. Siphon got close as well, but Shadow sent a throwing knife deep into his heart.

142

Elenyr turned away from the opportunity to strike at Zenif and resumed her place at the controls. She pulled levers and pressed runes, attempting to separate Shadow and Lorica from the other cells, all while Bartoth reached Mimic's cell and ripped a portion of the roof free. She expected him to help the woman exit her cell, but instead he pulled a dark green cloak and tossed it to her. Mimic didn't hesitate, and donned the cloak. Elenyr did the only thing she could think to do, and reached for the rune that would break the chains holding Mimic's cage.

"Elenyr!" Zenif shouted.

She heard the anger in the mage's voice and turned to see Zenif standing at the edge of the courtyard on top of the low wall. He had his hand around Rune's throat, the girl's eyes fluttering, as if she were struggling to stay awake. The acid had burned Zenif's arm, and the flesh was mottled and damaged.

"You drop mine, I drop yours," Zenif growled.

Elenyr held his gaze, her hand on the rune that would sentence Mimic to death. Out of the corner of her eye she watched Mimic begin to change, the cloak sinking into her flesh and skin, turning her into the final general. Mimic did not scream, but rather clenched the bars of her cage, her eyes darkening inside the cowl.

"You drop her and I'll cut you to shreds," Sentara shouted, and Elenyr heard Zoric strike at her flank, the two battling for dominance in the doorway leading to the road. Zoric used his magic to anticipate Sentara's blows, sensing enough to prevent Sentara from landing a lethal blow, or intervening with Zenif and Rune.

Elenyr! I cannot wake Rune!

Elenyr flinched as the voice of the Unnamed echoed in her thoughts, and she heard the panic in her voice. Zenif's greatest skill was a sleeping charm, and he kept Rune subdued, even as the Unnamed fought to wake her. Elenyr locked eyes with Zenif and the man's lips curled into a sneer of triumph. Then Elenyr shook her head, and pressed the rune.

The chains holding Mimic's cage snapped, and it dropped toward the lake of acid. Bartoth growled and leapt to a neighboring cell, just managing to catch the edge. Zenif bellowed his fury and released Rune, who dropped down the side of the cavern. Elenyr turned ethereal and plunged into the floor, speeding downward and reaching out of the stone wall. Her fingers turned corporeal just as they closed over Rune's arm. She grunted as the girl's weight pulled on her, but managed to retain her grip. The unconscious girl hung above the acid, and Elenyr forced them upward.

She rushed upward, her body ethereal inside the stone, her corporeal hand extended out, lifting Rune up the side of the cavern wall. She angled her path to go to the window of the control chamber, allowing her to pull the girl over the controls and lay her on the floor. Then she heard a strangled cry.

Leaving Rune where she lay, Elenyr leapt to the closed portcullis and passed through it, arriving in the courtyard to find a shocking scene. Zoric leaned against the wall, holding a cut across his stomach, while Sentara stood behind Zenif, her sword through his back.

"Father!" Zoric cried.

Zenif gasped for breath, but Sentara's sword was through his lungs. She used the sword to push Zenif to the edge of the drop and leaned forward to speak in the mage's ear, her voice so savage it made Elenyr cringe.

"You killed my only family."

Zenif struggled to speak, to breathe, to push his magic on Sentara, but the old woman's fury kept him at bay. Sentara placed her boot on his back, and with a savage kick, pushed Zenif off her sword, and into the air. Still fighting to breathe, Zenif fell down the inside of the cavern, the exact fall Rune had just taken, but without Elenyr to catch him. He bounced off the stone and splashed into the acid.

Weak from the gash in his back, he swam to the surface and uttered a final shriek of pain, the acid seeping into his body through the wound, eating his armor. Again he screamed before finally slipping beneath the surface.

"*Father!*" Zoric screamed.

He'd stumbled to the wall and watched in horror as his father died. Sentara turned on him, her features forbidding. Zoric's eyes pulsed with rage and he raised a hand to point at Sentara, his arm trembling.

"You killed him."

"He killed Rune," Sentara snarled. "And she was worth far more than your wretched father."

"Sentara," Elenyr said. "Rune is alive."

Sentara whirled and spotted Rune behind the portcullis. Without a word she jumped to the courtyard wall and climbed above the acid lake to reach the open window, where she leapt inside the control chamber and crouched at Rune's side. Elenyr raised her sword to Zoric, who glared at her with unbridled hatred.

"You think yourself impervious?" he demanded, his chest heaving, his eyes glowing with hatred. "Sentara will pay for what she has done."

"Not if you are dead," Elenyr said coldly.

"Zoric!" Bartoth bellowed.

Elenyr risked glancing his way. To her dismay, the powerful rock troll had caught the chains of Mimic's cell, preventing her from falling into the acid. He swung the chain and the cage, building up momentum, swinging the cage towards the cavern entrance. His intention was obvious, to throw the cage to the entrance, where Zoric could help Mimic escape the cell. But Zoric bared his teeth in a snarl and stepped closer to Elenyr.

"Zoric!" Bartoth barked, his voice full of command.

The mind mage scowled, torn between battling Elenyr and Sentara, or helping secure Mimic's release. Elenyr too, was torn. She wanted to stop Mimic, but if she left, Zoric might overcome Sentara and kill her and Rune. And why was she sick to her stomach?

She clenched her waist as her last meal heaved. The prisoners that Bartoth had released were similarly struggling, with some kneeling in their cages to vomit. One lost consciousness and fell to his death.

Another managed to wrap a chain around his body before he lost consciousness. Another leapt to the outer wall, an impossible leap.

He caught the stone with nimble fingers, and climbed like a crab along the surface. As everyone else suffered from the sudden illness, the man did not seem affected. Without a backward glance, he dropped onto the road and slipped away, his escape unnoticed by anyone in The Melting.

"You feel that?" Zoric asked. "That's the birth of Plague, the final general. It cannot be stopped, and none of you will survive what she will do to you."

Elenyr turned ethereal but the sickness continued. She dropped to one knee and fought to hold her sword upward. Zoric regarded her with distaste and knelt to her level. Pointing to the swinging cage, he lowered his voice.

"Mimic is a disease now," he said. "And you cannot stop a disease with blade or magic. There's nothing you can do to prevent your end."

Elenyr cast about in desperation, but half the prisoners were dying, the other half retching and writhing. Lorica had managed to reach a further cage and Shadow had lashed her in position, but she was vomiting on the cage. Shadow alone seemed unaffected, but then again, Shadow could not get ill. His magic was weaker than every other type, but he was also immune to physical ailments.

"You forget your foe," Elenyr said in grim satisfaction.

Zoric frowned and turned. On the cages. Shadow abandoned Lorica and sprinted to the next, leaping from one to another with the agility of a night panther. Zoric shouted a warning but Bartoth could not move. Braced as he was, he could not fight Shadow without releasing the cage. Shadow leapt to his position. Bartoth swung a meaty arm, but Shadow slashed the rock troll's hand and then dropped down the chain toward Mimic's cage.

It was swinging upward, toward the entrance, and Shadow danced along the chain, sprinting its length like it was a tree limb, and then dove for the end. Bartoth growled and heaved, intent on throwing the

146

cage the remaining distance. But Shadow caught the pin where the cage connected to the chain, and yanked it free.

The chain parted, the cage flipping awkwardly. Mimic screamed her dismay as it tumbled towards the entrance of the cavern, and all eyes fixed on the spinning cage. With a great *clang*, the cage struck the side of the road . . . and fell into the lake of acid. Shadow managed to get his feet and jumped off the sinking cage, leaping into a flip that carried him to the road. He caught the edge and stumbled with a laugh of delight, before turning to watch Mimic sink beneath the surface.

The sickness vanished, the sound punctuated by Zoric's bellow of disbelief. Bartoth too, seemed stunned, and hung on the top of the cage as he stared into the acid lake. Zoric rotated to face Elenyr.

"Your victory will be short lived," he snarled.

"It's still a victory," Elenyr retorted.

Zoric didn't speak again, and his body seemed to fade into nothingness. Bartoth too, seemed to disappear, both obscured by Zoric's magic. Elenyr raised her sword, ready for an attack, but the rocking of the cages and the sounds of fading footsteps indicated Bartoth and Zoric had retreated. For now, at least, they had won a battle. Elenyr breathed a sigh of relief as Shadow sauntered into the courtyard.

"Looks like we win," he said.

Elenyr engulfed Shadow in an embrace. "Well done my son," she breathed.

But Shadow merely laughed. "I *love* The Melting."

Elenyr leaned back and tousled his hair. "Of course you do."

Chapter 18: Vanguard

At midnight, Water and Lira joined the small gathering at the edge of the alliance camp. Rynda was already present with a knot of rock trolls, a pair of dwarves, and a trio of dark elves. Fire arrived shortly afterward with two members of the Bladed. Mox, the rock troll that was first of the Bladed, and Dek, a slim woman with a knot on her shoulder showing her to be a mind mage. The group shifted and Water spotted the woman Rynda was speaking to, Alosia, queen of the elves. Rynda spotted Water and Lira and motioned the group together.

"About time you arrived," she said.

"We're right on time," Water protested.

"Then you're late," Rynda said, and then swept her hand to the group.

"With Alosia, Erisay, and Mox, we've come up with a plan for our assault." She pointed to the two dwarves. "Bint and Bellin are stone mages. They're going to get us up the cliff. We're going to avoid the road entirely, and go straight for the fortress. We have ten rock trolls, including Mox, Lira and Dek, as well as the two fragments."

Mox motioned to Dek. "We know Serak has two lieutenants, Zenif and Zoric, both powerful mind mages. It will be Dek's job to keep them from causing you harm."

"And causing them harm in turn," she said dryly, fingering the purple dagger on her hip.

"Erisay and her two guards have the task of insuring silence," Rynda continued, nodding to the dark elf queen.

"You're coming with us?" Water asked.

The small woman smiled faintly. "There is little point in hiding my magic now, and although there are some talented sound mages in the alliance, few can do what I can do, if I'm not being boastful."

"Not at all," one of her guards muttered, making it clear her guards were not happy about their queen's intention to secretly assault Xshaltheria.

"Once we breach the top of the volcano, it will be Lira's job to get us across the gap. Remember, there's a fifty foot gap between the mouth of the volcano and the top level of the fortress. If we fall, we'll enjoy a long drop through volcanic air until our flesh melts in the magma. Are you up for getting us across?"

Lira, the only air mage of the group, nodded, her jaw set. "You can count on it."

"The top of the fortress is mostly flat," Rynda said. "A few entrance points leading below, and if Serak hasn't moved it, the Dark Gate should be there. Our job is to destroy it and get out."

"What about the dragons?" one of the dark elf guards asked.

"Ten rock trolls and two fragments," Mox said. "One of which should be able to negate the dragon fire." She motioned to Fire, who grinned.

"A lovely jaunt into a foe infested volcano beneath a dragon filled sky," Bint exclaimed.

"Beautiful this time of year," Bellin said.

Alosia swept a hand to the alliance. "Dothlore is meeting with King Justin as we speak, and I will be with him. Our job is to keep the army unaware of your activity. We cannot risk this effort fracturing the alliance we have built. We protect the alliance, you destroy the Gate. If all goes well, the assault will begin tomorrow and we can destroy the Order of Ancients for good."

"And what if Draeken or Serak are guarding the Gate?" Lira asked.

Rynda laughed. "They're too arrogant to pull guard duty."

"Which is why this is our best chance to destroy the Gate," Mox said. "Rest assured, this group represents some of the best warriors and mages on Lumineia. Fight together. Survive together."

"And if you die, you die for Lumineia," Alosia said.

Rynda groaned. "Can we move this along? We aren't here to talk."

The elf smiled up at the towering rock troll queen. "Always to the point, my dear friend."

"I just want to kill what needs killing," Rynda said, and then pointed west. "Let's move."

The group slipped into the darkness, but Water noticed Erisay step to Alosia. The elven queen, fair and beautiful in her gown, and the dark elf queen, beautiful and imposing in her black armor. Erisay embraced Alosia.

"Be safe, sister."

"I'll try to get Rynda back," Erisay replied.

"The world needs her," Alosia said. "And you."

"My daughter can reign in my stead," Erisay said dismissively. "Rynda does not have an heir."

Erisay noticed Water watching and gave a final nod to Alosia. Then she joined Water. As the rest of the vanguard had pushed ahead, the two of them walked alone. Water lowered his voice so they would not be overheard.

"How is Princess Aranian?" Water asked.

"She is well," Erisay said. "And your brothers?"

Water grimaced. When he and Fire had joined the army, they'd informed the kings and queens of the events at Blackwell Keep, and how Draeken now stood apart as the fragment of Power. The news had not been received well, but Erisay had sat in the back of the room, and watched Water and Fire with curious eyes.

"My brothers are well," he said. "Alive, at least."

150

"Your presence among the living suggests you conquered Draeken in Blackwell Keep," she said.

"I didn't say that."

"You didn't have to," she replied. "I could see it on your face when you spoke of the separation. Since tonight may very well lead to the death and ruin of everything, I thought I'd let you know that I'm proud of you."

"For what?"

"For being strong enough to do what is necessary," she said. "Would that we all had such courage."

"I do not deserve such praise," Water said quietly.

She patted him on the arm. "Just make sure you keep that woman of yours alive."

"Lira?" he asked. "How did you know she was with me?"

"You're a loud kisser," she said.

He flushed and stuttered, "Sorry, I mean, I—'"

"I could hear you halfway across the camp," she said. "But don't worry, only the other sound mages would have noticed."

"How many are there?" he hissed.

"A few dozen," she said with a smile.

As he groaned, Queen Erisay accelerated a step and hurried to the front of the group, joining Rynda. Lira dropped back to Water's side.

"What's wrong? You're bright red."

"The queen of the dark elves just told me she could hear us kissing from across the camp."

Lira chuckled, and then stifled the sound when one of the rock trolls glared at her. They all fell silent as they reached the base of the cliff.

Bint and Bellin took the lead, and pulled footsteps out of the stone, forming a makeshift ladder up the steep incline.

For the next hour they climbed the outside of the volcano in near silence. Water vacillated between worry of discovery, and worry of failure. They stopped occasionally to rest, and Bellin pulled a ledge out of the mountainside so they could sit. Water's legs burned from the climb, but it was better than fighting their way through the gates on the road.

Minutes turned to hours as they climbed, one painstaking step at a time. All grew tired, especially the dwarves. Their armor darkened with sweat, and Rynda wisely called for another rest.

Water looked out over the valley. Pinpricks of light rose from campfires, light orbs, and torches, and even with the distance, he could hear a scattering of hammers on steel. It would have been almost beautiful if it's purpose had been different.

They slowed as they approached the top of the volcano. Just around the curve of the mountain, Water could hear the soldiers manning the final gate, the outer entrance to Xshaltheria. Their voices were muted and tense, and from their height, the whole of the valley stretched below them.

A fifty foot wall extended from the top of the volcano, the wall circling the summit. A handful of guard towers extended even higher, and occasionally soldiers patrolled the top wall. The two dwarves had taken the last few hundred feet of the ascent into a crevasse, allowing the darkness to hide their approach. Still, they probably would have been discovered if the fortress had a full garrison. Most of the forces had been placed further down the road at the smaller gates.

Water clung to the handholds the two dwarves had provided, wishing the wind was not tugging his cloak. He glanced backward and regretted the action. The ground seemed miles away, and if he fell, he would bounce his way down the slope for long enough to consider a multitude of regrets.

The two dwarves led the group to the base of the dwarven-made wall, where their magic could take them no further. Xshaltheria had been one of the first dwarven structures in Lumineia, and even then they

152

had been overly paranoid about their city defenses. The fortifications of the citadel had been enchanted so stone magic could not manipulate the rock.

From near the front of the group, Erisay whispered into Lira's ear, and she worked her way up the handholds to the front. Then she cast her magic, shaping the air into more handholds. Alone, she climbed the remaining distance and disappeared over the edge. Water watched the battlements, his heart constricting for each passing second until she reappeared and dropped a rope. One by one the others ascended to the battlements of Xshaltheria.

Water slipped over the edge, his eyes scanning the top of the fortress. Heated air washed across him, rising from the depths of the volcano, but the tension had already made him sweat. If someone spotted them they would sound the alarm, and Serak and Draeken would be the ones to come. Water shuddered at the prospect of them alone, especially after what had happened in Blackwell Keep.

"A handful of guards on patrol," Lira whispered as the last of the group joined them. "I eliminated one. The next should be passing in a few moments."

All turned when the faint humming of an approaching guard came through from the guard tower, and light bobbed on the torch. Erisay flicked her hand and an orange dagger appeared in her grip. She threw it at the open doorway, the dagger banking to the side and out of sight. The humming stopped and the torch dropped, extinguishing on the stones. No sound came from the impact.

Rynda pointed to the guard house. "Helliot," she ordered one of the rock trolls, "deal with the bodies. Then wait for the remaining guards. The rest of you, line up to follow Lira."

Water took his place next to Lira as she shaped her magic. The outer wall of the fortress had battlements on both sides. On the inside, Water peered onto the top of the hanging fortress, his eyes drawn to the two dragons.

Gorewrathian was perched on the outer wall just a few hundred feet to their right, above the main entrance. Serak's mount had claimed a spot on one of the three giant chains that held Xshaltheria aloft.

153

"There it is," Mox whispered, pointing to the top of the fortress.

As Rynda had described, the top of Xshaltheria was mostly flat, with a staircase descending into the interior. At the center of the circular platform, a hole extended through the structure, and smoke rose from the opening, suggesting it vented heat from the magma.

Adjacent to the vent, a large archway had been erected. The dark material seemed luminescent, and a quartet of guards stood watch. The four were obviously focused on the impending conflict, and spoke in low tones.

"Once we're inside," Rynda said, "we'll be visible to the dragons and everyone else. We need to act quickly and escape. Remember, if we fail to break the Gate, Erisay has a plan to destroy it that will take more time. We'll have to give it to her."

"Ready?" Lira turned away from where she'd been casting her magic. "You can't see it, but there's a slide of solid air that will take you to the inside."

Rynda reached out, her hand coming to rest on the invisible plank of solid air. She nodded to Lira, her jaw set as she lifted herself onto the battlement and knelt on the slide. She drew her sword and nodded to Lira.

"I'm ready."

"Wait," Erisay hissed. "Get down."

Rynda dropped from the battlement just as two figures appeared on the stairs in the middle of the fortress. Water scowled when he recognized them as Serak and Draeken, the pair advancing towards the Dark Gate.

"They're arguing," Mox said. "I want to hear what they are saying."

Erisay inclined her head and orange light sparked in her fingers, stretching into threads that extended to the ears of everyone in the group. As the light faded, Draeken's voice came into focus . . .

154

Chapter 19: The Fourth General

"I'm not waiting any longer," Draeken said.

"This plan is dangerous," Serak said. "We do not yet have the last general. You might not be able to stand against the Dark."

Draeken rounded on Serak. "Are you questioning my power?"

"No," Serak said hastily. "But I have planned every contingency for this moment. My servants will bring the final general by dawn, and then the Gate can open."

"*Your* servants?"

Serak lowered his gaze. "My apologies, master."

Draeken smiled at Serak's humbling and gave a dismissive wave. "I cannot fault you for your habits. After all, they were your servants prior to my arrival."

"Your mercy is admirable."

Draeken's voice hardened. "But I *can* fault you for your doubt. I know my former fragments. They will not wait until dawn, not when they know the alliance was a trap. Bring the two candidates."

Serak hesitated, but ultimately he nodded and called to a nearby guard. "Bring them."

Two captives were led to the top of Xshaltheria, both bound at the wrists. Lady Dentis was in the lead, her red hair in shambles, dirt on her gown. They failed to obscure the seething haughtiness to her gaze, her expression matching that of the second woman.

Princess Melora, second daughter to Queen Erisay, still wore her prisoner greys. Captivity, even for a few weeks, had not been kind to her, and several wounds and bruises were on her face and arms.

"What is the meaning of this?" Melora demanded.

"Nobles," Draeken said with smile. "You are most welcome in my fortress."

"Why are we here?" the Raven asked.

"To witness the dawn of a new kingdom." Draeken swept his hand to the Dark Gate. "When the portal is opened, a vast army will be released, an army leashed to my will, and the will of my generals."

The Raven scowled. "You mean Gendor and Bartoth."

"The same," Draeken said, pleased by their knowledge. That would make it so much easier. "But I have two remaining cloaks."

"For us?"

Draeken chuckled at Melora's response, and the trace of greed. Serak had indeed chosen wisely in the two, and he wondered which it would be. He held out a hand to Serak and the Father of Guardians placed a cloak into his hands. It rippled like liquid, but unlike the others, it was brown rather than black.

"Both of you possess an insatiable ambition," Draeken said. "A hunger for power and prestige, a craving for greatness. This is the moment that one of you will attain such a position."

The truth settled in and the women exchanged a look. One cloak. Two candidates. The Raven bared her teeth in a snarl, while Melora smiled at the Raven, the expression one of dark anticipation. Both had served Serak in the Order of Ancients, and both had used their positions to expand their influence.

"And to the victor?" Melora asked.

"More power than you can imagine," he said. "Each cloak is imbued with a unique magic, and touched by the Dark, the shadow on the other side of the portal. You will be my servant, but your power will be greater than you can imagine. The people will fear you, and flee from the mere whisper of your presence."

Both women eyed the cloak, their eyes bright. Draeken ordered their bonds cut and a blade given to each. There was no need to explain the request, and as the swords were placed in their hands, Melora snarled at her sudden foe.

"This will be a pleasure."

"You never did know how to recognize a superior," the Raven said coldly.

As the two circled, Serak lowered his voice to Draeken. "I do not understand the need for this."

"You said yourself," Draeken replied. "You do not know which is better suited for the cloak. What better way than to let them decide for themselves?"

Serak fell silent, and Draeken spared him a glance. For all his preparation for Draeken's arrival, he'd begun to express frequent doubts, and Draeken was irritated at his constant hesitation. For the first time, Draeken considered the possibility that he did not want Serak as his servant.

The Raven lunged, her blade striking low and to the side, a feint. Melora flicked her sword out, long enough to deflect the sword and giving her time to strike from above. The blade came within an inch of the Raven's throat, slicing several red hairs as it whipped over her shoulder.

The Raven rotated, her sword slicing a shallow line across Melora's waist, turning her smirk into a pained scowl. The duel quickly intensified, and Draeken watched with interest. He would have preferred a more ceremonial duel, but the circumstances did not permit such a display.

More blood spilled, and both women fought for dominance. Draeken didn't care who was the victor, only that they were stronger. The Raven was obviously more skilled, but she was human, and Melora had lived for hundreds of years. To Melora's discredit, she did not fight as one who had spent lifetimes in training.

Blades locked as the two combatants fought, and the Raven showed her skill and patience, leaving Melora bloodied, her grey prison uniform cut into tatters. Doubt flickered on Melora's expression, and in that moment Draeken knew.

"Stop toying with her," he commanded the Raven. "End it."

"With pleasure," the Raven said.

She unleashed a furious barrage of strikes, driving the woman towards the vent at the center of the platform. Melora struggled to defend, fear rising in her eyes as she was driven back to the edge, where a column of heated air rose from the hole. The Raven twisted and struck for Melora's throat. She threw her sword up, but the Raven dropped her swing, striking the sword from her grip. The blade tumbled into the hole with a *clang*.

"Please," Melora said, falling to her knees and raising a hand. "I've always lived to serve."

"You serve yourself," Draeken said. "You always have."

"I am loyal to you," she quivered as the Raven placed her sword on her throat.

"You betrayed your home and family," Draeken said. "Your mother and sister. I admire your ambition, but not even they would save your life."

"I would."

All four turned to face the small figure striding to them. She held two orange daggers in her hands, her cloak thrown back to reveal her dark elf features, and the small silver circle about her head.

"Queen Erisay," Draeken said, delighted by the sudden arrival. "I must say, you arrived just in time to witness the death of your daughter."

Serak hissed orders to the soldiers and they rushed about, searching for other intruders. Draeken ignored them, his gaze fixed on the approaching dark elf. Erisay's features were set in a hard line, and Melora looked to her with hope, tears in her eyes.

158

"I have no wish to see my daughter perish," Erisay said.

"I admit I am surprised," Draeken said. "After all she has done to you and your people, I would think her death would bring you peace."

"The death of a child never brings peace," Erisay said. "Even an errant one."

"Mother," Melora pleaded. "I'm sorry."

"Free my daughter," Erisay said. "Or you'll deal with me."

Draeken burst into a laugh as Gorewrathian landed behind Erisay. His jaws opened and flames trickled between his teeth, but Draeken raised a finger, holding the dragon at bay. He cocked his head to the side.

"And what threat do you pose to me?" he asked.

"Not to you," she said, "but I can still do you harm."

Draeken winced as a dull thrumming filled his ears, the sound rising and crashing over him. He reached to his ears to block the sound but it vibrated into his bones and blood, crashing through his skull. He grimaced as it continued to mount. Thirty feet away, the Gate was trembling.

"The Gate!" Serak screamed.

Draeken reached for the cloak and darted to the Raven, throwing it about her shoulders. Startled, she retreated, and then her eyes widened. She screamed as the magic sank into her flesh, empowering her hunger, her flesh turning weak and thin, hanging on her bones. Melora scrambled to Erisay, who caught her hand and bolted, sprinting away from the dragon's charge.

A bellowed roar echoed, and two rock trolls appeared behind the dragon. Rynda dropped on the creature's back and drove her greatsword into his flank. The dragon reared back, flames bursting from its maw at the sudden strike. But Mox came from behind, and brought his hammer down on the embedded blade like a hammer on a nail, driving the greatsword deep into the dragon's back.

The dragon bellowed in pain and thrashed about, nearly crushing everyone as it sought to dislodge the buried blade. Draeken ducked as the tail snapped above his head, but a wing caught Serak, knocking him skidding away.

And still the thrumming from the Dark Gate mounted.

Heedless of the battle, Serak raised the stone around the Gate like a shield, but the thrumming did not diminish. The stone cracked and crumbled, even as cracks appeared in the Gate arch. Serak shouted to Draeken, his voice tinged with fear.

"The Gate is imbued with anti-magic," he shouted. "It should be stopping her magic."

"She isn't using her magic to strike directly," Draeken said, watching the Raven transform into Famine. "She's using a rising shriek curse to break the very stone."

Draeken turned away from the writhing figure and the dragon battle. Even as more rock trolls dropped into view and struck the wounded dragon, he stepped to the side of the Gate, where the runes lay hidden.

"Draeken!"

His hand on the activation rune to Kelindor, Draeken looked back, and found Fire and Water rushing towards him. He smiled, pleased that they would be here for this. After all they had done to him, the very least they could do was witness his victory.

"You don't have to do this!" Water shouted.

"Ah, the one piece of me that remains apart," Draeken said. "Don't worry, I'll tear it from your corpse in time."

Fire gathered flames in his hands and struck the two human guards rushing his flank. "Opening that thing could destroy everything."

"I know," Draeken said.

"Then why would you do this?" Water demanded, fending off a trio of Order soldiers.

160

More appeared behind him, and two more dark elves engaged them. A pair of dwarves joined the battle, blocking the stairs leading below, where soldiers rushed to join the conflict from the barracks.

"I am the fragment of Power," Draeken snarled, rage abruptly spilling into his blood. "And I *deserve* to rule, to command the lesser races, to be lord over kingdoms and races. In the face of my power, even dragons kneel."

Gorewrathian had caught Rynda's sword and yanked it out. It tumbled away but Lira raced into view and caught the enormous blade. She heaved it across the expanding battlefield and Rynda caught the hilt just as the dragon's tail snapped, catching her on the chest, the spikes digging into her hardened flesh and knocking her sideways. The giant dragon dropped its jaws but Rynda rolled to the side and slashed across the dragon's teeth.

The sound from the Gate continued to grow, deep and resonant.

"Please don't do this," Water pleaded, extending his hand. "You were part of our family once. You can be again."

Draeken's features hardened. "I don't need your broken family."

He pressed the rune, and silver light took shape inside the arch. The liquid rippled with the rising shriek, and the Gate gained a dull whine, but the material of the arch did not crumble. Cracks formed and expanded. As the shrieking curse wailed, the Gate vibrated, and dragons roared, the first fiend stepped into view . . .

Chapter 20: Sacrifice

The Dark seeped through the opening like smoke, passing around the armored fiend, only to wither in the air. The Dark crumbled to dust and the cloud tried again, pressing outward, reaching for Draeken, coiling about his arms, its words piercing Draeken's consciousness.

. . . Your will is mine . . .

The voice of the Dark carried a disturbing timbre, like the dark laughter of a murderer on a cold winter night. But the voice faded as the Dark again withered. Even that brief touch sent a shudder through Draeken's body. The voice threaded into his consciousness, subverting his will, and Draeken was shocked to find himself terrified.

He clenched a fist as the Dark withered, his vision returning to the battlefield and the fiend standing in the opening. A kraka. He knew the name because the Dark had provided the name, because for one small moment their thoughts were linked.

The towering warrior had once been a dakorian, and still had the bone armor over much of his body. But the bone armor had gone stark white, his flesh turning black, like paper pulled from a fire. He carried a giant obsidian sword, the blade hanging behind him, still inside the Gate.

It did not move or look at Draeken, the disturbing stillness a contrast to the raging conflict on the top of the citadel. Shouts and cries, angry and pained, and still the thrum in the Gate mounted. The kraka captain stood like a statue, an appendage to the Dark.

"The cleansing worked," Serak said. "The Dark knows it cannot enter Lumineia."

"How do we claim the army of fiends?" Draeken asked.

"You must speak to the Dark," Serak urged. "Subdue its will, and the army will yield to you."

Draeken stepped in front of the kraka and the eyes dropped to him. Red and glowing, they seemed to burn through him like a branding iron. Draeken sneered and reached out with his consciousness.

I require the fiend army for—

YOU THINK TO CONTROL ME?

The voice returned like thunder in his skull, mighty and everlasting, the voice of a mind so vast Draeken could not comprehend its power. The Dark possessed an entire world, and who was he to offer challenge? He was an insect demanding a monstrous dragon to be its servant.

Bound by fear, Draeken trembled in place as more krakas appeared, followed by the smaller creatures. Quare. Once human and krey, the Dark had twisted them into spindly creatures, their bodies muscular and humanoid, but lacking any semblance of humanity. Their features were sunken onto their skulls, their fingers like hooked claws.

Draeken wanted to shrink before the Dark, to flee and never hear that terrible voice again. But three other minds were touched to his own, his three generals. The warmind, the assassin, the devourer. Their will was his own, and with their aid he gathered his courage, finally understanding why Serak had planned four generals.

More fiends poured from the opening, and large doglike creature appeared. Sipers. They were the size of lions, their skin shaped in thousands of triangular scales. Rising and flaring red, the beasts snarled and spread outward, circling Draeken.

Distantly he was aware of the raging battle, of Fire and Water attempting to reach him, but the thickening ranks of fiends forced them back. Serak stepped to the fragments and forced them to retreat. But still the Dark Gate vibrated, the cracks widening. The ranks closed about Draeken until he stood alone, a solitary figure in a sea of black and red creatures. They snarled inches from his flesh, only his will keeping them at bay.

The dragons leapt to the wall and launched into the sky, the Order members fleeing in terror. Still the fiends came, pouring from the Gate and filling the breadth of the fortress, spilling into the interior and crossing to the outer fortifications. Still they came, expanding and taking positions. Thousands. But the Gate continued to vibrate, and the cracks were deep and chunks began to fall off the sides.

"We must stop the curse!" Serak's voice was distant.

The Dark's will crashed against Draeken, mightier than a hurricane and just as fearsome, rending his vaunted strength to shreds. If he fell to the Dark, he would be destroyed, and the rest of Lumineia would suffer a brutal fate. He needed a fourth general, but it was too late for that, and he could only fight or fall.

Your army is mine, Draeken snarled.

The Dark recoiled, and Draeken growled in savage pride. The Dark was mightier than any normal being, but Draeken was the fragment of Power, and before him the Dark would kneel. He took a step forward, and the krakas parted, allowing him to reach the Gate.

"No!" Serak's voice barely touched his ears. "Do not touch the Gate!"

Draeken ignored him, and reached to the Gate, his fingers passing into the silver liquid. He reached to the world on the other side, and imagined all he could do if he possessed the Dark as his servant . . .

YOU THINK TO MASTER ME IN MY OWN WORLD?

The thundering voice crashed through his body, ripping his pride to shreds, a thousand times stronger than it had been before. Draeken instinctually realized the Dark's strength was diminished through the Gate. He lurched back, sweat beading his neck and forehead, and the fiends leaned in, eager for the kill.

Claws grasped his arms and throat, but he burst to his feet and they recoiled once again. They fell back into their ranks, all facing him, and he realized the truth. The Dark had twisted the army and reshaped them to its will. He'd even taken their minds. But instinct could not be taken, and when the Gate opened, the fiends saw the opportunity to escape

164

Kelindor. The moment they passed through, Draeken became their master.

The fiends poured from the portal, sipers, quare, kraka captains, and giant skorpians. Draeken's army. His weapon of victory. He sensed their will, their desire for blood and battle, and he gave them a goal. At the base of a mountain a conveniently placed army had come, and they needed to be humbled.

"Draeken!" Serak's voice seemed distant. "The Gate will not last! We must stop Erisay's Magic!"

But Draeken could not hear, his thoughts weighed by the weight of so many minds. He gloried in his newfound power, reveled in the might at his fingertips. No army could defeat him. No warrior could defy his rule. And the fiends poured through the Dark Gate, driving the allied vanguard back.

"And my reign will be endless," Draeken said.

A hand caught his elbow and yanked him about. The anger was quick and vengeful, and he raised a hand to kill the offender. Then he recognized Serak, the man's eyes wide with panic and fear.

"Draeken!" Serak shouted in his face. "If we do not stop Erisay, the Dark Gate is going to shatter!"

All at once Draeken saw the top of the fortress. The fragments fought for their lives but they were isolated, and half their allies were dead. The waves of fiends hardly paused in their rush out the gates and down the outer road. But it was the Dark Gate that commanded attention.

The trembling arch emitted a whine as if in pain. Cracks marred the stone, and with each passing second the cracks expanded, the wounds threatening to destroy the entire arch. Tens of thousands of fiends had entered Lumineia in just the last few minutes, but they were a fraction of Draeken's army.

"Where is Erisay?" Draeken demanded.

"She fled with her daughter," Serak shouted. "I'm trying to hold the Gate together but her charm is still building!"

Serak's features were drawn, sweat beading his forehead. He grimaced and then reached for the Dark Gate, holding it together by force of will. Draeken leapt into the air and soared over the conflict, ignoring the fragments and the others. Several launched weapons in his directions but he swatted them aside, his gaze searching the battlements for his target.

He spotted the two dark elves on the battlements, Erisay fighting a group of Order guards as she ushered her daughter towards safety. Draeken dropped into their midst, sending the Order members scattering.

"It's time your magic came to an end," he said, advancing on the queen.

The dark elf queen conjured two daggers of sound magic, the orange blades shimmering in the light. "You cannot stop it," she said.

"But you can," Draeken said.

The shadows behind the two woman reached out, muscled arms wrapping around Melora and Erisay. Wounded as she was, Melora could not evade, but Erisay sliced at the hands and twisted out of reach. Then she sent a dagger spinning at Draeken's chest.

Draeken swatted the weapon aside, but the dagger burst apart, and turned into a piercing wail. He grimaced at the assault on his senses and she threw another dagger, and then another, the weapons hurtling at his body. He knocked two aside but the sound just got louder. Then the fourth plunged into his body, and the sound magnified tenfold.

He laughed as he used his mind magic to focus his hearing. The din of battle, the shouts of the dying, the roars of dragons, all became muted, like he was listening from underwater. Then he began to advance again, causally pulling the daggers from his body. They clattered on the stone at his feet.

"End your magic on the Dark Gate," he said. "Or I will end you."

"I'm not afraid to die," she said.

"You should be," Draeken said. "For I am not a normal death."

166

He used a spark of fire and snapped it like a whip. Erisay leapt back but the fire coiled around her leg and then fastened to the stone at her feet. Draeken sent three more, the ropes holding her fast. Then they began to pull her apart. The dark elf queen cried out as the fire bonds pulled, lifted her off the parapet.

"Do you have any idea how much pain I can cause you?" Draeken demanded. "End your magic, and I'll spare your life."

"My life does not belong to me," Erisay spoke through clenched teeth. "It belongs to my people."

"Mother," Melora shouted, still bound in arms of shadow. "Just do what he asks!"

"I give my life for my people," Erisay said.

"But would you give your daughter's life?" Draeken asked.

He raised his arm and a trident of light formed in his hands. He pointed it at Melora and leaned into the blow. The three points turned as sharp as broken glass and he pointed them at the woman's heart.

"End it now!" Draeken barked.

The whine from the Dark Gate continued to mount and Serak's scream was audible as he fought to hold the Dark Gate from shattering. Melora called to Erisay but Draeken saw the truth on her face. She would not do it even to save her daughter.

"She clearly means nothing to you," Draeken snarled, and then leaned into the killing blow.

Erisay cast a dagger and sliced the bonds on her arms. As she fell, she twisted her body, and fell between the trident and her daughter, the trident piercing her heart instead of Melora's. Surprised, Draeken retreated, the bonds holding both women evaporating.

"Mother!" Melora cried, falling to her knees to cradle Erisay's head. "Why would you do that?"

"I give my life for my people," Erisay said. "And my daughter."

"You would die for her?" Draeken asked, struck by the sacrifice. "Even after all the times she betrayed you?"

"A family is worth any sacrifice," Erisay said.

She reached up and touched her daughter's cheek. Then she smiled, and her body relaxed in death. Draeken stared as Melora cried her anguish, unable to pull his eyes from the sight of Erisay's final act. Then another sound touched his ears and on instinct he turned.

The Dark Gate trembled, the cracks expanding across the arch. Serak abandoned his efforts and leapt back, just as the silver light shimmered to purple, and then sparked into thousands of tiny shards.

And the Dark Gate shattered.

Chapter 21: Fallen

Fire fought for his life on the summit of Xshaltheria, fiends dying on all sides. The Dark Gate lay in ruins, shattered into oblivion, but forty thousand fiends had exited before it had been broken, and Fire roared his challenge as the waves of dark creatures crashed against him. With fireflesh wrapped around his body, he charged through the horde and picked up Lira. In his other hand he picked up one of the dwarves. Rearing back, he hurled them to the outer wall, where Water caught them.

"We have to go!" he bellowed.

"What about Rynda?" Water shouted back.

The attempt to destroy the Gate had succeeded, but the fiends were already pouring down the mountain. Shouts and screams came from the valley, barely audible over the sounds of combat on top of the hanging fortress.

Rynda had lost most of her trolls, and both of Erisay's guards were dead. She'd managed to get her daughter to the outer wall, but the second dwarven engineer had been torn apart by the fiends. Rynda and Mox fought with unsurpassed valor, their weapons cleaving through the fiends as they raced for the gates. Then Gorewrathian dropped behind them and his jaws snapped over Mox. One moment the First Blade was sprinting and fighting, the next he was inside the dragon's maw.

Rynda snarled her hatred and turned, but Fire struck the stone, sending a blast of flames outward, knocking fiends away and allowing him to reach Rynda. He rushed to her and grabbed her arm. Wrapped in spitting and damaged fireflesh, he was as large as she was, but she was stronger.

"Flee or die," Fire said.

She bellowed her anger and turned with Fire, and the two of them sprinted for the bridge leading to the outer fortifications. Draeken had abandoned them and taken his dragon mount to lead the attack, while Serak stood before the shattered Gate, on his knees. Fire yearned to turn about and kill him, but there were too many foes.

They sprinted across the drawbridge and then turned aside, where the surviving dwarf had used his magic to create a thin path on the cliff. Fire jumped off the road and landed on the path. He wobbled and got an eyeful of the drop before he managed to catch a knob and push forward. Rynda landed with more poise, spreading blood on the mountainside as she pushed by. A handful of fiends tried to make the jump but the dwarf pushed the ledge back into the mountain and they fell to their deaths.

"We need to get back to the army," Water called, and they hurried to descend back the way they'd come.

Melora appeared, cradling the lifeless Erisay, and Fire groaned when he saw her body. Rynda accepted the body with gentleness, tears forming in her eyes. Without a word, the others gathered around her, and Melora spoke in a whisper.

"She died to protect me."

"You should have been the one to die," Rynda said.

"I know," Melora said, and then straightened. "But I will not be found again on the wrong side of this war. Please . . . allow me to stand with you."

Rynda's features hardened. "I'd rather take a blade to your—"

"We need to get down this mountain," Water cut her off before she would strike Melora.

The fiends rushed about, killing with abandon. The Order guards fled, but the sipers raced after and dragged them down, tearing them apart. Draeken did not seem to notice, and their cries for aid went unheeded.

A pair of krakas entered the Xshaltheria stables. They returned with blood on their obsidian blades, and left a disturbing quiet where the horses had been bucking in their stalls. The bulk of the fiends had reached the alliance and the battle had begun. The sun touched the horizon, and with each passing hour, the light continued to brighten, revealing the chaos.

"What is happening?" Lira asked.

A claw had ripped across her arm and blood seeped from the wound. Fire paused and tried to bandage it, but her eyes fluttered, and he noticed the blood darkening her hair. She was lucky Water had been nearby, and he'd wrapped a liquid bandage around the wound on her head.

"Draeken commands the fiends," Water said. "But I don't think he was prepared to control them. They're killing the Order soldiers."

"They're going to destroy half the alliance," Rynda said. "But at least the Dark Gate was destroyed."

"Only temporarily," Melora said.

"What do you mean?" Fire asked.

"My mother shattered the stone," Melora said. "But Serak is a stone mage, an extremely talented one. He will be able to rebuild the Gate."

"This was for nothing?" Rynda rounded on her, and the dwarf cursed as he was nearly knocked loose.

"Watch it, troll," he growled. "I'd rather not fall to my death after surviving that."

"Our purpose was to destroy the Dark Gate," Rynda snarled. "My people gave their lives for that. Mox gave his life for that."

Melora passed a hand over her features. "I'm sorry, but the only way to destroy the Dark Gate for good would have been to drop the pieces into the volcano."

Rynda reared back and punched the mountain, cursing with enough force to make even Fire wince. She cursed again, and then again. Fire saw her anger, but her hand trembled in regret and loss. Then she stabbed a finger at the dwarf.

171

"Get us down to the valley."

"I'm trying," the dwarf said.

"Try harder."

The dwarf growled and worked the stone, forcing it to bend out of the mountainside. Many of the ladder sections were still there from before, but some had been destroyed by dragon fire. It didn't matter. By the time the group reached the base of the mountain, the battle was over.

Fire jumped the last few feet and raced to the battle, but he slowed as it became clear most of the fiends were dead. He advanced through the battlefield, where healers rushed to care for the wounded. Five thousand krakas and sipers, and thirty thousand quare, as well as a handful of skorpians. The small army of fiends had been a quarter of the size of the alliance. In the smoke and wreckage of camps, it was clear the alliance had survived, but at a cost.

As the sun rose over the camps, clumps of scattered fiends were caught and killed. Archers and mages fired at Draeken on his dragon, forcing him to keep his distance. The black fury on his face was sufficient to make Fire smile.

"He looks angry," he said.

"We lost thousands of troops in the time it took for us to climb down the mountain," Water replied. "*I'm* the one that's angry."

Fire spared his brother a look, surprised by the anger on his features. Water was the calm fragment—or had been the calm one before the separation. But Water glared at Draeken with a baleful gaze.

The fiend assault had been straightforward, a charge into the heart of the camp. Fortunately the rock trolls had been at the center of the line, and they'd retreated, drawing the entire fiend army inward, allowing the cavalry and infantry to strike the flanks. The rock trolls had then turned on the fiends, shattering their ranks.

The dead were scattered across the ground, and healers rushed to care for the wounded. Other soldiers knelt at the sides of friends, and Fire spotted a father weeping over his son. He grimaced, and wished they'd been successful in their task. If they'd destroyed the Dark Gate for good, the battle would not have occurred.

"*You.*"

The word came from King Justin, who advanced across the battlefield like a charging warhorse, his nostrils flaring. He stabbed a finger at Rynda, Fire, and Water, his guards scrambling to keep up.

"Where were you?"

Rynda caught the hilt of her sword, bringing the man to a halt. "I don't answer to you," she said.

"My mother destroyed the Dark Gate," Melora said. "For now, at least."

"I don't speak to you, traitor," he barked. "Where's Erisay?"

Queen Rynda reverently placed the body of Erisay on the ground, and those present sucked in their breath. In the last few weeks Erisay had become a beacon of hope to the alliance, and her sudden loss would hit all races hard.

"She died to destroy the Gate," Melora said. She straightened. "She died to stop Draeken."

"Then she died in vain," Justin growled, and then turned to the group. "Have you gone mad? We barely survived their assault, while you were off trying to play hero."

"We saved this entire army." Fire folded his arms. "If we had not done what we did, the fiends would still be pouring from the Gate, and the alliance would be trod under their feet."

"No one asked you to intervene," he growled. "You and your fragments are the cause of all of this."

"We're stopping it," Water said with uncharacteristic heat.

King Justin took a step towards him. "You're the source of this war. You merely have to look at the dragonrider to see the truth."

173

The mighty dragon swooped to the ground and alighted on the opposite side of the river, his enormous wings sending gusts across the river and into their group. Draeken's expression had shifted from fury to cold calculation.

"I'm afraid the king is correct," he called. "The fragments were my host, and because of them, I exist."

"Elenyr should have killed you," Justin spat on the ground.

"Why?" Water demanded. "Because we existed? She taught us how to use our magic to protect the kingdoms. To protect *your* kingdom."

"You're *destroying* my kingdom," Justin snarled.

"Come now," Draeken said. "Your bickering is tedious. Perhaps you have forgotten that I am your foe. Do you require a reminder?" The dragon's jaw's opened and fire kindled in his throat.

"We destroyed your vaunted army," King Justin called. "You are nothing to us."

Draeken chuckled and patted the dragon's neck. "I'm afraid my former brothers are correct, King Justin. My servant will rebuild the Dark Gate, and when it is opened this time, I'll be prepared to control my army. We'll sweep across this land and destroy every city and village, until there is nothing left but broken streets and bones."

"Why?" Fire asked. "Why do this?"

"Because Serak gave me power," Draeken said, "and power is meant to be used."

Serak's dragon dropped from the clouds and landed next to Draeken's own mount. Serak tried to speak to Draeken, his features surprisingly full of doubt. Fire exchanged a look with Water, who shook his head in confusion.

"Serak says the dark army was never supposed to attack us," he murmured. "He says it was merely supposed to show the people their strength so they would relinquish their crowns to Draeken."

174

Draeken jerked his hand in dismissal, his features clouding with anger. "The army is *mine*, Serak, and I will use it as I see fit."

Serak's eyes flicked to Water and Fire, his features clouded, uncertain. Draeken straightened as if he could salvage the situation, and swept a hand to the battlefield, and Fire noticed that surviving soldiers had gathered and closed ranks, as if preparing for an attack.

"Serak brought you here so you could witness my might," he called, raising his voice so the soldiers could hear. "And you have witnessed but a fraction of the blood that will be spilt. When the Dark Gate opens again, we will flood these lands until any that oppose me are destroyed. Only those who swear allegiance to me will retain their lives."

"You seek to rule us all?" King Justin sneered.

"I do not seek," Draeken said, a scowl forming on his face. "I desire, and I obtain."

"You will never possess my kingdom," King Justin growled. "I am not afraid of you, your dragon slaves, or your supposed army. I think we destroyed everything you had, and you merely want us to cower in—"

Fire burst from Gorewrathian's maw and streaked across the river. The flames engulfed King Justin and the guards. Nearby soldiers leapt away. Fire stepped into the blast and sought to deflect it, but his magic was subdued, and he could only deflect a portion upward.

Water leapt to the river and brought his hands into a rising clap. The water rose upward at his command, extinguishing the flames in a wall of water. Steam burst from the contact, billowing upward until the dragon cut off its assault.

"Be my subjects," Draeken said coldly. "Or join your king."

The dragon launched into the sky. Serak stared at the burning corpse of King Justin before he too departed. Fire and the others gathered around the remains. Fire shook his head, confused and uncertain. They'd delayed defeat, but victory seemed even more daunting.

Chapter 22: Retreat

Without a human king, and their enemy certainly protecting against another attempt to destroy the Dark Gate, the alliance was forced to withdraw. Led by the trudging troops of Griffin, Talinor, and Erathan, the entire force retreated west. Dead were carried in wagons, while the wounded were also in wagons, the healers fighting to save their lives.

Fire conjured a horse of flames and rode it beside Water, his gaze fixed ahead, to where Rynda argued with the remaining monarchs. Many of the soldiers cast their eyes at their feet, and Fire wondered how they had so utterly failed.

For six days they worked their way through the middle cities on their way to Griffin, pausing each night to cook a meal and rest. Many cast their eyes into the dark night, and Fire read the fear in their eyes. How soon would the Dark Gate be opened anew? Were fiends even now spreading into the forest? Would they attack tonight?

Almost a week since the battle of Xshaltheria, the army reached Terros. Word had reached the city of their impending arrival, and many families lined the road, searching for their loved ones in the line of infantry and cavalry.

Fire and Water separated themselves from the march and ascended a small hill to watch the alliance return to their camps. Fire frowned as he surveyed the trudging soldiers, wondering what they were supposed to do now. Melora, Dothlore, and Rynda also joined them.

"We need a new plan against Serak and Draeken," Melora said.

Fire spared her a look. He'd been doubtful of the woman's loyalty. She'd been a member of the Order of Ancients, betrayed her people and her mother, even tried to become one of Draeken's generals, but her mother's sacrifice had changed her. She'd taken the lead of her people, since her older sister was absent, and done so with humility and conviction. Many had spoken in doubt, even to her face, but she had withstood their accusations, and Fire realized her dark ambitions had died on the summit of Xshaltheria. Some had called for her to be in shackles, but the haunted look in her eye was more pain than any imprisonment.

"We're scattered and broken," Rynda said. "And although I hated King Justin, he held the human kingdoms together. It's only a matter of days before this alliance crumbles into its former factions."

Fire grunted in agreement. "King Numen joined Serak and was killed, King Justin is also dead, and King Porlin has always been an ally of the enemy. Are there any *other* kings allied with the enemy?"

Water gave a sour chuckle. "I don't believe so, but we never know."

Fire looked back at the army trudging over the hill, wondering what they could have done differently. The human soldiers looked to their feet, their armor dusty and stained, their expressions fallen. They'd thought the battle easily won, a campaign against a criminal that had kidnapped their king. They'd been victorious, but only partially, and all understood the truth. If the Dark Gate was opened a second time, the next battle would be their last.

"I still say we should have attempted to destroy the Gate for good," Rynda sniffed in irritation. "We would not have failed a second time."

"We would have died," Lira said flatly.

"Better dead and the Gate destroyed, than alive and awaiting the fiend arrival," she retorted.

"We must press forward," Water said. "There must be a way to stop them."

Fire admired his brother's optimism, and didn't have the heart to disagree. Fire would have been the first to fight, and Water glanced his way for support, but Fire gave a small shake of his head. Not this time. Draeken and Serak, with their dragons and Gate, were just too strong. And perhaps it was time to think about surrender.

He looked ahead, to the city of Terros, a shining city of white stone walls and richly dressed people. Griffin's capitol had always looked formidable with its great walls and the abundant towers in the out fields. The army had built a wall around Outer Terros, making it even stronger, but Fire wondered how many days it would last against the fiend horde. A day? An hour?

"What will the human kingdoms do now?" Lira asked.

"Probably fight each other," Rynda said.

"Don't say that." Water cast a look at the line of soldiers, but the small group was ahead of the army, and none of the soldiers had overheard. "They are disheartened enough."

"It's true," Rynda said. "Some duke or noble will see this as an opportunity to seize the throne, and the alliance will break apart as quickly as it started. It was a fool's hope anyway."

"But it was hope," Melora said softly.

Fire's gaze swept across the trees on either side of the road. Spring had blossomed, and leaves grew on limbs. Flowers appeared in shrubs and other underbrush, and birds sang in the cool breeze. Scattered patches of snow lingered, but they were melting, the winter giving way to warmth.

Would the forest be destroyed by the fiends? Devoured by legions of dark creatures until only earth and ash remained? Fire disliked the image, and his thoughts turned to his brothers. What would Draeken do with the fragments if the kingdoms surrendered?

The army reached the camps of Outer Terros, where they had departed just weeks prior with the hopes of a quick campaign and victory. The despondent troops threaded their way back to their camps, their ranks noticeably thinner. The various armies kept a distance from each other, and Fire guessed that was just out of uncertainty. The three human armies were soldiers without a king, and would their swords now turn on each other?

"Who is that?" Water asked, squinting to the trio of horses riding out from the city.

178

Lira blinked and light flickered in her eyes. "That's Queen Alosia, and it looks like princesses Annah and Nelia?"

"Numen's daughter?" Fire frowned.

"And King Justin's daughter," Water said.

Fire exchanged a look with his brother, who seemed equally as surprised. Queen Alosia had been selected to ride back to Terros ahead of the army to give the surviving daughters the news. It was a token effort, as both daughters had been considered too young to assume the throne for either Erathan or Griffin. But as the trio galloped through the camps of human soldiers, they sparked a buzz that swept the allied forces. Soldiers stopped in their duties, craning for a look at the two women racing through the camp.

Their heads held high, the women rode in front of Queen Alosia, instead of behind. Their regal dresses and side saddles had been replaced with fitted white armor and soldier's mounts. Twin crowns graced their heads.

The news swept the army, and soldiers from every kingdom stopped in their tracks and turned, crowding closer to the apparent destination of the trio, the hill where Rynda, Melora, the fragments, and Lira had halted.

As they drew closer, the murmur became a shout, with soldiers from throughout the kingdoms calling the names of the two princesses. They looked neither right nor left, their gaze fixed on Rynda and the group arrayed around the rock troll queen. Their hair was tied back and hung down their armor, one blonde, one brunette, one from Griffin, one from Erathan. Then Fire noticed what hung about the neck of the daughter of King Numen.

The golden pendent of the Steward of Talinor.

"Is that what I think it is?" Dothlore asked.

"I think it is," Water replied. "Perhaps Jeric gave it to her?"

The trio arrived and the two women reined the horses to a halt. Alosia did the same, but remained behind the two girls, the position

179

obviously intentional. The smile on her features was knowing as she swept a hand to the princesses.

"I give you *Queen* Annah, of Griffin, and acting Steward of Talinor, *Queen* Nelia, of Erathan."

"Queens?" Rynda folded her arms. "Aren't you a bit young for the thrones?"

"As blunt as ever," Queen Annah said with a faint smile.

It was the obvious question. Annah looked to be in her late teens, while Nelia looked to be slightly older. Despite their youth, both conveyed an aura of strength that brought a smile to Fire's lips.

"You've been busy the last few days," Fire said to Alosia.

Water shot him an annoyed look. "Our condolences for King Justin."

"Grief will have its place," Annah said, "after the war. For now, we seek to retain the alliance formed by King Justin, and the support of the neighboring kings."

It was a pivotal moment, and Fire held his breath. If Rynda or Dothlore refused, the human kingdoms would look fragile and broken, and the returning army—most of which were soldiers trained by dukes and other nobles—would fracture to their old allegiances. In riding out so quickly, the newly minted queens sought to consolidate their power before the army could divide. A bold move.

At the same time, the two women were young and inexperienced in nearly every facet of conflict. In the coming weeks, the people needed strength, not youth, and if Rynda or Dothlore saw the two queens as incapable of such strength, they might push for a different leader to take the throne.

"You speak for Talinor?" Melora asked Nelia.

She reached up and touched the amulet. "I do."

"How did you gain such a rank?" Dothlore asked.

Nelia raised her chin. "It was given to me by King Porlin in my youth, as a promise of marriage to his son. Although King Porlin never had an heir, I have retained the Steward's Crest."

Whether true or not, the fact that she possessed the Talinorian crest was significant, and Fire again wondered if Jeric had given his to her. But Rynda continued to regard the two young women with her arms folded.

"Rynda," Water said, his tone urgent. "You must—"

"I don't need your help to be queen," Rynda snapped.

Water fell silent, and Rynda stepped toward the young women. Those nearest sucked in their breath as the towering rock troll advanced on the two young queens. To their credit, they stood their ground, but their horses fidgeted, and Fire noticed Annah had sweat trickling down her forehead. Nelia swallowed in fear and her hand tightened on the pommel of her saddle.

Rynda came to a halt close enough to strike, and then spoke in an undertone. Her words were not audible to Fire from where he stood, and he looked to Lira, but the woman just shook her head.

"If she wanted you to hear her words, she would have spoken louder."

"You heard them," he accused.

Lira smiled faintly. "Just because I can enhance my hearing doesn't mean I have to share what I hear."

Rynda stepped back, and then offered her metal hand to Queen Annah. The woman reached out and accepted the offering, her tiny hand resting in the metal grip of the rock troll. Rynda then offered her hand to the second queen. Nelia nodded in gratitude, and if Fire was not mistaken, a measure of relief.

Annah turned and looked to Melora, who gave a solemn nod. "Not that the opinion of a dark elf matters much to the surface races, but I too will support your appointment."

"You have our gratitude," Annah said.

181

Nelia nodded to Annah and then touched the Steward's pendant. Orange light sparked from the amulet and arced to Annah and Nelia, swirling about their throats and mouths, sinking into their flesh. Annah thanked her with a nod of gratitude and turned her horse to face the forces that had gathered. When she spoke, her voice stretched across the field and extended even into the walls of Terros, not a voice of thunder, but a rolling echo that reached every ear.

"People of Terros and Griffin," she called. "I am Queen Annah, appointed by the council of Dukes at the urging of Queen Alosia. I speak to you from the edge of the alliance camp, where Queen Rynda and Melora have just supported my right to rule."

"And I am Queen Nelia of Erathan," her companion called, her voice equally amplified. "I too, have had my ascension ratified, and speak with Queen Annah in full accord. I also carry the amulet of a Talinorian Steward, granting me all the rights and privileges of the Talinorian throne."

Annah smiled to her sister queen and then stepped forward. "At this time of conflict, we lead all three human kingdoms, but against foes like Draeken and Serak, the boundaries of our kingdoms must be set aside."

The words drew people out of the city. Men and women lined the battlements and poured from the gates. Soldiers of every race stood in silence, watching as the two queens spoke from the hilltop outside of Outer Terros.

"Until the threat is extinguished," Queen Annah said. "We must stand together. We have faced the most difficult of decisions. With the agreement of our neighboring kingdoms, we have decided to gather in Ilumidora for a final stand."

The proclamation sent a murmur through the gathered forces, who likely had assumed the gathering place would be Terros. Queen Annah raised her voice, the amulet's magic allowing her to speak over the doubt.

"Griffin is in no shape to defend against Draeken's army," she called. "And after speaking with my advisors, we have reached a decision. The kingdom of Griffin will evacuate to Talinor, where the people will be housed until we are able to return to our lands."

182

Fire looked to his brother, surprised by the bold plan. To abandon the entire kingdom to Draeken would allow his forces to invade. It also suggested they would be relying on more than just military might to stop Draeken. What did they know?

Queen Annah swept her hand to the gathered forces. "I now address you, my brothers and sisters of Lumineia. Whatever grievances you have had against neighbors, bury them. Whatever doubts or ambitions, forget them. There is only one aspiration that matters, and that is victory over Draeken and Serak. They think we will surrender," her voice hardened with anger, "but we will not relinquish our freedom. By blade and blood we stand together, an alliance of Lumineia."

Her words echoed into silence, and then a rising cheer swept the soldiers. It spread into the city and through the camps, expanding to engulf the entire alliance. The people shouted, roaring their approval, and Fire smiled.

"Draeken wanted a fight?" he murmured. "A fight he will have."

Chapter 23: The Warview

Mind prowled the spacious receiving room of their quarters in the Warview, struggling to keep his anger in check. Three weeks he'd been trapped in his quarters, his anger gradually building to a breaking point. What was happening on Lumineia? How long would they wait for the Bonebreaker to appear?

The quarters were unbelievably lavish. As large as a king's great hall, the room boasted a spiral staircase to a second floor where a trio of bedchambers overlooked the ridiculously expansive receiving space. Couches and desks were placed about the room, all positioned to view the enormous wall that depicted battles in the Bone Crucible.

The krey called it the vid, short for a name in krey that Mind did not understand. The screen never stopped, and showed battle after battle, rotating through individual duels and larger conflicts, a ceaseless array of blood and battle across the planet. If Mind had not hated the Empire before, he would have gained such hatred after watching the vid.

The Warview was an inn, but that was like calling a king's castle a hovel. Comprised of three towering buildings that stretched into the sky, the structure extended even higher than the clouds, taller than entire mountains on Lumineia. Gardens connected the three towers at various points in its height. Glowing green water gurgled down beautiful creeks and waterfalls, passing in and around a host of paths and ponds. The gardens attached to each of the three towers at thousands of intervals, a veritable labyrinth of light and greenery. Places to dine were abundant in the gardens, with krey and dakorians partaking of the small, open-roofed taverns that dotted the central structure. More vid screens were visible at the eateries, so the patrons would be able to wager on the never ending conflicts.

On the outside of the tower, a nearly invisible shield kept the volcanic air from reaching the gardens or the private quarters, the shield shimmering when dust or debris scattered across it. Mind had marveled at the sheer engineering of the structure, but knew the cost. How many lives had been paid to purchase such a building?

On the outside of the quarters, a second balcony overlooked the largest of the battlefields, the unforgiving region known as the Red Vent. Like a jagged scar, a breach in the surface allowed plumes of ash and smoke to rise skyward, the vent forming the center of the line between the two armies. Thousands fought for dominance with personal weapons, vehicles, and even larger war machines.

The only place to escape the scenes of battle was in his personal quarters, where Mind spent much of his time. At first he'd relished the opportunity to learn about the Empire, and once Ero had shown him how to operate the vid, he'd searched other channels. Of the millions available, he learned of worlds and history, ships and mighty krey houses. But throughout all the torrent of information, one thing was constant, a near reverence of the Empirical house, and the supreme power of the Krey Empire.

The days had turned into weeks, and despite countless offers to either buy Mind, or to entice him into more duels, the Bonebreaker did not appear. And it became increasingly clear that the woman might never arrive.

"Patience," Tardoq said.

"I'm always patient," Mind snapped. "But this is foolish. We cannot sit here while Lumineia falls to Serak and Draeken."

The dakorian leaned against one of the pillars in the room, munching on Jolisin, a type of food he'd retrieved from the kitchens. Mind glared at the dakorian, but the soldier continued to eat. Just as Mind was about to shout, Tardoq spoke in a voice of ice.

"Do not think you are the only one that is worried, human. I too, have friends on Lumineia."

Mind growled and looked away, annoyed and angry at his own helplessness. "Why has she not come?"

"She is probably already here," he said. "You must understand. This woman is cautious, and has evaded capture for ages. The price Ero

185

won for your victory is paltry compared to the bounty on the Bonebreaker's head. I would guess she is planning her assault as we speak."

The corner of the room that contained the ascender glowed, and Ero rose into view. He stepped off the ascender and motioned to the two of them, his expression bringing Mind to an abrupt halt.

"She is here," he said.

Tardoq gave Mind a pointed look, and he rolled his eyes. "How do you know?" Mind asked.

"I have a friend that works in the building," Ero said. "It's why I chose this particular place of residence. He informed me that the room adjacent to ours has been claimed by a mysterious party, one that wanted discretion for their arrival. While that is not uncommon, the fact that they insisted on the room next to ours indicates they are here for us."

"About time," Mind said.

Ero regarded him with a look of disapproval, and Mind abruptly realized his own impatience. As a fragment, he'd always been patient and calculating, but he'd lost his piece of Power, leaving him altered.

He grimaced. "My apologies."

He didn't explain the reason. He'd changed since the separation with Draeken, and he was still grappling with his new identity. Facets of his person that he'd always counted as immutable had been stripped, and he was not certain as to his own strength.

Ero nodded as if he understood and pointed to the south wall. "She's in that room, and her party is arriving right now."

Mind rose to his feet and drew his sword, eager for action after weeks of inactivity. Tardoq and Ero flanked him, both obviously agreeing to his assumption. The only reason to pick the adjacent room was because you did not intend to use the door.

"She's here," Mind said, sensing the minds on the other side of the wall, "but what can we expect?"

186

"She is too cautious to believe our words," Tardoq said. "She will want to ascertain our credibility, probably by combat."

After all the waiting, Mind was eager for the Bonebreaker to appear. At the same time, he found a measure of apprehensiveness—also a new attribute gained since parting with the fragment of Power. He disliked the uncertainty.

The seconds passed in silence and Mind wondered how long they would have to wait. Then the back wall began to glow faintly, the white material shimmering and turning silver in an arch. Tardoq nodded as if it were expected.

"A wall Gate," he said, and then glanced at Mind. "It's a weapon of thieves, and creates a Gate that passes through a single wall. Very useful. Very expensive. Very illegal."

The wall turned silver, and then translucent instead of the solid silver of a regular Gate. Through the liquid, shapes were visible, large and small, and Mind spotted blurry outlines of the room beyond, a matching one to their own quarters. One figure approached the Gate and stepped through, and Mind's eyes widened.

The Bonebreaker stood at thirteen feet tall, her armor thick and powerful. She carried herself with the grace of a gazelle and the might of a dragon. Her muscles rippled with strength as she hefted the great hammer in her hand. Her horns were long and twisted, and jet black. She did not seem surprised to find the three of them standing in greeting.

Her eyes passed over Ero and Mind, dismissing them as weaker, before settling on Tardoq. A faint smile formed on her features before she came to a halt. Four more dakorians came from behind, followed by two humans, a woman and a man. The humans were dressed as slaves, but Mind noted the spark of determination in their eyes, marking them as ones who did not bow to the krey. He also heard their thoughts.

The man and woman both worried about the danger, and feared that it was a trap. The woman cared deeply for the Bonebreaker. She'd been rescued by the dakorian several years past and viewed her akin to a queen. The man loved the woman, and his stance was more protective.

Mind had thought he would be unable to read the thoughts of the other dakorians, but none were Bloodwalls, and all were younger than a hundred years. Mind caught snippets from their thoughts, enough to recognize that they carried themselves with integrity and honor, as well as paranoia. They'd lived most of their lives being hunted, and would not hesitate to kill any threat.

"Bonebreaker," Ero greeted the woman.

"Krey," she said evenly, her eyes still on Tardoq. "Call me Belrisa."

"Belrisa," Ero said with a short bow. "I am grateful you have—"

"I wasn't talking to you."

Her eyes flicked to the four marks on Tardoq's horns, the same four marks that graced her own horns. Both were Bloodwalls, only Tardoq had come from a lesser house, while Belrisa had once been the personal guard to the emperor himself.

"Tardoq," she said. "Bloodwall for Wylyn, head of the house of Mor'Val, ranked ninth, but high enough be considered second tier. Your reputation precedes you."

"I am no longer the Bloodwall of house Mor'Val." Tardoq drew his sword and placed the point on the floor. "And Wylyn is dead."

Her eyes narrowed. "You have renounced your rank?"

"I have."

Her eyes flicked to the sword. "Why a sword? Our people have not used such an antiquated weapon in ages."

"My hammer was broken," he replied, "and I was given this sword as a replacement."

"I would have believed you until that," she said with a sneer. "No dakorian would choose a sword over a hammer lance."

"He speaks the truth," Mind said.

The Bonebreaker met his gaze, her scowl turning to curiosity. "It is uncommon for a human to speak to me without fear."

188

"I do not fear what I can defeat."

She burst into a laugh, her companions exchanging smiles. The two humans both smirked as well, and Mind again sensed their allegiance to the woman. He wondered how many more had been freed by the Bonebreaker.

"You are bold," she said. "I'll give you that."

"We need your help," Mind said. "I come from a world called Lumineia."

A flicker of recognition registered in the eyes of the human woman. "There are whispers of a world kept secret from the Empire, a place of free humans. But we know that such rumors are Empire lies."

The human man nodded. "They seek to draw you into a trap."

Belrisa sniffed and shook her head. "A pitiful attempt."

"Lumineia exists," Mind said. "And it is unique for what it possesses."

"Free humans?" one of the dakorians scoffed. "No such world exists."

"Free humans," Ero said. "And magic."

"Magic?" Belrisa scoffed.

"A power only possessed by the race of man," Ero said. "A power the Empire would fear."

"Another myth," the human jerked her head. "Tales for children so they do not see their plight as slaves. Mankind does not have any power."

Mind reached his hand out and gathered the threads of gravity magic to lift the woman off the ground. She called out in surprise as her feet lifted free and the man grasped her arm. Mind relinquished his magic and her feet returned to the floor.

"A clever trick," Belrisa said, but her smile was gone. "But gravity spheres can grant the same ability."

189

"We speak the truth," Ero insisted. "And we seek your aid."

"A krey, a human, and a dakorian Bloodwall," she shook her head in disbelief. "Every year the Empire gets more clever in their attempts to assassinate me."

"Belrisa," Tardoq said. "We are not with the Empire. Ero may be krey, but he protects Lumineia from discovery, and Mind is one of the most powerful mages on Lumineia. I've spent the last several months there, and learned the value of a free people."

"You expect me to believe you are a friend to humans?" she scoffed. "A dakorian Bloodwall?"

"As hard as it is to believe," he said, "it's true."

She raised her hammer and pointed it to him. "Prove it."

Tardoq took a step forward and raised his sword, taking a combat stance. Mind noticed he placed his thumb on the highest rune, activating the magic embedded in the blade. Light flowed up the sword, making it heavier than normal. Belrisa noticed the enchantment and smiled as she started forward.

Chapter 24: The Bonebreaker

Mind retreated as the Bonebreaker charged Tardoq and the two dakorians locked into a duel. He'd battled dragons and reavers, great warriors and renowned kings, but the duel between the two Bloodwalls surpassed them all.

The Bonebreaker swung her hammer in a swing that would crush Tardoq's chest. Tardoq sidestepped, narrowly missing the blast of power that erupted from the head of the hammer. Tardoq swerved around her flank but she spun and twirled her hammer, swiping for Tardoq's legs.

Tardoq leapt into a rolling flip and retreated up the stairs to the second floor. Belrisa pressed the assault, driving him back, her hammer crashing through the railing and sending glass and metal cascading onto the floor. Tardoq swung his sword at her shoulder but she blocked, and then struck him with her free hand, sending his giant form tumbling into Ero's quarters.

She lunged out of view, her hammer shattering the wall and knocking Tardoq through the next wall into Mind's quarters. Tardoq bounced off the bed and caught the edge, heaving it into the woman's path. She blasted it with her hammer, the energy tearing a hole through the mattress and sending it bouncing off the far wall. But Tardoq leapt and caught a fixture on the ceiling, an ornate swirl that allowed him to grasp the edge. Swinging his legs over the tumbling mattress, he struck back, his now weighted sword coming down across her arm, drawing first blood.

"Perhaps a sword has merit," she said, and lunged, driving the hammer at his back.

Tardoq rolled forward, the hammer passing above his body. The motion carried him through the open door to the receiving room, the spikes on his armor bones catching the glass and shattering the door. He came to his feet on the balcony overlooking the room and leapt into a flip that carried him back to the floor by a couch. She skidded to a halt on the balcony and fired her lance, the power deflecting off his sword to burn a hole through the wall into the Bonebreaker's quarters. Tardoq sprinted to the side, using his sword to deflect each subsequent lance, the deflections burning into cloth and glass, wall and stone.

"This room was expensive before the damage," Ero said with a sigh.

"You're worried about the cost of the room?" Mind scoffed. "She's going to kill him."

Ero swept a hand to the four dakorians and the two humans, all of whom had weapons pointed at them. The dakorians also carried lance hammers, while the two humans carried smaller weapons that fit in their hands, the end of which glowed with red light.

"Are you ready?" Ero asked.

"Of course," Mind replied.

He started forward, and the group of dakorians raised their weapons. The one with a bone missing on his shoulder shook his head. "She will decide your fate."

Mind realized the group had no idea about magic, just like the dakorians that had come with Tardoq through the Gate. All their training, all their vaunted skills, had not prepared them to find mages. Ero realized it as well because he reached to the two hilts hidden in the folds of his cloak and snapped them outward, the aquaglass enchantments flowing into two swords. The humans stared at the weapons in astonishment, while the dakorians scowled.

Mind took advantage of their confusion and reached for his magic. The gravity in the room extended through all of the combatants, but he reached for the gravity touching their weapons—and yanked the weapons to the ground.

The dakorians cried out as their hammers suddenly became four times heavier, the weapons thudding into the floor. One tried to pick his up, straining on the handle, while a second abandoned the weapon and

192

charged. The remaining two joined the second, and Mind faced three furious dakorians.

They were too heavy to lift without the fragment of Power, so Mind reached for the objects in the room, the broken glass and metal. Raising them off the floor, he turned them into a whirlwind of sharp objects, the lethal wall rising up and carving back and forth. The lead dakorian tried to charge through the barrier, raising his hands against the glass and steel. They slashed him across his body, leaving him bloodied when he came out the opposite side. Mind leapt to his shoulders and jumped, flipping over the sharp wall and swinging the deadly whirlwind at the two dakorians, both of which darted to his two flanks.

Ero had engaged the two humans, and had destroyed their strange weapons, both of which sputtered on the floor, sliced into pieces by Ero's aquaglass swords. They'd fired several times, burning holes into the walls. Mind turned the shards of glass and steel into long spears which hovered at the dakorian's throats. They shifted and attempted to evade, but the six foot weapons drove them backward. One by one they were pinned against the wall.

The last swung his arm, attempting to bat the hovering weapon aside. It shattered, the shards turning into a dozen smaller weapons that leapt forward, pressing against the dakorian's throat. His eyes widened in shock and confusion and he leaned away from the shards hovering a hairsbreadth from his vulnerable neck.

Tardoq and Belrisa crashed through the wall Gate. Both were bloodied, but Tardoq had suffered the worst of the damage. Belrisa took the room at a glance, her eyes narrowing in anger before she kicked Tardoq in the chest, knocking him into the wall. He swung his sword but she caught the weapon against her hammer and twisted, driving the blade against Tardoq's own throat. Also trapped against the wall, Tardoq growled, his muscles bulging as he tried to push Belrisa away. But the sword inched closer to his jugular.

"Stop!" Mind shouted.

"You would spare this dakorian's life?" Belrisa snarled. "Do you have any idea how many humans he has killed?"

She used her chin to point at one of her companions, and the man shouted at the vid screen. It glowed to life, filling the wall, but instead of displaying battles in the Bone Crucible, it showed Tardoq.

He stood over a pair of dead human slaves, growling at other humans cowered in the corner of the room. He pointed his hammer to one and they fled, all except a woman, who tried to reach the two bodies.

"You are all the same," Tardoq sneered, and swung his hammer.

Mind grimaced and turned away, but the image shifted to another scene, where Tardoq killed a man because he would not leave his child. Another image. Another death. The images filled the room, spilling rage in Mind's gut.

"Enough!" he snarled.

"I know his kind," Belrisa roared. "Because I *was* his kind. He will kill any who oppose the Empire. He would kill me and you, every slave and dakorian that defied him."

"No."

Tardoq's voice was broken, drawing all eyes to him. He stared at the screen, his features twisted in the agony of regret. Shocked by the expression, Belrisa retreated, but Tardoq crumpled on the wall. Every wound he'd endured did not compare to what the vid showed. Actual tears formed in his eyes.

"I'm sorry," he said, his eyes settling on Mind. "For everything that I have done."

"Tardoq," Ero said softly. "That's not you anymore."

"But it was," Tardoq spoke with sudden vehemence, and his sword fell from his fingers. "What you see is a fraction of the blood on my hands."

Mind shook his head. "And yet I trust you, just as Queen Rynda does."

He grimaced and looked away, and Belrisa shook her head. "Who is this queen you speak of?"

"A member of a race called rock trolls," Ero said.

"She has the highest caliber of anyone I have ever met," Tardoq said.

Belrisa made a motion and the vid ended. In the ensuing silence, Belrisa shifted to regard Mind, who suddenly realized he still held the other dakorians pinned against the wall. He swept his hands wide and the lethal shards turned aside from their lethal positions and swirled to him. They merged together, binding into a spear in his hand.

"You speak the truth," Belrisa marveled. "Magic exists?"

"It does," Ero said.

Her eyes flicked to him. "Then Lumineia is real?"

"It is," he replied.

Belrisa released a long breath. To Mind's surprise, she reached down and offered her hand to Tardoq. He stared at her and shook his head.

"I am not worthy."

"Neither am I."

Her soft response conveyed a wealth of pain, a reminder that she too, had killed in the name of the Empire. Tardoq regarded her for a long moment and then accepted her hand. She pulled him to his feet.

"Belrisa?" one of the dakorians asked, rubbing his throat, where a shard of glass had cut a shallow line.

"Prepare our departure," she said, jerking her head at the wall gate. "Someone will have heard the conflict. They will come to investigate."

The four dakorians nodded in unison, and departed through the wall Gate. On the other side, Mind spotted them erecting a portable Gate. The two humans remained, and Belrisa pointed to them.

195

"This is Merana and Drogil, descendants of a woman named Quin, the woman that taught me what it meant to be a protector. She had more dignity than any royal."

"I learned on Lumineia," Tardoq said. "We called them slaves, but the more time I spent with them, the more I learned their caliber."

"I am sorry," Belrisa said, and then grimaced. "For ages I have lived in caution, and it seems that caution has made me blind against true allies."

"The guards have been summoned," the human said, cocking his head to the side as if he were listening. "We must hasten."

She nodded and pointed to the wall Gate. "If you wish to speak further, we should go. House Torn'Ent likes to punish guests that damage rooms by putting them into the Crucible."

Mind and Ero exchanged a look, and then followed her from the room. They passed through the wall Gate and into the room beyond. It too had been destroyed by the duel between Belrisa and Tardoq, the walls scorched, the furniture broken and scattered. One balcony had broken, and wind whistled into the interior. A small Gate had been erected in the corner of the room, and the dakorians activated it. One by one they departed, and just as Mind stepped to the Gate a crash echoed in their own quarters. Mind looked back to see several dakorians rushing the room. They caught sight of the wall gate and sprinted to it, but Belrisa tossed a small pulsing object to the Gate. It detonated against the wall, destroying the wall Gate. Belrisa activated another small pulsing sphere and dropped it at their feet. Then she stepped through the Gate. Mind didn't need to be invited, and stepped into the unknown.

The opposite side proved to be lower in the same structure. Mind looked out the window and upward, where he spotted their previous quarters. Both their and Belrisa's chambers were in ruins, smoke billowing as guards searched the interior, attempting to find the occupants. Mind grunted in approval. Belrisa had planned her escape with care before setting foot into the room, and her tactical mind was one to be admired.

Belrisa motioned to her soldiers who were setting up a new Gate. "It won't take them long to figure out where we went. By then, we'll have departed from this world. You have until then to tell me of Lumineia, and why you think I would help."

Chapter 25: Rebirth

Draeken watched as Serak assembled the pieces of the Dark Gate. The stone fragments had shattered from Queen Erisay's magic, and the powerful artifact had been reduced to rubble. As Serak labored, the pieces rose and shifted. Serak had feverishly worked to reassemble the broken arch, and the two sides were now whole, only the curve and keystone still absent.

"This is taking too long," Draeken said.

"It must be perfect," Serak said wearily. "I'm rebuilding a mechanism that transports objects through the stars. One error could be catastrophic."

"Why aren't we just using another Gate?" Draeken asked. "The Eternals certainly have access to Gates, and I was even a member."

"Do you have the keys to their halls?" Serak asked.

Draeken frowned and struggled to recall where he'd placed the keys. He remembered possessing the two keys, and then they were absent. Why could he not remember? It was maddening, as if the memory had been taken.

Serak grunted in understanding. "We cannot access their Gates without keys, and so we must rebuild."

Draeken scowled, disliking his tone. Ever since the battle at Xshaltheria, Serak had been withdrawn and taciturn, bordering on sullen. He'd immediately set to rebuilding the Dark Gate but he spoke little, and Draeken knew Serak did not agree with his actions at the battle.

They'd moved the pieces of the Dark Gate deep into the fortress so it would not be so easily attacked. The chamber Draeken had chosen hung at the extreme base of the citadel, beneath the vent that rose through the structure.

Fifty feet across, the circular floor of the chamber lacked walls or railings. Another fifty feet from the edge, the wall of the chamber stretched to the ceiling high above, where the vent extended through the heart of the fortress. The platform hung from invisible chains fashioned of heat.

Draeken walked to the edge and reached into the plume of sulfuric air rising from the magma. The air rose up the wall and curved into the central shaft that pierced the fortress from bottom to top, where the air vented into the sky.

The entrance to the chamber was high on the wall. Stairs of fire extended from the entrance corridor and bridged the gap. If an attacker sought to reach the platform, the stairs could be extinguished, leaving them to fall into the magma below.

Draeken turned and strode to the center of the platform, where the Gate was being erected. He looked upward, through the central shaft and to the dark sky. Then he turned to Serak, who sought to find a sliver for a crack in the stone. Serak sifted through the pile and then a sliver of rock rose and settled into place, the material melting and merging to become whole.

"Tell me your impression of the battle with the alliance," Draeken said.

Serak glanced his way. "What do you wish to know?"

"It obviously did not go as intended."

"I believe the alliance knows what they face," Serak said. "And that was the primary purpose of the fiend army."

Serak's voice carried a tinge of rebuke, a reminder that the fiends were only supposed to intimidate the gathered force, not attack and kill them. It confirmed that Serak thought Draeken had erred in his sending the fiends into battle.

"When the Gate is restored, we will be able to bring the full fiend army through," Draeken said. "Such a force possesses a single purpose, to conquer."

"They may serve that purpose," Serak said. "But they can also protect the people."

"Only if that is my will," Draeken said.

Serak glanced his way, and Draeken read the regret in his eyes. Serak was just beginning to see the truth, that he had brought Draeken into being, created him to become a master, but in so doing, he had relinquished control. Serak's intention was not Draeken's intention.

Draeken sensed a gulf between him and Serak, a subtle shift in their connection, and began to question if Serak needed to be killed. If Draeken continued on his current course, the day might come that Serak became a foe. Draeken faced the Gate, recognizing that only Serak could assemble the mechanism. Draeken still needed Serak. For now.

A hurried set of footsteps approached in the entrance corridor, and Draeken turned as Zoric appeared. He'd obviously rushed to arrive, because his clothes were still muddy from the road, and he hurried down the fire steps to reach the platform.

"Master Draeken," he said. "I bring news. Bartoth and I went to the Melting but the Hauntress was already present with Shadow and others. They managed to stop us from obtaining Mimic." His features contracted, the grief and anger tightening his muscles.

Draeken frowned. "Where is my fourth general?"

Zoric grimaced. "Bartoth managed to give Mimic the cloak, but Shadow dropped her into the acid beneath the prison." Zoric hesitated, and then said. "She is dead."

"Where's your father?" Serak asked.

Zoric's features hardened. "Sentara killed him."

"Zenif is dead?" Serak spoke with uncharacteristic force, drawing Draeken's gaze.

"You worry more for Zenif than Mimic? We needed her."

Draeken passed a hand over his face and then stabbed a hand to Zoric. "With your father dead, I will need your aid to complete the Dark Gate."

"Mine?" Zoric asked, clearly surprised.

Draeken scowled. "What do we do about Mimic?"

"If she became the fourth general, she is not dead," Serak said.

"I saw her fall into a lake of boiling acid," Zoric said. "No one could survive."

Serak straightened, his features clouding with anger. "Stand forth and do as I command."

Zoric flushed and advanced, mumbling an apology. Serak directed Zoric to stand at the center of the arch, and to use his magesight to search for tiny purple threads connecting the Gate pieces. Draeken reluctantly retreated, disliking Serak's forceful demeanor. Was he hiding something?

"I don't know what I'm looking for," Zoric said.

"Gate energy is a magic of the mind," Serak said. "Only special tools used by the Krey Empire—or a mind mage—can see this type of power. Your father helped me build the Gate in the first place, and you're going to help me finish it now."

"*I* possess mind magic," Draeken said.

Serak hesitated, and in that moment Draeken made his choice. Serak could not remain. Then Serak pointed to the other side of the Gate, directing him to stand opposite Zoric. Draeken took his place, careful to keep his decision from showing on his features.

"As I move the stones into place, make sure the threads all point into the center," Serak said. "It should look like a spiderweb, with all the threads converging."

"I see it," Zoric said.

Draeken blinked into his mage sight and squinted, the chamber turning into swirls of colors. Mages could only see the energies to which they were attuned, so he saw the magic of light and shadow, as well as fire and mind. He'd gained only a touch of water magic when separating from the fragments, but there wasn't much moisture in the room. As he examined the partially assembled Gate, he noticed faint lines of purple light connecting the outer arch to a central point.

"Is this how every Gate looks?" he asked.

"I cannot see it," Serak said, "but I would assume that to be true."

There was a touch of evasiveness in Serak's tone, and again Draeken felt like Serak withheld the truth. But when their eyes met Serak's expression was earnest, and Draeken was not certain if it was just his imagination.

"As I assemble the stones, make sure the threads do not cross," Serak said. "It is imperative they all connect together into a single web."

They set to work, with Draeken and Zoric guiding Serak where to place stones. Many of the already placed sections needed to be shifted, and the painstaking effort quickly grew tiresome. Piece by broken piece, the arch continued to rise.

The hours passed, but Draeken and Serak did not require food. Both were impatient, and although Zoric grew fatigued, they pushed forward. Gradually the top of the arch came together, the pile of pieces at the base quickly shrinking.

As the last pieces lifted off the ground and socketed into place, the web of Gate energy seemed to sparkle, as if it sensed the completion of the arch. After a day and a half of continuous effort, the last piece lifted and slid home the stone merging over the cracks.

"It is done," Zoric breathed.

The man teetered on his feet, his eyes drooping, his face drawn. Irritated, Draeken motioned in dismissal and he stumbled to the stairs, where he sat and stared at the Gate.

"Will it work?" Draeken asked.

In answer, Serak reached for the runes embedded on the sides of the arch and pressed the largest. Silver liquid flowed from the sides, filling the interior and covering the threads Draeken had helped place. It shimmered once, and then went still. Draeken's eyes glowed with triumph as the Dark Gate became whole once again.

A small figure appeared in the silvery liquid, stepping into view and looking about with interest. Draeken resisted the urge to recoil from her appearance, even as he contained his rising anticipation.

Her skin was mottled and diseased, her flesh covered in sores. Her eyes were sunken, enhancing the force to her gaze. A tattered cloak hung about her shoulder, much of it burned, as if by acid.

"Mimic?" Zoric called, lurching to his feet.

She looked to him, and he crumpled to the floor, retching and gasping, his skin turning a shade of green. Delighted with the woman's newfound power, Draeken began to laugh, the sound tinged with pride.

"She is every whit as powerful as you promised," Draeken said.

Serak made a motion to Mimic. "Enough. There is no need to kill our own."

Mimic didn't move, but Zoric sucked in a breath and gained enough strength to retreat. Draeken motioned in dismissal and the mind mage gladly fled, retreating up the stairs into the fortress.

"What am I?" Mimic asked evenly.

"You are the general of Plague," Draeken said. "And from this day forth, arrows and swords cannot harm your body. The disease that ravaged your body in life now grants you this power, to destroy with a look, until your prey withers to aching sickness in your very presence."

"I thought I perished in the acid," Mimic raised a hand and examined her flesh. "Then I found myself in a endless cloud, and heard a mighty voice in my thoughts."

"As you died the Gate pulled you back to Kelindor," Serak said, glancing to Draeken. "Only a direct opposite magic could permanently kill you now."

Mimic faced Draeken. "And I am to serve you." A statement, not a question.

"You have always wanted to destroy," Draeken said and pointed west, towards the allied lands. "Go, and wreak havoc on the people."

She regarded him with unblinking eyes, her disconcerting gaze only bringing more delight to Draeken. Aside from Bartoth, she was the most dangerous of the four generals, and was nearly impervious to any damage. But because she'd been made using the cloak, her will belonged to him.

"I sought healing my whole life," Mimic said quietly. "I never considered that my fate was to *become* my disease."

"Embrace your fate," Draeken said. "And destroy your foes."

She smiled, the expression wonderfully sickening on her diseased features. "My plague is yours to command."

She turned and ascended the steps, and Draeken listened to the cries from the guards above, pleased by the sweet melody. He did not notice Serak standing near the Gate, or his expression. Rather than triumph or pride at his creation, a different emotion flickered on his features.

Regret.

Chapter 26: Betrayal

Draeken basked in the sensation of riding a giant dragon, the beast soaring above the landscape like a god. He had no allusions to Gorewrathian's allegiance. The dragon would obey until the moment he saw a chance to retaliate, and in that moment Draeken would have to kill the beast. But for now, he relished the wind on his face astride the king of dragons.

Behind and lower, Serak rode his own mount. Draeken caught several lingering looks from the Father of Guardians, but ignored them. Serak would learn their destination when they arrived. Draeken fleetingly considered if his plan was sound, but discarded the doubt. He'd seen the truth in Serak's gaze after the battle at Xshaltheria, and the horror on his face had been unmistakable. Serak had raised Draeken to his position and called him master, but he would not remain a servant for long.

Draeken spotted their destination and directed the great red dragon downward. The beast did as ordered, but his mind conveyed an air of seething hatred. Draeken smiled, pleased that the king of dragons knew his place.

They passed through giant peaks and descended into a hidden valley, a shelf of rock surrounded by mountains. A great chasm marked the east side of the city, one surviving bridge reaching to the opposite side, where a canyon cut through the mountains, the narrow passage the only point of ingress to the ruins. Once a mighty fortress, the city had long since fallen to decay.

Verisith.

The city had inspired wonder and mystery among all nations, the stronghold at the heart of the powerful guild of Verinai. Few non-Verinai ever set foot in the city, and fewer still survived to speak of their experience. Since the fall of the Verinai, many had sought its secrets, but none returned, the adventurers falling to the hands of the guardians still tethered to the city foundations. None were as strong as Draeken or Serak, but they were powerful enough to protect the city. Even if they were going mad.

"Why are we coming here?" Serak called as they landed.

The two dragons alighted on the city battlements that overlooked the gorge. Draeken dropped from Gorewrathian's neck and surveyed the decaying city, a small smile on his features. He recalled exploring its alleys and buildings as the fragment of Shadow, relishing the dark recesses.

Verisith was just a few miles from Cloudy Vale, the place where the fragments had spent the bulk of their youth, and where Draeken recalled so many memories. The fragments remembered the Vale with fondness, but Draeken remembered the Vale as his prison.

"There is one secret we must unearth." Draeken strode to the stairs and pointed to the keep at the back of the city. "It lies within Elsin's own chambers."

Serak's eyes clouded at the mention of Elsin, and Draeken turned away so Serak would not see his smile. The fragment of Mind had discovered a great deal about Elsin, and her relationship to Serak. The woman had been guildmaster of the Verinai, brought Serak to Lumineia, and turned him into the Father of Guardians. She'd also spent much of her life experimenting with magic, creating numerous spells that many of the guilds still feared.

Draeken descended the steps of the battlements and advanced up the main throughway of the city, marveling at how he'd feared the denizens in his youth. The guardians had been forged from beast and man with various magics. As Shadow, he'd escaped their clutches on countless occasions. Light had disliked the ruins, while Fire had occasionally tested his mettle against the guardians. Now, Draeken walked among the legacy of the Verinai, and knew that he was the greatest.

He advanced up the center of the road, unhurried. One guardian barred the way, a man imbued with the magic of fire. The statue turned to flesh as Draeken and Serak approached, and fire spilled into his hands. Then he caught sight of Draeken and did not strike. Draeken smiled as he passed the guardian, and it turned back to stone. Even they sensed his superiority.

"What do we seek?" Serak asked.

"Did you know that I was originally bonded to a human youth?" Draeken asked.

"I know everything about you," Serak replied.

"Elsin was the boy's mother," Draeken continued as if he had not heard. "I have a few scattered memories of him and know what Elsin looked like. What was most vivid in those child's memories was Elsin's determination."

"It was her defining characteristic," Serak said.

Draeken swept a hand to the ruins of Verisith. "This city is a testament to her greatest triumph, the power of the guild of Verinai, and her greatest failure, believing she was invulnerable."

"It was not her fault she failed," Serak said. "She fought against Elenyr, the most powerful oracle in ages, perhaps in our entire history."

Draeken flew them up the face of the keep, elevating to enter through a window on the fifth floor. From there he made his way to the stairs where he ascended to Elsin's private office. The keep had been carved directly from the cliff face, with the base level a great, open hall. The second hall also contained large windows and a wide promenade, a place for receiving kings and dignitaries. Vines now grew across the ground, and dust and grime coated the surfaces.

Above the halls, the rooms were split, with the front chambers overlooking the city, and the rear chambers set inside the mountain, the windowless rooms providing a secure place for masters to teach apprentices more damaging magic. A corridor separated the back and front sides of the keep, and Draeken led Serak to its topmost level.

Passing the once elegant bedchamber that had belonged to Guildmaster Elsin, Draeken stepped to the office. He swung the door open and came to a halt, where he surveyed the chamber. A desk sat at the back, and a handful of books were placed neatly on a shelf.

207

Paintings had once graced the walls but they were covered in dust and grime, the images worn away. He stepped to one of the paintings and caught the latch, swinging the secret door open.

Draeken advanced down the dark corridor. Light orbs had long since gone dark, so he gestured upward, infusing them with light. Serak strode in his wake, his step hesitant, reserved, but he did not again ask about their purpose.

Draeken reached the chamber at the end and breathed deep of the cool air. Bowl shaped on the ceiling and flat across the floor, the circular room contained a large hole at the center. An enormous sphere of swirling water hovered above the hole, perpetually fed by four small waterfalls trickling down from above.

"The room where you were created," Serak said, coming to a halt at his side.

"And the one where you professed your love to Elsin," he replied.

"What secrets lie in here?" Serak asked.

Draeken advanced to the sphere of magic and gazed upward, recalling the moment he was separated from the boy, the first time a guardian had been parted from the flesh that had been its host.

"The secret was not present before," Draeken said.

"I don't understand," Serak replied. "I thought you said it was here."

"It is," Draeken said, and turned to Serak. "It just arrived."

Serak stared at him, and understanding ignited in his eyes. "You think I have kept a secret from you?"

"Of course," Draeken replied.

"Master," Serak scoffed, "I created you. I will forever be your most loyal servant."

"Even when I do not follow your plan?"

A touch of doubt appeared in Serak's eyes as he shook his head. "I serve you."

"Even when I use the fiends to destroy the people of Lumineia?"

"Always."

Serak retreated as Draeken began to advance. "Even when I want to conquer the kingdoms of Lumineia and become their king?"

"You are my master," Serak insisted.

Draeken chuckled, the sound echoing in the confines of the chamber, a dark reminder that Draeken knew the truth. Serak swallowed and looked away, unable to hold Draeken's gaze. Then suddenly his jaw clenched and he came to a halt.

"I did everything for you," he growled. *Everything*. I prepared the Gate and manipulated the fragments to Blackwell Keep, trapped them so you could *become* the fragment of Power. I studied and learned, built an Order for thousands of years to bring about a singular opportunity, the chance to protect Lumineia from the Krey Empire."

"You assumed I would want what you desired," Draeken said.

"How could you not?" Serak shouted. "That is what Elenyr taught you to do!"

"I was *never* her puppet," Draeken snarled.

Serak reached to the source of water and the liquid burst forth, but Draeken incinerated his magic with an explosion of fire. Serak cried out and gathered the stone at his feet, striking at Draeken. Stone rose in needlelike spears, but Draeken shattered them with a clench of his fist. Then he leapt, using gravity to fly over Serak's head and land at his back. Serak spun but a burst of light temporarily blinded him, causing him to stumble. Serak reached for the earth again but Draeken drew power from the light. The light flowed inward, wrapping around Serak's body, binding him fast. Both guardians growled as they fought for dominance, but the light continued to thicken, forcing Serak to his knees.

209

The floor of the cavern trembled but Draeken reached to it, using gravity to hold it fast. Veins bulged on Serak's neck as he fought, his fury gradually turning to desperation. All the while Draeken regarded him with contempt.

"You cannot do this!" Serak cried.

"You know I can."

"The people of Lumineia will always fight. They will resist you."

"Then I will kill them all," Draeken said.

Serak's eyes widened. "You would slaughter the races?"

"I am the fragment of *Power*." Draeken spoke with such vehemence that Serak flinched. "I was born to *rule*, not to *serve*. Why would a being of such greatness allow the kings of Lumineia to retain their thrones? You wanted a master, but you wanted me to be their servant."

Serak's eyes widened. "You're just like the Empire."

"No," Draeken said. "I am greater than the Empire, and my power will be endless. After I've conquered Lumineia, I'll use the fiends you have given me to strike the Empire. If they, too, will not yield, I will release the Dark on their worlds. I'll open a Gate to Kelindor and watch them destroy each other. For every world that refuses my reign, my fiend army will grow, until the emperor himself kneels at my feet."

Serak stared at him in shock, his features frozen in horror. Draeken used his distraction to press the portion of magic he'd gotten from the fragment of Water to bind him to the water source. Serak screamed, the sound echoing and reechoing as the water cut deep into Serak's soul. Draeken hooked the magical tether and then released his power. The water splashed away and Serak fell to his knees, gasping for breath.

"What have you done?"

"I'm not heartless," Draeken said. "After all you've done, you deserve to see for yourself what you have created. Of course, I cannot have you interfering, so this chamber will be your home. You are now chained to this source, and not even your significant magic will permit you to break free."

"Don't do this." Serak lifted his gaze to Draeken. "Please."

"You have my gratitude," Draeken said, "but you must understand. Elsin did not perish because she faced the oracle. She perished because she was betrayed by those she believed loyal. You claim that you're my servant, but we both know you would have one day turned against me. And so I ask a final sacrifice. Enjoy your solitude, Father of Guardians, and bear witness to what you have wrought."

Serak remained on his knees as Draeken turned and departed. A glowing chain of water leashed Serak to the source of magic. Broken and alone, Serak screamed and struck the floor in his anguish, sending cracks all the way to the walls. But Draeken was already gone. As Draeken exited the keep, he turned his gaze forward. He had an empire to build. His attention focused on his dragon and the future, he failed to notice the shadow flitting out of sight.

Chapter 27: Serak's Shadow

As Draeken emerged from the keep of Verisith, one figure dropped from under Gorewrathian's wing and darted into an alcove of a structure, disappearing from sight just as Draeken climbed onto the dragon's back and barked an order.

Bendelinish swung its head towards the keep. *Where is Serak?*

"Serak has a new assignment," Draeken said. "You will come with me."

Even you cannot ride two dragons, Bendelinish growled.

"I'll need you if I have to kill Gorewrathian," Draeken said.

Both dragons snarled, but did as requested. From inside the darkened recess of the ruins, the visitor watched as the two dragon's rose into the air, a smile on his face. When the dragons were gone, Shadow stepped into the open and made a rude gesture at the departing beasts.

"And you thought you were mighty."

He turned and threaded his way into the ruins, avoiding the host of guardians chained to their sources. The darkened streets and alleys loomed above his head, vines and brush growing against the molding stones. He shivered in delight. Let the elves have their bright cities. He preferred the ruins of a forgotten city, where powerful guardians lurked.

He recalled the events leading up to his precarious flight under the dragon's wing. A few hours before Draeken and Serak had departed Xshaltheria, he had infiltrated the fortress. He'd witnessed the rebuilding of the Gate, and the emergence of Mimic in her new form as the general of Plague. Then Draeken had ordered Serak to follow, and on a whim, Shadow had crept beneath the great dragon and turned into his shadow form. As Draeken mounted, he grasped the shadows under Gorewrathian's right wing, and it carried him aloft.

He caught a glimpse of Elenyr's astonished face as they passed over the battlements, and he dropped a shard of darkness, a glittering object that she would be able to follow. She'd leapt away, her ethereal form allowing her to speed through stone and tree. She'd kept pace with the beasts on the land below, her Hauntress form streaking across the landscape, a wraith in the night.

Shadow wondered if Elenyr had been able to keep up. The dragons had flown throughout the night and the next day, and Elenyr would not have been able to sustain a sprint for two days. He'd dropped a few shadow shards during the night, but during the daylight hours he couldn't, so Elenyr might have lost his path.

Shadow ascended the steps to one of the high roads curving across the ruins, and just as he leaned against a support post, Elenyr burst from the cliff adjacent to the city and alighted on the city wall. She spotted him lounging on the roadway and turned in his direction, gasping for breath. Her tunic and armor were wet with sweat, and her hair was wild. Black fury marred her features.

"Have you *completely* gone mad?" she demanded.

He grinned at the higher pitch to her voice. She must really be furious. It had been many years since he sparked such anger in Elenyr, and he relished the moment. Then he noticed the tinge to her gaze and realized she was close to throttling his life from his body.

"It was a gambit," he said. "But wasn't that the reason we returned to Xshaltheria?"

"You were *supposed* to learn if the Gate had been rebuilt," she snarled. "*Not* climb onto his dragon and fly into another country. Do you know what he would have done if he found you? He would have cut you to shreds, and I would have watched the pieces fall to the earth."

"You were worried about me?" Shadow feigned mock surprise. "I'm touched."

"Shadow . . .," she rubbed the roof of her nose. "I love you as a son, but that doesn't mean I will not kill you."

"Trust me," Shadow turned and pointed to the keep. "When you hear what occurred here, you'll be glad of the risk I took."

"What?" she demanded. "What could be worth your life?"

"Victory."

She regarded him with anger and, he noticed, a lingering fear. He grimaced as he realized she'd just sprinted for nearly a day, because she feared for his life. Elenyr could travel leagues without tiring, but now sweat darkened her clothing, and her hands trembled from the run.

"I'm sorry," he said earnestly. "I didn't mean to worry you so much. I saw an opportunity and I seized it."

She blinked in confusion. "You've never apologize like that."

Shadow cocked his head to the side, and a slow smile lit his features. "Well that's new."

"What?"

"I can feel remorse now," Shadow said, and his expression soured. "I don't think I like it."

Elenyr began to laugh, the sound rolling out of her before she engulfed him in a long, sweaty embrace. He hoped that meant she forgave him. He didn't like the twinge in his chest that made him think he'd been wrong. He was never wrong.

"Tell me what happened," Elenyr said, retreating a step.

Shadow briefly outlined what he'd witnessed at the base of Xshaltheria, and the completion of the Gate. When he detailed Mimic's rising, she sighed and leaned against the railing of the roadway.

"We cannot even kill Serak," she said. "How can we possibly defeat the generals?"

"I think the answer lies in there." Shadow pointed to the keep.

Elenyr raised an eyebrow. "There's more?"

"All I know is that Draeken and Serak entered the keep, and only Draeken departed. He looked rather pleased with himself."

"And Draeken took Serak's dragon with him?" she asked, looking about as if she'd just realized they were alone.

"Exactly." Shadow rubbed his chin as he recalled the events at the base of Xshaltheria. "And Serak was acting fishy, like he and Draeken were not on the same terms after the battle in the valley."

Her eyes widened. "You think Draeken turned on Serak?"

"If he did, it would mean Serak might help us," he said. "If he's not dead, that is."

Elenyr's gaze turned calculating, and for several moments she stared at the keep like it held all the answers she sought. Then she nodded to herself and motioned to that direction.

"We should see if he is alive."

Shadow frowned. "I just hid on the underbelly of a dragon as they flew across an entire country—all while dropping signals for you to follow." Shadow folded his arms. "A little gratitude would be in order."

Elenyr sighed and rubbed her forehead. "Thank you, Shadow. I'm sure that was difficult."

"It was *epic*," Shadow breathed. "They could have noticed me at any moment, but Gorewrathian is so big, he didn't see me clinging to the shadows under his wing."

"I'm proud of you," she said. "Now don't ever do that again."

"No promises."

She regarded him with irritation, and then laughed sourly. "I suppose it is your greatest gift."

"That and inciting anger," Shadow said.

"That too," Elenyr replied.

215

The pair turned off the road and advanced up the street towards the fortress, detouring around a pond with various pieces of broken armor rusting on its banks. A pedestal at the center was empty, but the green water rippled and the top of a gigantic alligator head briefly surfaced. Shadow pointed to the pond, where he'd swum in his youth, but Elenyr jerked her head.

"You no longer possess a piece of the fragment of Power," she said. "I'm not sure you would survive against the guardians of these ruins."

He rolled his eyes but softened his footsteps so they could enter the keep. He took a peek at the rock troll statue, wishing he could fight it again. Instead of weapons, the rock troll guardian had gauntlets of spiked chain, weapons meant to damage and maim.

"Next time," Shadow murmured, and followed Elenyr up into the fortress.

"What are the others doing?" he asked.

"I sent Sentara, Rune, and Lorica to join the alliance," Elenyr said. "They couldn't keep up with me, and I didn't want them to be discovered while we are away. Rune is still adapting to the companionship of the Unnamed, and her actions can be chaotic."

Her words were faint, as if she were pondering the revelations Shadow had shared. Then he realized it was caution, and Elenyr pressed into the wall, advancing in silence up through the fortress.

"You think it's a trap?" Shadow asked in a normal voice.

She paused to roll her eyes. "How can you be so good at infiltration, and so terrible at the same time."

"I think Serak is dead," he said with a shrug.

"You just *hope* he's dead," she hissed. "Don't forget this could be a trap."

"Then you escape through the wall and I fade to shadow and depart." He shrugged like it was easy. "It's not like they can stop us."

"Serak has already trapped you twice," she said. "I don't think you'll survive a third imprisonment."

He frowned, but could not refute her logic. The pair gradually searched the keep, working their way up through the structure. As they approached the final corridor, the one containing Guildmaster Elsin's private office, Shadow pointed ahead.

"You really think Draeken left him alive?"

"Draeken has separated from you," she said. "But I believe he still retains a measure of personality from all the fragments. From Mind he gained ambition, from Fire he gained arrogance. From you, he obviously acquired recklessness."

"Hey!"

She smiled and patted him on the shoulder. "We both know it's the truth."

He grinned. "It's true. But why would he not kill Serak?"

"Because Serak helped create him," she said. "And the fragment of Light was ever loyal. For Draeken to kill Serak would require a ruthless lack of loyalty, and none of the fragments possessed such a trait."

"Perhaps that trait belonged to Draeken," Shadow reasoned. "We have both seen what he has done."

"We have."

Shadow heard the wealth of regret in the woman's voice and stepped in front of her. "You feel like you failed him, don't you."

She held his gaze. "How could I not? I raised the fragments. All six of them."

"You cannot save those who do not wish to be saved," he said.

"I know." She looked away, the anguish on her face. "But you were all my sons. I hoped that by teaching you five, Draeken would learn to overcome his darker impulses."

"It is because of you that five fragments survived," he said.

217

Moisture collected in her eyes and she wiped at the tears. "You're kinder than you used to be," she said.

He cursed. "Blasted remorse."

She laughed and leaned in to kiss him on the forehead. "You have my gratitude."

The bellow caused them both to turn. Muffled by distance and stone, the sound was nevertheless filled with anguish, the sound of a broken man. They exchanged a look and advanced to the door of Elsin's private quarters. There the stone trembled, a vibration as if someone nearby sought to shift the very mountain.

"I don't think it's a trap," Shadow said.

"At least not for us," she mused.

"You think Draeken trapped Serak?" Shadow whistled in appreciation. "That's brutal, after everything Serak did for him."

"You saw Serak after the battle at Xshaltheria," she drifted into the room. "He looked on in horror. I don't think he ever intended to unleash the fiends on the alliance. Surround them and show his might, yes. Intimidate them into submission, yes. But slaughter?" She shook her head. "That's never been his goal."

"That doesn't mean he's going to help us," Shadow said.

He found himself apprehensive about approaching Serak. If Elenyr was right, Serak had just been betrayed and probably imprisoned. He would be violent and angry, and unpredictable, perhaps even try to kill Elenyr in retribution.

At the same time, Shadow could not deny the appeal of speaking to Serak. The man had built the Dark Gate, created the cloaks that had forged the four generals, and knew the most about the fiends of Kelindor. If anyone possessed knowledge of how to stop Draeken, it would be him. If he would help.

Shadow caught Elenyr's arm, and when he turned back, he shook his head. "I'll talk to him."

She slowly removed his fingers and turned to face him, offering a faint smile. "Not this time, my son. I'm not risking your life, even for this."

"But he's tried to kill you," Shadow protested.

"And failed," she replied. "Besides, I am the Hauntress, and his magic cannot harm me."

She reached up and lifted her cowl, her body turning ethereal, green smoke cascading off her skin. She smiled at Shadow and then turned and passed through the secret door into the corridor beyond. Shadow leapt to the door and caught the latch, but a dull clanking suggested Elenyr had locked it from within. She was alone. With the Father of Guardians that had sought her life. Shadow grunted in irritation and raced from the room, hoping to find another entrance to the chamber.

Chapter 28: Serak's Secret

Elenyr advanced down the corridor, wary of another trap. In her ethereal form very little could harm her, but Serak had proven cunning enough to exploit her weaknesses. He'd also failed three times, and this might be a changing of tactics. But it was worth the risk.

She slowed as she approached the end of the corridor, where the tunnel opened into a large cavern, the cavern where Draeken had been torn from the body of a young child. She drew her sword and came to a halt on the threshold.

Light orbs circled the room, illuminating the enormous source of water at the center. She fully expected to find a small army arrayed against her, bearing blades of lightning, and a wall of lightning closing off her escape. But there was only Serak, on his knees.

The Father of Guardians knelt on the hard stone, staring into his hands. They trembled, but with fury or grief she could not tell. Then Elenyr noticed a nearly invisible chain extending from his body to the source of water.

Her eyes widened as she understood. Guardians were either chained to a source, or left unchained. Chained guardians were more powerful and stable, while those on their own were usually quick to fall to madness. Serak and Draeken were exceptions to that rule, their power greater than their chained cousins. Yet here Serak was, shackled.

"Have you come to gloat?"

Serak spoke in a whisper, the voice of a broken man. Elenyr did not advance, her eyes searching the room. Even now, after all Serak had done, she remained wary. But there was nothing, only Serak chained in a way that even Elenyr could not break.

"I cannot blame you for your caution," Serak said. "But you have won, and my creation has turned against me."

"I have hardly won."

He gathered the chain and stood, thrusting it towards her. "You don't call this a victory? Here I am, caged like a beast. I sacrificed for *ages*, and this is my reward."

His voice turned savage, his chest heaving, his eyes sparking with rage. The stone floor trembled and crackled, and the water source roiled, turning white as it churned. But Serak's rage departed as quickly as it had appeared, and he grimaced.

"Where did I err?" he whispered. "I planned for every contingency, every possible turn of events. But never this."

"We made the same mistake," Elenyr said. "We both thought Draeken could be tamed."

His eyes snapped to her. "*You.*" The word was like gravel from his teeth. "It's *your* fault the fragment of Mind pushed Draeken out." He advanced upon Elenyr, his features contorting. "I planned on a Draeken with the fragments intact. He was supposed to retain the influence you had created. Instead my master was left alone."

Serak reached out and clenched a fist. The walls of the corridor smashed together. Unharmed, Elenyr remained in place, the stone passing through her ethereal form. Serak opened his fist and the walls opened—before smashing together again, and then again. The Father of Guardians screamed as he sought to destroy Elenyr, the very mountain quaking as he feverishly crushed the corridor.

Elenyr didn't move as the stone turned to spikes that pierced and shattered through her body, only to reform and attempt to crush her anew. His chest heaving, Serak brought his hands together, cleaving the ceiling apart and pummeling Elenyr, the stones grinding through her, cracking and parting from the pressure. Then he collapsed to his knees with a roar of primal rage.

"YOU STOLE MY VICTORY!"

Elenyr took a single step out of the blocked tunnel. "You sought to kill my sons."

Her voice was cold, and she turned her sword outward. Serak's eyes lifted to the blade, and the pain in his gaze elicited a measure of pity. But not enough to spare Serak's life. Not after what he'd done.

"So you're here to kill me?" he asked.

"I am, but I'd rather have your help."

Serak released a rancid bark of laughter. "You think I would help you? I'd rather die."

"I think you would rather see Draeken destroyed," she said quietly.

"HE IS MY CREATION!" Serak charged to the end of his chain, his face just inches from hers. But he did not reach for her again. His eyes blazed, his chest heaved, but his expression conveyed an ache.

"He is going to destroy everything," Elenyr countered.

"Then kill me," he sneered. "Do what you have sought since the moment we met."

"No."

"Draeken would have killed your sons," he snarled. "*I* would have caused their end."

"Dying will not end what you have begun."

He stared at her, the anger gradually melting from his features, to be replaced by shame. He turned away and took several steps, his trembling fingers rising to his face. His shoulders hunched, he spoke without turning.

"You helped kill my beloved Elsin," he whispered. "You destroyed her attempt to protect Lumineia, and now you come to destroy mine."

"Draeken has destroyed your plan," Elenyr said. "I would have, given the chance, but Draeken has always been the foe you did not see. Even if he possessed my fragments inside, the darkness of his soul would not be suppressed."

Serak shook his head, but his silence spoke volumes. Serak could not disagree with her statement because he'd seen the truth with his own

222

eyes. He'd failed, and to his utmost shame, his creation would use his plan to destroy everything Serak had wanted to protect.

"I have hated you for ages," Serak ground the words out. "Hated you for what you did to my Elsin, and the guild of Verinai. I will not help you."

"Then your shame will last an eternity," she said.

He finally turned and met her gaze. His eyes were hollow, his features shattered with guilt. Anger could not hide the truth, that by bringing Draeken into being, Serak would be the destroyer of Lumineia.

Elenyr's features hardened as she advanced to him. "Draeken will obliterate the kingdoms. He will kill the people, slaughter soldiers and innocents until nothing remains but his fiends and his slaves. This free world—the only free world in the Krey Empire—will be left desolate."

He retreated from her ethereal form, wincing at her words. She did not relent, her voice rising as she proclaimed his guilt, laid bare his greatest failure, and with every word Serak stumbled away.

"*You* will be known as the creator of this holocaust," she said, "and until my dying day, I will make certain the people know how *you* created Draeken, and all of the blood on his hands—will be on *your* hands. I will erect monuments and pillars with the tale, I will write it on walls of stone and paper, in books and in memory. And if Draeken destroys them all, I will *invite* the Krey Empire to Lumineia, and *help* them destroy Draeken and his army of fiends. Then your failure will be remembered in the Empire, and your shame will be *eternal*."

Serak retreated and reached to the stone, the floor rising into spikes. But this time they were pointed at himself. She turned corporeal and slashed the spikes, shredding them as quickly as they formed. Serak bellowed and tried all the harder.

"*Let me die!*"

"Your shame will remain!"

She slashed her sword through the last spikes and no more appeared. Tears formed in Serak's eyes, spilling down his cheeks and staining his tunic. He reached his hands out to her sword and gently placed it on his throat.

"Please," he pleaded. "Please remove my shame."

Elenyr withdrew her sword and shook her head. "Shame is not removed by the sword," she said.

He swallowed and wiped at his face. The conflict passed through his features, the muscles contracting and releasing, his lips trembling as if in pain. Helping Elenyr went against everything he'd built, but it was his only chance of repairing the damage of his failure. His shoulders slumped . . . and he spoke in a whisper.

"Two thousand years ago, I opened the Dark Gate myself. The Dark of Kelindor entered Lumineia, nearly consuming me. It did kill my four lieutenants in the room."

"That's where you got the cloaks for Draeken's generals," Elenyr said.

He nodded. "The Dark is a power of its own, and I managed to insert my will upon the cloaks, turning them to my command."

"Why did Mimic not die in the acid?" she asked. Serak's jaw worked but no words came out, and she advanced a step, her voice hardening as she repeated, "Why did Mimic not die?"

"Because I built a contingency into the Dark Gate," he finally said. "I linked the four generals to the Gate, so if they perished, they would merely be Gated back to Kelindor."

"Only the generals?"

He grimaced and refused to meet her gaze. When he spoke, his voice was hollow. "After the battle in the valley, I feared what Draeken would do, so when I rebuilt the Dark Gate, I ensured the same magic will attach to anything that passes through the portal."

"How does this contingency work?" she pressed.

"The krey control the Gate energy through machines," he said. "But it is an energy like any other, and that means it is magic—magic that can be manipulated by mind mages."

"Like my son," Elenyr said.

Serak nodded in agreement. "Zoric unknowingly created a web of Gate energy across the Gate, so anything that passed through it would be linked to it. Every fiend that enters Lumineia will be leashed to the Dark Gate. If the portal is closed, they will be drawn back to Kelindor."

It was the truth she'd sought for, the secret that gave them a chance at victory. It seemed so simple, destroy the Gate and the army would disappear. A spark of hope kindled in Elenyr's chest.

"So closing the Gate will draw the generals back through as well?" she asked.

Serak shook his head. "Their link is only partial. If the Gate is closed before the generals return, they will remain on Lumineia. You must kill them before you close the Gate."

"How do I kill them?"

Serak shook his head. "An opposite magic will kill them for good, but any normal death will simply push them back through the Gate."

Elenyr saw the path to victory form in her mind. Tenuous and dangerous, she imagined killing the four generals, and then shutting the Dark Gate. Permanently. If they did it right, the Draeken War would be over.

"Does Draeken know about this?" she asked.

Serak held her gaze. "No."

"And Zoric?"

"I told him it was part of the function of a Gate," he said. "None but you and I know this secret."

"Then I will use it to stop him," she said.

He reached a hand to the broken entrance corridor and the stones shifted and lifted, reforming the exit. She could have departed with ease as the Hauntress, but she recognized the gesture for what it was, an act of trust.

"Please, Elenyr," he pleaded. "Please, remove my shame."

Elenyr inclined her head. "I will try."

She turned and departed up the corridor, her step lighter than at her approach. For the first time in months she saw a way to victory. The Gate could be closed, the fiends destroyed, the war ended. She paused and looked back, wondering if she should kill Serak. But she had no thirst for his blood, so she turned and walked away.

"That was interesting."

She nearly leapt from her skin when Shadow materialized at her side. "You watched?" she demanded.

"Of course," he spoke like the question was ridiculous. "I came in through the hole at the base of the chamber. Did you really think you could lock me out of anything?"

She smiled and reached out to tousle his hair. "I guess not."

He smiled and jerked a thumb back at Serak's prison. "Are we going to kill him?"

She paused and looked back. "No. Draeken has chosen his fate, and on this, we have an accord."

She faced forward and advanced up the corridor to the secret exit, a plan forming in her mind. It would work, of that she was certain, but the timing would have to be flawless. For the first time in months, a smile spread on her features.

"When you get that look, someone always dies," Shadow said.

She grinned and motioned to him. "Can you get a message to the other fragments?"

"Of course."

"Then it's time for us to end this war."

Chapter 29: A Tale of Brothers

The Gate glowed to life, silver liquid shimmering into place and turning solid, illuminating the dark chamber. Two figures stepped through, and Mind breathed a sigh of relief as he returned to Lumineia.

"You did not care for the Empire?" Ero asked.

"I have little taste for the darkness in krey souls," he said.

"It is disheartening to witness the depravation of my kind," Ero said, and touched the amulet on his neck, altering his flesh back to Jeric. The now-elf gave a wry smile. "Can you fault me for wanting to spend time on a free world?"

"I suppose not," Mind said, and then motioned to the Gate. "Do you think she will really come?"

"I believe she will," Jeric said. "My previous doubts aside, Tardoq is committed, and he has convinced her of our cause. Belrisa desires the downfall of the Empire as much as I do, and she sees the merit of protecting Lumineia."

Mind recalled their conversation, and the demonstration of magic he'd provided. She'd been impressed, but also wary. Mind wasn't sure if she liked the idea of mankind possessing such power. She'd promised to come when needed, and Ero had given her a set of keys that would connect to Lumineia, allowing two individuals passage. Ero had further warned her that in using the keys, he would know of her presence.

"You're as paranoid as I am," Belrisa had said.

"I'll take that as a compliment," Ero had said.

She'd inclined her head in respect, and then departed with Tardoq. Mind and Ero had departed another way, slipping out of the main Gates of the Bone Crucible before the guards discovered their presence. They exited the basement from beneath the fort in Orinfall. The moment they set foot in the street, it was obvious something had occurred.

Men and women rushed about, loading wagons with supplies. Children cried, and sheep bleated. Caravan leaders shouted as the people departed Orinfall in a steady stream. Mind frowned as he picked the truth from the panicked minds of the commoners.

The Alliance failed at Xshaltheria . . .

Thousands are dead because of Draeken. Who is next?

What will we do without King Justin? Surely his daughter is too young to hold the throne . . .

"Who ordered the evacuation?" Jeric asked.

"His daughter, Annah," Mind replied. "It appears she has ascended to the throne, and with the support of the other monarchs, has ordered the entire kingdom to evacuate north or south."

"A bold strategy," Jeric said. "They must fear the arrival of more fiends."

Mind spotted a captain barking orders, and he reached into the man's consciousness. "Someone destroyed the Dark Gate," he said. "But it's only a matter of time until it's rebuilt."

They joined the throng and pushed their way south. Jeric glanced his way, his next words unspoken. *I'm surprised the people obeyed the order to flee.*

Don't be, Mind replied in kind. *All four of Draeken's generals are abroad, spreading disease, famine, and death. The people flee out of fear.*

Mind wrestled to control the flood of fear from the commoners, their thoughts piercing his own like shouts in his ears. A mysterious disease in the eastern villages. Thousands dead by famine in the south. Food stores turning moldy in seconds, and large men withering away to bones and skin.

"Death rides the surface of the earth," a woman wailed. "He is the reaper of souls, and will come for you as he came for my husband!" Her family sought to quiet her and load her into a wagon, but she resisted. "You cannot escape the coming calamity!"

"Sit, woman," an older man said, exasperated.

As the village evacuated, many mounted horses and gathered armor and swords, the soldiers threading through the gates of Orinfall. They were headed north, to protect the refugees on their way out of Griffin. Most of the soldiers had already departed to join the final stand at Ilumidora, and the remainder were the young and the old.

"At least we are not too late," Jeric said.

"We should hasten," Mind said. "It won't take long for Draeken and Serak to repair the Dark Gate."

"It might already be open," Jeric said.

He found himself gripped by a need to find his brothers. They'd been fighting for weeks, and he had no way of knowing if they had succeeded, or if they'd been killed. His worry mounted as they sought for a pair of steeds. Most were being used by the forces moving south, a herdsman saddling every available mount to the soldiers. Mind and Jeric managed to acquire two and rode ahead, where Mind set a blistering pace.

The road was packed with soldiers heading south and people heading north. All of Griffin was being evacuated, and the people hastened to flee before Draeken's army descended upon Griffin.

"Mind," Jeric said, his voice labored from the ride. "We cannot reach Ilumidora in a single day."

"You want to slow down?" Mind shot over his shoulder. "Be my guest."

"Your horse cannot keep this pace," he said.

Mind looked down to find his horse lathered in sweat, his breathing labored. He reluctantly pulled on the reins, allowing the horse to slow to a walk. Jeric caught up and then pulled on his reins.

230

"I know you're worried about your brothers and Elenyr," Jeric said. "But sometimes you just have to be patient."

"This is my family," he said. "I'm not going to let them die, not by Draeken."

"How do you intend to stop him?" Jeric challenged. "He's more powerful than all of the fragments combined."

He sighed and stared down the road, realizing that was the greatest question. Knowing his brothers and Elenyr, they would have figured out how to stop the generals, perhaps even destroy the Dark Gate. But it was Draeken that was the greatest threat. If he survived, he would be unstoppable. He didn't even need the fiends to conquer, he could do it all on his own.

"I don't know," he finally said.

"You're the only one that can."

He shifted in the saddle to regard Jeric. "What makes you say that?"

"Because you already did so at Blackwell Keep."

"I didn't destroy him," Mind said. "I *made* him."

"You cannot create what already exists," Jeric said. "And he was always part of you. If he were stronger, he would have killed you and your brothers, and you would have all become a distant memory. But it was you that proved victorious, and it's you that can defeat him again."

"His magic is stronger than mine."

"True," Jeric said. "But you didn't use magic to defeat him the last time."

"What am I supposed to do? Hit him with a spoon?"

Jeric chuckled. "Of course not. You are the fragment of Mind. Outthink him, and then use your magic to stop him."

"You say that like its easy."

Jeric shrugged. "It's simple, not easy. But you should be grateful you have your brothers to help."

"You haven't talked about your brothers," Mind said.

Jeric gave him a measuring look and then seemed to decide it didn't matter. "Krey family life is not like here. There are usually over sixty houses in the Empire, although when I was born there were more than a hundred. The stronger houses control a multitude of worlds, and in order to maintain that order, the head families frequently have dozens of children, and each are placed in positions of power. Mine was to control Kelindor as Primus."

"You controlled an entire world?" Mind asked.

He grappled with that idea, of a single head for all the people on Lumineia. How many millions, or more likely billions, had served Ero?

"My house was a mid-tier house," he said. "I was the Primus, with my two brothers as Secondus and Tertious."

"You still owned a world."

"It's not like what you think," he replied. "Although billions of individuals were directly under my authority, my position was similar to a duke of Griffin." He swept his hand at the forest of oak and pine. "Our house was our kingdom, and as a son of the king, I controlled a region."

"A region the size of a world."

"It didn't stop our destruction," Jeric said.

Mind saw the parallel to Draeken's invasion. It didn't matter the size of the province or kingdom, there were always greater threats. It was actually comforting, in a way, to know that the Krey Empire experienced upheavals and conflicts like any other government. The only difference was how many lives were lost, and that elicited a frown.

"Were you close to your siblings?" Mind asked.

"Some were rivals," he said. "Some were friends. Skorn and Thengor were those I trusted. After Kelindor, my house was punished, and my parents lost their status. My house resources were divided

232

among rivals, and Skorn and I were bereft of home. All houseless krey are called mercenaries, because they are paid to work for other houses."

"From Primus to mercenary," Mind said.

"A sad tale," he replied, "but one that ultimately led to all this." He swept his hand to trees bordering the road.

"Lumineia was your new house," Mind realized.

"It was. And then it became so much more."

"And Skorn?" he asked.

"A tale for another day," he replied. "Suffice it to say, the Dawn of Magic saw the loss of my second brother."

The sun had set and shadows filled the road. Most of the travelers had shifted to camps along the side of the road, subdued affairs where the people ate quick meals and retired to uneasy rest. Guards were plentiful, and soldiers huddled around their campfires as if the flames would protect them from Draeken's generals.

Mind and Jeric continued on the road, which grew quiet, a dark lane bordered by scattered camps. Both required less sleep, and Mind intended to push the steeds as long as they could. As the moon began to rise, he pondered Jeric's revelations, and the deeper meaning to the story.

It was clear why Ero guarded Lumineia with such zeal. It had become his home when he was homeless. At one time Ero had thought it would return him to his power, but then the people had become his family, and he'd become more than a Primus. He'd become their protector.

A shape appeared ahead, crossing the road and flitting into the darkness. Mind reined his steed and peered into the gloom. Jeric caught the handle of one of his sword hilts and drew the weapon, the aquaglass hardening into a longsword.

"Gendor?" Jeric murmured.

Mind reached out with his consciousness, into the dark forest. He couldn't breach the assassin's mental shields, but he should be able to sense the man's presence. Nothing. Mind drew his own sword, the tension rising as he turned his horse to the side. He caught a glimpse of movement, closer than before, and scowled.

"If it's Gendor, don't hesitate," he said. "He was a lethal assassin before he became Draeken's puppet."

The seconds ticked by and Mind scanned the trees with sight and magic. Distant clanking of a ladle over a stewpot, and a muffled whinny from a horse. Whoever it was, they didn't care about the camps . . .

A large shape leaped from the darkness and Mind whirled, raising his sword. But it collided with him and carried him to the road. He landed with a grunt as large jaws clamped on the sword and yanked it from his grip. Then it dropped its jaws to his face.

And licked him.

He cursed and shoved the shadow panther away, but it nuzzled against him, shoving him deeper into the mud. Jeric lowered his sword and grinned as Shadow's messenger continued to lick his clothing.

"I'm going to kill Shadow," Mind said.

Is that any way to treat my messenger? the panther asked, and Mind caught the remnant of thoughts. It was an echo, but Shadow had obviously known what the panther would do when they met.

Mind shoved the panther aside and stood to wipe the mud from his clothing. "Just tell me your message so you can dissipate."

What I have to say is too important to reveal through a messenger. Shadow's voice came from the shadow cat. *Just come to Ilumidora. You'll want to hear Elenyr's plan. We discovered something, and trust me, it's big . . .*

Chapter 30: A City Destroyed

The farther Mind and Jeric journeyed south, the more bleak the region became. Wind whistled through empty villages, the vacant structures dark and forlorn. Animals were gone, some barn doors left open in haste. Then they reached Terros.

The city was gone.

Stone walls and wooden houses, castle and hovel, even the waterfront, all had been reduced to a pile of rubble. The outer fortifications were unrecognizable, the farms rent and torn until the land looked broken. The cobblestone streets and gilded manors of the rich were nothing but a sea of broken stones and scorched beams.

"It's been erased." Mind stared in horror at the destroyed city.

"This is the work of Draeken's army," Jeric said.

Mind knew the people had evacuated to Ilumidora, but the devastation would not have been stopped, not even by the allied forces. Anything powerful enough to cause such damage would not be stopped, not by a million soldiers.

"We must hasten." Mind pointed to the road south, where trees were torn up, the gravel ripped apart by the passage of thousands of fiends. "The fiends are already on their way south."

"How are we going to get through Draeken's army?" Jeric asked.

"Leave that to me," Mind said.

They flicked the reins and hurried south until finally a bend in the road took the disturbing sight of Terros from view. Struck by a renewed sense of urgency, both pushed their steeds, driving them through the night and into the next morning. For two days they hastened their journey, until they reached the fiend army.

Mind and Jeric left their horses and crept through the trees, advancing to the edge of a short cliff overlooking the valley. The sun had begun to set, and in the darkness Mind watched the earth ripple with moving bodies of millions of fiends, the dark creatures marching south. Trees in their way were uprooted or hacked to splinters, boulders were shoved aside.

To the east, more fiends poured from the hills, cascading down the slopes in a wave of flesh. Sipers, the doglike creatures the size of lions. Quare, the spindly humanoid beings that had once been krey or human. And krakas, the captains wielding giant obsidian swords. Then Mind spotted a fourth type.

"What's that?" he whispered.

The beast resembled a scorpion, with a long pointed tail extended over its back. Larger than a wagon, it had dual pincers and thick, scale-like armor. The tails flicked, and then one snapped, sending a bone spear streaking into a boulder laying in its path. The spear plunged into solid stone, the boulder cracking from the impact.

"Skorpians," Jeric murmured. "They were once beasts of burden on Kelindor. The Dark twisted them into creatures of war, giving them tails and claws."

Mind's features darkened and he pointed east, towards Blue Lake. "There are trails between the fiends and the lake. If we hurry, we should be able get ahead of the fiends and reach Ilumidora in time."

Jeric nodded and the two returned to their horses. Wheeling their mounts west, they worked their way around the fiend army before taking a thin trail through the rolling hills adjacent to Blue Lake. Scattered fiends, separated from the main army, frequently crossed their path, and Mind altered their thoughts, sending them in different directions. The body of a dead fiend would be discovered and investigated, but he doubted anyone would notice if a fiend wandered away.

They raced through the night, the horses laboring to maintain the pace. When the sun rose, Mind's gaze lifted to the haze that hovered over the fiend army. Like a storm cloud, it wafted off the fiends and blurred the clouds, obscuring the rising son.

"The Dark may not have been able to enter," Jeric said, "but the fiends are infused with it."

Mind nodded, and tried not to think about the enormous breadth of the cloud. If the army was even half the size, it was larger than Mind feared. He realized that unless Elenyr had a plan to stop them all, Ilumidora would end up like Terros. He shuddered at the thought and urged his flagging steed to greater efforts.

The horses gave out the next day, but Mind managed to subvert a pair of elk. Moving the saddles over, they left the horses and continued their path on the unusual steeds. Far less sturdy, the animals didn't last long, but after two days, they managed to pass the front of the fiend army. Just as they reached the forest of Orláknia, they encountered a vanguard of the alliance.

Mind dropped from his saddle and approached the scouts. "We're half a day's ride ahead of them," he said.

The elf eyed the docile elk. "You got around the fiend army on that?"

"Just the last day," Mind said. "Do you have a pair of horses we can use? We need to reach Ilumidora."

The officer called an order to a lieutenant to fetch some steeds, and two were brought forward. The captain offered food and drink, and Mind slaked his thirst from the water skin. Then he shook his head clear of fatigue and nodded his gratitude.

"Did you see Terros?" the captain asked. "Scouts said it was destroyed."

"It's gone," Mind said.

"All of it?" another elf asked. "How is that possible?"

A dull reverberation came through their boots, and as it mounted, all eyes turned towards the road. Winding east and north, it passed over a hill several miles away. As they watched, a dark wave crested the rise and poured down the slope, its sheer size eliciting muttered curses and a prayer from the other scouts.

"Ero save us," one archer breathed.

"He can't save us this time," Mind said, glancing at Jeric. "We're going to have to do it on our own."

He mounted and pulled the reins. "I'd suggest you retreat, captain. You don't have much time."

Mind and Jeric flicked the reins and their horses accelerated south. They again set a pace that would devour the miles. Mind rubbed his eyes, smearing dirt across his face as he fought to stay awake. He'd never been so fatigued.

They did not camp or rest, and only paused to water the horses at the numerous streams. Ilumidora sat in the heart of Orláknia, several days from the exterior of the forest. The empty road wound through towering trees and crossed beautiful bridges, but there was a noticeable absence of animal life, as if they too had fled in the face of Draeken's army. Several times the shadow of a large dragon passed overhead, and Mind lifted his gaze to Gorewrathian, wondering what he could do to end Draeken for good.

They encountered more scouts as they neared the elven capital, and managed to trade for fresh steeds. The soldiers were of every race and kingdom, but in the various colors of skin and under different armors, one thing was constant in the eyes of the men and women, a gripping fear of the impending battle. Although it was fear on their faces, Mind heard a different emotion from their thoughts.

Resolve.

They knew the threat, they knew to fear. But these men and women were prepared to fight, to die to protect their homes and families. One man thought of his wife and young child, his jaw set in a determined line. The woman beside him thought of her husband, who'd lost a limb in a war several years ago. She had taken his place because he had trained her, and she thought of his kiss on her lips. She fought for him.

As the bright city of Ilumidora rose in the distance, they passed through thousands of elves laboring to increase the city defenses. Men dug holes and set traps while dwarves placed war machines and stonesap barrels. All labored with courage in their hearts, and Mind

238

could not help but feel the swell of hope. Mind had once considered joining Serak, even seen the merit to his plan, but as they made the final approach to Ilumidora he finally understood what Elenyr had tried to teach. To fight on the correct side was more important than retaining one's life.

They rode to the city gates and dropped from their weary mounts. Elven mages sought to strengthen the charms on the city gates, and reinforce the walls themselves. Unlike standard stone walls, the city of Ilumidora contained walls of aquaglass, the material granted every possible spell by the powerful elven guild of magic. Ten feet thick and fifty feet high, the wall had further been strengthened by the lake at the heart of the city, the water having previously been raised and added to the aquaglass walls.

Barricades blocked city streets, and tens of thousands of soldiers prepared arrows and swords. Dwarven ballistae, taken from Terros, had been placed on the inside of the wall, the large bolts pointed at the wall itself. Crossbowmen lined the base, with hundreds of crates of crossbows. Elven archers ascended the wall to place more arrows above.

Homes, taverns, inns, and other structures ringed the exterior of the lake. All had been converted into barracks or armories. The ring of hammers on anvils gave the bright city a dwarven air, with many of the bearded race laboring in outdoor forges.

At the center of the lake, Urindilial, the queen of trees, held the fortress high above the lake, its massive roots growing into the island at its base. Branches from the queen tree extended over the lake, merging with the trees on the opposite shore to form roads and sweeping paths. Smaller branches had been grown into railings, providing a host of balconies and overlooks. They too, had been converted for war, with mounted ballistae and catapults placed beneath flowering trees, the purple petals floating down to land on the steel-tipped weapons.

Water flowed out of the lake, swirling upward and parting into a myriad of floating waterways. Small watercraft provided transportation in and through the upper city. The crystalline water carried boats filled to the brim with supplies and weaponry. The bright lights of thousands of light orbs clinging to hanging branches, illuminated the tremendous armament, and the soldiers rushed to complete final preparations.

At the heart of the city, the three-sided fortress sat nestled in the branches of Urindilial. A plume of water rose through the center of the fortress and curved into streams that arced around the exterior, making it seem like the castle was contained in an orb of glass. But the water was expanding and hardening, forming a protective sphere around the queen's castle, a final redoubt in case the outer defenses crumbled.

Mind and Jeric threaded their way through the harried soldiers and ascended a plume of water to reach the upper city. Mounted crossbows and mage catapults equipped with stonesap barrels or explosive fireballs were being fastened to the roofs of inns, taverns, and homes. Some had their walls removed to make room for more ranged weaponry.

As they approached the castle, Mind spotted Elenyr talking to a knot of officers from various races. She wore armor over her customary cloak, the green enhancing her fearsome look. The soldiers nodded and departed to obey her orders, and then she turned. Their eyes met and Mind smiled.

"Elenyr," he said. "Are we late?"

Elenyr looked up at him. "You are right on time."

Tears formed in her eyes and she closed the gap in a rush, engulfing him in an embrace. He'd never been effusive, but he hugged her just as fiercely. How could he have ever thought to betray this woman? He whispered into her ear.

"In case I have never said it aloud, I love you mother."

They parted and he fought the sudden tears. She smiled at him. "I love you too, my son."

Tears dripped down her cheeks and Mind caught the tinge of hope from her thoughts. She believed in her plan, but it would be for naught if she did not have her sons. In that moment, Mind felt sorry for Draeken. The fragment of Power had been raised with the other fragments, been taught and trained by Elenyr, but had never seen how much Elenyr believed in them. He was alone by choice, and Mind felt pity for his fallen brother.

"Tardoq?" she asked, glancing to Ero.

"With the Bonebreaker," Jeric said, nodding in greeting. "We believe she will come, and I provided means for her arrival."

Elenyr motioned to the castle. "Come. There is much to discuss."

Chapter 31: Elenyr's Plan

Elenyr guided Mind to the queen's castle and through the aquaglass sphere that surrounded the fortress. With the branches holding the fortress and protective shield, the castle resembled a clawed hand grasping an orb. Only this orb was several feet thick and could absorb tremendous damage.

She cast frequent glances at Mind. He looked different, more mature. He'd always been tactical, but his cunning had carried a darker tint. Now he seemed almost happy, despite the circumstances. And he'd never expressed love for her or his brothers. It seemed unnatural in the face of such opposition to feel such a sense of joy, but that was what she felt. Her family remained intact, and although the separation had changed her sons, all signs pointed to the changing being for their good. Her sons were here, and she would rather fight beside them than anyone else in Lumineia.

If they survived.

Her joy at Mind's return seeped away as she listened to their tale of the Krey Empire. The final battle was upon them, and although she had a plan to fight Draeken, the chance of defeat remained significant.

"Draeken devastated Terros," Jeric said, and briefly described the city.

Elenyr winced, but nodded. "We expected as much. That's why we gathered here. Queen Alosia agreed to use her city and nation as a focal point for Draeken's army, drawing them here so others had time to escape to Talinor and into the north."

"The fiend army will reach the city by morning," Mind said.

"We should be ready by then." Elenyr swept her hand to the armament of Ilumidora. "Ero knows we have turned this city into a weapon."

Jeric grinned at her use of his krey name. "Is everyone here?"

"They are," she said. "You are the last, and you arrived just in time for our war council. I'm sure you're tired, but you you'll have to rest after the council."

"Can we at least change?" Mind wrinkled his nose. "I'm fairly confident we reek."

"We do," Jeric said.

A tug at her consciousness came from Mind, and he provided glimpses of what he'd experienced at the Bone Crucible. More importantly, he shared the conversation with Tardoq and Belrisa, and their final words. Elenyr motioned to Jeric.

"Will they come?"

"They will," Jeric said. "When we're ready, I will send a message and tell them the hour has arrived."

They entered the fortress, where a quartet of gnomes used their staves to examine every person entering the castle. Elenyr endured the examination as well, and raised her arms as they passed the staffs around her torso.

"We are employing every caution to prevent Draeken hearing our plans," she said. "These gnomes are the highest ranked members of their guild and are making sure that everyone that enters the fortress is not using the persona of another."

"What if we have another Porlin?" Mind asked.

Elenyr frowned at the reminder of King Porlin, a king who had never existed. The man had been placed as a spy in infancy, and raised with an allegiance to his father, Zenif, and Serak. Porlin had served Serak for four decades, and had never been in the royal bloodline.

"We can protect against magic covering the identity of another," she said, "but we cannot prevent one who is already a servant of Serak. Some elements of our plans are not being disseminated in an effort to protect the truth. We are also limiting the number of people allowed at the council."

"A wise precaution," Mind said, and then lowered his voice. "Except for Jeric, of course."

Elenyr grinned. "Jeric's persona is based on krey technology, so the charms we have placed should have no effect on him."

"*Should* is not comforting," Jeric murmured. "I would rather not become Ero in front of the entire council of kings. I wager that would create quite a stir."

The trio finished passing the inspection of the anti-magic gnomes and entered the fortress, passing through the thick, icy sphere of aquaglass. Elenyr shivered at the cold vapors wafting off the shield and crossed the bridge to reach the great hall.

With sweeping architecture and great chandeliers of pure, solid light, the great hall now contained crates and goods, the great tables for guests having been moved to the side of the room. Elenyr, Mind, and Jeric endured two more checkpoints as they ascended the steps to reach the council chamber, situated in the left wing of the fortress. Elenyr motioned to a side chamber and waited while they changed into clothes less filthy. When they stepped back into the hall, they looked worlds better.

She ascended the final steps and nodded to the guards as she entered the turret. Wide and vaulted, the chamber contained banners of every kingdom on Lumineia, a symbol of the elven view of unity. Now, contingents of every race occupied the chamber, and stood in front of their respective banners, the first time in Ilumidora's history that it had seen such a varied council.

Elenyr spotted Queen Alosia standing with her chosen advisors, the Princess Devina, first in line to the throne, and surprisingly Princess Serania, third in line to the throne. As her personal guard, she had chosen Horn, the towering elf and firstborn of the House of Runya.

Queen Rynda stood in front of her own banner. She stood flanked by Warshard Toril, the two speaking in low tones. Beyond the rock trolls stood the gnome king and orc king together, both sitting silent, their expressions forbidding, each with a single advisor.

The three human kingdoms had two young queens, Queen Annah of Griffin and Queen Nelia of Erathan. Elenyr met their gaze and nodded, pleased by their courage and wisdom. Without them, the alliance would have crumbled. Sentara and Rune stood behind Queen Nelia, while the heads of the House of Runya, and a soldier Elenyr did not recognize stood behind Queen Annah.

Melora occupied the seat on the opposite side of the chamber, and spoke to Willow and Light, her chosen advisors. She'd sent for her older sister to take her place, but the woman had surprisingly permitted Melora to stand in her stead. Elenyr had been present when the message had come, and seen the tears in Melora's eyes. Tears of shame and gratitude that her sister believed in her.

King Dothlore of the dwarven race occupied the last chair, and two of his sons were with him, both capable warriors. As Elenyr entered the room, the dwarf inclined his head, the motion drawing the gaze of the four standing in the center of the space, the other four fragments.

Light's eyes lit up when he spotted Mind, but he did not bound over. "You made it back," he exclaimed, the lack of impulsiveness demonstrating his change since the separation.

Mind shot Elenyr a look. *Does the council know my task in the Krey Empire?*

Elenyr also spoke through Mind's magic. *They only know you sought reinforcements, not the source.*

Mind nodded. The other fragments greeted Mind while Jeric slipped to the back of the room. Water raised an eyebrow and looked about, obviously searching for Tardoq. Mind spoke in an undertone.

"My assignment appears successful."

"And what assignment was that?" the orc king demanded. "You have spoken very little and asked a great deal."

"My apologies," Elenyr said. "But in this, we cannot risk Draeken hearing the whole of our plan, or he will take measures to stop us."

"Is that why there are so many charms placed on this room?" Dothlore asked.

Elenyr motioned for the doors to close, and when they clanked shut, there was an audible hiss, like the sound of air escaping a broken seal in a pouch. Elenyr smiled at the sound, recognizing it as sound of magic sealing them inside.

"Until the door is opened, not even a sound mage can overhear what is spoken during this council."

The gnome king grunted. "No magic can pierce the charms in the wall. For the moment, we are safe."

"Even with these protections," Water said. "The truth must be guarded by each of you."

"Just tell them your plan," Rynda said, annoyed.

Elenyr inclined her head to the rock troll, and then rotated to meet the eyes of the gathered leaders and their commands. Pride gripped her as she witnessed the alliance of nations, all against Draeken.

"Gathered kings," she began, "honored dignitaries. Although I desire to share the whole of our plan, that would be unwise. During this council, I will be sharing only the portion you are allowed to know."

"And why can we not know the whole of it?" the orc king demanded, jutting his chin out.

"Because Draeken and Serak have a powerful mind mage, you thick brained moordraug." Rynda rolled her eyes as if it were obvious. "They could pick the truth from your thoughts faster than you can swill a mug of grog."

The orc growled and rose to his feet, but Elenyr raised a hand to Rynda. "Let us not permit insults in this alliance."

Rynda shrugged and pointed outside. "We've got fortifications to complete. Can we get on with this?"

"I agree with Rynda," Queen Alosia said. "Let us dispense with the formalities."

Elenyr recognized the wisdom to their words, so she led with the most important piece of information.

246

"Serak is no longer our adversary."

That brought them to their feet. The alliance had been formed to stop Serak and his Order of Ancients, and until recently, had been their principle foe. It was not until the battle at Xshaltheria that they'd learned how Draeken had risen to become Serak's master.

"You killed him?" Rynda nodded in approval.

"No," Elenyr said. "Draeken thought he would eventually betray him, so he cast him into a prison, one from which even he cannot escape."

She'd considered withholding the truth of Serak, but had decided it did not matter. Draeken didn't know Serak's secret about the Gate, so he wouldn't care that Elenyr knew of Serak's imprisonment. But for Elenyr, she needed the alliance to accept her plan, without revealing the truth about the Dark Gate. Only her fragment sons would know everything.

"But the army of fiends is still coming," Dothlore stated.

"They are." Elenyr gestured to Mind. "They will arrive tomorrow morning."

"What does Serak's absence change in the conflict?" Queen Nelia asked.

The relief in her voice was palpable, and inspired a note of pity for Elenyr. The girl had lost her father to Serak—twice. Once when he'd betrayed their kingdom of Erathan and again when he'd actually perished. To be rid of Serak probably set her mind at ease.

"I spoke with Serak," Elenyr said. "And have learned a critical piece of information."

"He turned on Draeken?" Rynda leaned forward, her eyes bright with curiosity.

"Did he tell you how to stop Draeken and the fiends?" Princess Serania asked, drawing a frown from the first princess of the elves.

247

Elenyr kept her smile in check. Princess Serania was not one to hold back, and Elenyr liked her courage and bluntness. It reminded Elenyr of Queen Alosia. With two princesses ahead of Serania, it was unlikely that she would take the throne, but Elenyr appreciated her lack of fear in a war council of such magnitude.

"Serak shared a secret that can change the war," Elenyr said.

Excitement buzzed through the room, with several leaning over to speak to their chosen advisors. The surge of hope was palpable, and Mind smiled, probably at what he'd overheard in scattered thoughts. Then Elenyr noticed Dothlore's frown.

"So your plan is based on knowledge from Serak?" He jerked his head. "I am uncertain we can trust him so much."

"Then trust me," Elenyr said, rotating so she could meet the eyes of everyone in the room. "This is our only way of defeating Draeken, his generals, and his army."

"Where is Oracle Senia?" Queen Annah asked.

Others looked about as if suddenly realizing the oracle was not present. Before their confusion could turn to doubt, Elenyr swept her hand upwards, into the castle. "The oracle has withdrawn to explore possible futures. Time is short, and she seeks to ascertain the best course for one aspect of our plan. Rest assured, she agrees with my plan, or I would not be here."

"What can you tell us?" Melora asked.

"In order to be victorious, we must kill the four generals, and then we close the Dark Gate, all within a few minutes."

"At the same moment?" the orc king scoffed. "How? The Gate is in Xshaltheria under heavy guard, and the four generals are sure to be here."

"We will send a small force to destroy the Gate," Elenyr said.

"I understand that was already tried," Queen Annah said.

"Not when Draeken's focus is here," Rynda said, rubbing her steel hand against the table, lost in thought. "Then we faced Draeken, Serak, fiends, even his dragons. This time they would all be here."

"But at the same time?" The gnome king's voice was full of doubt.

"We strike when the sun is at its zenith," Elenyr said. "The generals will be on the battlefield, so we merely need to locate them, and attack at the right moment. To succeed, we must endure throughout the morning."

"Can we do that?" Dothlore asked.

"Are you doubting our defenses?" Queen Alosia asked.

"Not our defenses," Dothlore exclaimed. "But from what our scouts say, the fiend army already numbers in the millions, and it's still growing."

"Surely we will be swept aside," the orc said.

"We must survive until noonday," Elenyr repeated. "And there are several elements in motion to assist with that." She gestured to the fragments. "Water has a task, as does Mind. Both may bring reinforcements."

"Who can help us now?" Rynda asked, a frown on her face. "We have already gathered all our forces."

She wants to know if the Bonebreaker is joining us, Mind spoke into Elenyr's thoughts.

Tell her the truth, Elenyr replied in the same manner. *She deserves the truth.*

"That I cannot reveal," Elenyr said to the group, even as a small smile formed on Rynda's features. "Just know that we will not stand alone on the morrow."

"I don't understand," Queen Nelia exclaimed. "If we kill the generals and close the Gate, we will still have to contend with the millions of fiends already through the Gate. Surely we cannot stand against so many."

249

"The fiends will no longer be a threat to us," Elenyr said.

"What about Draeken?" Rynda asked.

Elenyr looked to her sons, and they held her gaze. Mind inclined his head, a confirmation that they would do what is necessary. She faced the kings and swept her hand to her sons.

"If you can hold the city until noonday, my sons and I will help with the generals and Draeken himself. If we fail in this, the city and all of Lumineia will fall to Draeken." She turned to each, meeting their eyes, hoping they would accept her plan. "In this I ask for your faith and trust. If we follow this plan, we have a chance at ending this war. Permanently."

Chapter 32: For Elenyr

Water ascended the spiral staircase that wrapped around a thick limb, the city gradually falling away as he climbed to the highest point in Ilumidora. Situated in the lofty branches of Urindilial, the small overlook extended above the aquaglass sphere that held the fortress. Water reached the barrier and placed his hand against it, opening a portal so he could pass above the protective sphere. Higher and higher he climbed, until he could see the great breadth of the elven forest.

The overlook at the top of the limb sat nestled in a crook between two branches, the small hut containing only a peaked roof and wide windows. Water stepped to the eastern side of the hut, his eyes drawn to the destruction in the distance.

Draeken's fiend army was drawing closer by the hour. Dragon fire from his two beasts poured from the sky, burning the trees of Orláknia, and allowing the fiends to rip them from the earth. By the time they reached Ilumidora in the morning, a third of the forest would be ravaged.

A great cry rose from the elves of the city as their forest was destroyed, the lamentation a deep keening of anger and loss. Water clenched his fist on the railing of the overlook and knew Draeken destroyed the forest out of spite.

The other fragments appeared behind him, one by one joining him in the overlook. Light brought up the rear, panting from the climb. They took places at the window to survey the destruction in the distance, all falling silent as more fire erupted from Gorewrathian, briefly illuminating the great dragon in the twilight sky.

"I can't believe it's come to this," Water motioned to the approaching army. "After all we've been through, now we battle the fragment of Power."

251

"Elenyr said he was our brother too," Fire said. "But I don't believe that."

"He could have been one of us," Mind murmured. "He has chosen his own path."

"I liked having such power."

Shadow's voice was disappointed as he reached to the dark night and shaped the shadows into a dragon. The beast was smaller than he'd previously cast, and lacked the sharp definition. Water placed his hand on Shadow's shoulder.

"The fragment of Power no longer binds us, but that does not mean we are divided."

"I don't want to lose you," Light said softly.

"You won't," Fire smiled at Light. "We've always come out as victors before. It's not about to change this time."

"We've never faced a threat like this," Mind said.

Water chuckled as his words elicited a memory. "Do you remember when we went with Elenyr to fight a nest of reavers for the dwarves?"

"The silver reavers," Light's eyes brightened as he recalled. "The one where I—"

"Yes," Shadow groaned. "The one where I lost my arm."

"It grew back." Fire grinned and poked his left shoulder, the one that Shadow had been forced to regrow.

Mind's expression was fond. "As I recall, Light lost his temper because the beasts weren't playing nicely. He killed two with a giant spear."

"And cut off my arm," Shadow said flatly.

Water laughed at the memory. "You picked up your arm and shook it at Light," he said. "Your face turned purple you were so angry."

"You were rather upset," Light said.

252

"Not as upset as when you tried to fix it." Fire grinned at Light.

Shadow chuckled sourly. "I'm glad you found my arm amusing."

"Didn't Light keep the arm for a while?" Water asked. "Whatever happened to it?"

"Elenyr burned it," Shadow said, shaking his head sadly. "She caught me trying to attach it so I could have a third arm."

They all laughed, and Water tried to imagine his brother with three arms. It was exactly the type of thing Shadow would attempt, or at least would have attempted, prior to losing the fragment of Power.

He looked at his brothers, laughing and talking about their lives together, and it reminded him of the memories Elenyr had saved, and used to help Mind fight Draeken in Blackwell Keep. She'd always seen them as family, even when they had not seen it in themselves.

He looked back on their life, of how much she had taught and guided, always with patience and compassion. Had she ever wavered in her dedication to their strange family? Had she considered a different course?

His brothers were laughing about another incident, this time between Shadow and Mind, when Shadow had gotten Mind ejected from a guild of mercenaries who thought he'd stolen their prized blade collection. Mind smiled as Shadow described Mind's indignation. Mind reminded them of Shadow's punishment, to return the blades and complete five contracts for the guild. For free.

"Elenyr always did take care of us," Water said.

The amusement faded as they all turned their thoughts to Elenyr, the woman that loved them. Light's shoulders hunched, his brow furrowed in thought. Shadow looked out over the approaching fiend army, while Mind and Fire exchanged a look.

"I wish there was something we could do for her," Light said.

"She's shouldered more than anyone," Fire nodded in agreement.

"And saved our lives more times than we can count," Mind said. "She even saved us from ourselves."

Shadow folded his arms. "Plus we might die tomorrow, so whatever we might get her, we have to do tonight."

"Like a dress?" Light rubbed his chin.

Fire snorted in amusement. "She's the type of woman that would prefer a new set of armor."

"Perhaps a sword?" Water suggested.

"No," Mind said. "It is us she cares most about, and there is something we can give her that she will value."

"A hug?" Light seemed confused.

Mind shook his head. "We survive."

"You're saying the best gift we can give Elenyr . . . is us?" Shadow smirked. "I knew I was special, but I didn't realize I had such value."

Mind pointed to the fiend army and Draeken, their adversaries. "We all know what we face, and she fears for our lives. If we survive this war, it is the greatest gift we can give her, to not die at the hands of Draeken."

"She thinks she failed us," Water nodded to Mind. "She thinks that she failed to protect us from Draeken. If we defeat him, we will show her how much she has done for us, how much she means to us."

"So we give her a victory," Fire said. "A victory and her family."

"For Elenyr?" Water asked.

"For Elenyr," Shadow said.

Fire inclined his head. "For Elenyr."

Light smiled. "For Elenyr."

Last of all, Mind held their gaze. "For Elenyr, our mother."

Five brothers, standing united for the mother that had raised them. The sight brought a tear to Water's eye, and he swallowed at the sudden knot in his throat. This was his family, the family he fought for, would die for.

"This could be pointless," Shadow finally said. "We could all die tomorrow and Elenyr will be in mourning forever."

"Way to ruin the moment," Fire said with a sigh.

"What?" Shadow shrugged. "We all know it's true."

"It is true," Water said. "But this time, we aren't fighting just to win. We're fighting for each other, for Elenyr, for the ones we care about. Draeken has nothing to fight for."

Fire shrugged like it would be easy. "Destroy the fragment of Power, end the fiend army, kill the four generals, and seal the Dark Gate at the same moment from miles apart."

"And not die," Mind said.

Water chuckled at their words. "Until recently, we were always part of the same soul, so I don't think I ever said it. But I love you. You are my brothers and family, and I would die for you."

"But you won't," Light said, obviously concerned. "Because we just made a pact to survive for Elenyr."

"Yes, Light," Water said with a smile. "That is our plan."

Shadow groaned. "You know I love you. Now can we get on with this? This war won't be won with us gushing about our feelings."

Mind's jaw tightened in determination. "I will see you the morning."

"As will I," Water said.

He embraced the other fragments, all laughing when Shadow pretended to panic when Water approached. Then he nodded to Mind and Fire before turning to Shadow and Light, the only two fragments to remain in Ilumidora.

255

"Keep Elenyr safe," he said.

Light straightened. "Always."

Water smiled and then descended the steps to the aquaglass shield around the castle. He allowed his brothers to pass. Mind brought up the rear, and their eyes met. They did not speak, either in voice or magic, but Water understood the resolution. It didn't matter how, but they would be victorious.

They left, and Water sealed the shield, closing off the opening. Then he stepped onto the shield and used his magic to pass above the aquaglass, falling down the side to reach the main gates of the fortress.

The guards cried out as he dropped in their midst, but a captain barked for order. His arrival caused Lira to turn, a smile on her face as she pointed to the sphere.

"Couldn't take the stairs?"

"I was already running late," Water said.

"True," Lira said. "But you're always running late."

"My apologies," Water said, not rising to her tease.

"Did you speak to your brothers?" she asked.

"I did."

"And?"

The two turned away from the fortress and Water collected liquid from a nearby stream, fashioning a wheel of water. Larger than normal, it had spikes on the curve, allowing it to dig into the bark of the limb. He climbed inside and she claimed the second seat inside the wheel.

"We have an accord," he said.

They sped down the sloped limb, curved around a trunk, and then threaded through the ranks of soldiers to reach the southern gates. Once outside the city, he poured his magic into the wheel, the circle of water spinning so fast the landscape blurred by. Dirt and mud kicked up into their wake.

"What sort of accord?" she had to shout over the sound of the spinning wheel.

"The type that brings victory," he called back.

"To have that, we're going to have to be successful," she shouted. "And those we seek to enlist will be reluctant to join our cause."

"We'll find out soon enough!" he called back.

They streaked through the trees, speeding their way down the wide road. Behind them, the fiend army gradually swallowed Ilumidora, ripping the forest apart as it surrounded the alliance. Water set his magic into the wheel, knowing that life on Lumineia hung in the balance.

The hours of the long night sped by, and Lira managed to fall asleep. Water kept his gaze fixed on the road ahead, unwilling to pause or rest. This time, they would be victorious. This time they would stop Draeken for good.

"For Elenyr," he whispered, and pushed the wheel to even greater speed.

Chapter 33: Draeken's Kingdom

Draeken surveyed the forest of Orláknia, a sneer spreading on his features. He'd thought the allied races would have gathered at Terros, an easy victory. But he'd found the city abandoned, and in anger, he'd ordered it destroyed. Then he'd set his sights on Ilumidora. When the fiends had reached the forest, he'd burned it, using his dragons to rend great furrows in the beautiful elven woods. The fiends had leveled the trees, leaving burning logs and limbs scattered in piles across the region.

Destroying the forest did little to the alliance, but they were watching, and to witness their beloved forest be destroyed would strike fear into the hearts of elves and man. Such destruction required power, and Draeken wanted them to know exactly what they faced.

Already his army of fiends was halfway around Ilumidora, the sound of snapping wood and rending earth filling the air. By dawn, the bright city would be surrounded by a sea of fiends, an island from which there would be no escape.

Draeken could feel the weight of the fiends pull on his willpower, an omnipresent anchor against his mind. The burden was shared by four others, his four generals. He shouldered the bulk of the load, but without them, he could not endure for long.

He fleetingly considered the prospect of ordering his generals to remain away from the battlefield. They were his greatest strength, and his greatest vulnerability. If they were killed, it would force Draeken to shoulder the entire weight of the fiend army, at least until they managed to return to Lumineia through the Dark Gate. (Return to Lumineia? Or Kelindor?)

Draeken shook his head and directed Gorewrathian to swerve around Ilumidora. The generals were almost impervious, their magic greater than any mage. Only a handful posed a threat to the generals, and if they were killed, they would not truly perish. He smiled, pleased that Serak had possessed such foresight to ensure the generals would endure. For all of Serak's weakness, he'd laid the foundation for Draeken's future.

From his vantage point, Draeken could see the alliance gathering on the walls. They'd obviously left traps and dangers in the mile outside the city. The fiends halted at the invisible barrier, leaving Ilumidora ringed by the final trees. The dangerous ground of traps and pitfalls had been covered, a needless gesture, as the fiends would not attempt to avoid the traps. They would just perish, and the fiends behind would trod their corpses underfoot.

Draeken chuckled to himself. The alliance thought the fiends were sentient, but they were more like limbs to his mind. They obeyed his will, and when he gave the order, they would charge the city and continue to assault the walls until all those within were dead or the survivors surrendered.

At his command, Gorewrathian came to a hover high above the city. Moonlight filtered through the cracks, but against a backdrop of dark clouds Draeken and his mount were almost invisible.

Why do we hold the assault? Gorewrathian rumbled his displeasure.

"We attack at dawn," Draeken said. "The alliance cannot stand against us, and I want them to see their destruction in the light of day."

Your pride will be your undoing.

"Isn't that what they say about dragons?" he retorted.

The dragon released a plume of flame, and Draeken smiled at his irritation. Draeken didn't care what the beast thought. He may be the king of dragonkind, but he was still just an animal, and his vaunted strength did not compare with his own.

Draeken turned his mount away from the city and flew to a camp erected at the middle of the fiend army. Above the camp, Draeken slid off the beast and dropped toward the earth, flying on his own. He could feel Gorewrathian's baleful gaze on his back. The dragon could strike, of course, but both knew the attempt would be lethal. Again, Draeken

259

smiled, pleased that he could remind the mighty king of his inferiority. Draeken didn't need the dragon to fly.

Draeken descended to the earth, the fiends stilling at his approach. He landed on a hill that had once held beautiful oak trees and flowers. Now the earth was rent, the trees fallen on their sides, their leaves and branches stripped bare. Zoric greeted him with a smile, but Draeken ignored him.

Draeken was surprised to find that he missed the trees. He'd always liked the forests, and decided that once he'd conquered the kingdoms, he could have the elves rebuild their forests, after they built him a seat of power.

He nodded to himself as his feet touched the ground, liking the idea of a mighty fortress. Not Xshaltheria, for that citadel reeked of sulfur, and Draeken had no love for ancient dwarven architecture. No, he needed a giant and spacious fortress. Perhaps one that floated above the earth, a constant reminder that his power exceeded that of the people. He could blend his magic with krey technology, ensuring none would ever dare to attempt an attack.

"We attack at dawn?" Zoric asked.

"We attack at dawn," Draeken replied. "But you will stay here, out of the conflict."

Zoric's eyes narrowed. "Why?"

"Because your father is dead," Draeken said. "And I don't want to risk your loss. A mind mage will be useful in my new empire."

Zoric inclined his head, obviously pleased that Draeken needed him. Alone, Draeken approached the summit of the hill and mentally summoned the four generals. Much like tugging on a string, he sensed their acknowledgement and response. Bartoth was nearest, and the armored rock troll ascended from the east. Raven and Mimic came next, their two forms approaching and coming to a halt beside Bartoth. Last to come, Gendor reluctantly appeared from the darkness.

Draeken frowned at Gendor's continued resistance. The man had been a murderer, a killer of soldiers and innocents, a man who took lives for coin and ambition. Why did he resist Draeken's will?

"My horsemen," Draeken said. "You have ridden on the four winds, destroying the earth, preparing the region for my new reign. You have my gratitude for your loyalty."

"We are grateful for the power you have granted," the Raven said.

Draeken smiled at the pleasure in the woman's voice. "After all you have endured, I believe it's only fitting that you discard your old names. They represent your past lives, and you no longer need them."

He advanced to Bartoth and looked up at the towering rock troll. He'd removed his helmet, revealing his tattooed features, and his savage smile. The troll may have failed in gathering Mimic, but Draeken believed that was because he'd tried to be subtle, and left his armor behind.

"You will never again remove your armor in battle," Draeken said. "In time, the people will not even know you were a rock troll, and will simply know you as the general of War."

He stepped to the next in line. The Raven hardly looked human anymore, her skin sunken against her bones, her features hollow, her body seemingly unable to stand on its own. Even Draeken could feel a touch of hunger at the proximity.

"Your ambition turned you into the essence of hunger," Draeken said, "and so you will be known as Famine. By the end of this war, the people will remember you every time their harvest is slim and teach their children to flee at your return."

The Raven smiled and accepted the new name, and Draeken advanced to Mimic. The woman looked diseased, her skin covered in sores and patches of purple and green. She regarded Draeken with dispassionate eyes.

"So much disease," Draeken said. "It haunted you in life, and now it will haunt our foes. Your new name is Plague, the source of disease and infection. No blade can harm you. No magic can damage your flesh.

261

On the morrow, you will ride across the battlefield and the soldiers will wither and die in your mere presence."

"And your brothers?" she asked.

"Kill them," Draeken said. "They are no part of me anymore."

She smiled, and Draeken stepped in front of Gendor. The assassin held his gaze, his glowing red eyes somehow cold. Draeken chuckled at the resistance against his cloak. Gendor may not be on his side, but his sheer willpower was admirable.

"Why do you continue to resist me?" Draeken asked. "You are a killer. Is that not what you do for me?"

"My blade is mine," Gendor said. "Even if you force me to strike in your name, that does not mean I belong to you."

Draeken's features hardened. "Tomorrow you will have the privilege of killing Elenyr."

His red eyes pulsed, and Draeken smiled, sensing the truth to his assumption. The assassin had hoped Elenyr would find a way to free him from bondage. It might even be possible, given her history of aiding those in need. But not this time.

Draeken closed the gap, his voice turning to steel. "You will kill Elenyr tomorrow. When you set your gaze upon her, you will engage in a duel, and will not retreat until her body lies in pieces. If anyone gets in your way, you will kill them as well. Any soldier, any woman, any child, any king or fragment, you will kill anyone in your way to get to her."

Gendor's cloak shimmered as Draeken imposed his will, and Gendor glared at him, his red eyes pulsing in hatred. Draeken had considered his words with great care. Gendor would obey his command.

"You are the essence of Death," Draeken said. "And when Elenyr dies, that will be your name forevermore. No one will remember Gendor, the once fallen assassin. But the people always remember Death. You will give voice to those fears."

Gendor did not acknowledge the new name, by bowing his head or by speaking, but Draeken knew he would obey. The man may try to find loopholes in Draeken's orders, but he could not outright disobey. The power of the cloak required absolute loyalty. By not bowing, he demonstrated his resistance.

Draeken retreated and examined his four new horsemen. They were men and women to be feared, beings of power, nigh impervious to any attack. Draeken imagined statues placed on the four corners of his fortress, each depicting the four horsemen.

Yet as Draeken regarded them, a touch of worry crept into his heart. His brothers had a way of victory. He'd seen it a thousand times in a thousand conflicts, and if anyone could destroy him and his generals, it was the fragments.

But how? The question nagged at his thoughts. How would Elenyr and the fragments stop such might? It seemed inconceivable, and yet the fragment of Mind had used cunning to defeat foes of great strength and power. Could they do it again?

Draeken chuckled to himself. His caution was prudent, but Draeken could not permit himself to fall to paranoia. He had a crushing army and power unmatched across Lumineia. And they possessed only the allied races and the weaker fragments.

His gaze settled on Death, and his eyes narrowed. "Have you seen any of the fragments?"

Compelled by the cloak, he answered, "Yes."

The other three generals turned on him, and Plague growled. "When?"

Death remained silent until Draeken repeated the question. Then he said, "earlier this night."

"Tell me everything you saw," Draeken growled. "And tell me now."

Death's red eyes pulsed, and then he reluctantly said, "One departed west, alone. One went south with a single companion. One went east, with two companions. I did not see their identities."

Draeken scowled, disliking the news. Three fragments had departed on the eve of the greatest battle in recorded history. Why? What could they hope to achieve in a single night? He barked an order and the four horsemen departed, leaving him alone. When they had left, Draeken growled and discarded his doubts. The fragments had been mighty only when they had possessed the fragment of Power. Now they were weak, and they sought a fool's hope.

Draeken turned and surveyed the battlefield, and the bright city in the distance. Visible through the haze of smoke, the encased castle and the high aquaglass walls seemed to sparkle. One last battle, and then the kings were his. The dawn of his reign. The beginning of his empire.

Chapter 34: The Ancient Warrior

Mind leaned over the neck of Light's wolfsteed, the animal devouring the miles. Midnight had passed hours ago but he urged the enchanted mount to greater efforts, rushing across the waving grass of eastern Talinor.

The steed glowed in the night and Mind scanned the sky, hoping Draeken did not appear. He guessed the fragment of Power would remain with his army, gloating over the impending kill. But if Draeken possessed a portion of Mind, that meant he was not bereft of strategy. Mind shifted the cloth he'd draped over the glowing mount, obscuring the bulk of the wolfsteed from view. But there was little he could do about the horse's legs.

Mind leaned in, driving himself to greater efforts, pushing past the fatigue of the last several days. After three weeks languishing in the Krey Empire, he'd been thrust into the conflict without a moment's rest.

As the predawn glow appeared on the horizon, he spotted Herosian. Rushing the flagging wolfsteed across the earth, he galloped straight to the eastern gates. He reached out with his magic and caught the distant thoughts of the guards left to care for the city, and ordered them to open the gates.

Responding as if the order had been spoken by an officer, the soldiers caught the handle of the mechanism that opened the door. As they spun the wheel, the long bars swung upward, and the doors opened. Mind raced through, not slowing as he rushed down the crowded streets.

Tents and other makeshift structures lined both sides of the street, housing the innumerable refugees from Griffin. Anyone able to fight had gone to Ilumidora, leaving those too young, old, or infirm. The older guards stood watch, offering aid to the overflowing inns.

Mind's haste elicited a swell of noise, and he used his magic to send comfort to the people. *The battle will begin at dawn, and we are prepared for Draeken's invasion.* Mind did not reveal the size of Draeken's army, unwilling to stretch their tenuous hope.

Mind banked his steed down a street and turned into the wealthier rings of the city, closer to the castle. His destination loomed above the others, the spherical structure prominent among its neighboring shops. Mind raced to a stop and leapt from the saddle. He reached the door just as it opened.

"What's wrong?" the older man demanded. "I could hear your mental shouts from a mile out."

"Moren," Mind greeted the man. "I need you and your daughter to come with me, right now."

"Is this about the war?"

Moren turned and called back into the spherical building, shouting his daughter's name. Above the door, a sign described the location as Requiem. Mind caught a glimpse of shelves of memory orbs, the glass spheres enchanted to contain memories. Well known for his magic, Moren and his daughter plied a thriving trade in Talinor, and used their skills to place memories into the glass balls.

Mind glanced to the sky as Moren exited the structure, wincing as he noticed the light approaching dawn. The battle would begin within the hour, and he was three days ride away from Ilumidora. The wolfsteed had faded significantly, and Light's magic was already beginning to disintegrate.

Moren pulled his cloak about his shoulders and called again for his daughter. "Stella!" he shouted again.

Mind had met the man a few times, but never his daughter. From what Elenyr had said, he expected to see an accomplished woman. But the woman that stepped into the open was not what he expected.

Dressed in armor with purple accents, Stella carried a beautiful cloak, also purple. Her hair was black, her eyes a striking green. She tightened the strand on her cloak while Moren stared in shock.

"Why are you dressed for combat?"

"Someone called the Unnamed told me I would need to fight." Her expression turned disapproving. "I did tell you to gather your armor."

"I thought you spoke in jest," Moren said, still staring at his armor clad daughter.

"Hurry up, father," she said. "We don't have much time."

Her eyes settled on Mind, and he realized that he too, had been staring. He flushed and looked away, but her beauty remained fixed on his consciousness. And that was before she smiled.

"You must be the fragment of Mind," she said.

"I am," Mind said.

"Well?" she asked, striding down the steps. "What's the plan?"

He wrestled with the surge of attraction. This was not the time or place to find a woman so captivating. He glanced to the horizon, using the approaching sun as a reminder of the importance of his task.

Moren appeared in the doorway again, muttering under his breath as he tied the fastenings on his leather armor. Covered in dust, it was obviously rarely used, and Stella shook her head, her brow furrowing.

"Father, I did tell you to get better armor."

"I'm a mind mage with a business," he huffed. "I have no need of armor."

"Until the day you do," she said. "And that day is today."

Mind stifled a laugh. Moren glared at him, and then shut the door. He fumbled for a key and then locked it. He paused, and looked to Mind, his expression pensive. Then he began unlocking the door again.

"Perhaps we should get some supplies."

"Father," Stella groaned, at the same time Mind spoke.

"No need."

267

Mind motioned them to follow and threaded his way back into the street. He crossed the road, and led the two mind mages deeper into the second ring of the city, to a certain hidden door behind a large estate. Activating the secret entrance, he guided them into the underbelly of the city.

"Where are we going?" Moren asked.

"Up until recently, this led to the Assassin's Guild," Mind said.

"Epic," she breathed.

Moren paled. "Surely they will kill us for entering their sacred hall."

"Those still living are at Ilumidora," Mind said. "Besides, the new head of the guild has moved them to a new location."

As he hurried them down the corridor, he could not help but test the limits of Stella's magic. The young woman raised an eyebrow as he subtly tested her mental shields. He realized she'd sensed his efforts and was grateful for the darkness to hide his flush.

"If you want to know my ability, you have but to ask."

"I'll do that," Mind said.

They advanced down the winding corridor that made its way deep into the earth. The direction pointed to the great fortress of Talinor, and Mind sensed Stella's excitement. Despite the situation, he was eager to show her what lay in the Assassins' guildhall.

After their war council, Mind had decided there was one possible person to recruit, and upon speaking to Elenyr, had asked Light to craft him a wolfsteed and departed. He'd escaped just before the fiend army had closed the gap.

The end of the corridor culminated in a giant cavern. Mind dropped onto the stairs as his companions came to an abrupt halt. Stella sucked in her breath, her eyes sweeping across the footings of the castle, the lake and island, where seven destroyed towers lay in ruins. Then her eyes widened when she spotted the enormous statue leaning half in the lake water where it had fallen.

"What is that?"

Mind pointed to the statue. "That is a Titan."

Moren cursed, drawing Stella's gaze. "You know of it?"

"In the Mage Wars, the Verinai built four Titans," Moren said. "They represent the crowning achievement of the guild of Verinai. They were devastating war machines, intended to wreck castles and uproot city walls."

"You want to bring it to life," Stella guessed.

Mind smiled at the touch of excitement to her tone. "Yes," he said.

"How?" She hurried to catch up to him on the stairs. "It's five thousand years old. Surely it cannot function."

"This Titan was unlike the other four," Mind said, recalling Elenyr's tale. "This was the first, the largest and greatest. When it failed, the Verinai built four smaller Titans, their magics more fluid. This was left here, forgotten."

"But if it didn't work then, why would it work now?" Moren was breathing hard as they reached the floor of the cavern and crossed the bridge to the island.

"Because it *did* work," Mind said.

"I don't understand," Stella said. "Why did the Verinai think it didn't?"

Mind crossed the island and came to a halt at the edge of the statue's enormous foot. "The Titans were so large, and possessed so much magic threaded into their makeup, that they could not operate without a cost. One soul, their mind imbued into the Titan, brought the war machine to life."

Moren raised a hand and retreated a step. "You cannot mean for—"

"Of course not," Mind said. "I'm not going to sacrifice either of you. That's why there are three of us."

269

"And you think we can shoulder the burden together?" Stella asked, her eyes wide and eager.

"You cannot be considering this," Moren said. "This is madness. I know the war is grave, but this could destroy us all."

"Your ancestor fought in the Mage Wars," Mind said. "Did you know that?"

Moren blinked in surprise at the shift in conversation. "My ancestor disappeared during the war. How do you know her fate?"

Mind stabbed a finger at the Titan. "She was the one chosen to become this Titan."

Moren's eyes widened. "How can you know this?"

"Your ancestor was forced to become this Titan," He said. "The Verinai believed that a mind mage was required. She did in fact empower the Titan, but she did not move or speak, and died to prevent the Verinai from knowing their success."

"She fought?" Moren seemed stunned.

"And won," Mind said. "Elenyr found her, and spoke to her in the final moments of her life. She brought her child so she could say goodbye. And that is why your bloodline is beholden to her."

Moren's entire ancestry had served Elenyr without understanding why. Mind was giving the man the reason. Mind chafed at the man's struggle to understand. Dawn was just moments away, and they still had to make the return journey. In the Titan, they could cross the distance in just a couple of hours, but every second counted.

"I never knew," Moren breathed.

"This is your chance," Mind urged. "If you do this, your family's oath to Elenyr will be fulfilled."

Moren stared at the Titan, the truth settling on him like a mantle. His jaw tightened and he looked to his daughter, who nodded her head, an unspoken accord. Then Moren straightened and turned to Mind.

"What do we do?"

Mind directed them to climb up the Titan, to the access panel in the chest. Using his magic, he unlocked the latch inside and it swung open with a creak. Inside, the space was hardly large enough for a single person, the walls of the space glowing faintly, pulsing with long buried power.

Mind reached into the threads of power. The musculature of the war machine had been patterned after a rock troll, and beneath the thick armor and great skeleton, the chest cavity contained a reservoir of power that still survived to this day. Mind used his gravity magic to compress the reservoir, shaping a new space inside, a place for two more occupants.

"Get inside," Mind said.

The two mind mages clambered into the opening and squeezed into the recess Mind had created. Mind then claimed the center seat. He reached to the panel as he gave the final instructions.

"This Titan carries an enormous load," he said. "If I were alone, it would probably kill me. But the three of us can share the burden if we blend our magics into a single focus."

"A melding?" Stella abruptly appeared nervous. "Are you certain?"

"All will be well," Moren said. "Do as he says."

Sitting so close their shoulders touched, Mind met her gaze. "Anything I see in your mind, I will never reveal."

She hesitated, and then nodded, and Mind shut the latch. Then he closed his eyes and reached to the other two mind mages. After a lifetime of holding strict mental barriers, Mind lowered his shields, allowing the three to meld.

As they merged, Mind caught glimpses of Stella's life, events and places, joys and embarrassments. He saw Moren as well, his pride of his daughter, his fear of the battle they would face. They, in turn, saw him. Mind fought the urge to shield his vulnerability, but felt Stella smile when she saw his attraction for her.

271

He reached for the Titan, his magic empowered by the two mind mages. The energy coursed through the Titan's flesh, flooding into limbs and extremities, filling the armor and sinews. The melding was only as strong as the mind mages that performed the joining, and all three were committed. Mind delved deeper into the magic, giving himself into the Titan's enormous reservoir of power. A smile spread on his face and he opened his eyes—but his eyelids did not lift.

On the outside of the statue, the eyes of the Titan began to glow.

Chapter 35: Return to Xshaltheria

"It's almost dawn," Fire said, peering into the clouds below. "Are we almost there?"

"We are close," Senia said. "I can foresee our arrival."

"How many fiends are still in the fortress?" Fire asked.

"Too many to fight," Senia said.

"I can fight a lot of foes," Fire retorted.

"They are still coming through the Dark Gate," Senia said.

"Still?"

The news shocked Fire. Before the clouds had obscured the earth, he'd watched the entire landscape undulate and shift as the fiends advanced to the southwest. Much of southern Griffin was covered in their dark forms. If they were still coming through the Dark Gate, that meant they numbered well into the millions.

We will be victorious, Isray rumbled.

"I like your optimism," Senia said, patting the white dragon on the neck.

"As long as the Dark Gate shuts, we will be fine," Lachonus said from the back of the group.

"Easy," Fire said.

Lachonus laughed. "Then what are we waiting for? Let's do this."

"Don't take this lightly," Senia said, her tone filled with disapproval. "Everything hangs on us."

"I'm not taking it lightly," Fire said. "Life is just better when you focus on the amusing bits."

Lachonus grinned, and Fire decided he liked the man. Fire wondered how he'd been born of such a terrible woman, but perhaps his better qualities had come from his father's side. Isray rumbled in irritation and banked to the side, dropping into the clouds in order to stay hidden.

"What's the plan to get inside the fortress?" Fire asked.

"Draeken and his generals were spotted at Ilumidora," Senia said. "Unless they have one of Serak's Gates, they cannot return to Xshaltheria."

"So it's just us and a million fiends," Fire nodded. "That's not so bad."

I can land on the east side of the mountain, Isray said. *There are less defenses there, and we should be able to ascend to the fortress unseen.*

"And what about getting inside?" Lachonus asked. "From what you've described, there is a large gap between the rim of the volcano and the fortress. If we fall, we fall into the volcano."

"It's nice this time of year," Fire said.

"Says the one who is immune to heat."

Fire grinned. "I should be able to shape the heat into a bridge we can use to reach the fortress."

Senia agreed with a nod. "Once we are inside, I'll watch our immediate future so we can sneak inside the fortress and find the Dark Gate. When we get there, Lachonus will need to do his part."

"And what part is that?" Lachonus asked. "You've been irritatingly silent on the matter."

"All I know is that Draeken placed a sentry at the Gate," Senia said. "One he crafted with his own hands."

"So it will be powerful," Fire said. "Probably some sort of golem. Possibly a sentient."

"I thought a sentient takes years to craft," Lachonus said.

"For a normal mage," Fire said. "Not a guardian, and Draeken is the most powerful guardian ever created."

"How am I supposed to kill a sentry like that?" Lachonus tapped the hilt of his sword. "I like my blade, but it's not like it will do much against a being of magic."

"Look at your sword," Senia said.

Lachonus frowned and pulled his sword partly out of its scabbard. His eyes widened at the dark metal and he pulled it the rest of the way free. He touched the smooth black blade and whistled in appreciation.

"It's my sword."

Senia smiled at his surprise. "A new sword would not have had the same balance as yours. Plus it's rather hard to find a katsana with anti-magic attached to the steel."

"When did you do this?" Lachonus asked.

"I had it crafted last night," Senia said. "My friend did not have time to cast an enduring charm, but it will last for a few weeks, or long enough for a single battle."

"Don't touch me with that thing," Fire said.

Lachonus abruptly cursed, drawing their attention. His hand was empty, and he was looking over the side of the dragon. He grimaced and turned to Senia, his expression apologetic. Senia's features clouded with anger.

"Did you *drop* it?"

"Is it bad if I did?" Lachonus asked.

"I don't have a replacement in my pocket," Senia snapped.

I'll get it.

275

Isray folded his wings and dropped out of the sky. Fire sucked in his breath as the wind billowed past them. Passing through the clouds into open air, he scanned the earth, and recognized the mountain range. It was the same that connected to Xshaltheria, and bordered the southern side of the valley where the alliance had fought the fiends.

"I can't believe a swordsman dropped his sword," Senia fumed.

"I would never drop my sword," he protested. "But I would test the oracle's skill."

Fire spun in his seat, just as Lachonus pulled the sword into view. He began to laugh as Senia glared at him. Isray opened his wings and pulled out of his dive, the rumble in his chest indicating he was less than pleased.

"You want to test me?" Senia's voice turned dangerous.

"Not when you ask like that," Fire said.

Her eyes flicked to him, and Fire regretted speaking. Then his smile faded as he looked beyond Isray's spiked head and through the gap between two peaks. He could just make out Xshaltheria.

"Down," he hissed.

"I'm not falling for that again," Senia snapped.

"*Down*," Fire snarled.

Hearing the warning in his voice, Isray dropped lower, falling behind the string of peaks. Suddenly tense, the three remained silent as the white dragon found a roost behind a ridge. Fire dropped from the saddle and sprinted up the slope, slowing as he reached the top.

The peak on his right rose into the clouds. Fire took a place behind a boulder and surveyed the valley beyond, and Xshaltheria rising in the east. Senia and Lachonus joined him, and the oracle lowered her voice.

"What did you see?"

Fire didn't respond. The remains of the scattered tents and war machines were still present in the valley, visible in the horde of fiends marching west. The river that ran through the center of the valley was almost invisible beneath their sheer mass.

The volcano sat at the eastern end of the valley, a dark haze rising from its mouth. The road and battlements had more fiends, the creatures marching from the gates at the western side of the volcano's mouth.

Isray morphed into Rake and he joined them, but Fire motioned them to silence. All four scanned the fortress, and then a large shape dropped out of the clouds and settled on the rim of the volcano. Rake sucked in his breath.

"Gorewrathian is here?"

"That's what you saw?" Lachonus asked.

Fire nodded. "I saw his wing as he turned back. Both of Draeken's dragons are here."

"He must have sent them back to guard the fortress," Senia said.

"You didn't see it?" Rake asked.

She cast him a withering glare. "As Lachonus has just irritatingly demonstrated, I do not foresee everything. I can only catch glimpses of the future."

"Is this a bad time to point out that I saved us all?" Lachonus asked.

"How did you do that?" Rake asked.

"If I hadn't pretended to drop my sword, we would have flown around the fortress and come from the east, where we surely would have been discovered by the two red dragons."

Fire grinned. "He has a point."

Senia rolled her eyes. "If I didn't need you, I would kill you."

"So what do we do?" Rake motioned to the red dragons. "Gorewrathian is the king of dragons for a reason. He's four times larger than Isray, and that doesn't include Bendelinish."

Serak's dragon appeared out of the clouds and curved around the fortress, obviously on patrol. Gorewrathian dropped from the volcano and flapped for altitude before turning into the valley. It soared south, towards the foursome, before sweeping along the mountainside.

Fire ducked behind the boulder, crouching with the others as the great shadow passed above them. Senia grimaced and shook her head, but Fire realized why she was angry. She blamed herself for not seeing the dragon's presence.

"We need a new plan," Fire said.

"And it needs to be fast," Lachonus said. "Noonday is only a few hours away."

"Can you see another way in?" Rake looked to Senia.

Fire watched the doubt on her features. The entire plan hinged on them destroying the Dark Gate. They'd counted on Draeken retaining the bulk of his forces at Ilumidora, leaving Xshaltheria open to attack.

Senia's jaw set in a firm line and she settled into a hollow between the boulder and the rock. "I'll have to," she said.

As Senia dropped into her farsight, Fire returned his gaze to Xshaltheria. The presence of the dragons changed everything. The four of them would be hard pressed to kill a single dragon, let alone a second—or the fiends. And that didn't include Draeken's mysterious sentry.

His thoughts shifted to his brothers. The sun would rise soon, and when it did, the final battle would begin. Elenyr, the other fragments, everyone had hung their hopes that he and the others could destroy the Gate at the appointed hour. He grimaced as another person came to mind.

He hadn't seen Soreena since before the Stormdial, but she came often to his thoughts. He hoped she was in her druid village north of Erathan, far from the war. If they failed, there was no place far enough, but it was a consolation that the woman he cared for would not have to witness the end. He smiled as he realized such a hope was fool's hope.

Soreena was a leader and a soldier. She was probably already at Ilumidora, ready to fight for her tribe.

He put his hand on the boulder and felt the cold stone, ignoring Lachonus and Rake arguing about different options. Fire set his gaze on the dragons in the distance, and accepted that whatever the cost, he would make sure the Dark Gate was destroyed.

Chapter 36: Walls of Glass

As dawn approached, Shadow dropped from the aquaglass wall and threaded his way through the lethal field of traps and pitfalls. From there, he entered the ranks of fiends. Disturbingly, they stood silent, or occasionally rocked in place, their blank eyes fixed on the city of Ilumidora. Some were still occupied in tearing down trees, but the rest resembled statues of flesh, waiting on the order of their master to attack.

In his elemental form, Shadow slipped among them, using the darkness to weave threads of magic from krakas and sipers, to quare and skorpians. The threads of magic were invisible in the dark, but they would be as binding as chains until the sun came up. More and more he cast, binding them together, wrapping the cords around broken trees and under fallen logs.

He stifled a chuckle as he wrapped a shadow rope around a kraka's horns and then tossed a loop over the sword of its neighbor. Then he fastened the thread to the claw of a skorpian. When the predawn glow touched the eastern horizon, he retreated back through the landscape of pitfalls and scaled the aquaglass wall. On the other side, the ranks of soldiers tasked for the night watch failed to see him, even when he passed right in front of their eyes.

Shadow reached the top of the wall and clambered over, and found Elenyr leaning against the battlements. Shadow chuckled to himself as he straightened, but did not wonder how the Hauntress had known his intention. She always knew.

"Did you enjoy yourself?" she asked.

"Not as much as I will at sunrise," he said.

She inclined her head. "We don't have long to wait."

They both turned to watch the fiend army gradually materialize as daylight approached. The fiends began to stir, a swell of motion across the landscape as far as Shadow could see. Captains and officers barked orders, and archers notched arrows. Crossbowmen laid bolts into place and ballistae operators armed their war machines. The grinding of stone echoed across the city as boulders were rolled into catapults.

"Where's Light?" Shadow asked.

"While you were out playing, he built his own war machine." She pointed to the cavalry ling up behind the northern gates.

One contraption stood out from the rows of horsemen. The machine had been built atop a wagon, and looked much like a carver, a spinning wheel of spiked blades that could cut through steel and bone, only this wagon had three carvers, all pointing in opposite directions. Willow sat on the front of the wagon, holding the reins of two wolfsteeds, the animals of light stomping their horse hooves on the road. They tossed their wolf heads, as if eager for the coming conflict.

Light was atop the wagon, his feet in the air as he ducked under the top of his machine. Elven light mages lined up with imbued light orbs, and he sucked them dry, using their magic to finish crafting the machine. The depleted orbs were taken away, making room for elves and a new supply.

"Ten gold says it doesn't work," Shadow said.

Elenyr smiled. "Make it twenty."

"You think his machine will function?" Shadow snorted in disbelief.

"I will always bet on my sons."

Shadow chuckled at that. "But aren't you betting against me?"

"Perhaps," she allowed. "Does that mean you are rescinding?"

"Twenty gold it is."

Her smile turned smug, causing him to frown. "What do you know?"

"King Dothlore and two of his engineers helped in the design." She smiled and turned to Rynda, approaching along the battlements.

"That's not fair," he protested.

"You didn't ask," she replied.

Rynda reached Elenyr and swept a hand to the stirring fiends. "Let them come."

"You sound excited," Shadow said.

"Why should I not be?" Rynda asked. "This is the greatest battle in the history of our world. I wouldn't miss it for anything."

"Me either," Shadow said.

Rynda regarded him and then grunted her approval. Then the light pierced the horizon, a sliver of yellow that signaled the charge. The fiends began to paw the ground, a rising snarl filling the landscape. Shadow shivered in excitement as the horde charged—and promptly fell on their faces.

The shadow ropes went taught, the ropes catching on leg and pincer, arm and horn, hand and neck. Quare flopped awkwardly as krakas landed upon them, crushing them under their bulk. Sipers tripped and went down, while skorpians were tossed onto their sides, pincers and spear tails stabbing and impaling. Shadow burst into a laugh at the thrashing horde of fiends, and to his surprise, Rynda joined.

"It appears your mischief has a purpose," she chuckled. "When it's pointed in the right direction."

A distant roar rumbled across the writhing mass of bound bodies, and Shadow spotted Bartoth standing atop a nearby log. His roar signaled another charge, this time by the second rank. Heedless of the damage, the second rank charged, carving their way through the first line as if their lives meant nothing.

Quare were torn apart as krakas used their heavy obsidian blades on their bodies, the shadow ropes snapping under the assault. Thousands were slain in minutes, and the second wave trod them underfoot.

282

"I get credit for those kills," Shadow said.

"Are you counting?" Elenyr asked.

"Of course," Shadow said. "How else will we know that I killed more than Queen Rynda?"

She smirked. "Let the best troll win."

She reached to her back and unstrapped a giant bow. The weapon was as tall as Shadow's entire body, the string as thick as his thumb. The arrows were odd, a mixture of wood, metal tips, and wind magic, the air swirling around the shafts. She notched the arrow and aimed at the charging horde.

The bow released, the arrow soaring farther than even an elven longbow. Then it splintered, the arrows separating in all directions, turning into a lethal volley that pummeled a pack of sipers. One embedded into a neck, bringing it down, others sank into flesh, but most soared right down their throats.

"A thousand to fifty," Shadow said. "You've got some ground to make up."

The horde plunged into the sea of pitfalls, falling into holes and tripping over hidden wires. Many were impaled by buried spikes. Treewalkers rose up and bashed the ranks of fiends before kraka swords cleaved their trunks apart. The charge slowed, but again the fiends continued to advance over their fallen brethren.

The fiends approached the outer wall, seemingly oblivious to their fallen dead. Quare screamed in pain, sipers fell into pits, and a pair of skorpians died in an explosion of stonesap, the fireball sending a plume of smoke across the charge. Then the skorpians formed a line and their tails snapped forward, sending black spears soaring through the air.

"Get to cover!" Queen Nelia's voice filled the city, and everyone ducked beneath the shelters they had built.

The black spears thudded into the aquaglass walls, the smooth blue momentarily cracking, the spears sinking deep. Others clattered across the battlements while many fell into the forces behind the wall. One man made the mistake of poking his head out to watch the barrage, and a spear took his life.

In his elemental form, Shadow leaned out over the battlements and watched the city wall push the spears out, the enchantments forcing the weapons back. They clattered to the ground and the crystalline blue became smooth once again.

"Archers ready!"

Again Queen Nelia's voice filled the city, and archers raised their weapons. Crossbowmen and ballistae behind the wall also took aim, the bolts pointed directly at the wall, and the charging fiends beyond.

The fiend charge flowed across the dead, shrieking and screaming, the sounds punctuated by the dull roar of krakas and the clacking of skorpian pincers. On all sides of the city the fiends closed the noose, sipers taking the lead, their scaly skin shimmering from black to red. A hundred feet closed to fifty, and Rynda raised her bow, bellowing an order.

The archers released their arrows, filling the first wave with a lethal volley. Sipers died by the thousands, falling to their knees and tumbling to a halt. Those that came behind snarled and charged the city walls, just as those behind the barrier fired. But they didn't fire over the wall. They fired *into* the wall.

Crossbow bolts and ballistae exploded from weapons. Where they touched the aquaglass wall, the enchantment opened small holes, allowing the bolts to pass through. From just feet away, the crossbowmen unleashed a devastating volley, the barbed shafts thudding into siper and quare flesh, sinking deep and bringing the charge to its knees.

A handful of krakas made it through and the armored soldiers swung their obsidian swords, bashing the aquaglass barrier. Cracks spread across the surface, but the magic healed quickly, the cracks turning smooth. The ballistae operators turned their weapons on the krakas, the large bolts bursting through the wall and striking them in their sides.

From above the wall, dwarves ignited fuses and dropped small barrels on the remainder. The barrels exploded, covering the remaining captains in fire. Rynda raised her splinter bow and fired, the arrows bursting apart and thudding into the next wave, which was already drawing close.

"I *love* this wall," Shadow breathed.

"It's enchantments are powerful," Rynda said, aiming with her bow and sending another splinter arrow into the leading ranks. Then she pointed to a section farther north. "But it has a cost."

Shadow followed her direction and saw where three krakas had survived the initial charge. All three pummeled the wall, spreading cracks across its surface. A skorpian bolt had further damaged the section before the captains were slain. The cracks had begun to repair, but the wall could not finish repairing before the next assault slammed into the barrier.

"If the wall shatters, we won't last long," Elenyr said, turning and heading to the stairs.

"Where are you going?" Shadow called.

"To make sure I win my bet," Elenyr said.

Shadow grinned and followed her down the stairs. Despite her banter, Shadow noticed the tension in her shoulders, and the crease to her forehead. Elenyr feared the worst, and although the battle had just been joined, both knew their chances were slim. Especially when the generals joined the fray.

They reached the north gates just as Light poked his head from above his war machine. "Done!"

"It's beautiful," Willow said.

"But will it work?" Shadow asked.

Shadow eyed the three circular blades placed on the outside of the machine. All three contained spikes that arced away, resembling the circular saws the dwarven iron mages favored. All three were attached to the top of the wagon by glowing chains, each link fashioned by Light.

285

King Dothlore and two engineers appeared from the other side of the wagon, checking the mechanisms made out of solid light. Dothlore grunted in approval and then stepped to Elenyr's side.

"Get to cover!"

The entire group retreated to the back of the wagon, where they remained underneath the shield Light had crafted to protect his machine. Shadow couldn't help but grin as the spears bounced off the shield.

"Are you really going to ride this out there?" he asked.

"Elenyr said we have to protect the wall," Light said. "And I'm going to join the cavalry charge."

He had to shout over the sound of thousands of crossbows and arrows being released, and the shrieks and cries of the dying fiends. More cracks appeared on the wall, most healing, but some remaining, the white lines a stark reminder that the city was not impervious.

Skorpian bolts thudded into the sphere protecting the castle, driving deep. The enchantments pushed them out and they fell to splash into the lake. Others thudded into the great mother tree, and the wood shuddered in pain.

"Time to go!" Light called.

Shadow grinned and turned to Elenyr. "Can I come?"

Elenyr reached for the mechanism and leapt to the top. "Could I stop you?"

Willow sighed, the sound implying she was regretting her life choices. "One day you are going to be the death of me."

Light grinned. "Not today."

Shadow climbed to the top and found a place where Light could sit and operate the three saws. "Don't worry, Willow. It's going to be fun."

"We're going to ride out into a giant horde of fiends bent on destroying our very existence, and you think it's going to be fun?"

Shadow's smile matched his brother's. "This is the very definition of fun."

Chapter 37: Light's War Machine

Light checked his machine and called out his gratitude to Dothlore. Normally he would never have used such a contraption, but Elenyr had convinced him that since his magic was weaker, perhaps he would enjoy crafting a war machine.

"This is actually rather clever," Shadow said.

"It was Elenyr's idea," Light replied.

Shadow looked daggers at Elenyr, who suddenly seemed very interested in the controls. Light was too busy to notice the exchange and hurried to explain the machine, but Shadow cut him off and stabbed a finger at the doors.

"I'll figure it out as we go, the cavalry is ready."

"Ready when you are, captain," Elenyr called.

"Are you sure about this?" Captain Horn asked, mounting a steed.

"We'll find out soon enough," Elenyr said.

The next wave slammed into the aquaglass wall. Thicker than the previous attacks, many made it through the withering volley of arrows and crossbow bolts. The fiends struck the glass and climbed on the bodies of the fallen, clawing at the material. The krakas slashed at the glass and spearmen stabbed through the wall, the weapons striking the fiend captains. One yanked the spear through and tried to stab the owner, but the enchantment only went one way, and the spear bounced off. The kraka growled in dismay and caught a ballistae bolt in the gut, knocking him backwards.

"Now!" Willow called, and the gates swung open.

Light's excitement mounted as the gates opened. The sudden breach in the wall was seen as an invitation, and the fiends rushed to the opening. Talinorian and elven cavalry charged the four entrances to the city, bursting into the open. With spears pointed down, the armored riders slammed into the fiends and turned right, all four groups sweeping around the exterior of the city.

Skorpian spears flew thick in the air but the riders on the outside of the charge raised their hands, calling on the wind to knock the spears from the air. Instead of falling among the riders, the lethal volley dropped in the next wave of fiends, killing their own and slowing the advance. Jumping the bodies of the dead, the cavalry arced around the city, their combined shout sending a cheer through the defenders.

Willow snapped the reins and the wagon lurched forward, falling into line behind the last of the cavalry from the north exit. Its wheels were spiked and made of light, allowing it to ride over the dead fiends on the outside of the city. The moment they were in the open, Light reached for the three levers, and yanked the center one.

His carver began to spin, the entire machine vibrating. The central carver leapt from the wagon and streaked away, spinning so fast the spikes became a blur of sharpened steel. It struck the leading edge of sipers and cut through, plunging into the dark horde. Fiends screamed and cried out, falling in both directions as the carver cut a lethal line deep through the rank.

The chain connecting the carver to the machine went taught, jolting the wagon. Then Light used the two other levers, one to move sideways, one to move up. The spinning carver reacted to the command and turned sideways.

Shadow crowed with delight as he sent his own carver spinning away and used his own levers to turn it one way or another, directing its angle of attack. The spinning blade cut through two krakas and then a skorpian before catching a knot of quare.

"This is worth twenty gold," Shadow called.

"What?" Light glanced to his brother, but he shook his head.

"Nothing."

"I knew you liked puzzles," Elenyr said, activating the third carver. "But this is brilliant."

Light grinned, pleased by her praise. "Like you said, I created my own puzzle."

When Mind, Fire, and Water had departed the previous night, Light had been worried, so Elenyr had suggested he create a puzzle to occupy him until morning. She'd even suggested he create a new type of war machine, a prospect he found appealing. And once he remembered the carver used by the Order of Ancients, the idea had fallen into place.

"Can you three focus!" Willow shouted. "We're drawing a lot of attention."

The fiends were turning away from the cavalry ahead of them and flooding in their direction. Light pulled his two levers, shifting the carver in one direction and then the other, and raising it to cut through the tails of several skorpians behind a rise of earth.

A large mass collected to their left and Willow turned them right, the wheels bouncing over the rough earth as they rotated to follow the curve of the city wall. Light leaned to the right, cringing as the wagon tilted. Shadow laughed and kept turning his carver, clearing the path ahead.

"Just keep going!" Light shouted.

"I plan to," Willow said grimly.

Light noticed her features were tight, her grey skin a shade darker. "Willow?" he called. "Are you well?"

"No!" she shot over her shoulder. She grimaced as the wolfsteeds carried them over a group of wounded quare, who were trampled beneath the hooves and wheels. "Do you have a plan when they catch us?"

"I hadn't thought of that." Light tapped his chin in thought.

"They're getting closer," Elenyr warned.

The fiends were jumping and charging past the spinning carvers, which leapt back and forth. Some were getting through. A siper fell into their wake, its powerful legs allowing it to leap a stump and a dead kraka. He closed the gap in a burst of speed and lunged, its jaws reaching for a wheel.

Elenyr turned ethereal and leaned out of the wagon. She drew her blade and sliced the beast across its face. It gave a wounded cry and fell to the ground, but Elenyr's carver had not moved for a few precious seconds, and the enemy took full advantage of the lapse. They charged around it and sprinted into the dust cloud kicked up by their wagon.

"Faster!" Shadow warned.

"I'm going as fast as I can," Willow snapped. "You want to drive?"

"Of course," he said. "I didn't know that was an option."

"It wasn't," Light said apologetically. "We both know what happens when you drive anything with wheels."

"I crash," Shadow said. "But it's so worth it."

"Can you keep them off us?" Willow called, her voice tense.

They bounced over dead fiends and ruts in the earth. Trees had been torn up, their giant logs forming a labyrinthine network of large holes, fallen trees, and giant roots. Willow yanked on the reins, turning them away from the city because the wagon wouldn't fit through a gap. The cavalry continued on, leaving Light's wagon more exposed.

"We need to get out of here!" Elenyr called.

Sipers turned on them as they circled the city, and Light swung his carver, slicing through the next rank of fiends. But thousands were filling their wake, with more coming. Several quare got past Light and leapt for the wolfsteeds, but such an assault was a mistake, as the wolf part of the horses snapped at the quare, their jaws clamping shut.

"I told you they were useful," Light called.

Shadow rolled his eyes but did not respond as the sipers converged on his side. They darted in, struggling to avoid the shrieking carver. Several got past and charged, leaping for Shadow's chair.

A splinter arrow exploded from several feet away, the smaller arrows pummeling the sipers, killing them so closely that one fell beneath the wheels. Light raised a hand and waved his gratitude to Rynda as they bounced over the siper body. Rynda made the symbol for Light in the air, making it clear the assist was for Light.

"I don't think she likes me," Shadow lamented.

"She doesn't," Elenyr said.

Elenyr relinquished control of the carver to Light, who turned in his seat to work both. Elenyr jumped to the back of the wagon and swung her sword, cutting a quare that had caught a grip on a section of the upper shield.

"Look out!" Willow cried.

Hundreds of skorpian spears streaked for their position, the black weapons bouncing off the upper shield, some narrowly missing the wolfsteeds. Light ducked as one came for his head. The sheer volume of spears caused the wagon to tip, and Shadow cast a thread into the haze. The shadow caught a stump of a tree, dropping them back to the ground.

"We're running out of time," Willow called.

"Especially now," Shadow said.

He pointed to the figure that had appeared in their path. The giant form swung his sword in lazy arcs, his armor seeming to absorb the light. Bartoth stepped into the only route the war machine could pass. Then he picked up a stray obsidian blade and hefted the weapon like it was a toy. Leaning forward, he hurled the heavy sword.

Willow yanked on the reins, attempting to swing them up a slope and into the open ground closer to the city walls. The kraka sword caught them on the corner of the war machine, slicing through the mechanism before coming to a stop next to Light's leg. It lodged in the controls of Elenyr's carver, severing the magical link. The spinning wheel at the end of the chain went wild, hurtling west before slamming through two kraka and thudding into a tree.

"Hang on!" Willow called.

"Time to get back in the city," Elenyr said, stabbing a finger at the eastern gates, which had just appeared around the turn. Tens of thousands of fiends had just crashed into the wall, and they died by bolt, arrow, and spear.

"Don't stop," Light said.

His own carver responded sluggishly, but he directed it into their path, the chain extending above the heads of the wolfsteeds and darting about. The war machine slammed into the flank of the fiend wave. Elenyr slashed at their unprotected side while Shadow spun his carver about, keeping them from climbing aboard. Despite their efforts, more and more caught the wagon and its wheels. They began to slow.

Arrows flew overhead, quare snapped and shrieked, sipers darted through the haze of smoke from stonesap explosions. Krakas appeared and disappeared, charging the wall. Skorpian spears streaked by, thudding into the glass walls of the city.

Light winced as he saw the breadth of the damage. Cracks spread across the city walls, some so dense the wall appeared white. They'd been fighting for less than an hour, and already the city walls looked like they were about to fall.

He glanced over his shoulder to Elenyr. "How are we—"

A wounded kraka burst from the haze and crashed into the side of the war machine. Already teetering on the top of a slope, the wagon rolled into a shallow ravine between fallen trees, shedding enchantments, gears, and splintered wood on its way to a bruising stop. Light caught a glimpse of a wolfsteed disintegrating, a large root protruding from its flank. He grunted in pain and dragged himself from beneath the broken wagon.

"Everyone alive?" Shadow groaned and pulled himself free.

Light shook the confusion from his thoughts and sought for Willow—and found her half buried in the dirt. Panicked, he scrambled

293

to her side and pulled her free. Blood seeped from a gash in her side, and a wound on her head looked ugly.

"Willow!" he cried.

Her eyes fluttered and focused on him. Then she grimaced and reached to her stomach. He tried to stop her, but she pulled the small hand crossbow from her flesh, the ink pooling in her hands. She raised it over her shoulder and fired.

A quare whined and collapsed adjacent to Light, the bolt through his mouth. Willow grimaced.

"You were always bad at watching your surroundings."

Elenyr appeared and slashed her sword, killing a siper that found them. She caught the reins of the remaining wolfsteed and slashed the bonds holding it to the wrecked wagon. Then she reached out and pulled Shadow to his feet.

"Shadow, help Willow get back to the city. Light, you need to follow them and make sure they make it. They're going to close the gates at any moment, so hurry."

Light helped Willow onto the steed, his worry bordering on panic. Willow slumped against him, and he had to lash her to the wolfsteed so she wouldn't fall. He'd never seen her so injured. Then Light noticed the urgency in Elenyr's voice and followed her gaze.

A cloaked figure advanced from the haze, his eyes burning red beneath the cowl. A splinter arrow exploded just feet from his body and he swung the scythe, absently slashing through the missiles.

"Go," Elenyr said. "I'll meet you in the city."

"Are you sure?" Light asked, casting an uncertain glance at Willow.

"Stay with Willow," Elenyr said, stepping between them and Death.

"I'm not leaving you," he said.

"Yes we are," Shadow said. "This isn't a duel we are part of."

The normally amusing Shadow had a serious expression, and Light realized he was right. Reluctantly, he slapped the side of the wolfsteed and then leapt into a sprint, rushing to keep up with his brother and Willow. He cast a look over his shoulder, and watched Elenyr draw her sword as she prepared to face the mightiest assassin on Lumineia.

Chapter 38: Allies

As Light raced away with the heavily laden wolfsteed, Elenyr circled Gendor, looking for an opening. But the assassin came to a halt. The sounds of battle cascaded over them, yet the fiends did not seem inclined to attack Elenyr, and flowed around the gully containing the two combatants. Elenyr flicked her sword out and bared her teeth.

"What are you waiting for?"

Gendor was turned toward her, and seemed to be looking at Ilumidora. She frowned, disliking his lack of attention. What was he looking at? She began to circle him but he rotated in place, never meeting her gaze.

"You cannot win this battle," Gendor said.

"I know," Elenyr replied, frowning at his posture. "But we have a plan to succeed."

She glanced skyward. Three hours until noonday. Three hours to locate the four generals, and kill them at the precise moment the Dark Gate was destroyed. But the walls of Ilumidora were already cracking. The cavalry charge had given the walls time to heal, but not enough. The next wave crashed on the city walls like a wave on a boulder, each blow sending more cracks spreading across its surface.

"Will you be triumphant?" Gendor asked.

"I do not know." She came to a halt and regarded him. He still would not meet her gaze.

"Would you trust me?" the assassin asked.

"Why would I do that?" Elenyr asked.

"Because it's the only way you can win."

"I bet on my sons," she replied.

She began to advance on the assassin but his hand shot up, barring the way. His pulsing scythe hung behind him, low and ready. She came to a halt, and then recognized the reluctance to his frame.

"You are choosing not to fight," she guessed.

"I'm choosing not to look," he replied. "I must obey Draeken's commands, and he ordered me to kill you—and anything that stands between us. I must strike the moment I *see* you."

Elenyr realized the man's clever interpretation of the order. He had to strike and kill Elenyr, but only when he saw her. Until he did, his will remained his own. But if his focus lapsed for even a moment, if he so much as glanced in her direction, he would turn against her.

"What do you want?" Elenyr asked, a skorpian spear passing through her ethereal body.

"I know you cannot heal me," he said. "And I have accepted my fate. This is my penance for my life of blood. My one chance at redemption is to destroy Draeken from within. We were once foes, but if you will allow it, I would be your ally."

Elenyr recognized the weight behind the question. Gendor could have simply attacked the fiends, or even the other generals, but he'd come to Elenyr. The man was smart enough to recognize that killing fiends was not the purpose of the battle, and if he wanted to offer aid, he could only do so if he understood Elenyr's plan.

But to share the truth with Gendor represented a massive risk. If Draeken asked, he would be forced to respond, and their slim chance at victory would crumble. And there was the chance he would look at her, and then go for the kill.

"We must endure until noon," she admitted.

"You will not," he said simply, and pointed to the nearest wall.

The aquaglass cracks had spread between the tree towers, and from the base all the way to the top. Fiends hacked at the barrier, bits of magic flying in all directions. Even beneath the blistering fire from ten

297

thousand archers and crossbowmen, they pushed through and struck the barrier. The cavalry swept by in another charge, clearing the ground once more, but many riders were torn from their saddles by the next wave of fiends.

"When the time comes," she said, "I will ask for your aid."

"I cannot help you if your walls crumble," Gendor said. "Your forces are too small."

"Not all of our army has arrived," she replied.

Over the din of battle and the screams of the dying, one sound gradually rose, the sound of an enormous object charging across the ground. Both Gendor and Elenyr turned as a giant form burst over a western hill and plowed into the back of the fiends. So dense were their bodies that for a moment the fifty foot Titan disappeared from view. Then it swung its sword, the blade cleaving through the ranks of fiends and sending them flying.

"The Titan from the Assassin hall?" Death sucked in his breath. "You got it working?"

"That would be the fragment of Mind," Elenyr said.

A distant roar pierced the battle din. Deep and throaty, the roar signaled a challenge, and many of the fiends slowed. Defender and attacker turned their eyes to the sky, where from a cloud descended a large golden dragon. Two figures sat on its back, and the sight of them drew a smile to Elenyr's lips.

The great golden dragon roared its challenge, and another dragon dropped from the clouds at his side. And then another. And another. Dragons abruptly filled the sky, all dropping from the clouds and landing on the ground outside of the city, their maws opening and spilling fire and frost into the ranks of fiends. Lightning exploded from the throat of a blue, while acid came from a black dragon. Thousands of dragons, all come to join the war against Draeken.

"*Now* our forces have arrived," Elenyr said.

"Draeken may have the might," Death said, his tone tinged with praise, "but you have the cunning to win. I will be your ally when you say the word."

He retreated back into the ranks of fiends, still keeping his gaze averted. Then he was gone. Elenyr turned and sped toward the Titan, relishing the cheer swelling up from the defenders. Thousands of dragons had come, their combined breath filling the battlefield with lethal elements, scorching the broken trees and earth. Elenyr phased to flesh and back, slashing across fiends as she sprinted for the Titan. For the first time, she dared to hope.

***

Deep in the thrall of the magic, the fragment of Mind did not control the Titan, he *became* the war machine. He stood fifty feet tall, his head even with the battlements of Ilumidora. A hundred men could not have lifted his blade, but he swung it with ease, slashing across the ranks of fiends as he raced for the fortress.

He felt more powerful than he ever had, even as Draeken. The sheer power in the Titan's flesh made him invincible, and he savored the swing of the sword, the strength of his legs as he kicked a skorpian. The beast flipped end over end, flailing before it crushed a pair of quare leaping over a streambed.

He roared his challenge, the voice carrying the joined timbre of three speaking as one. Merged as he was with the girl and her father, Mind could feel their excitement and fear. Fiends clawed at their legs and scaled their back, digging their claws into the ancient flesh, but Mind dove to the ground and rolled, crushing hundreds before he regained his feet.

He charged through the ranks, avoiding the dragons. Skorpian bolts soared in his direction, plunging into his body or bouncing off his armor. A kraka swung at his leg but Mind stepped on him like he was an insect, and then Mind dragged his sword through the fiends charging his flank.

He picked up a tree in his free hand and used the entire tree like a club, bashing fiends on all sides. Mind had trained for combat for thousands of years, and used both weapons to the pinnacle of his skill, slashing and striking, moving with such agility and speed that fiends could hardly touch him.

He hurled fallen trees, leveled thousands with a sweep of his sword, and shattered an entire charge. A boulder from a catapult fell nearby and he picked it up and sent it hurtling into a collection of skorpians, the great stone crushing hundreds before it finally came to a stop.

He felt the kinship with Stella and her father, their unity empowering the Titan to greater efforts. The host of fiends were like insects scratching and biting his skin, but his might would not be constrained.

He expected one of the generals to appear, but the minutes stretched into an hour. Wherever the fighting was thickest, he fortified the defenders. He saved dragons and city walls, and held the horde at bay. Several times he spotted the generals, and once Bartoth came in his direction. Each time he glanced to the sky, and knew it was not yet time. He kept his distance from Plague and Famine, and never saw Death. In his great black armor, War seemed content to watch the Titan, and Mind made no move to engage. Between the Titan, the dragons, and the alliance, they stood against the endless horde and refused to yield.

Twice he spotted Draeken flying above his fiend army. He did not engage on his own, and Mind was grateful. For now, it seemed Draeken wanted to wait until the walls were destroyed before risking his generals. But as the second hour passed it seemed Draeken grew impatient, and Bartoth appeared in his path.

Unhurried, Bartoth advanced across the ground. At twelve feet tall he'd always seemed enormous, but not this time. Now he seemed small and insignificant. He spun his sword in lazy circles.

"You want me?" he called. "Come and get me."

Mind charged, sprinting through the ranks of fiends and tossing them aside. Others were trampled beneath his boots. Bartoth did not deviate, he accelerated his sword until it began to whine.

Mind closed the gap in a rush and swung his sword like a woodsman chopping a tree. Bartoth jumped and flipped over the blade.

Landing on his feet, he darted in and slashed once, cutting deep into the Titan's knee.

Mind sucked in his breath. Connected as he was to the Titan's magic, he could feel the pain in his own knee. He spun and lashed out, and this time his sword struck Bartoth on his side. The general blasted through a group of quare, bouncing and tumbling until he slammed into a boulder. He fell to his knees and Mind raised his hand, motioning an invitation. Bartoth rose to his feet with a snarl and charged, closing the gap in a rush.

Mind swung his sword again, but Bartoth swung his own blade, knocking the giant weapon upward. Mind leaned down and struck the ground, but Bartoth dodged and swung, slicing deep across Mind's hand.

For several furious seconds they dueled, their conflict spilling into nearby fiends. Mind possessed the greater strength, but Bartoth's magic gave him agility and speed, both elements that the Titan could not match. But what the war machine lacked in speed, it made up for in brute strength.

Mind leaned down and punched the ground, the earth bursting in all directions. Fiends were knocked into the air, a pair of logs were thrown thirty feet, where they collided with a trio of krakas. Even War was tossed onto his back, and Mind raised his sword. He brought it down and drove it into the ground, just missing the general as the troll rolled to the side.

Bartoth jumped to Mind's arm and scrambled up his elbow. Mind released his sword and swatted at the rock troll. Bartoth ducked and jumped, and managed to catch the ridge of armor at Mind's throat. With his weapon in hand, he plunged the heavy blade into the Titan's shoulder, driving the sword all the way to where Mind and his friends were locked in a meld.

Mind instinctively ducked as the sword entered their chamber, narrowly missing his ear. Still deep in the Titan's magic, the war machine also ducked, and Bartoth yanked his sword free. With a savage burst of strength, the rock troll swung. The sweeping attack came from under the war machine's shoulder, and cut deep into Moren's leg.

All three cried out, the pain transferring. The Titan stumbled and fell to its knees. Bartoth leapt away and landed nearby. Mind released the meld and reached for Moren. Like a doll dropped by a child, the Titan fell forward, landing on a contingent of krakas and rolling down a slope into a shallow recess. Mind yanked a section of cloth from his shoulder and tied it around the gushing wound.

"He needs a healer in Ilumidora," he said.

"We're five hundred feet from the wall," Stella said, her voice worried.

"Hit the rune," he said.

"Mind!" Bartoth called. "I must say I'm impressed."

"When he's distracted," Mind said, "get your father to the city."

"I'm not abandoning you." Her jaw tightened.

"You're not leaving me," he said. "You're saving your father."

Moren's eyes fluttered and the cloth Mind used to wrap around his leg was already dark with blood. Stella grimaced at the choice but nodded, so Mind opened the hatch and climbed out. The Titan had rolled down the slope onto its back, and Bartoth stood on the giant statue's stomach, his armor bent but not broken. Mind stepped into view and noticed the ring of fiends.

"A valiant effort," Bartoth said. "But not even a Titan can stop me."

"That's why I brought someone else," he said.

Behind him, Stella slammed her hand onto the rune he had placed, and a crackle of energy appeared above the Titan, the threads brightening as an arch drew power from the flesh of the Titan to create the Gate. Bartoth charged, but the Gate shimmered to life, and two figures stepped into Lumineia.

Tardoq and the Bonebreaker.

Chapter 39: Breached

Shadow spun and cut his sword through two quare that had climbed the wall, darting between them to strike at another just appearing over the battlements. Above him, Lorica dove in front of the wall and slashed her sword across several climbers before banking away from a skorpian bolt.

The battlefield lay in ruins. Dragons roared and breathed their deadly breath. Fiends stampeded in every direction. Cavalry raced about, their ranks in shambles as they fought scattered fiends that made it past the dragons. One aquaglass wall was on the verge of crumbling, the blue material so damaged that crossbow bolts could no longer pass through. Drawn to the weakness, the fiends rushed the spot, led by Famine.

Shadow spotted Famine and shouted to Lorica. The assassin folded her wings and dropped to his side, both sprinting to intercept the general. As they did, Shadow began to feel the hunger, forcing him to turn into shadow form.

All around, soldiers of every race began to wilt. They cried out and grasped their stomachs, their food stores molding before their eyes. Shadow shouted for Light and his brother darted to his side.

"I'm hungry," he said.

"I know," Shadow said. "Famine is attacking the wall. Are you ready?"

"I think so."

His brother grimaced and then turned to his elemental form. Shadow and Light raced together, one a body of smoke, the other a body of light. Shadow grinned and accelerated, motioning Lorica away.

"You know what to do!"

"I didn't forget," Lorica called.

Obviously grateful to leave, she leapt into the sky and banked away, flying for Dothlore, the dwarven king. Someone recognized Famine and began shouting orders, calling for a retreat from the breaking wall. The elven mages, lathered in sweat from their efforts to hold the wall, stumbled back, and in seconds the krakas on the other side shattered the glass.

The wall cracked from the battlements to the foundation, water pouring from the crack and flooding inward, washing away crates and weapon stands. A pair of elves were caught in the flood and carried forty feet.

"Retreat!" Captain Horn bellowed, and the entire group raced away from the wall.

Shadow and Light reached the breach as the others departed. Shadow gave Captain Horn a mock salute, and noticed the female elf fighting at his side. Was that Princess Serania? The captain clenched his stomach with his free hand.

"I hope you know what you're doing," he called.

"We do," Shadow said.

Horn nodded and then barked an order before retreating with the rest of his forces. Alone, Shadow and Light stood in the center of the breach as the remainder of the wall section cracked again—and then shattered. The entire wall collapsed, flooding in both directions. One ballista was crushed as another crate fell from the battlements above. Krakas appeared and hacked at the wall, expanding the breach, but one figure stood in their midst.

Famine.

"Shadow and Light," she sneered. "I did hope I would get to kill you."

"I know," Shadow said. "But sadly, you won't get the chance."

"Greetings, Lady Dentis!" Light waved, and then squinted. "It's still you in there, right?"

Famine pointed to them and clenched her fist, and Shadow grimaced as his hunger spiked. Even in shadow form, the woman's power was tremendous. The woman began to advance, and by unspoken accord Light and Shadow retreated, stumbling backwards from the powerful general.

"You think your brotherhood can stop us?" Famine asked, her voice rising. "That you can survive what Draeken and Serak have built?"

Light tripped and Shadow caught his arm, dragging him down the street. "Did Draeken tell you he was going to make you ugly?" he taunted. "Or was that just a surprise?"

The woman's eyes flared with anger and she pointed to them. Light groaned, and Shadow pulled him harder, down the street and away from the breach. Soldiers circled behind Famine and filled the gap, rushing to erect temporary fortifications. She didn't spare them a look, and continued to advance on Shadow and Light.

"I am more powerful than you can imagine," she said. "And everything strong in you was taken when Draeken came into being."

At the perimeter of Famine's power, Queen Rynda raised her bow and fired, the arrow splintering apart, the splinter arrows arcing for Famine. The woman picked up a shield and held it aloft, catching the bolts before pointing to Rynda. She clenched a fist, and the powerful rock troll queen collapsed, gasping for breath.

"When I'm done with you," she said, turning back to Shadow and Light. "I'm going to watch your entire alliance wither and die."

Light was slowing, so Shadow pulled his brother into an overgrown yard. Kicking the door into an abandoned home, he shoved Light into the interior and hurried him towards the back exit. Famine ascended the steps, the wood beginning to rot beneath her feet.

"You think to escape?" she called. "There is nowhere for you to go."

Shadow leaned against the wall, gasping for breath. Light whimpered at his side, holding his stomach. Famine advanced across the space and raised her hands, a smile spreading on her sunken features.

"When I touch you, every bit of flesh in your bodies will die, and your magic will have nothing left. Two of the five fragments will be dead, and Mimic will deal with the others."

Shadow managed a smile and raised his voice. "Lorica?"

From outside the house—Elenyr's house, to be exact—Lorica and Dothlore pulled a lever the dwarves had installed. The floor dropped out from under Famine, and she fell into the ascender shaft.

She screamed as she fell, and the farther she went, the better Shadow felt. He rose to his feet and pulled Light to his. Light smiled weakly, and the pair stepped to the edge. Shadow peered into the dark abyss. Lorica reached the doorway and breathed a sigh of relief.

"You cut it a little close," Shadow said.

"I almost died just being that close to her," Lorica said.

"Do you think she survived the fall?" Light asked.

"Of course," Shadow said, and then listened for the distant snarls. "But I left a few hundred shadow creatures for her to play with. I doubt she'll make it out before noon."

Light chuckled. "I love your plans. They are always so devious."

Shadow clapped him on the back. "And Mind said our plan would never work."

"He said it was dangerous," Lorica corrected him. "Not that it would never work."

Snarls erupted from the dark shaft, followed by a shout of anger, sweet sounds of a foe being assaulted by a wealth of shadow creatures. Satisfied that the Raven would be occupied for a while, Shadow caught his brother's arm and jerked a thumb back to the city.

"We still have three more generals to deal with."

"Make that two," Elenyr said, entering through the wall.

She turned corporeal and leaned against the wall. Blood stained her clothing from a host of wounds but her features were fixed and

306

determined. She peered down into the dark shaft and nodded in satisfaction.

"Gendor is temporarily on our side," she said.

"No," Lorica scowled and jerked her head. "You cannot trust him."

"For now, we can," she said. "And we need all the help we can get."

"Are you certain?" Shadow asked.

"As much as I can be," she said. "We just need to find Mimic. Last I saw, Mind was in the Titan fighting Bartoth."

I could use some help out here. Mind's words entered Shadow's consciousness, rushed and annoyed. He gave an image of his current situation, of Tardoq and the Bonebreaker in a frenzied duel with Bartoth, and Mind half carrying Moren toward the city gates. He managed to force a riderless horse to him and loaded the wounded mind mage into the saddle before helping the girl up as well.

"Looks like Mind has a girlfriend," Shadow crowed.

"Shadow," Elenyr warned. "Can we please focus?"

"I am focused," Shadow said as they raced out of the house and back towards the conflict. "I'm focused on his girlfriend."

Light began to laugh. "Shadow's not wrong."

"I'll meet you there," Elenyr said. "There's one thing I need to do first."

She leapt away in another direction, while Shadow, Light, and Lorica sprinted toward Mind. A dragon rose over the wall and roared. As he sought to fly, a kraka on his back plunged his sword into the beast's spine. It crumpled, another dragon pouncing and engulfing the killer in dragon fire.

Arrows, catapult stones, and skorpian bolts filled the haze of smoke. Fiends shrieked and snarled as men shouted, the clang of swords and cracking glass a sharp counterpoint to the meaty thud of large

307

bodies. Nowhere was the fighting more fierce than at the breach, where fiends and alliance fought for dominance. Shadow then looked skyward and spotted Water astride the great golden beast, and wondered why he was the one that got to ride a dragon . . .

Chapter 40: Defiance

Astride his dragon, Water surveyed the battlefield. The arrival of the dragons and Mind's Titan had thrown everything into chaos, and the fiend charge had stalled. Aside from the one breach in the Ilumidora city walls, there had been no more breaks. Some of the walls were even repairing.

His dragon, Kinselithen, spoke into Water's thoughts. *I'm sending the reds to strike the north ranks of skorpians.*

"A wise tactic."

Water watched a dozen red dragons rise into the air before descending toward a group of thousands of skorpians. Sweeping above the giant creatures, the dragons rained dragonfire upon the fiends. Skorpians deeper in the fiend army retaliated, and the bolts darkened the air. The attack forced the dragons upward, but one was not so lucky, and a host of black spears pierced his scales. He landed hard, and fought with teeth and claws against the horde of fiends that swarmed his body.

I do not see Gorewrathian, Kinselithen rumbled, the anger evident in his voice. *You promised me a chance to slay the coward king.*

"He should be here," Water said.

Do not make me regret my choice to join your war, the dragon growled.

"You joined us because it was the only smart choice," Water said. "We both know that after Draeken finished with us, he would come for you. Our only chance was to fight together. And do not forget that your father was already killed because of this war."

The throne is mine by right, Kinselithen said, his voice as hot as his fire.

"And if we survive, you have the oath of the Hauntress and the oracle that you will regain what belongs to you."

We are allies of circumstance, the dragon replied. *When the circumstance changes . . .*

The implication was clear, but Water had known the danger when he'd agreed to speak to the dragons. Elenyr had wisely seen them as allies, if they could be convinced of the threat. It turned out that Draeken had done what no other in history had accomplished, and taught the dragons to fear. And that was why they had come, not because they wanted to conquer, but because they wanted to retain their freedom.

"Then let's make sure we win," Water replied.

Flames kindled in the dragon's throat as he dropped from the sky, unleashing his breath on a charge of krakas. Water poured his own magic into the fight, deflecting skorpian bolts and striking at fiends attacking the dragon's flanks.

He coughed in the smoke and haze that covered the battlefield, cringing when the shatter of glass indicated another section of wall had fallen. At the breaches, the fighting was the most intense, with blood spilled on both sides. But the fiends had blood to spare and gradually pushed their way into the city. Talinorian cavalry rushed into the breach, charging into the field of dead outside the wall before retreating.

The orb around the castle was cracked and broken, the abundance of black spears protruding from its surface. Fire had broken out inside, the flames licking at the limbs of Urindilial. Elves fought to extinguish the flames and save the castle, but Queen Alosia sent them to the defenses, abandoning the castle to its fate.

A skorpian bolt grazed Water's side and he grimaced before raising a wave of water from a nearby stream, forcing the fiends into a funnel. His mount unleashed his fire, burning the focal point to a deadly inferno.

Elenyr appeared below. As the Hauntress, she passed through fiend and friend, turning to flesh just long enough to slice deep. Where the fighting was fiercest she burst from the earth, her blows so strong that even krakas died in fear. Many sought to kill her, their claws reaching for her body, but she leapt and twisted, avoiding attacks and somehow avoiding the bulk of the damage.

Water caught glimpses of Mind, Tardoq, and the Bonebreaker battling with War but could not offer aid. He and Kinselithen led the dragon charge, dropping into the thickest knots of fighting, and then flying into the air to search for more. Each conflict left them bloodied, but the city survived for a little longer.

He cast his gaze to the sky. Hours had passed, and the city looked on the verge of collapse. A third of the walls were destroyed, the people retreating into the upper boughs of the city. Could they last another hour? And where was Mimic? The thoughts were fleeting, his attention focused on survival and his brothers.

***

Tardoq flanked Bartoth and lunged, driving the heavy sword for the rock troll's back. With impossible reflexes, the armored behemoth whirled and deflected the blade before spinning back and striking at Belrisa.

The woman danced out of reach and then charged. She swung her hammer upward and then flipped it over, the shaft striking Bartoth in the chin. The blow rocked his head backwards, and would have killed a human. But the troll recovered and swung his sword, cutting a chip from the bone on her thigh.

"Who are you?" he demanded.

"One who breaks bones," she said.

She feinted, and took advantage of Tardoq's swing, which forced the general up a slope. He bared a savage smile as she reversed her motion and stepped on a fallen log, leaping high. Her hammer came down on Bartoth's arm, the weapon striking so hard that even nearby fiends flinched. Bartoth bellowed in pain, the arm twisted at an awkward angle, obviously broken.

"You'll pay for that," Bartoth hissed.

"How many more bones can I break?"

311

Tardoq grinned and leapt at the rock troll's unprotected flank. He swung his sword in an overhand blow, but even wounded, War managed to deflect the attack. Then Tardoq lightened the weapon, allowing him to spin at impossible speed. At the last moment, he raised the weight again, driving the sword into War's waist. The armor split, and the sword cut into flesh. Bartoth snarled and kicked Tardoq in the chest, forcing him back.

Bartoth raised his good hand and clenched a fist, and fiends charged their position. Belrisa withdrew pulsing orbs and tossed them in a ring around them. The orbs detonated in plumes of fire, earth, and broken bodies. Other fiends rushed into the breach, but the orbs pulsed again, the explosions turning into fountains of fire.

"You are alone," Tardoq said, ignoring the sting from his own wounds. "And your fiends cannot help you."

"You think you are great warriors?" Bartoth snarled. "Victory of two against one is no victory, it is cowardice. If you are truly great, fight me alone, and prove your might."

Belrisa laughed and darted in, driving Bartoth towards the fallen Titan. "My proof is victory."

Tardoq attacked the other flank, lightening the sword and allowing him to unleash a blistering volley of blows. Bartoth growled as he fought to keep him at bay, but with one arm broken he could not withstand the assault. Belrisa attacked the opposite side, and together, the two dakorians battered the general of War.

Tardoq grimaced as a wave of weakness washed over him, and noticed a matching look on Belrisa. She fought through the attack, but the weakness mounted. Tardoq spun, and then spotted a figure striding into one of the gaps between the pulsing explosions.

Plague.

Tardoq's perfect body could not suffer disease, but Mimic's power was no normal illness. She advanced, her hands outstretched towards Belrisa and Tardoq. He sucked in his breath, willing himself to stand even as spots appeared in his vision.

"You think yourself so perfect," Mimic said mildly. "But your body is still made of flesh, and all flesh can wither."

Nearby fiends groaned and collapsed, but Tardoq and Belrisa kept their feet. The weakness was strong but not overpowering, and Tardoq focused on breathing. He turned away from Bartoth to face Plague.

"You were right about magic," Belrisa said, her voice strained. "It is more powerful than I thought."

Bartoth tried to attack Belrisa when she was distracted, but she ducked and spun, and used her hammer on War's knee. He cried out when his knee buckled, and Tardoq bared a savage smile. He spun his sword and advanced on Plague. The woman reached a hand outward, and yellow liquid flowed from within her flesh. Shimmering green and black, it shaped into curved blades that extended from her fingernails.

He swung his sword, carving a deep line across her chest. She did not flinch or retreat, and the mottled flesh began to reknit. She swung her arm, the tip of the poisoned nails grazing his waist as he retreated.

The cuts were hardly a scratch, but they quickly turned red and infected. A fever spread through his body. He had not felt physical weakness since becoming a Bloodwall, and he stumbled back, snarling at his foe.

"Weapons do not harm one like me," she said, stalking forward. "And there is nothing you can do to stop me."

She slashed again, the attack almost lazy. Normally he would have evaded with ease, but in his weakened state he only managed to prevent the worst of the damage. His fever mounted, and it was all he could do to keep his stomach from ejecting its contents. He shivered and retreated, his vision cloudy, his body spiking aches from within his organs.

"You're going to die here," Mimic said softly. "Alone and far from home."

"I'm not alone," he said as he caught a glimpse of a swirl of green smoke rising at his side . . .

***

313

Elenyr burst from the ground and turned to flesh long enough to slash her sword across Mimic's body. The impact drove her back, forcing her away from Tardoq. It also exposed her to Plague's magic. She grimaced and returned to ethereal.

Flickering to flesh and back, she attacked Mimic with a flurry of blows. Each time she turned corporeal she felt the sting of the disease magic, but Elenyr succeeded in pushing her back to the edge of the clearing, granting Tardoq space. As she did, Light, Willow and Shadow leapt over the fallen Titan and charged, sending bursts of magic at Mimic.

She growled as beams of light plunged into her body, followed by a knife hurled by Water. Shadow then conjured a bow that looked remarkably like Rynda's splinter bow, the haze and smoke granting him enough power to craft the weapon. He fired, the splinters parting and then plunging into Mimic's body like a thousand needles. Willow pulled a whip from her waist and attached the ink from a dagger. She snapped it, slicing deep across Plague's forearm. Mind appeared last and joined Elenyr, the two striking on both sides.

Pride filled Elenyr's chest as she fought beside her sons. They fought together, battering Plague and driving her back. Even her vaunted magic could not stand against the bond of brotherhood. But before they could press the assault, the ring of explosive geysers died, the flames extinguishing and crumbling. In the ensuing haze and smoke, Elenyr braced for a new fiend charge, but only one figure appeared.

Draeken.

The fragment of Power advanced into the group, and Elenyr called an order. Her sons retreated, joining Belrisa and Tardoq against the Titan's side. War and Plague stumbled to Draeken's flanks.

Fiends appeared and formed a new circle, krakas at the front. A hundred soldiers deep, their obsidian swords held high, they stood ready to descend upon Elenyr and her family. Gendor glided at Draeken's side, his scythe low, his burning eyes glowing. Elenyr retreated from the wounded Mimic and Mind followed, the two retreating to join the others.

Draeken chuckled as he advanced. "You think your defiance is honorable?" He swept a hand to the city, where fiends flooded through several breaches. The allied races had retreated to the upper boughs, and shouts came for a retreat. Thousands fled into the fortress, but the mother tree was on fire, and a deep keening came from the other trees.

"You could end this," Elenyr said. "You know you could."

"I could," Draeken held her gaze. "But why would I? I stand on the verge of victory, and the world will be reshaped into my realm. Magic—and all it possesses—will belong to me."

"It's not yours yet," Mind said, advancing to stand behind Elenyr.

Elenyr snorted at Mind's brash statement. Shadow actually laughed, as did Belrisa. Draeken merely stared at Mind like he'd gone mad. Disbelief washed across his features and then hardened to anger.

"Do you not understand?" Draeken spit the words at them. "You cannot stop me! You cannot kill me! You cannot defeat me! All of you live at my will, and if I desire, I could slay you all!"

He raised his hands and hundreds of spears appeared. Some rose in lengths of fire, others in light, all hovered around Elenyr, her sons, and the dakorians. Too many to evade. Too many to block.

"When will you kneel?" Draeken demanded. "How many must I kill before you accept my rule?"

Elenyr looked skyward, and saw the sun nearing its zenith. Just a few minutes until midday, and they were out of time. She hoped Fire was ready. She shifted her feet and subtly drifted to the side. Then she sent a mental order to Mind.

"Last chance," Elenyr said.

Draeken burst into a laugh and swept his hand at Elenyr's collection of allies. "You have nothing that can harm me. I will crush you, and then your alliance will shatter."

"Then I'm sorry," Elenyr said, and then raised her voice. "Death? It's time for you to look at me."

315

Draeken blinked in confusion and turned to the assassin, but Death was already turning his head. He met Elenyr's gaze—and leapt into a charge. He crossed the space in a burst of speed, rushing to Elenyr. But one individual stood in his path.

Plague.

"No!" Draeken roared, but the order came too late.

The scythe swung through Mimic's body, slicing from spine to ribs. Her magic had withstood steel and shard, arrow and lance, but Death's blade was unique, and it killed even a disease. Without uttering a sound, Plague crumpled to her knees, her body turning to dust.

"What have you done!" Draeken shrieked.

He stared in horror at the pile of dust, even as Gendor closed the gap to Elenyr. She turned ethereal and leapt backward—passing through the fragment of Mind, who raised his sword. His sword passed through her stomach and pierced Gendor's chest.

Death fell to his knees, his scythe falling from his fingers, his cloak falling into the dirt, his cowl falling back to reveal Gendor's stark white features and burning red eyes. Gasping for breath, he looked up to Elenyr, his fingers disintegrating to dust.

"Thank you," he breathed.

Death faded to dust and the wind brushed him aside like a broom. The shocking kills left everyone speechless. Mind stepped free of Elenyr and she nodded her gratitude. Draeken stared at the spot of their demise.

Draeken groaned and fell to one knee, the weight of the fiend army falling upon him. He passed a hand over his face, his fingers trembling in rage. Even with many of the fiends disappearing, Draeken still struggled to carry the load.

"This place is more exciting than you described," Belrisa said to Tardoq, who chuckled.

"You have no idea."

Draeken clenched a fist and rose to his feet before turning to Elenyr. "That was a mistake, one for which you will be punished." His eyes glowing with hatred as he advanced.

Chapter 41: Plummet

"Are you sure about this?" Lachonus asked uneasily.

Fire peered over the dragon's side, a smile spreading on his features. "Doesn't it sound like fun?"

"No," Lachonus said.

I have to agree with him, Isray said, flapping his wings to maintain a hover. *This plan is madness.*

"Mine usually are," Fire said.

"It's the only one we have," Senia said, her breathing labored.

They had flown above the clouds, rising to such a height that the air was thin and all four struggled to breath. Fire carefully extricated himself from spikes on the dragon's spine and leaned over his wing. Lachonus did the same.

"If we survive this," Lachonus said. "I don't ever want to follow another of your plans."

"If we survive, I won't either," Fire said.

They stood side by side, and Fire checked the pack he'd fastened onto Lachonus's back. Bound with leather straps, the pack resembled a long cylinder, with rigid handles that extended forward, so Lachonus could hold them for stability.

"You ready?" Fire asked.

He laughed nervously. "Can anyone be ready to jump off a perfectly good dragon from several thousand feet in the air?"

Fire glanced to the sky. "We're out of time. Let's do this."

"Nothing good ever comes from saying that," Senia said.

"See you at the bottom," Fire said with a grin.

"If we aren't flattened into oblivion by the impact." Lachonus eyed the drop and shuddered.

"Trust me," Fire said, and jumped. "It will work!"

Lachonus drew in a breath, looked to Senia, and then jumped. Fire turned his head downward and squinted through the blasting wind. He fell freely, quickly accelerating as he plummeted through the clouds.

"She was right!" Lachonus shouted as he fell. "This is madness!"

The fear in his voice matched the thudding in Fire's chest, and Fire realized that for the first time he was afraid. Water had been right, and with his reduced magic, this attempt was as likely to get them killed as get them inside the fortress of Xshaltheria.

He closed his eyes and fought the tremble in his fingers. He was weak, not broken, and despite the separation, his magic would keep him alive. Or he would be dead. He gathered his courage and fought the burgeoning panic.

They breached the clouds and Fire lost all sense of direction, except down, because he could feel the earth reaching for his body, like it wanted to drag him to a crushing demise. The clouds passed in a blur and the wind whipped at Fire's cloak, the material snapping above his head before abruptly ripping free. Lachonus flailed nearby, struggling to keep his feet pointed downward. The clouds came to an end and the pair burst into the open.

Directly beneath them, Xshaltheria approached at shocking speed. Their tiny forms were quickly noticed by Gorewrathian, which sat on the lip of the volcano. He released a below of warning and leapt into the air, fire kindling in his throat.

"It's going to be close!" Fire shouted.

He extended his hands but the motion caused him to spin. He used bursts of fire from his fingers to help stabilize his fall. The surface of the fortress approached and he sucked in a breath, cringing at the approaching impact. Then he brought his arms into his chest just as they streaked past the battlements—and plunged into the central vent.

Fire pointed downward and released a blast of fire from his hands. Above him, the pack he'd crafted for Lachonus did the same, the flames exploding downward and filling the vent that passed from the top of the fortress to the base.

Fire strained to push the fire downward, the superheated current of flames slowing their descent. The fortress was tall, but arresting their plummet required all his strength, and they gradually began to slow.

"Brace yourself!" he bellowed.

He shoved every ounce of fire he possessed down the vent. They passed through the opening at the base of the column and entered the great chamber at the base of the citadel. They fell the last hundred feet through the flames Fire had conjured and slammed into the ground, waves of fire exploding outward.

The impact drove Fire to his knees, the explosion scattering fiends like leaves caught in a cyclone. They were tossed in all directions, and tumbled over the edge of the platform. Their shrieks were lost in the roar of fire and flame, their bodies falling into the magma of the volcano.

Fire groaned as he stood, his body aching. He stumbled to the side, grimacing in pain and sharp relief. Then he noticed Lachonus. The man was on his hands and knees, the pack on his back spurting flames. Wincing, Fire closed the gap and reached for the soldier, and then heard him laughing.

"Are you well?" Fire asked.

"I can't believe that worked," Lachonus said.

Fire extinguished the magic on the man's back. "That was the easy part."

"The *easy* part?" Lachonus grunted as he stood. "We just dropped from five thousand feet into a hole barely ten feet across and landed on a platform filled with fiends hanging above a live volcano."

Fire grinned. "Like I said, the easy part."

He pointed to the Dark Gate. The arch rested at the edge of the platform, the silver liquid visible behind the inferno still burning. Defiant screams came from within, suggesting the blast of fire had passed through the Gate.

"The firewall won't last long," Fire said. "You need to shut the Dark Gate."

"And you?" Lachonus asked.

"I give you time," Fire said.

He clapped Lachonus on the shoulder and then hurried to the stairs ascending to the chamber's entrance. At the top of the stairs, howls came from the fortress, and Fire could hear the fiends rushing to reach the intruders. Fire stepped to the entrance and gathered the abundance of heat from the volcano and filled the tunnel with fire.

Fiends turned the corner at the end and charged into the flames, dying by droves. Fire stood his ground, knowing that if he failed to protect Lachonus, there would be no victory this day. Lachonus had to shut the Dark Gate, and Fire had to keep him safe until he did.

Fire cast a look over his shoulder—and then snapped around to get a better look. Lachonus had approached the Dark Gate, but a new figure had materialized on the circular platform. Crafted from light, shadow, heat, water, and mind magics, the figure resembled Lachonus, right down to the frown on his features. The mirage stood across from Lachonus.

"What's going on?" Fire shouted.

"I don't know," Lachonus called back.

The soldier stepped to the side, and the golem matched the motion with exactness. Fire grimaced as a siper leapt through his firewall and his jaws clamped shut on his arm. He blasted the beast down the throat and kicked him over the edge. Then he poured his magic into the opening, strengthening the barrier against the charging fiends, who had grown so thick their bodies pressed against each other in their haste.

321

Fire turned back and watched Lachonus circle the mirage, and it was impossible to tell which was real, and which was replica. More disturbing, the mirage duplicated the motions of Lachonus with absolute perfection.

Lachonus closed the gap in a rush and swung, almost losing his head when the mirage attacked with the same technique. Fire sucked in his breath as the two combatants placed their swords on each other's throats, and he realized the purpose of the sentry.

"It's Draeken's final defense," he shouted.

Lachonus reached his sword out and cautiously nicked the mirage's arm, the mirage nicking his own arm in turn. On the top corner of the Dark Gate, the black material cracked, like a blade had cut the stone.

"I think it's linked to the Dark Gate," Lachonus called.

"What's that supposed to mean?" Fire shot over his shoulder, straining to keep the fiends at bay.

Lachonus didn't answer, and Fire realized the truth. Draeken had laid a singular trap. To close the gate required killing the mirage—but killing the mirage required the ultimate sacrifice. Fire cursed Draeken's tactic and called over his shoulder.

"You have to fight," Fire called. "Draeken is powerful but not perfect. Surely he left a flaw in that thing. You can find it."

The clang of blades indicated Lachonus had begun to duel, and Fire turned the whole of his attention to the entrance corridor. Lachonus needed time, and Fire would give it to him. As fiends poured in his direction, Fire shoved them right and left, using fire hammers to knock them over the edge of the steps. They fell past the edge of the platform and into the magma. Distantly he heard dragons roaring and Senia's scream, but could not join their aerial duel. He had his place, and he would not be moved.

***

Senia pulled on the dragon's spines, and Isray responded to her mental direction. The white dragon folded one wing and rolled into a dive, evading blasts of fire from two red dragons. They swung above the

322

fortress and Senia caught a glimpse of Lachonus through the vent shaft. But there were two soldiers, fighting each other. Then Isray was forced to bank left when a volley of skorpian bolts came for his wing.

Is Lachonus battling himself? Isray asked.

"Draeken has left a golem as a defense," she said. "But we have to keep the dragons occupied."

Isray flew upward and twirled between Gorewrathian and Bendelinish. Superheated flames scorched the air and Senia coughed in the smoke. Isray banked out of the dive and rotated, sending a burst of icy breath at the second red. The ice coalesced on its tail as it swooped away, and then Gorewrathian was upon them, its huge form obscuring the sunlight.

You think to fight me little one?

The king's voice was mocking, the fire pouring from its maw and reaching for Isray. Senia had seen it coming, and directed Isray upward, out of the path of the second red that sought to cut them off.

You are almost a child. The king gave a sinister chuckle. *If you were any younger, your snout would still have fragments of shell.*

I'm old enough to survive against you, Isray retorted.

You have the oracle on your back, Gorewrathian replied. *And she is the sole reason your flesh is not burning as you plummet to your death.*

The king's words pricked the dragon's pride and Senia sensed the dragon's intent. She shouted a warning, but the beast whirled in the air, lifting its claws to strike at Gorewrathian. The king's own claws raked deep furrows in the white dragon's body, and the second red scorched Isray's wings. Isray leapt away, flapping for altitude.

"Will you stop letting them bait you?" Senia winced as she examined the wounds. "He's just trying to get you to fight him."

I am a dragon of Lumineia! Isray roared.

"You're going to be a *dead* dragon if you don't listen to me." She turned her head to watch the two dragons giving chase. "You're faster than them both, but if you tangle again, they're going to rip your head from your body—and currently I'm riding on your neck."

She sensed the dragon's arrogance warring with Rake's wisdom, the bonding of the two eventually cooling the dragon's bloodlust. Isray turned his head and bellowed a warning at the two dragons, the great reds responding in kind.

"Get low and fast," she said. "I know just where to take them."

Isray did as requested, and folded his wings. The white dragon dropped to the earth and banked north, along the river through the valley. Isray converted the height into speed and hurtled toward the foothills. Skorpian spears were launched in their direction but fell short, the white dragon's speed preventing any from striking.

Senia reached over the dragon's neck and to the river water. A simple charm lifted the river in plumes of steam that billowed upward, through the ranks of marching fiends and filling the lower valley. Gorewrathian chuckled at the effort.

You cannot hide from me.

Who says I want to hide? Isray retorted.

Senia directed the white dragon into the foothills of the mountain, and then south, banking around the valley. They flew so close to the mountain cliffs that their passage sent stones and leaves bouncing downhill. The wind through the valley picked up the clouds of steam Senia had created and pushed them to the side, into Isray's path. Ahead, the cliffs and crags of the mountains gradually disappeared from view, and Isray flapped for altitude.

"No," Senia said, a grim smile spreading on her features. "Go into the fog."

I cannot see, he replied.

"I will be your eyes," Senia said.

The dragon reluctantly continued his path, and Senia closed her eyes, mentally directing the white dragon into the mist. A cliff rose up on their right, and they turned inward and up, sweeping through a narrow pass and then rising to an escarpment that resembled a blade. Invisible behind a curtain of mist and fog, she guided Isray through the cliffs and crags before bursting into open air.

"Now!" she shouted.

Isray flared his wings wide, slowing and turning him into a flip. Bendelinish came through the mist. He'd gone slow enough to avoid the crags, but his body clipped the knifelike escarpment. He roared in pain and rose through the fog, directly under Isray.

The white dragon dropped onto the red dragon's back, his claws grasping his wings. He leaned down and poured frost breath onto the wing joints, the wings growing brittle. The dragon roared its fury—and crashed into the mountainside.

Frozen solid, the wing joints shattered, and the dragon fell into the fog. A thousand feet he fell, the impact driving the life from his body. Isray roared his victory just as Gorewrathian came through the fog and hovered a short distance from Isray.

A fool's death, he snarled. *But I've lived long enough to know every trick of dragon combat. You cannot defeat me, not with the oracle, not with anyone. You are but a hatchling, and I am the king of dragonkind—*

A deep groan drew all eyes upward. When Bendelinish had struck the cliff, the impact had dislodged several boulders at the top. They rained down on Gorewrathian like enormous catapult stones, and one struck his back.

Bones cracked as the dragon was taken into the fog. Gorewrathian twisted and turned, painfully dodging the remainder before alighting on a ridge. He roared his pain and defiance, but Isray laughed.

What were you saying about being able to defeat an oracle? Isray taunted.

The red dragon unleashed a blast of flames so hot the fog burned away. Isray swerved to the side and then dove. Senia cried out as she nearly lost her seat, and clung to the bony spikes on the dragon's neck.

The white dragon flew above the great red dragon and unleashed his breath, leaving a frozen line across Gorewrathian's spine. The king whirled, but injured as he was, he could not turn fast enough.

Again and again Isray scored the great dragon's body, the ice forming on his wings, back and tail. Gorewrathian's breathing was labored and blood mingled with the fire in his throat. His fury turned desperate, and even with Senia's farsight, the great king managed to burn Isray across the side. Isray landed hard and Senia tumbled from his back, injuring her arm.

I'll rip your spine from your body and hang it on my wall, Gorewrathian snarled, stumbling after Isray. The white dragon bellowed and hid the burned wing behind his body, snapping his jaws and unleashing more ice, the breath burning into the king's throat. Gorewrathian sought to turn away but the white dragon pounced and used its claws to hold the red dragon's mouth open. He leaned in and unleashed a blistering blast of ice right down the red dragon's throat.

Throat and stomach, heart and lungs, the inside of the red dragon turned to ice. He clawed at Isray, scoring lines in his flesh and ripping scales free, but Isray continued pouring ice down the red dragon's throat. In desperation, Gorewrathian swung his head and bashed Isray against the stone wall, finally knocking him free. Isray tumbled away, but the damage had been done, and Gorewrathian collapsed.

Impossible, the red dragon screamed, his voice fading into silence.

With a great groan, the king of dragons slumped to the side, his weight carrying him over the edge. He fell in silence, but when he landed below, the ice inside his body shattered, claiming his life.

Senia picked her way across the battlefield, holding her elbow where it had broken in her fall. She regarded the fallen king as Isray began to change shape, the white scales turning to flesh, until Rake lay in the grass. He touched the large burn on his side and sucked in his breath.

"Did we win?"

"We did our part," she said, turning to Xshaltheria in the distance. "Now it's all up to Lachonus and Fire."

326

Chapter 42: Empowered

Mind held his arm, grimacing as he scooted along the ground, pushing himself further from Draeken. He reached to the shard of light and yanked it from his elbow, tossing the bloody shard aside. He clenched his teeth to prevent crying out and ripped the remainder of his sleeve, using it to tie around his arm. He used his teeth to tie it off and then picked up his sword with his good hand.

Draeken stood in the open, daring the others to strike him down. Shadow lay on the ground at his feet, unconscious, while Light lay crumpled against the Titan's hand, whimpering in pain. Willow sought to staunch the blood seeping from Light's wounds.

Water darted in and swung his staffblade, but Draeken conjured his own staffblade out of fire and deflected the blow. Then he leapt into the air and soared above Water. He gathered the light around his form, his body shimmering into dozens of replicas, the images soaring above Water.

"The one piece of Power that remains in a fragment," he said. "But you are not wise enough to recognize your failure."

A geyser of water burst from the ground and Water stepped on it, leaping into the air and spinning, slicing through mirages on all sides. The copies shattered from the blows—and Draeken plunged a blade of fire into Water's back.

Water shouted as he fell to the ground, the blade protruding from his chest. Rune leapt to him and yanked the sword free, allowing Water to reach to the still rising geyser and pull the liquid to help knit the wound.

Draeken dropped to Rune and swung, a blade of light forming in his hand. Sentara shouted a warning and Rune whirled, instinctively raising her hands. The blade shattered on an invisible barrier, and Rune retaliated.

Her sword darkened as anti-magic suddenly appeared, her blade cutting deep. Draeken snarled and leapt into the air. Impossibly, Rune did the same, and soared after Draeken, maintaining the assault.

Mind saw the coil of fire rising. "Rune! Beneath you!"

Too late. Like a snake, the fire reached up and snapped, catching Rune's leg. She screamed as the long teeth buried in her thigh, most of her leg disappearing in the snake's throat. Draeken darted in—but Rune spun her blade, and plunged it into Draeken's chest.

The snake dragged her to the ground as Draeken bellowed in pain, the anti-magic sword sparking and spitting, his body darkening. He reached up and snapped the blade sticking out of chest. Then he dropped to Rune and lunged. The young girl raised a wall of earth, but Draeken shattered it. Needles of light appeared above Rune and Draeken clenched his fist. Mind's hand shot out, slowing their fall, but Draeken was stronger. As the needles fell on Rune, Sentara suddenly appeared and shoved Rune out of the way, the needles sinking into the old woman.

"Sentara!" Rune yanked the snake of fire away and clawed her way to Sentara.

Sentara's hand trembled as she touched Rune's face. "You are my greatest memory, my beautiful Rune," she smiled, and then her eyes shut. Rune cradled the old woman, tears streaking down her dirty cheeks.

"You live at my mercy!" Draeken bellowed, turning to face them all.

Rune whirled, lightning crackling on her fingertips as tears streamed down her face. "You killed her!"

Draeken swung his hand in dismissal and the ground turned into a hand that struck Rune. The girl went soaring into the air, flipping end over end before she collided with a dragon and fell. Mind jumped beneath her and caught her unconscious body. He placed her on the ground, grateful to find her still alive.

"When will you learn?" Draeken shouted as he hovered in the air. "You cannot harm me. You cannot kill me. My army will defeat you all, and you will either serve in my empire or die on this battlefield."

"It seems unfounded arrogance exists on every world." Belrisa wiped blood from her cheek.

"A universal rule," Tardoq agreed, grimacing as he pulled a spike of fire from his shoulder.

Elenyr leapt from the ground and whirled, her sword slicing across Draeken's cheek. He winced as the blade split his flesh and tried to backhand her, but she'd gone ethereal. She reached the zenith of her jump and flipped. She turned to flesh and sliced again across his side, dragging her sword down his leg as she fell.

"Elenyr," Draeken snarled. "You have been a thorn in my side for too long. Fortunately I know what can kill you, and so I brought a friend."

A dragon abruptly dropped from the sky, bursting through the haze and smoke. She landed twenty feet in front of Elenyr, her jaws opening wide. Her azure scales marked her as a lightning dragon, and pure lightning crackled in its throat. Elenyr leapt backward, but the dragon was too close, and Draeken had chosen his moment well.

"Elenyr!" Light screamed.

Water stumbled to reach her, but they were too far. Willow sought to strike the blue dragon. All was in vain. Mind bellowed his helplessness as the lightning burst across the battlefield, streaking for Elenyr's body. The blast was as thick as a tree trunk, raising Mind's hair as it passed—and slammed into Queen Rynda's wide sword.

Rynda held her blade with her metal hand, the lightning ricocheting off the wide greatsword and exploding into the nearby ranks of fiends. Black bodies were shredded by the lightning, and Rynda straightened.

"Is that all you've got?"

330

The blue dragon leaned in and again lightning kindled, but Tardoq and the Bonebreaker struck, their weapons plunging into the blue dragon's throat. The dragon died in seconds under the assault, and Draeken roared his anger. Mind sagged in relief.

Rynda sniffed as she turned to Draeken. She'd arrived at the head of an alliance army. Flanked by Jeric and Captain Horn, and followed by Thorilian and his wife, Venia, they were surrounded by dozens of others. Warshard Toril and a druid riding a moordraug, members of the Bladed, Moren and Stella, they all advanced to stand with the fragments.

King Dothlore and a contingent of dwarves, standing with Queen Alosia and her elven guard. Queens Annah and Nelia, both stood with soldiers of men and troll. Lira strode through a gap and stood next to Water, nodding to him as two dark elves joined him. Cutter and Black, the last surviving members of the Queen's Hand.

"You are nothing compared to me!" Draeken shrieked.

Mind looked beyond the army, and realized why they had been able to come. Fiends had begun to disappear, the ranks thinning as quare and kraka evaporated from view. With two of the generals gone, many of the remaining fiends had fallen upon each other, the ranks roiling in a cascade of battle.

"My army is greater than you!" Flames and light sparkled off Draeken's arms and shoulders, his eyes wild with rage. "Kill them! Kill them all!"

The surrounding fiends raised their obsidian blades and charged, lunging down the slope. They flooded toward the allies, and Mind shouted for his family to close ranks. Draeken looked on with a disturbing triumph in his gaze. Mind raced to Elenyr—but stumbled when a screaming ball of fire dropped from the sky and landed in the midst of the kraka charge. From the flames a beak and wings appeared, and a phoenix issued a thundering warcry.

"Archeantial!" Elenyr shouted.

They killed the Ancient, the great firebird replied, her tone as dark as midnight. *Did you really expect us to miss this?*

Another ball of fire landed, and another, the entire flock of phoenixes plummeting into the ring of foes. They exploded in their midst, filling the region in blinding fire. Last to land, a smaller bird swooped into the krakas, flames pouring off his wings to scorch their armored bodies.

My apologies for being late, Reiquen said. *We came as soon as we received Fire's message.*

"You're right on time," Mind said.

Waves of heat washed across them, the entire group surrounded by flames as tall as the walls of Ilumidora. The firebirds swept through the flame wall, appearing and disappearing with a tip of a wing, or a terrifying current of fire from an open beak.

Mind caught Elenyr's gaze. "Did you know they were coming?"

She had tears in her eyes. "I had no idea. Fire must have sent a message on his own."

Cut off from his army, and with only Bartoth at his side, Draeken's scream of rage was barely audible over the inferno. He turned about, his hands trembling, his eyes wild. Mind thought he would attack the firebirds, but his shock carried a trace of fear, as if he realized that he stood in the jaws of defeat.

"You cannot win here," Mind said, drawing Draeken's focus. "The people will not accept you as their ruler." He picked his way across the broken ground towards Draeken, raising a hand as cinders washed across the battlefield.

"Then I will turn them into fiends," Draeken snarled. "I still have two generals."

A large shadow panther appeared from a cavity next to the fallen Titan and slunk into the group, carrying the body of Famine. Shadow smirked as Famine was dropped to the ground. She reached for Draeken with trembling fingers before her body disintegrated.

"Make that one," Mind said. More fiends went mad, the entire charge faltering.

"War!" Draeken barked, the fear now apparent in his voice. "Kill them!"

But War hesitated. His broken arm still hung at his side, his armor dented and cracked from battling Belrisa and Tardoq. He glanced between Elenyr, the ring of fire, and Draeken, but did not attack.

"You obey my will!" Draeken dropped to the ground and struck War, knocking him back. "These people are insects to be squashed."

"In the Dawn of Magic there was one lesson I learned," Jeric said. "When you give people freedom, you grant them valor."

"You are all born of flesh!" Draeken whirled and stabbed his finger at them. "And not one of you can kill me!"

He reached to the sides and clenched his fists, and shards of light formed in the air. Each as large as a ballista bolt, the shards hovered over everyone. They dropped from the sky. Willow rolled Light out of the way, while Tardoq and the Bonebreaker jumped aside. Mind darted to Shadow and caught his arm, yanking him beyond the spear, but the weapon sliced across his shoulder.

Draeken charged and caught Mind about the throat, his voice savage and desperate. "You think you can protect your brothers? You think you can stop my power? Have you not learned what I have become?"

Draeken began to squeeze, and Mind's vision flickered. Others struck at Draeken but he swatted them aside, his eyes fixed on Mind. Tardoq swung his sword but Draeken caught the blade in his bare hand and wrenched it from his grip.

"You will die witnessing your failure," he snarled to Mind.

Mind then looked beyond Draeken and managed a smile. *You first.*

A group of fiends managed to get through the firewall, but their bodies disintegrated as if they were made of smoke rather than flesh. Through a gap in the fires, more fiends evaporated, their bodies turning to smoke and fading from sight. Draeken's eyes widened in shock.

"What is this?" he demanded.

"Serak told us his secret," Elenyr said from nearby. "He threaded the Dark Gate with magic that linked to every fiend, and when the Gate is destroyed, they are drawn back to Kelindor."

Draeken's eyes widened and he spun. "Where is the fragment of Fire?"

"Destroying your Gate," Shadow said.

Shadow darted into view and drove a dagger into Draeken's stomach. Draeken snarled and kicked Shadow, sending him tumbling away. Shadow cried out as he collided with a stray kraka blade, the weapon shearing through his shoulder and taking his arm. Draeken turned his baleful gaze on Mind and reached into a pouch at his side, to withdraw a small mirror.

"Looks like I have an infestation to eradicate. I'll be back in a moment."

Draeken turned his eyes away from Mind and to the mirror, his thumb rising to press the rune that would open a Gate to Xshaltheria. Mind recognized the moment as his final chance to stop Draeken, to prevent him from killing Fire and returning to destroy them all. Draeken still had his hand around his throat, his fingers like an iron vice.

Mind reached into his magic and saw Draeken for what he was, a being of almost pure magic. He was the fragment of Power, his body and flesh infused with four energies, that of the fragments. Including Mind's.

Mind reached his hand toward Draeken and connected to the power that had once been his. Like an old friend, it turned and reached back. Draeken grimaced as if he'd been struck, and dropped Mind to the ground. The small mirror tumbled from his grip and fell into a pile of ash.

Draeken touched his chest, and his eyes snapped to Mind. "What did you do?"

Mind clenched a fist and stepped in, driving his fist into Draeken's chest with all his might. At the point of impact, he summoned the piece of mind magic inside Draeken's soul. Draeken threw his head back and screamed, the sound of mortal pain. Mind clenched his fist and pulled, wrenching the mind magic from Draeken's soul. Threads of purple light were torn from Draeken, the light gradually fading to white as it hardened in Mind's hand.

Draeken fell to his knees, staring in horror at the black hole in his chest, where the magic of mind had been rent from his body. Groaning, he looked up at Mind, who stood over him with the pulsing orb of white in his hand.

"You think to take back my power?" Draeken demanded.

"Never," Mind said, sensing the power in his palm. "But this amplious can empower anyone. And if I fall, another will wield it."

A great swelling of sound erupted across the battlefield, and more swaths of fiends disappeared. Inside the city, tens of thousands simply evaporated, leaving stunned defenders with empty streets. Draeken swept his eyes about and saw the truth. His army was being taken before his eyes.

War turned and fled, sprinting to a gap in the firewall. Belrisa stepped on the hilt of an obsidian blade and it spun upward. She caught the hilt and tossed it to Rynda, who stood behind the fleeing general. The rock troll queen leaned forward and hurled the obsidian blade at War's back. The giant blade plunged into War, piercing the armor and dropping the rock troll to the ground. He bellowed as his armor disintegrated, his body crumbling to dust. Belrisa grinned at Rynda, who nodded in satisfaction.

"Are females stronger than males on this world," she looked to Tardoq, who laughed.

As the final general died, Draeken gasped and fell to his knees. His generals were dead, his Gate was falling, and the fragment of Mind advanced upon him with a piece of his own power. Draeken gasped for breath, his features frozen in disbelief.

"You would kill your own brother?" he asked.

"You were never my brother," Mind said.

Mind leapt in, the light in his palm going blinding as he swung his fist, a shard of purple extending from his knuckles. But Draeken extended his hand towards the pocket Gate and it flew into his hand. He pressed the rune and silver light poured into shape beneath Draeken. He fell, disappearing from sight before Mind could stop him. Mind lunged for the Gate but it closed, and he landed in the dirt.

"No!" he shouted.

He knew where Draeken had gone, to Xshaltheria. If he could destroy Fire and repair the Gate, he would return even stronger than before, and the alliance would have lost its one chance at victory.

Elenyr wearily stepped to his side and placed a hand on his shoulder. "It's up to the others now."

More fiends disappeared, and fear entered the hearts of the remainder. Shrieking and screaming, they scattered, sprinting in all directions, the battle forgotten. They swept away from the battlefield, fleeing the mysterious foe that caused their neighbors to turn to smoke and dissipate, and the dragons and firebirds in the sky.

Mind held the orb in his hand, hoping it had been enough, hoping Draeken was injured enough that Fire could survive. Hoping he and Lachonus could triumph. Shadow, Light, and Water approached and nodded.

"We've done our part," Water said.

"Let us hope it was enough," Mind said.

Chapter 43: The Final Trap

Fire fought with every ounce of power he possessed, blasting the fiends left and right, scorching them to death, and even pinning them to the wall in the hopes they would bar the opening. But still the fiends came. They pulled the bodies of the dead back and charged the steps leading to the platform where Lachonus fought, their claws, teeth, and obsidian swords reaching for Fire's body.

"Lachonus!" Fire shouted. "You're running out of time!"

Lachonus spun and twisted, attempting to swing his blade through the mirage, to find a weakness in the magic. He searched for any irregularity in the floor but the surface of the platform was perfectly round. Lachonus fought with unmatched ferocity, a hundred small cuts marking his flesh—and that of his opponent. For every drop of blood spilt, he suffered the same fate.

For every cut on the mirage, the Dark Gate endured a wound, it's very shape linked to the mirror soldier. Some of the fiends evaporated, their flesh turning to smoke and drifting away. Each time it helped to save Fire from being driven back, but Fire knew he could not last forever. The only way to destroy the Gate was to kill the mirror—and die.

"I can't find an opening!" Lachonus shouted, his tone desperate.

"Keep trying!" Fire shouted.

Fire conjured a giant leg and stomped his foot, kicking two krakas from the ledge. One managed to hurl his obsidian sword, the blade passing over Fire's shoulder, slicing deep across his arm. He grimaced and pulled the magma from the volcano, lifting it into a golem of magma that charged the corridor, melting and crushing the packed fiends.

Abruptly a silver light burst into shape at the edge of the platform, and Fire spared a look. He hoped to see Elenyr, or perhaps one of his brothers. Instead it was Draeken himself that stumbled into sight.

Draeken came to a halt and took the room at a glance. Lachonus standing close to the mirror, while Fire fought at the top of the stairs. Fire's eyes widened when he spotted the dark hole in Draeken's chest, and the pain on his features.

"What did they do to you?" Fire asked.

Draeken stared at Lachonus, and then surprisingly began to laugh. He kept his distance from Lachonus, but began to circle the outer perimeter of the platform to reach the Dark Gate. He motioned to the soldier.

"Elenyr is almost as clever as the fragment of Mind," he said. "But in this, you have lost—without even realizing your defeat."

"What are you talking about?" Lachonus asked.

Lachonus held his sword on the mirror's heart, and the other blade rested on his own chest. The fact that Draeken kept his distance made it clear that Lachonus was a threat, but his haughty expression filled Fire with fear.

"Your generals must be dead," Fire called to Draeken. "How many of your fiends have begun to disappear?"

Draeken's features twisted with hatred but he remained fixed on Lachonus. "The prophecy spoke of one born to human, elf, and dwarf, and your mother said you were from the right lineage."

"The prophecy was real," Lachonus said. "You cannot deny that."

"It was true," Draeken said. "But the lie came from your mother. She wanted the pride of your victory."

"You lie," Lachonus growled.

"You know your mother." Draeken stabbed a finger to him. "You know her ambition. It was your cousin that was born to the right lineage, but it was your name I gave to Elenyr."

Fire's eyes widened in shock, and he punched the ground, sending fire billowing into the corridor. He sucked in the heat and sent a blast at Draeken, but he swatted it aside with ease. Fire grimaced as he was forced to turn back to the next wave of fiends.

"Don't listen to him!" he called to Lachonus. "Elenyr believed in you."

Draeken snarled at Fire's words. "I made her *think* you were the one person that could defeat me," Draeken said. "But you are just a warrior destined for obscurity."

Draeken crept closer to the Dark Gate, his hand rising. Fire guessed he was going to attempt severing the link between the mirror and the Dark Gate, allowing him to slay Lachonus and Fire at his leisure.

Lachonus stared at Draeken and then looked over his shoulder to Fire. "Tell my mother I'm sorry," he said.

Lachonus closed his eyes . . . and drove his sword into the mirror's chest.

"NO!" Draeken roared.

He leapt to the Dark Gate, but the damage had been done. The silver liquid sparked and shimmered, and the arch began to crumble. The fiends in the corridor evaporated, the sounds of snarling fiends fading into silence.

Draeken leapt to the Dark Gate and raised his hands, purple light flowing from his fingers as he sought to keep it from collapsing. Fire sprinted down the stairs and skidded to a stop at the body of Lachonus. He grabbed his body and retreated.

"I am the essence of Power!" Draeken roared. "I cannot be defeated by fragments!"

The Dark Gate began to collapse, but Draeken remained in the center, desperately trying to keep the portal open. Fire caught a glimpse of War through the breach, as well as Plague, Famine, and Death. War sought to push his way through the portal but the Gate was crumbling, and they were trapped.

Abruptly realizing he could not stop the end, Draeken leapt back—only to find that the threads of magic binding the Gate were linked to him as well. He began to scream as the threads pulled him into the Dark Gate, but no amount of magic could stop the destruction of the Gate, and he was pulled into the center. A rising whine came from arched Gate and Fire sprinted up the stairs to the exit.

The Dark Gate detonated, the pieces of the arch flying upward and embedding into the wall of the chamber. Caught in the center of the portal, Draeken was slammed into the wall with the remnants of the Gate, the remaining magic lashing Draeken to the stone, partially in Lumineia, partially in Kelindor.

The blast rocked the entire fortress of Xshaltheria, flames spilling up the vent. Fire raised his arms to shield himself, the flames washing over and around them. For a terrifying moment Fire worried they would fall into the volcano. Then the fortress settled and Fire lifted his gaze.

Draeken was bound to the wall, his body ethereal, his eyes open but not seeing. He turned his head left and right, calling Fire's name, the sound filled with seething anger. Draeken's body shifted but the chains had been of his own making, and were remnants of the destroyed Gate. His effort to prevent the destruction of the portal had left him trapped between the two worlds. His body was no longer of flesh, and seemed to swirl with white and purple energies.

"*I cannot be caged!*" Draeken roared, his voice like it came from a great distance. "*I am the fragment of Power! The mightiest of any being to ever live! I will have my revenge . . .*"

Fire lifted the body of his friend and turned away. Without a word, he exited the chamber and departed through the fortress, the sounds of Draeken's ranting fading in the distance. Fire ascended to the top of the hauntingly empty fortress, where he found Isray and Senia waiting for him.

"Draeken?" Senia cradled her elbow, which bent at an odd angle.

Fire carefully placed Lachonus on the back of Isray. "It is finished."

Senia nodded soberly, and the two climbed onto the white dragon's neck. Painfully, Isray flapped his wings and they rose above the volcano. As they departed, Fire looked back at the disturbingly empty fortress.

Doors hung askew, gates lay broken, and the valley below had been stripped of all greenery. A solitary catapult remained on the field, miraculously having survived the conflict and the fiend march. Fire guessed that, in time, the ground would be covered in trees and Xshaltheria would fall to ruin. Draeken, for all his power and ambition, had been defeated.

Chapter 44: A Mother's Request

Elenyr glided through the ground outside the city of Ilumidora, searching. She crisscrossed the earth, scanning the scorched soil and roots of destroyed trees. As much as she felt the need to find all the victims, she dreaded any more discoveries. When she was satisfied she had found them all, she rose to the surface next to Water.

"That was the last area," Elenyr said. "There are more dead."

"A terrible task," Water said, inclining his head. "But the families are grateful."

She faced Ilumidora. Most of the walls were destroyed, with only a trio remaining standing, all permanently damaged from the assault. The homes, taverns, inns, and shops were nothing but ruins and piles of wood, thatch, and broken glass. Most of the trees had burned.

The upper city, unprotected by the city walls, had suffered the brunt of damage from skorpian spears. Limbs were splintered and broken, some hanging by slivers. Many of the buildings nestled into the branches had fallen into the lake, and they remained half submerged in the water.

The sphere protecting the castle had shattered, and two of the three sections to the fortress were reduced to rubble. Entire wings had fallen next to the trunk, and Elenyr had searched the wreckage for those that had survived. Then she'd searched for the dead.

Elves still labored on the mother tree of Urindilial, working to remove the thousands of skorpian spears still embedded into the trunk and limbs. The bark was splintered, the wood beneath rent in gaping wounds. The tree had not spoken to elven mages since the battle, and they feared the worst.

"Do you think the elves will rebuild?" Water asked.

"I hope so," she said. "But not here. This site has suffered enough."

One section of the city had caved into the earth, falling upon the ruins of Dawnskeep that lay buried. Queen Alosia had ordered many to remain outside until dwarven engineers had determined it was safe.

Outside the city, a sprawling camp occupied the space of the battlefield. Well organized by Queen Alosia, the camp cared for the host of wounded, and prepared the dead for a final rest. Weapons had been set aside, and members of every race moved freely through the camps.

Beyond the camps, the forest had been devastated. Trees lay on their sides, some covered by earth. The rent soil and broken limbs stretched in every direction, with most of the elven forests reduced to ash and charred trunks.

Despite the damage, the camps around the city contained an air of hope. Elves spoke to dark elves and humans joined orcs for a midday meal. Draeken may have come to destroy, but he had succeeded in uniting the people.

Elenyr spotted Melora caring for a gnome injured during the battle. She applied a cool cloth to his forehead and spoke words of encouragement before moving to the next cot, where an elf held a bandage over his chest. Water noticed her gaze.

"I admit, I never expected Melora to become so kind."

"A mother's sacrifice leaves a mark on a soul," Elenyr said. "And I believe Princess Melora to be irrevocably changed."

"A mother's mark *did* leave a mark on a soul," Water said.

Elenyr turned with a smile. "Oh?"

"You have my gratitude." Water reached around Elenyr's shoulders and squeezed. "For everything."

"You have my gratitude for surviving," Elenyr said fervently.

"Not all in one piece," Shadow said, climbing the hill. He grinned and pointed to his missing arm. "I still say you should have let me reattach it."

"You aren't a full guardian anymore," Elenyr said. "The attempt would have failed."

"I can always try later," Shadow said. "And Rune said she would help."

"You kept the arm?" Water groaned and look skyward. "Why am I not surprised."

"If you lost a toe, wouldn't you keep it?"

"No," Water said fervently. "I would not keep any appendage."

"Your loss," Shadow said.

Elenyr smiled at her sons, tears forming in her eyes. In the week since the battle had ended, The first night, Elenyr had slipped away, and found a private corner where she could cry her gratitude and relief. Shadow, of course, had found her. Without a word, he'd simply hugged her. Elenyr had thought Shadow would tell his brothers, but he kept the moment to himself.

"Looks like Fire and Light are almost finished with the caravans," Shadow said.

A long collection of wagons was placed on the outside of the camps, all filled with the honored dead. Light and Fire had covered them in coffins of light, allowing the thousands who'd arrived since the battle to mourn for their passing. The wagons were crafted of fire that would not burn, a glittering tribute to the thousands who'd paid the ultimate sacrifice. At their head, two wagons carried a single occupant each. Sentara and Lachonus Dralen.

"Where's Mind?" Elenyr asked.

"He's still working with Stella," Water said with a broad smile. "And anyone can see the budding attraction."

"I knew we all changed since the separation," Shadow said, "but honestly, watching Mind flirt is, what's the right word? Oh, that's right, disturbing."

Elenyr chuckled. "Maybe, but you cannot deny his happiness."

344

"Has Jeric returned?" Elenyr asked.

Shadow shook his head. "I don't know why he was so disturbed. So one prisoner escaped from the Melting. Why does it matter?"

"He was no normal prisoner," Elenyr said.

"You know him?" Water asked.

Elenyr shook her head. "I only know that Jeric doesn't want him found."

She recalled Jeric's disturbing expression when he'd discovered one had escaped from the Melting. With little explanation, he'd departed, intent on locating the man. Elenyr had wondered before if Ero had imprisoned someone on Lumineia, and now she was certain. But what was his identity? And why did Ero fear his freedom?

"We could use the amplious to find him," Water said. "Mind said it can empower any mage, even us."

"True," Shadow said, and wrinkled his nose. "But Mind already hid it."

Elenyr smiled at his irritation. "You tried to steal it, didn't you."

"Of course," Shadow said. "Do you know where he put it?"

"The one place it will not be found," she replied.

"So you *do* know where it is." Shadow leveled an accusing finger at her.

"It is not prudent to have a piece of the fragment of Power in easy reach," she replied.

Captain Horn appeared at the edge of the camp and spotted them at the top of the hill. He turned in their direction and hurried up the slope. Princess Serania raced at his side, taking two steps for every one of his.

"Elenyr," Captain Horn called. "There's something you need to see."

345

Catching the urgency in his tone, Elenyr dropped from her spot and joined him. "What's wrong?"

"Urindilial is speaking." Serania said.

Elenyr's eyes widened and the five of them returned to the city. Threading through the fallen buildings and soldiers working in the ruins, they crossed an aquaglass bridge to reach the island at the center of the city.

Queen Alosia was there, as were Queen Nelia of Erathan, and Queen Annah of Griffin. The three women stood around the trunk of the tree, talking in low tones. As Elenyr and the others arrived, Alosia turned to her.

"I'm glad you've come. Urindilial is asking for you."

"Me?" Elenyr asked, surprised. "Why?"

"She's very weak," Alosia said. "I don't know how much time she has."

Water frowned. "You mean . . ."

Alosia's features constricted. "She is dying. And there is nothing we can do."

The grief was evident in her face. Urindilial had lived for ages, and even been transplanted from their former capital. It had seen ages and eras pass, and survived wars and conflicts that had ravaged the elven kingdom.

Elenyr approached the tree and placed her hand against the bark. Rough to the touch, the bark had been burned, and Elenyr could feel the sense of pain. A consciousness stirred, and then Elenyr sensed a faint voice touch her thoughts.

Hauntress . . .

"I am here," Elenyr said softly.

You have my gratitude for protecting my people, the tree murmured.

"I fear I have done very little."

346

. . . I see much, Urindilial said, *and I have witnessed your devotion to your sons. They survived because of you, and now I witness their integrity . . .*

I did not do enough, Elenyr silently replied. *For one of my sons was the cause of this war.*

. . . A greater mother has yet to live, the tree replied, the voice growing faint. *And it is to a mother I must make my request, for I need one of your caliber . . . to protect my daughter . . .*

"Daughter?" Elenyr blurted.

The bark shifted beneath her hand, a small branch pushing outward. Leaves extended from the tiny extension as the wood unfurled, revealing a tiny seed. Alosia sucked in her breath as Elenyr accepted the seedling.

Plant my daughter where she will thrive, Urindilial said. *To this I entrust the mother I respect, the protector of our world . . .*

The voice withdrew, and the bark of the tree darkened. The nearby elves sensed the passing, and heads bowed, tears wetting the earth. But Elenyr held the tiny precious seed in her hand, and watched as a tiny sapling extended and shaped a leaf.

"She needs a home," Elenyr said reverently.

"Don't we all," Alosia said dryly.

Queen Nelia stepped forward. "You can have mine."

Water swiveled to face her. "What do you mean?"

Queen Nelia looked to Annah, and the woman smiled and nodded. "Tell her, Nelia."

Nelia swept her hand to the ruined city. "Queen Alosia, in drawing Draeken here, your people paid the heaviest price. Your forests are destroyed, your cities are broken, and your people are homeless. After speaking to Annah and my advisors, we have made a decision. Erathan now belongs to you."

347

Elenyr exchanged a look with Water, shocked to silence. Was Nelia giving her entire kingdom to the elves? The enormous gift could not be quantified, yet it was evident by Nelia's smile that she was sincere.

Stunned, Alosia stared at her. "What about your people?" she asked.

"We are moving to Talinor," she said. "After my father's betrayal, my people are divided and I see conflict in our future. By joining Talinor, and unifying our kingdoms, we can preserve our heritage, and also save Talinor. Wellith, son of Duke Relis, is well respected, and a marriage between us will seal our kingdoms."

"Plus he's rather attractive," Shadow said with a smirk.

"That did not factor into it," Nelia said, but a touch of pink appeared in her cheeks. Elenyr hid a smile, pleased by the plan for the future. She sensed Senia's hand in the arrangement. When she'd been high oracle, she'd helped orchestrate such unions, and appreciated the elegant solution.

King Dothlore grunted in agreement. "I support this arrangement if you do, Alosia. I will even bring my race to build you a mighty citadel. Heth currently rests on the Giant's Shelf, but we can turn that cliff into a refuge that will never fall, even to an army the size of Draeken's.

Tears formed in the elven queen's eyes as she looked to Dothlore, Annah, and Nelia. She tried to shake her head, but a refusal failed to escape her lips. Elenyr saw the weight she'd carried and hidden, the cost her people had paid, and now her neighbors were willing to shoulder the same burden.

"This has been our homeland for ages," Alosia said.

"Are you really going to refuse a free citadel?" Dothlore sniffed. "I thought your response would be different."

"You have my deepest gratitude." Alosia laughed and wiped the tears in her eyes.

Nelia embraced the woman. "It is our deepest honor."

Elenyr smiled and looked to the seed in her hand. "You hear that little one? It looks like you have a new home."

Chapter 45: A Given Name

Two Years Later

"It's time," Mind said.

"Already?" Elenyr asked.

Elenyr looked up from the desk and peered out the door of the tent. The sun was nearly at its zenith, exactly two years since Draeken's defeat. Excited, she placed the quill next to the parchment and stood. With great care she picked up the small pot that never left her side. The sapling extended from the soil, its strong limbs reaching upward to coil around her hand.

"Yes, it's time," she said.

The young sapling seemed to shudder in excitement, and Mind grinned. "She seems excited."

"She won't stop chattering," Elenyr said.

"She only talks to you and Alosia," he said, his tone one of admiration. "I must say, I think Urindilial chose wisely."

"Come *on*," Stella appeared next to Mind. "Everyone is waiting."

Mind grinned and threaded his hand into hers, prompting the next visitor to groan. "You guys are disgusting."

"Love you too, Shadow."

Stella tousled his hair, and he brushed her away. Elenyr carried the pot to the door and they made space for her, allowing her to step into the open. Elenyr breathed deep of the cool breeze, her gaze sweeping the top of the plateau known as the Giant's Shelf.

Camps dotted the top of the cliff, the tents occupied by members of every race, visitors who had come to see the planting. Most were already in the new city being constructed, and Elenyr made her way in that direction.

A river from the north split to either side, the two channels sweeping around the city being built by the dwarves. Tens of thousands of dwarves labored to shape the city out of the very cliff, forming curving tiers of stone descending toward the base of the city.

The center had been hollowed out and the dwarves had turned their attention to the structures. But at the base of the city, gardens filled the level, and plant mages had grown an assortment of flora. Waterways curved through the plants, flowing to a pool the elves called Horizon's Edge, the pool overlooking the large forest below the citadel.

Over the last two years, citizens of Erathan had moved from their kingdom and into Talinor, where they were given lands and homes. The elves had gradually taken their place, filling the breadth of the new elven kingdom.

The many visitors climbing scaffolding or sat in half carved windows. Others packed the streets and steps, craning to get a look at the garden at the base of the city. All began to cheer when Elenyr entered the gardens.

She raised the pot in her hands as she approached the center of the gardens, and turned a circle so all could see. The kingdoms of Lumineia raised their voices in a mighty shout, their voices mingling with clapping and cries of praise to Ero, whom many attributed to have saved them from Draeken. Elenyr caught Jeric's eye, and he stifled a grin.

Gathered in a circle around the small hole in the earth, an assortment of individuals had come by invitation. Light, Fire, and Water all stood together, and Mind and Shadow joined them. Stella took her place with them, as did Lira, Willow, Lorica, and Soreena. Fire kissed the druid woman, and Shadow groaned and looked away.

"Disgusting," he muttered.

On the opposite side of the circle, Jeric stood with Tardoq, and surprisingly Belrisa, who'd come at Tardoq's request. Tardoq had become an Eternal, and although Belrisa had not accepted the invitation, she remained an ally and friend. Elenyr caught her gaze and smiled, and the towering dakorian smiled in turn.

Rune stood a little apart, but she looked very little like the girl she had during the war. Elenyr had not seen her in over a year, and had no idea where she'd gone, but the girl looked older, her eyes firm and steadfast. Elenyr fleetingly wondered if she would become an Eternal.

The monarchs of Lumineia occupied the next arc of the circle, with Queen Nelia standing beside her husband, the newly crowned King Wellith. He waved to the people and smiled at his young bride. The wedding had been a few months ago, but Elenyr was pleased to note the growing affection in their eyes. A good pairing.

Queen Annah stood beside her friends, a small smile of triumph on her face. She'd spent the last few months rebuilding Terros and Griffin, but had still managed to send aid to help in the construction of the new elven capital.

Now Queen Aranian, and her sister, Princess Melora, stood together, both smiling as Elenyr met their gaze. Melora had remained true to her word, and sought to repair the damage she'd caused as a member of the Order. She'd regained the trust of her people, and proven to Elenyr that she lived up to her mother's hopes. Erisay would be proud.

The orc king, who'd succeeded his father after the war, and the gnome king stood with Queen Rynda. Towering over most of the group, she stood with her arms folded, tapping her feet impatiently.

Queen Alosia claimed the last section of the circle, and stood with Thorilian and Venia, as well as Captain Horn and Princess Serania, first in line for the throne when Alosia passed. The house of Runya had distinguished itself in the war, and when it was discovered that one of the two ruling houses had been destroyed, the house of Runya had taken its place. Captain Horn and Princess Serania were regarded highly by all races and Elenyr liked the idea of the new monarchy.

Elenyr advanced to the hole, where Senia, Alosia, and Dothlore joined her. Alosia activated the amulet on her neck and raised her voice to the city. Her booming words gradually quieted the noise.

"People of Lumineia, on this day we have much to celebrate. Our lands are healing, our people have begun to rebuild, and as of this moment, The Great Draeken War is part of history. As we plant our new mother tree, let us never forget the sacrifice of those who died for our freedoms. In this, the city of Azertorn, we welcome you, and hope our nations can forever be allies."

Elenyr knelt beside the carefully groomed hole and removed the sapling from the pot. She placed the sapling in the hole, whereupon the roots wiggled into place and shivered in delight. Elenyr smiled and spread the soil around the plant.

"Welcome home, little one."

The leaf caressed her hand. Elven plant mages stepped forward and infused their magic into the tree, the trunk swelling in size, the roots thickening and diving deep. Limbs stretched into the sky, and leaves blossomed from sudden buds. Ten feet, twenty, and then thirty feet. The elves retreated and the tree stretched to its newfound strength.

Alosia stepped forward and reverently placed her hand on the trunk, listening for the name the tree had chosen for herself. Many looked in Elenyr's direction but she kept her features fixed. Elenyr had helped the sapling pick a name, but there was no need for that truth to be known.

"Le Runtáriel!" Alosia raised her voice. "She has come home!"

A cheer went up, the sound sweeping across the city of Azertorn. It spread all the way to the tenth tier, where tens of thousands waved and shouted. Elenyr smiled at the gathering, and felt their joy in her bones. They had been victorious against Draeken's might, and all felt the triumph keenly.

When the noise had subsided, Queen Alosia motioned to Elenyr, and she stepped in front of the group. Unable to constrain her smile, she used her own sound pendent to address the gathering.

"Many have been honored in the last two years, for their bravery, valor, and sacrifice. Today there are five who deserve a special honor, the five fragments of a single shattered soul. Please step forward, and accept your reward. Her sons shifted in surprise, and then took places at her side.

353

What are you doing? Mind spoke into her thoughts.

You'll find out soon enough, Elenyr said.

She then turned to the crowd, which had fallen to widespread chatter and speculation. Few knew that the fragments and Draeken had once been one and the same, and most thought Draeken had been created by Serak. At Senia's urging, the truth of Draeken's origin had not been recorded, and so the people viewed the shattered soul as heroes.

"These five mages were born as guardians," Elenyr said. "And today they gain one thing they have always lacked. A name."

She stepped in front of the fragment of Shadow, who grinned, obviously excited at the prospect. Elenyr smiled in turn, and proclaimed the first of the names that she'd carefully crafted.

"Jerison Myst," she said, handing an amulet to Shadow. "Your new name is granted to you by the kingdoms of Lumineia. Do it honor."

"Not if I can help it," Shadow said with a smirk.

Elenyr smiled and stepped to Fire. "You have fought with firebirds and dragons, and so your name will be Firehawk, soon to join the clan of druids."

Soreena smiled broadly at that, and Fire accepted the offered medallion. Elenyr advanced to the next in line, the fragment of Light. He was veritably bouncing on his feet, his excitement causing his skin to shimmer.

"Light," she said tenderly. "You have distinguished yourself in battle, and called down light from the sky to fight the enemy. Your new name I give to you, that you will be known as Teril Gaze."

"Epic," he breathed, accepting his amulet.

She stepped to the next in line. Water's expression was concerned, probably because he retained a portion of Draeken soul. He might think he did not get a name, but Elenyr swept a hand to her son.

"You have enlisted dragons and battled foes across the four corners of Lumineia. Your new name is Davin Whitethorn."

Water inclined his head in gratitude and accepted the medallion. Elenyr stepped to the last of her sons, who regarded her with a curious expression. Elenyr removed the last amulet from the pouch and held it aloft.

"And to you, I give the name Keldon Braon."

His lips tugged into a smile as he interpreted the last name. "A victor's mind."

"Indeed," she replied, and then stepped to the side. She swept her hand to her five sons, the shattered soul that had ultimately conquered Draeken. "I present your champions, the five warriors of Lumineia."

The cheers were deafening, the sound reverberating off the stone walls of Azertorn. Elenyr's smile was as bright as her sons', and she gazed upon them in pride. She never imagined when she'd taken charge of the fragments that it would lead to this, but watching her sons stand with pride before the people they had served and protected filled her with joy. This was her family. This and Lumineia.

She noticed Belrisa's eyes upon her. The dangerous dakorian bore a curious expression, and Elenyr realized the woman recognized that Lumineia was an oasis, one still under threat by the Krey Empire. In that moment Elenyr understood why Belrisa had chosen to help in the fight against Draeken. Lumineia possessed the one weapon that could topple the Empire, and if Lumineia survived, it gave her hope.

Belrisa caught her gaze and nodded, and Elenyr nodded in turn. Then she faced forward and smiled, her thoughts turning to the future. She'd protected Lumineia before, but she sensed her time among the people had come to an end. It was time to prepare for the conflict with the krey.

It was time to join the Eternals.

Epilogue: Master and Servant

Zoric limped his way down the stairs of Xshaltheria, wincing as his twisted leg came in contact with each step. He cursed the fragments and the Hauntress. They had destroyed everything, and now only he remained.

He'd been hurt in the battle at Xshaltheria, and woken in one of the healing tents. The soldier that had found him had thought him a member of the guard, and had tried to heal his wounds. But the gash to his leg had gone too deep, and it had taken him months before he could walk, months where he'd languished in healing halls, manipulating the memories of all those he encountered.

When he was finally able to walk, he'd worked his way east, passing the many caravans threading their way to Azertorn. Their excitement elicited anger, but Zoric held the emotion in check. Alone, he was vulnerable, and his foes would not hesitate to kill him.

He'd searched the breadth of Blackwell Keep and now Xshaltheria, driven by a desperate hope that he would find Serak or Draeken. The Father of Guardians had disappeared, and Draeken had Gated out of the battle, never to be seen again. It was a fool's hope, but his only hope.

He reached the base of the fortress and leaned against the wall to survey the pockmarked platform at the base of the hanging citadel. Then he noticed the shimmering chains on the wall and his eyes widened.

"Master?"

An ethereal body gradually took shape, and Draeken appeared. He growled, his features fading and then returning. He looked to Zoric with burning eyes, and Zoric wiped furiously at the tears on his cheeks.

"Master," Zoric said, dropping to his knees, "I thought you were dead."

"They cannot kill me," Draeken snarled, but the sound seemed distant.

"Tell me what I can do and I will free you," Zoric said.

"I am not on Lumineia or the Dark World," Draeken said. "They trapped me here, where only time can touch."

"Tell me how—"

"I CANNOT BE FREED!" Draeken's body shimmered to solidity, and then faded again, bits of silver and purple floating through his flesh.

"You live," Zoric protested. "Surely there is a way we can return to power."

"I have become the Dark Gate now." Draeken's voice was suddenly bitter. "I control a broken Gate, and it has become my prison."

Draeken began to fade from sight, his features twisted in anger, and Zoric surged to his feet, his desperation leaking into his voice.

"The world of Lumineia celebrates your defeat," Zoric shouted. "Give me time, and I will find a way for us to have our revenge."

"Time," Draeken gradually appeared, and then his eyes narrowed. "Perhaps you can be of use. I am bound to the Dark Gate, but that does not mean it cannot be repaired. Go to Blackwell Keep, and learn what you can of my plans there. Repair the Gate and I will reward you with accolades and gold, positions and power."

Zoric bared his teeth in a grim smile. "I would settle for the death of the fragments, and the Hauntress."

"That I would gladly give," Draeken said. "I grow weak, but the Dragon's Sleep will help you survive through time. Prepare the way, my servant, for one day my four generals will again walk this land, and then the people will learn to fear what rises from obscurity. My return will be my victory, and the end of Lumineia."

The Chronicles of Lumineia

By Ben Hale

—The Shattered Soul—

The Fragment of Water
The Fragment of Shadow
The Fragment of Light
The Fragment of Fire
The Fragment of Mind
The Fragment of Power

—The Master Thief—

Jack of Thieves
Thief in the Myst
The God Thief

—The Second Draeken War—

Elseerian
The Gathering
Seven Days
The List Unseen

—The Warsworn—

The Flesh of War
The Age of War
The Heart of War

—The Age of Oracles—

The Rogue Mage
The Lost Mage
The Battle Mage

—The White Mage Saga—

Author Bio

Originally from Utah, Ben has grown up with a passion for learning almost everything. Driven particularly to reading caused him to be caught reading by flashlight under the covers at an early age. While still young, he practiced various sports, became an Eagle Scout, and taught himself to play the piano. This thirst for knowledge gained him excellent grades and helped him graduate college with honors, as well as become fluent in three languages after doing volunteer work in Brazil. After school, he started and ran several successful businesses that gave him time to work on his numerous writing projects. His greatest support and inspiration comes from his wonderful wife and six beautiful children. Currently he resides in Missouri after completing his Masters in Professional Writing.

To contact the author, discover more about Lumineia, or find out about the upcoming sequels, check out his website at Lumineia.com. You can also follow the author on twitter @ BenHale8 or Facebook.

www.ingramcontent.com/pod-product-compliance
Lightning Source LLC
Chambersburg PA
CBHW020823180626
46814CB00001B/88